DATE DUE

A Background Note about *The Virginian*

The true story of the Wyoming cowboy began on June 25, 1876, at a place called Little Bighorn. There, 210 soldiers under the command of General George Custer were surrounded and killed by Indian warriors. In the next ten years, the U.S. Army destroyed or brought under control every tribe of the Plains Indians.

By 1879, the high flat plain east of the Bighorn Mountains was no longer Indian land. Instead, the region became open range for thousands of cattle owned by organized cattle companies. The growing cities of the East wanted beef, and the railroads would deliver it. Cowboys managed the herds on the range and then drove them to the railheads for shipping to the stockyards.

But the same open range that brought the cattlemen also brought homesteaders. Families staked claims on land for small farms where they could raise a few animals. The fences that marked their properties would soon mark the end of the open range. In the meanwhile, enterprising villains among the cowboys and homesteaders learned how to take advantage of the vast plains. It was easy to find unguarded calves, steal them, and mark them with your own brand.

Conflict was inevitable between the ranchers, the homesteaders, and the rustlers. The climax in Wyoming was the Johnson County Cattle War of 1892, which ended open range cattle operations.

The Virginian presents Wyoming from 1874 to 1890, when it became the forty-fourth state. Twelve years later, when Owen Wister published the novel, the Wyoming he knew had vanished. Barbed wire divided the land. Cattle could no longer roam freely on the plains. The true story of the Wyoming cowboy had ended. But thanks to Wister's novel, the legend of Wyoming cowboys like the Virginian was just beginning.

THE
VIRGINIAN
OWEN WISTER

Edited, and with an Afterword,
by David Kleiner

 THE TOWNSEND LIBRARY

THE VIRGINIAN

TP THE TOWNSEND LIBRARY

For more titles in the Townsend Library,
visit our website: **www.townsendpress.com**

ISBN 13: 978-1-59194-065-4
ISBN 10: 1-59194-065-6

Library of Congress Control Number:
2005910999

CONTENTS

ENTER THE MAN

Some notable sight was drawing the passengers—men and women—to the window. I got up to see. Near the tracks was a corral. Around it, men were laughing. Inside, dust whirled. In the middle of the dust some cow ponies ran about, huddled for a moment, and then darted away. One of them could not be caught, no matter who threw the rope.

We had plenty of time to watch this sport. Our train had stopped to be filled from a water tower only minutes from the station. We were six hours late and starved for entertainment.

The pony in the corral was wise, and quick.

Have you ever seen a skillful boxer keep a constant, but secret, eye on his opponent? The pony kept just such an eye on whoever took the rope. Pretending to look at the weather or to chat with a bystander was useless. The pony saw through it. His eye stayed fixed on the enemy. The serious look on his face made the matter quite comical. Someone would hurl a rope. The pony was already somewhere else. If horses laugh, snickers must have filled that corral.

For a moment, the pony stood alone. Then, in a flash, he slid in among his brothers. Suddenly, they whipped around the corral like a school of playful fish, kicking up the dust, and (I imagine) roaring with laughter. Through the window glass we could hear the thud of their mischievous hoofs and the curses of the cowboys.

For the first time I noticed a man looking on from the high gate of the corral. At that moment, he climbed down, moving like a tiger, smooth and easy, as if his muscles flowed beneath his skin. Where the others had whirled their ropes as high as their shoulders, I never saw his arm move. He held the rope down low, by his leg. But, as sudden as a snake his noose flew out and fell true. The thing was done. The captured pony walked in with a sweet, church-door expression. Our train moved slowly on to the station, and a passenger remarked, "That man knows his business."

Medicine Bow was my station. I descended, a stranger in this great cattle land. And here, in less than ten minutes, I learned news which made me feel even more a stranger. My baggage was lost. It was loose somewhere back in the two thousand miles that lay behind me. The baggage man remarked that passengers often got separated from their trunks, but the trunks mostly found them after a while. Having offered this encouragement, he returned to his business whistling and left me planted in the baggage room at Medicine Bow. I stood deserted among crates and boxes, blankly holding my baggage check, hungry and miserable. I stared out through the door at the sky and the plains. I could not see the antelope shining among the sagebrush or the great sunset light of Wyoming. Annoyance blinded my eyes to everything except my annoyance. I saw only a lost trunk.

I was muttering half-aloud, "What a forsaken hole this is!" when suddenly from the platform came a slow voice. "Off to get married *again*? Oh, don't!" The voice was Southern and gentle and drawling.

A second voice answered, cracked and cantankerous. "It ain't again. Who says it's again? Who told you, anyway?"

And the first voice responded affectionately, "Why, your Sunday clothes told me, Uncle Hughey. They are speakin' mighty loud of a wedding."

"You don't worry me!" snapped Uncle Hughey.

And the other gently continued, "Ain't them gloves the same you wore to your last weddin'?"

"You don't worry me! You don't worry me!" screamed Uncle Hughey.

Already I had forgotten my trunk. I had never heard conversation like this in my life. I stepped to the door and looked out on the station platform.

Lounging there at ease against the wall was a slim young giant. His broad, soft hat was pushed back. A loosely knotted, dull red handkerchief sagged from his throat. One thumb was casually hooked in the cartridge belt that slanted across his hips. The dust on him showed he had come many miles. His boots were white with it. His overalls were gray with it. His weather-beaten face shone through like ripe peaches on their trees in a dry season. Neither the dinginess of travel nor shabbiness of his clothes could tarnish his youth and strength.

"Who is the lucky lady this time?" he drawled.

The old man seemed to shake. "I tell you there ain't been no other! Call me a bigamist, will you? Then name some of my wives. Name two. Name one. I dare you!"

"—that widow from Laramie promised you—"

"Shucks!"

"—only her doctor suddenly ordered Southern climate and—"

"Shucks! You know nothing."

"—so nothing but her lungs came between you. And next you'd almost got united with Cattle Kate, only—"

"You don't know nothing!"

"—only she got hung."

"Where's the wives in all this? Show the wives! Come now!"

"That corn-fed biscuit-shooter at Rawlins you

gave the canary—"

"Never married her. Never did marry—"

"But you come so near, Uncle! She was the one left you that letter explaining how she got married to a young card player the very day before her ceremony with you was due, and—"

"Oh, you're nothing. You're a kid. You don't amount to—"

"—and how she'd never, never forgot to feed the canary."

"This country's getting full of kids," stated the old man, wearily. "It's doomed." He hoped this declaration would end the conversation. But his tall tormentor continued with a serious face and a gentle voice, "How is the health of that unfortunate—"

"That's right! Pour your insults on a sick, afflicted woman!"

"Insults? Oh, no, Uncle Hughey!"

"That's all right! Insults don't last!"

"Why, I was mighty relieved when she began to recover her memory. Last time I heard, they told me she'd got it pretty near all back. Remembered her father, her mother, her sisters and brothers, her friends, her happy childhood. Everything except your face. The boys was bettin' she'd get that too in time. But I reckon after such a terrible sickness as she had, that would be expectin' most too much."

At this, Uncle Hughey jerked out a small package. "Shows how much you know! That's my ring she sent back. So she don't remember me? Ha-ha!"

The Southerner put more fake concern in his voice. "And so you're a-takin' the old ring right on to the new one? Oh, don't get married again, Uncle Hughey! What's the use of being married?"

"What's the use?" echoed the bridegroom, with scorn. "Hm! When you grow up you'll think different."

"I expect to think different when my age is different. I'm havin' the thoughts proper to twenty-four, and you're havin' the thoughts proper to sixty."

"Fifty!" shrieked Uncle Hughey, jumping in the air.

"Now, how could I forget you was fifty," he murmured, "when you have been telling it to the boys for the last ten years!"

Uncle Hughey seemed to swell up from all the insults. Without another word he boarded the Eastbound train, which had just arrived. He could have escaped long before. But the old man had evidently got a sort of joy from this teasing. He had reached that age when we are tickled to be linked with romance, no matter how.

I stared at the older man's train until only a faint wisp of smoke against the evening sky was visible. Then the lost trunk came back into my thoughts, and Medicine Bow seemed a lonely spot. I felt marooned in a foreign ocean. How was I to find Judge Henry's ranch? Where in this wilderness was Sunk Creek? My host had written he would meet me at the station and drive me to his ranch. This was all I knew. He was not here. The baggage man had not seen him lately. The ranch was almost certain to be too far to walk to, tonight.

At the same instant, I became aware that the

tall man was looking seriously at me—as seriously as he had looked at Uncle Hughey throughout their remarkable conversation. It was unsettling to see him staring at me, his thumb still hooked in his cartridge belt. I recalled some terrible tales about people who had traveled to the West. Was I about to be invited to dance on the platform to the music of pistol shots aimed at my feet?

"I reckon I am looking for you, seh," the tall man now observed.

"WHEN YOU CALL ME THAT, SMILE!"

We cannot see ourselves as others see us, so I do not know how I appeared after hearing the tall man speak to me. I said nothing, feeling uncertain.

"I reckon I am looking for you, seh," he repeated politely.

"I am looking for Judge Henry," I now replied.

He walked toward me. At about six feet tall, he was no giant. But in his eye, his face, his step, the whole man, there was something powerful.

"The judge sent me after you, seh," he now explained, in a courteous Southern voice. He handed me a letter from my host. Outwardly, his appearance was unwelcoming. But, having witnessed his humorous performance with Uncle Hughey, I felt I knew a bit about him below the surface. I found it quite pleasant to be easygoing with a large stranger, who very politely handed me a letter instead of shooting at my heels.

"You're from old Virginia, I take it?" I began.

He answered slowly, "Then you have taken it correct, seh."

A slight chill passed over my easiness, but I

went on. "Find many oddities out here like Uncle Hughey?"

"Yes, seh, there is a right smart number of oddities around. They come in on every train."

As the only person who had come in on the last train, I dropped my method of easiness.

"I wish that trunks came on the train," said I. And I told him my predicament.

I didn't expect him to be greatly moved at my loss. He made no comment whatever. "We'll wait in town for it," said he, always perfectly civil.

Now, what I had seen of "town" was, to my newly arrived eyes, altogether horrible. If I could possibly sleep at the judge's ranch, I preferred to do so.

"Is it too far to go there tonight?" I inquired.

He looked at me, puzzled.

"For this valise," I explained, "contains all that I need right away. I could do without my trunk for a day or two, if it is not convenient to send. So if we could arrive there not too late by starting at once—" I paused.

"It's two hundred and sixty-three miles," said the Virginian.

I was dazed. How did they count distance in this country? The cowboy just said, "Supper will be about ready now." He took my valise, and I followed his steps toward the eating-house in silence.

As we went, I read my host's letter. He was very sorry not to meet me himself. He had been getting ready to drive over, when the surveyor appeared and detained him. In his place he was sending a trustworthy man, who would look after me and drive me over. They were looking forward to my visit with much pleasure. This was all.

Drive me over? It meant—I did not know yet how many days. And how many miles would be considered really far? I avoided asking the "trustworthy man." My questions had not fared too well so far. He did not propose making me dance, to be sure. But neither did he propose we become friends. What had I done to deserve his skillful sarcasm about oddities coming in on every train? Having been sent to look after me, he would do so, would even carry my bag. But this handsome, uneducated son of the soil kept his distance with cold and perfect courtesy. No polished person could have done it better. What was the matter?

I looked at him and suddenly it came to me. Had he been too friendly to me the first two minutes of our acquaintance, I would have resented it. Yet I had tried to be friendly with him. I had been patronizing. He had come off the better gentleman of the two. Here in flesh and blood was a truth I had long believed in words, but never met before. A true *gentleman* can just as easily be someone born without the chance to learn the outward trappings.

Between the station and the eating-house I did a deal of straight thinking. But my thoughts were soon forgotten in my amazement at the extraordinary man I had just met.

Town, as they called it, pleased me less and less

the longer I saw it. I will call it a town only until our language invents a better word to describe a place like Medicine Bow. I have seen and slept in many like it since. They littered the frontier from the Columbia River to the Rio Grande, from the Missouri to the Sierra Mountains. Each was like the next, as one old five of clubs resembles another: houses, empty bottles, and garbage, sadder than stale bones. They seemed to have been tossed there by the wind. And they were waiting till the wind would blow them away. Yet above each such town shone a pure and quiet light the East never sees. Beneath sun and stars their days and nights were gleaming and wonderful.

Medicine Bow was my first of these towns. It consisted of twenty-nine buildings in all, including one coal chute, one water tank, the train station, one store, two eating-houses, one billiard hall, two tool-houses, one feed stable, and twelve others that for one reason and another I shall not name. For all its simplicity, some thought had been put into the town's appearance. Many buildings wore false fronts to make them seem two stories high. From their ragged doorways into a land without end a road wandered. It ran over a hill and down out of sight, and up again smaller in the distance, and down once more, and up once more, straining the eyes until it disappeared.

Someone greeted my Virginian. He came rollicking out of a door, trying to grab the Virginian's hat. The Southerner dodged him with tigerlike movements once again. "How are you Steve?" he said to the rollicking man. And in his tone I heard instantly old friendship speaking.

Steve looked at me, and looked away—and that was all. But it was enough. In no company had I ever felt so much an outsider. Yet I liked the company, and wished that it would like me.

"Just come to town?" inquired Steve of the Virginian.

"Been here since noon. Been waiting for the train."

"Going out tonight?"

"I reckon I'll pull out tomorrow."

"Beds are all took," said Steve. This was for my benefit.

"Dear me," said I.

"But I guess one of them salesmen will let you double up." Steve was enjoying himself, I think. With his saddle and blankets, beds were nothing to him.

"Traveling salesmen, are they?" asked the Virginian. He set down my valise, and seemed to ponder. "I did want a bed tonight."

"Well," Steve suggested, "the one selling potions looks like he washes the oftenest."

"That don't matter," observed the Southerner.

"It will be when you see 'em. Two of 'em are selling cigars. One's peddlin' jewelry. The other's got a cure for what ails you."

"I'm expecting a bed to myself."

"Then you'll have to build one."

"Bet you I have the jeweler's."

"He scares too easily. Bet you drinks you can't have the medicine man's."

"I'll have his bed without any fuss. Drinks for the crowd is the bet."

"I suppose you have me beat," said Steve, grinning at him affectionately. "You're such a son-of-a—Well, so long! I got to fix my horse's hoofs."

I had expected that the man would be struck down. He had used a heavy insult. I was amazed to hear it from Steve's friendly lips. Stranger still, he had meant no harm. And no offense had been taken. In fact, this language was plainly complimentary. I had stepped into a new world indeed. There was hardly time to catch my breath between curious events. As to where I should sleep, I had forgotten that problem altogether in my curiosity. What was the Virginian going to do now? I already knew that beneath the quiet of this man was a volcano.

We were at the door of the eating-house. He set my valise inside.

"Will you wash first, seh?"

In my tenderfoot ignorance I was looking indoors for the washing arrangements.

"It's out here, seh." His accent seemed to grow stronger when he was being lighthearted. At other times he hardly had any special accent or errors in grammar.

A trough was to my right, slippery with soapy water. Hanging from a roller above one end of it was a rag of discouraging appearance. The Virginian grabbed it, and whirled it around on its roller. Not a dry or clean inch could be found. He took off his hat, and put his head in the door.

"Your towel, ma'am," said he, "has been too popular."

Out came a pretty woman. Her eyes rested upon him for a moment with favor, then upon me with disfavor. Then they returned to his black hair.

"We use one a day," said she, very quietly. "But when folks are particular..." She completed her sentence by removing the old towel and giving a clean one to us.

"Thank you, ma'am," said the cowpuncher.

She looked once more at his black hair and without any word returned to her guests at supper.

A pail stood in the trough, almost empty. This he filled for me from a well. I used my own soap. In a tin basin I removed as many of the stains of travel as I was able. It was not much of a washing, but it had to do. I took my seat at supper.

Canned stuff it was—corned beef. One of my table companions said the truth about it: "When I slung my teeth over that, I thought I was chewing a hammock." We had strange coffee and canned milk. I have never seen more flies.

I made no attempt to talk, for no one in this country seemed favorably disposed to me. Was it my clothes, my hat, my accent? Whatever it might be, I had a knack for setting people against me at first sight. Yet I was doing better than I knew. My strict silence and attention to the corned beef made me look better in the eyes of the cowboys than the talkative salesmen.

The Virginian's entrance produced a slight silence. He had done wonders at the wash trough. He had even brushed his clothes. With all the roughness of his dress, he was now the neatest of us. He nodded to some of the other cowboys and began his meal in quiet.

But silence is not natural for a salesman. An average fish can live longer out of water than this breed can live without talking. One of them now looked across the table at the flannel-shirted Virginian. Somehow, he thought he had an understanding with the man.

"Good evening," he said briskly.

"Good evening," said the Virginian.

"Just come to town?"

"Just come to town," the Virginian responded suavely.

"Cattle business jumping along?"

"Oh, fair." And the Virginian took some more corned beef.

"Gets your appetite going at least."

The Virginian drank some coffee. Presently the pretty woman refilled his cup without his asking.

"Guess I've met you before."

The Virginian glanced at him for a brief moment.

"Haven't I, now? Ain't I seen you somewhere? You been in Chicago, ain't you? Remember Ikey's, don't you?"

"I don't reckon I do."

"Chicago. Four or five years ago. Or maybe it's two. But I never forget a face. Yes, sir. Him and me's met at Ikey's, all right." We were supposed to be witnesses of how well he had proved old acquaintanceship. "Ain't the world small, though!" I believe he had attained that high perfection when a man believes his own lies.

The Virginian did not seem interested. He attended to his food, while our landlady moved between dining room and kitchen, and the salesman went on. "Yes, sir! Ikey's over by the stockyards. That's where all cattlemen that know what's what go. And he rolled a cigar across to the Virginian's plate.

"Selling them?" inquired the Virginian.

"Solid goods, my friend. Havana wrappers, the biggest tobacco proposition for five cents yet. Take it, try it, light it, watch it burn. Here." And he held out a bunch of matches.

The Virginian tossed a five-cent piece over to him.

"Oh, no, my friend! Not from you! Not after Ikey's. I don't forget you. See? I knowed your face right away. See? That's straight. I seen you at Chicago all right."

"Maybe you did," said the Virginian. "Sometimes I'm mighty careless what I look at."

Now it was the potion salesman whose bed the Virginian had his eye on. He was a sensible man who talked less than his brothers in the trade. I was confident who would end up in his bed. But I was very interested in learning how the deed would be done.

The Virginian looked good-naturedly at his intended victim, and made one or two remarks regarding patent medicines. There must be a good deal of money in them, he supposed. The victim was flattered. No other person at the table had been favored with the cowpuncher's attention. He responded, and they had a pleasant talk. I did not realize the Virginian's genius was already at work. But Steve knew. He stuck his head into the dining room. Seeing how the Virginian was engaging his victim in conversation, he remarked aloud, "I've lost!" and closed the door again.

"What's he lost?" inquired the potion peddler.

"Oh, don't mind him," drawled the Virginian. "He's harmless. Well," he broke off, "I reckon I'll go smoke. Not allowed in here?" This last he addressed to the landlady, with special gentleness. She shook her head, and her eyes followed him as he went out.

Left to myself, I wondered about my lodging for the night. Then I walked around smoking a cigar. There appeared to be no hotel in Medicine Bow. But connected with the eating-house was that place where, according to Steve, the beds were all taken. I went to see for myself.

Steve had spoken the truth. It was a single room containing four or five beds, and nothing else. When I looked at these beds, I grew less sorrowful that I could not sleep in one. To be alone in one would have been bad enough, but this doubling up—!

"Well, they got here ahead of us." This was the Virginian standing at my elbow.

I agreed.

"They have staked out their claims," he added.

On each bed lay some article of travel or dress. Two of the salesmen came in. They arranged their bags, and folded and refolded their linen dusters. Then a railroad employee entered and began to go to bed though dusk had not yet darkened into night. For him, going to bed meant removing his boots and placing his overalls and waistcoat beneath his pillow. He had no coat. His work began at three in the morning. Even as we still talked, he began to snore.

"The man that keeps the store is a friend of mine," said the Virginian, "and you can be pretty near comfortable on his counter. Got any blankets?"

I had no blankets.

"Looking for a bed?" inquired the medicine salesman upon arriving.

"Yes, he's looking for a bed," answered the voice of Steve behind him.

The Virginian looked thoughtfully from one bed to another. "I didn't know I'd be spending the night. Well, I have sat up before."

"This one's mine," said the salesman, sitting down on it. "Half's plenty enough room for me."

"You're mighty kind," said the cowpuncher. "But I'd not think of disconveniencing you."

"That's nothing. The other half is yours. Turn

in right now if you feel like it."

"No. I don't reckon I'll turn in right now. Better keep your bed to yourself."

"See here," urged the peddler, "if I take you I'm safe from drawing someone I might not care so much about."

"Well," said the Virginian (and his hesitation was truly masterly), "if you put it that way—"

"I do put it that way. Why, you're clean! You've had a shave right now. You turn in when you feel inclined, old man! I ain't retiring just yet."

The salesman should not have said "old man." Perhaps this kind of sham friendship works with the city crowd. But not so with the sons of the sagebrush. They live nearer nature, and they know better.

But the Virginian blandly accepted "old man." He had a game to play. "Well, I certainly thank you," he said. "After a while I'll take advantage of your kind offer."

I was surprised. Possession being nine tenths of the law, this seemed the best moment to stake his claim. But the cowpuncher was prospecting for a bed in his own way. Besides, he had no plans of retiring early the first time in weeks he'd been in town. All of us, including the potion peddler, walked over to the store, where my sleeping arrangements were made.

This store was the cleanest place in Medicine Bow. It would have been a good store anywhere. The proprietor placed both counters at my disposal. On the grocery side stood a cheese too large and strong smelling to sleep near comfortably. I chose the other side. Thick quilts were unrolled for me. The only request he made was that I remove my boots, because the quilts were new, and clean, and for sale. My rest was assured. Not a worry remained in my thoughts. Now I could turn my thoughts over to the other man's bed, and how he was going to lose it.

Steve was more curious than I was. Time was flying. His bet must be decided, and the drinks enjoyed. He stood against the grocery counter, contemplating the Virginian. But it was to me that he spoke. The Virginian, however, listened to every word.

"Your first visit to this country?"

I told him yes.

"How do you like it?"

I expected to like it very much.

"How does the climate strike you?"

I thought the climate was fine.

"Makes a man thirsty though."

This was what the Virginian had expected. But he, like Steve, addressed himself to me.

"Yes," he put in, "thirsty while a man's still soft. You'll harden."

"I guess you'll find it a drier country than you were given to expect," said Steve.

"If your habits have been that way," said the Virginian.

"There's parts of Wyoming," pursued Steve, "where you'll go hours and hours before you'll see a drop of wetness."

"And if you keep a-thinkin' about it," said the Virginian, "it'll seem like days and days."

Steve clapped him on the shoulder with a joyous chuckle. "You old son-of-a!" he cried affectionately.

"Drinks are due now," said the Virginian. "My treat, Steve. But I reckon your suspense will have to linger awhile yet."

Now they addressed each other instead of using me for their telephone.

"Any cards going tonight?" inquired the Virginian.

"Stud and draw," Steve told him. "Strangers playing."

"I think I'd like to get into a game for a while," said the Southerner. "Strangers, you say?"

Before leaving the store, he got ready for poker. He took his pistol from its holster, examined it, shoved it between his overalls and his shirt and pulled his coat over it. He might have been combing his hair for all the attention anyone paid to this, except me. As the two friends went out, I thought again of that expression Steve had used for the Virginian. Clearly this wild country spoke a language other than mine—the word here was a term of endearment. Such was my conclusion.

"See you later, old man!" said the potion peddler to his prospective bedfellow.

"Oh, yes," returned the bedfellow, and was gone.

The salesman winked triumphantly. "He's all

right," he observed, jerking a thumb toward the Virginian. "You got to know him to work him. That's all. He might not buy any goods off you or me, but he'll talk them up. I ain't done with him yet. Say," (he now addressed the proprietor), "what's her name?"

"Whose name?"

"Woman runs the eating-house."

"Glen. Mrs. Glen."

"Ain't she new?"

"Been settled here about a month. Husband's a freight conductor."

"Thought I'd not seen her before. She's a good-looker."

"Hm! Yes. The kind of good looks I'd sooner see in another man's wife than mine. She come here with a reputation. But there's been general disappointment."

"Then she ain't lacked suitors any?"

"Lacked! Are you acquainted with cowboys?"

"And she disappointed 'em? Maybe she likes her husband?"

I left them and their leering stories, and sought the saloon. It was quiet and orderly with beer in quart bottles at a dollar. Expensive certainly, but I had no complaint otherwise. Through folding doors I passed from the bar with its bottles and elk head back to a hall with tables. I saw a man sliding cards from a case, and across the table from him another man laying counters down. Nearby was a second dealer pulling cards from the bottom of a pack. Opposite him sat a solemn old fellow putting coins on the cards which lay face up.

But now I heard a voice that drew my eyes to the far corner of the room.

"Why didn't you stay in Arizona?"

Harmless looking words as I write them down here. Yet at the sound of them every eye went to that far corner. I didn't hear the answer.

"Well, Arizona's no place for amateurs."

Both card dealers started paying attention to the group that sat in the corner. I had an urge to leave this room. Before this, everything in Medicine Bow had been easygoing. Suddenly, this was gone, like the wind changing to north in the middle of a warm day. But I stayed, too ashamed to go.

Five or six players sat over in the corner at a round table where counters were piled. Their eyes were fixed on their cards. Someone dealt out a card at a time, with pauses and betting between. Steve was there and the Virginian; the others were new faces.

"No place for amateurs," repeated the voice. It was the dealer. His face echoed the ugliness his words conveyed.

"Who's that talkin'?" said one of the men near me, in a low voice.

"Trampas."

"What's he?"

"Cowpuncher, broncobuster, gambler, most anything."

"Who's he talkin' at?"

"The black-headed guy."

"That ain't safe, is it?"

"Guess we're all goin' to find out in a few minutes."

"Been trouble between 'em?"

"They've not met before. Trampas don't enjoy losin' to a stranger."

"Fellow's from Arizona, you say?"

"No. Virginia. He's recently back from havin' a look at Arizona. Went down there last year for a change. Works for the Sunk Creek outfit." And then the dealer lowered his voice still further and said something in the other man's ear, causing him to grin. After which both of them looked at me.

There had been silence over in the corner; but now Trampas spoke again.

"*And* ten," he said, sliding out some chips. Even those words were a personal taunt. The Virginian was looking at his cards. He might just as well have been deaf.

"*And* twenty," said the next player, easily.

The next threw his cards down.

It was now the Virginian's turn to bet or leave the game, and he did not speak at once.

Instead, Trampas spoke. "Your bet, you son-of-a—"

The Virginian's pistol came out. His hand held it on the table, unaimed. With a gentle voice and a drawl that put considerable space between each word, he issued his orders to Trampas, "When you call me that, *smile*." And he looked at Trampas across the table.

His voice was gentle. But in my ears it seemed as if somewhere the bell of death was ringing. Silence fell on the room. I stood still. Others crouched or shifted their positions.

"Sit quiet," said the dealer scornfully to the man near me. "Can't you see he don't want trouble? He has handed Trampas the choice to back down or draw his steel."

With equal suddenness the room relaxed. Voices and cards, the click of chips, the puff of tobacco, glasses lifted to drink betrayed nothing of what had gone on before.

Trampas had made his choice. And that choice was not to "draw his steel." He had taken the measure of his opponent. Trampas would speak no more of "amateurs." He knew now the black-headed man was no beginner at the art of self-preservation.

But what kind of a man was Trampas? A public back-down is an unfinished thing. I looked at his face, and judged him more tricky than courageous.

Once again I had heard applied to the Virginian that expression which Steve so freely used. The same words, but this time they had produced a pistol. "When you call me that, *smile*!" So I witnessed a new example of the old truth: the word means nothing until the spirit gives it life.

CHAPTER 3

STEVE TREATS

The card dealer who had already spoken so wisely now took his turn at sermonizing.

"What did I tell you?" he remarked to the man for whom he continued to deal, and who continued to lose money to him.

"When?"

"Didn't I tell you he'd not shoot? You got ready to dodge. You had no call to be concerned. He's not the kind of a man you need feel anxious about."

The player looked over at the Virginian, doubtfully. "Well," he said, "I don't know what you folks call a dangerous man."

"Not him!" exclaimed the dealer with admiration. "He's a brave man. That's different."

The player seemed to follow this reasoning no better than I did.

"It's not a brave man that's dangerous," continued the dealer. "It's the cowards that scare me." He paused so this might sink in.

"Fellow came in here last Tuesday," he went on. "Got into some misunderstanding about the drinks. Well, sir, before we could put him out of business, he'd hurt two perfectly innocent onlookers," the dealer explained.

"Were they badly hurt?" I asked.

"One of 'em was. He's died since."

"What became of the man?"

"Why, we put him out of business, I told you. He died that night. But there was no occasion for any of it; and that's why I never like to be around where there's a coward. You can't tell. He'll always go to shooting before it's necessary. But a man like that black-headed guy (the dealer indicated the Virginian) need never worry you. And there's another point why there's no need to worry about him: *it'd be too late.*"

These good words ended the sermon of the dealer. He had given us a piece of his mind. He now gave the whole of it to dealing cards.

The Virginian still sat playing his stud poker. After a decent period of losing and winning, which gave Trampas proper time for a change of luck and a repairing of his fortunes, he looked at Steve and said amiably, "How does bed strike you?"

I was beside their table, learning gradually that stud poker has in it more spice than our Eastern game. The Virginian answered his own question, "Bed strikes me."

Steve pretended he didn't care. He was far more deeply absorbed in his bet with the Virginian than he was in this game. But he took out a fat gold watch, consulted it elaborately, and remarked, "It's only eleven."

"You forget I'm from the country," said the black-headed guy. "The chickens have already been roostin' a right smart while." His sunny Southern accent was again strong. In that brief passage with Trampas it had been almost completely absent.

"A while ago," said Steve, "you had won three months' salary."

"I'm still twenty dollars to the good," said the Virginian. "That's better than breaking a leg."

Again, in some voiceless way, most people in that saloon had become aware that something was in the process of happening. Several left their games and came to the front by the bar.

"If he ain't in bed yet—" mused the Virginian.

"I'll find out," said I. And I hurried across to the dim sleeping room, happy to have a part in this.

They were all in bed. In some beds two were sleeping. The potion man had come in recently and was still awake.

"Thought you were to sleep at the store?" said he.

I invented a little lie and explained that I was in search of the Virginian. At this point I stumbled sharply over something.

"It's my box of Consumption Killer," explained the salesman. "I hope that man will stay out all night."

"Bed narrow?" I inquired.

"For two it is. And the pillows are mean. Takes both before you feel anything's under your head."

He yawned, and I wished him pleasant dreams.

At my news the Virginian left the bar at once and crossed to the sleeping room. Steve and I followed softly, and behind us several more. "What is this going to be?" they inquired curiously of each other. And upon learning the nature of the event, they clustered in silence outside the door.

We heard the voice of the salesman, cautioning his bedfellow. "Don't trip over the Killer," he was saying. "The Prince of Wales bumped his shin just now." It seemed my English clothes had earned me this title.

The boots of the Virginian were next heard to drop.

"Can you make out what he's doin'?" whispered Steve.

He was plainly undressing. The rip of swift unbuttoning told us that the black-headed guy must be removing his overalls.

"Why, thank you, no," he was replying to a question of the medicine man. "Outside or in's all one to me."

"Then, if you'd just as soon take the wall—"

"Why, certainly." There was a sound of bedclothes, and creaking. "This here pillow needs a Southern climate," was the Virginian's next observation.

Many listeners had now gathered at the door. The dealer and the player were both here. The storekeeper was present, and I recognized the agent of the Union Pacific Railroad among the crowd.

"I should think," said the salesman, "that you'd feel your knife and gun clean through that pillow."

"I do," responded the Virginian.

"I should think you'd put them on a chair and be comfortable."

"I'd be uncomfortable, then."

"Used to the feel of them, I suppose?"

"That's it. Used to the feel of them. I would miss them, and that would make me wakeful."

"Well, good night."

"Good night. If I get to talkin' and tossin', or what not, you'll understand you're to—"

"Yes, I'll wake you."

"No, for God's sake!"

"Not?"

"Don't touch me."

"What should I do?"

"Roll away quick to your side. It don't last but a minute." The Virginian spoke with a reassuring drawl.

There fell a brief silence. Then I heard the potion salesman clear his throat once or twice.

"It's merely the nightmare, I suppose?" he said.

"Lord, yes. That's all. And don't happen twice a year. Was you thinkin' it was fits?"

"Oh, no! I just wanted to know. I've been told before that it was not safe for a person to be waked suddenly out of a nightmare."

"Yes, I have heard that too. But it never harms me any. Don't want you to run risks."

"Me?"

"Oh, it'll be all right now that you know how it is." The Virginian's drawl was full of assurance.

There was a second pause, after which the medicine salesman said, "Tell me again how it is."

The Virginian answered very drowsily, "Oh, just don't let your arm or your leg touch me if I go to jumpin' around. I'm dreamin' of Indians when I do that. And if anything touches me then, I'm liable to grab my knife right in my sleep."

"Oh, I understand," said the medicine man, clearing his throat. "Yes."

Steve was whispering delighted oaths to himself, and in his joy applying to the Virginian one unprintable name after another.

We listened again, but no further words came. Listening very hard, I could half make out heavy breathing and restless turning. This was the wretched salesman. He was waiting. But he did not wait long. There was a light creak, then a light step. He was not even going to put his boots on in the fatal neighborhood of the dreamer. The observers conveniently formed two lines, making an path for him when he got out the door. And then the commercial traveler forgot his Consumption Killer. He fell heavily over it.

Immediately from the bed the Virginian gave forth a dreadful howl.

Everything happened at once. The door burst open. Out flew the commercial traveler in his stockings. One hand held a lump of coat and trousers with suspenders dangling. His boots were clutched in the other. The sight of us stopped his flight short. The boots fell from his hand. The men of Medicine Bow began to send him down the line in the style of the Virginia reel. The other occupants of the beds had already sprung out of them, clothed chiefly with their pistols, and ready for war. "What is it?" they demanded. "What is it?"

"I'll set 'em up all night!" Steve shouted, as the reel went on. The salesman was bawling to be allowed to put at least his boots on. "This way, Pard," was the answer and another man whirled him around. "This way, Beau!" they called to him, and he was passed down the line.

They were now shouting for music. It seemed like half the population of Medicine Bow swept in like a cloud of dust to where a fiddler sat playing in a hall. Gathering up fiddler and dancers, they swept out again, growing all the while. Steve told us to order whatever pleased us, and as many times as we should please. He ordered the town to be searched for more citizens to come and help him pay his bet. But he changed his mind, and kegs and bottles were now carried along with us. We had found three fiddlers, and these played busily for us. We set out to visit all the houses where people might still by some miracle be asleep.

The first man put out his head to decline. But such a possibility had been foreseen. The storekeeper dragged out some sort of apparatus, helped by the Virginian. The cowboys cheered. They knew what this was. The man in his window recognized it and immediately joined us. What it was, I also learned in a few minutes. We found a house where the people refused to answer. Then the infernal machine was set to work.

Its parts seemed to be no more than an empty keg and a plank. Some citizen informed me that I should soon have a new idea of noise. I expected something like gunpowder. But the Virginian and the proprietor now sat on the ground holding the keg braced, and two others got down to play seesaw over the top of it with the plank. But the keg and plank had been rubbed with rosin, and they drew the plank back and forth over the keg. Recall the worst sound you have ever heard. That noise is a lullaby compared with the staggering, blinding bellow that rose from the keg. If you were to try it in your native town, you would not merely be arrested, but you would also be hanged, and everybody would be glad, and the clergyman would not bury you. My head, my teeth, the whole system of my bones leaped and chattered. Out of the house like drops squirted from a lemon came a man and his wife. They were swept along with the rest. Routed from their own bed, they now became most determined that everyone in Medicine Bow was to come out.

Suddenly there was quiet. I did not see who brought the message. Word ran among us that there was a woman—the engineer's woman down by the water-tank—very sick. The doctor had come from Laramie to see her. Everybody liked the engineer. Plank and keg were heard no more. Medicine Bow went gradually home. I saw doors shutting, and lights go out. A late few reassembled at the card tables. The salesmen gathered together for sleep. I heard Steve urging the Virginian to take one more glass.

But the Virginian, the black-headed guy who had set all this nonsense going, said no to Steve. "I have got to stay responsible," was his excuse. And the friend looked at me. Therefore I supposed that the judge's trustworthy man found me an embarrassment to his holiday. But if he did, he never showed it. He had been sent to meet a stranger and drive him to Sunk Creek in safety. No temptation would endanger his mission. He nodded good night to me. "If there's anything I can do for you, tell me."

I thanked him. "What a pleasant evening!" I added.

"I'm glad you found it so."

Medicine Bow was quiet as I went to my quilts. So still that through the air the deep whistles of the freight trains came from below the horizon across great miles of silence. I passed cowboys, whom half an hour before I had seen prancing and roaring, now rolled in their blankets beneath the open and shining night.

"What world am I in?" I said aloud. "Does this same planet hold Medicine Bow and Fifth Avenue, New York?"

And I went to sleep, pondering my native land.

CHAPTER 4

DEEP INTO CATTLE LAND

Morning had long since come to Medicine Bow when I left my quilts. The new day began around me, chiefly at the grocery counter. The early rising cowboys were off to work. Those with any dollars left were spending these for tobacco, or cartridges, or canned goods for the journey to their distant camps. Portable ready-made food plays a necessary part in the opening of new country. Cans were only the first indication that civilization would soon arrive on Wyoming's virgin soil. Now the cowboy is gone. The wind has blown away the ashes of his campfires. But empty sardine boxes lie rusting over the face of the West.

When each horseman had made his purchase, he would trail his spurs over the floor. The sound of his horse's hoofs would be the last of him. Fragments of talk, heard in half-sleep, sometimes brought useful bits of knowledge. I learned the true value of tomatoes in this country. One fellow was buying two cans of them.

"Meadow Creek dry already?" commented the storekeeper.

"Been dry ten days," the young cowboy informed him. He would not reach any water much before sundown. The tomatoes were for drink. They have refreshed me many times since.

"Thanks," said a new voice, rousing me from a new doze. "She's better this morning, since the medicine." His was the sick wife who had brought a hush over Medicine Bow's rioting. "I'll give her them flowers soon as she wakes," he added.

"Flowers?"

"You didn't leave that bunch at our door?"

"Wish I'd thought of it."

"She likes flowers." He walked out slowly, with no one to thank. He returned soon with the Virginian who had two or three blossoms in his hat-band.

"It don't need mentioning," the Southerner was saying, embarrassed by this expression of thanks. "If we had knowed last night—"

"You didn't disturb her any," broke in the engineer. "She's resting easier this morning. I'll tell her about them flowers."

"Why, it don't need mentioning," the Virginian again protested. His eyes fell upon me on the counter. "I reckon breakfast will be over shortly," he remarked.

I was soon at the wash trough. It was only half-past six, but many had been there before me. One glance at the roller towel told me that. Afraid to ask the landlady for a clean one, I uncovered a fresh handkerchief. The salesmen joined me. They used the community towel without hesitation. Filth was nothing to them.

We sat at breakfast together.

Then, by seven o'clock, Medicine Bow stood silent and empty. The cowboys had melted away. Looking in at the store, I saw the proprietor sitting with his pipe. Looking in at the saloon, I saw the dealer dealing noiselessly to himself. Up in the sky there was neither cloud nor bird. Nothing stirred.

I saw the Virginian at an open door, talking to the golden-haired landlady. I strolled out on the plain. I lay down, to daydream in the sagebrush. Herds of antelope roamed in the distance. Nearby prairie dogs studied me. Before I knew it, five lazy imperceptible hours passed as all that had happened merged in my thoughts: Steve, Trampas, the riot of horsemen, my lost trunk, Uncle Hughey and his brides. Then I noticed the Union Pacific train.

Its approach was silent and slow. I easily reached town and the platform before it had finished watering at the tank. It stopped briefly and I saw my trunk come out of it. Then it moved away silent as it had come, smoking and retreating into the distance.

Medicine Bow was now ready for dinner. This meal would be my last here for a long while. Duty drove the judge's trustworthy man to take care of me again. He had not sought my company that day. He held onto his distaste for what he supposed me to be. (I don't exactly know what this was.) I believed that one's dress or speech should not be cause for mistrust in our democracy. Thieves are presumed innocent until proved guilty. Anyone with a starched collar is condemned at once.

The Virginian harnessed the horses, got my trunk, and gave me some advice about what to take on our journey. I bought quite a parcel of treats, sure he would despise both them and me. I took my seat beside him in the wagon, wondering what we would talk about for two hundred and sixty-three miles.

In those days, farewells were not said in Cattle Land. The nearest to "goodbye" was the storekeeper's "so long." But I caught sight of one wordless farewell.

As we drove by the eating-house, the shade of a side window was raised, and the landlady looked out at the Virginian. Her lips were faintly parted. Her eyes plainly said, "I am one of your possessions." Her glance caught mine, and she backed into the dimness of the room. What look she may have received from him, if any, I could not tell. His eyes seemed to be on the horses. He drove with the same masterful ease that had roped the wild pony yesterday.

We passed the boundary line of Medicine Bow, thick heaps of tin cans and mounds of bottles cast out of the saloons. In a moment we were in the clean plains, with the prairie dogs and the pale herds of antelope. The still air bathed us, pure as water and strong as wine. Sunlight flooded the world. Shining on the Virginian's flannel shirt lay one long gold thread of hair!

We must have traveled five miles in silence. Then I looked back, and there was Medicine Bow,

seemingly a stone's throw behind us. One half hour later I looked back again, and there sure enough was Medicine Bow. A size or two smaller, I will admit, but visible.

Today and all the days of this first journey, the Virginian preferred his own thoughts to my conversation. I would have greatly preferred his conversation to my thoughts. He dismissed my attempt to discuss Uncle Hughey. I didn't have the courage to touch on Trampas. I wondered if I should ever see him, or Steve, or any of those people again. And this wonder I expressed aloud.

"There's no tellin' in this country," said the Virginian. "Folks come easy, and they go easy. In settled places, like back in the States, even a poor man mostly has a home. So if you want him you can find him. But out here in the sagebrush, a man's home is apt to be his saddle blanket. First thing you know, he has moved it to Texas."

"You have done some moving yourself," I suggested.

But this word closed his mouth. "I have had a look at the country," he said, and we were silent again. I discovered later he had set out for a "look at the country" at the age of fourteen. By his present age of twenty-four he had seen Arkansas, Texas, New Mexico, Arizona, California, Oregon, Idaho, Montana, and Wyoming. Everywhere he had taken care of himself and survived. He had yet to feel any hunger for home. He was one of thousands drifting and, as you shall learn, one in a thousand.

When next I thought of Medicine Bow and looked behind, nothing was there but the road. We were swallowed in a vast solitude. A little while before sunset, a cabin came into view. Here we passed our first night. Two young men lived here, tending their cattle. They were fond of animals. By the stable a chained coyote rushed nervously in a circle, or sat on its haunches and snapped at gifts of food ungraciously. A tame young elk walked in and out of the cabin door, and during supper it tried to push me off my chair. A half-tame mountain sheep practiced jumping from the ground to the roof. Skins of bear and silver fox lay upon the floor. Until nine o'clock one man talked to the Virginian, and one played on an accordion. Then we all went to bed. The air was like December, but in my blankets and a buffalo robe I kept warm. Going to wash before breakfast at sunrise, I found needles of ice in a pail. It was hard to remember that this quiet, open, splendid wilderness (with not one mountain peak in sight) was six thousand feet high. By the time the Virginian and I were ten miles on our way, it was June.

We never passed a human being this day. Some wild cattle rushed up to us and away from us. Antelope stared from a hundred yards. Coyotes ran skulking through the sagebrush. At our noon meal we killed a rattlesnake and shot some young sage chickens, which were good roasted over our campfire that night.

By half past eight we were asleep beneath the stars, and by half past four I was drinking coffee and shivering. The horse, Buck, was hard to catch this second morning. I was hot as July by the time we had him safe in harness, or, rather, unsafe in harness. Later Buck, in the mysterious language of horses, proved a bad influence on his partner. About eleven o'clock they decided to break our necks.

We were passing through the foothills in a country where trees grew and water ran. The road had steep places in it, and places here and there where you could fall off and go bounding to the bottom among stones. But Buck selected an even more dramatic moment. We emerged from a narrow canyon to find ourselves among five hundred cattle. Some cowboys were branding calves by a fire in a corral. Though this was a sight Buck knew by heart, he acted shocked. I saw him kick seven ways. I saw Muggins kick five ways. Our furious motion snapped my spine like a whip. I grasped the seat.

Something gave a pitiful jingle. It was the brake.

"Don't jump!" commanded the trustworthy man.

"No," I said, as my hat flew off.

Help was too far away to do anything for us. We passed unscathed through the herd. Then some earth crumbled, and we plunged downward into water, rocking among the stones. We headed upward again through some more crumbling earth. I heard a crash, and saw my trunk land in the stream.

"She's safer there," said the trustworthy man.

"True," I said.

"We'll come back for her," said he, with his eye on the horses and his foot on the crippled brake. A dry gully was coming, with no room to turn. The far side was covered with rock. We were bound to fall backward, if we did not fall forward first. He steered the horses straight over and just at the bottom swung them to the right with astonishing skill. They took us along the stream bed up to the head of the gully, and through a thicket of quaking aspens. The light trees bent beneath the wagon as it went over them. Their branches enmeshed the horses' legs, and we came to a harmless standstill.

I looked at the trustworthy man, and smiled vaguely. He considered me for a moment.

"I reckon," said he, "you're feelin' about halfway between 'Oh, Lord!' and 'Thank God!'"

"That's quite it," said I, as he got down on the ground.

"Nothing's broke," said he, after a searching

examination. You, Buck," he murmured gently. "Some folks would beat you now. I'd do it myself, only it wouldn't be no cure."

I now told him that I supposed he had saved both our lives. But he detested words of direct praise. He made some grumbling answer, and led the horses out of the thicket. Buck, he explained, was a good horse, and so was Muggins. Both of them generally meant well, and that was the judge's reason for sending them to meet me. But these broncos had their off days. "They are just like humans," the Virginian concluded.

Several cowboys arrived to find how many pieces of us were left. We returned down the hill. When we reached my trunk, it was surprising to see the distance our runaway had covered. My hat was also found, and we continued on our way.

Buck and Muggins behaved with discretion through the rest of the mountains. That very night, Buck was allowed to graze loose, instead of being tied to a rope. With the hard work that he was gallantly doing, the horse needed more pasture than a rope's length would permit him to find. Therefore he went free, and in the morning gave us little trouble in catching him.

We crossed a river before noon, and far to the north of us we saw the Bow Leg Mountains, pale in the bright sun. Sunk Creek flowed from their western side, and our two hundred and sixty-three miles began to grow small. Buck and Muggins, I think, knew that tomorrow would see them home. They recognized this region. Once they turned off at a fork in the road. The Virginian pulled them back rather sharply.

"Want to go back to Balaam's?" he inquired of them. "I thought you had more sense."

I asked, "Who was Balaam?"

"A maltreater of horses," replied the cow-puncher. "His ranch is on Butte Creek over yonder." And he pointed to where the diverging road melted into space. "The judge bought Buck and Muggins from him in the spring."

"So he maltreats horses?" I repeated.

"That's the word all through this country. A man that will do what they claim Balaam does to a horse ain't fit to be called human." The Virginian told me some particulars. I almost screamed at the horror of it.

We were interrupted by a mild-mannered traveler riding an equally sober horse.

"Mornin', Taylor," said the Virginian, pulling up for gossip. "Ain't you strayed off your range pretty far?"

"You're one to talk!" replied Mr. Taylor, stopping his horse and smiling pleasantly.

"Tell me something I don't know," retorted the Virginian.

"Hold up a man at cards and rob him," pursued Mr. Taylor. "Oh, the news has got ahead of you!"

"Trampas has been here, has he?" said the Virginian with a grin.

"No, it wasn't him that brought the news. Say,

what did you do, anyway?"

"So that thing has got around," murmured the Virginian. "Well, it wasn't worth such wide repeatin'." And he gave the simple facts to Taylor, while I sat wondering at the powers of rumor. Here, through this voiceless land, this desert, this vacuum, it had spread like a change of weather. "Any news up your way?" the Virginian concluded.

Importance came into Mr. Taylor's countenance. "Bear Creek is going to build a schoolhouse," said he.

"Goodness gracious!" drawled the Virginian. "What for?"

"To educate the offspring of Bear Creek," he answered with pride.

"Offspring of Bear Creek," the Virginian meditatively repeated. "I don't remember noticin' much offspring. There was some white tail deer and right smart jack rabbits."

"The Swintons have moved up from Drybone," said Mr. Taylor. "They found it no place for young children. Uncle Carmody's got six, and Ben Dow. And Westfall has become a family man, and—"

"If this here Territory is goin' to get full of family men and empty of game, I believe I'll—"

"Get married yourself," suggested Mr. Taylor.

"Me! I ain't near reached the marriageable age. But Uncle Hughey has got there at last, you know."

"Uncle Hughey!" shouted Mr. Taylor. He had not heard this. Rumor is unpredictable. Therefore the Virginian told him, and the family man rocked in his saddle.

"Build your schoolhouse," said the Virginian. "Got your eye on a schoolmarm?"

CHAPTER 5

ENTER THE WOMAN

"We are taking steps," said Mr. Taylor. "But Bear Creek ain't going to be hasty."

"Sure," agreed the Virginian. "The children wouldn't want you to hurry."

But Mr. Taylor did not take lightly the problem of educating his children. "Bear Creek," he said, "don't want the experience they had over at Calef."

"Sure!" agreed the Virginian again.

"Nor do we want a flirt," said Mr. Taylor.

"She must keep her eyes on the blackboard," said the Virginian, gently.

"Well, we can wait till we get a guaranteed article," said Mr. Taylor. He now drew a letter from his pocket, and looked at me. "Are you acquainted with Miss Mary Stark Wood of Bennington, Vermont?" he inquired.

I was not acquainted with her at the time.

"She's one we're considerin'. She's a friend of Mrs. Balaam." Taylor handed me the letter. "She wrote that to Mrs. Balaam, and Mrs. Balaam said the best thing was to let me see it and judge for myself." Taylor handed me the letter. "Maybe you

47

can give me your opinion how it sizes up against the letters they write back East?"

The communication was businesslike but also personal and freely written. I do not think its writer expected it to be exhibited. The writer wished very much to see the West. But she could not accept this invitation for that reason alone. Teaching school was something she would very much like to do. But she did not think it right to accept a position in which one had had no experience. "I do love children, boys especially," she went on. "My small nephew and I get on famously. But imagine if a whole bench full of boys began asking me questions I couldn't answer! What should I do? For one could not spank them all, you know! And mother says that I ought not to teach anybody spelling, because I leave the *u* out of 'honor.'"

It was a letter which I could assure Mr. Taylor "sized up" very well against letters written back East. And it was signed, "Your very sincere spinster, Molly Stark Wood."

"I never seen 'honor' spelled with a *u*," said Mr. Taylor, over whose not highly civilized head certain portions of the letter had lightly passed.

I told him that some old-fashioned people still wrote the word so.

"Either way would satisfy Bear Creek," said Mr. Taylor, "provided she knows 'rithmetic and George Washington, and them kind of things."

The Virginian was now looking over the letter with awakened attention.

"'Your very sincere spinster,'" he read aloud slowly.

"I guess that means she's forty," said Taylor.

"I reckon she is about twenty," said the Virginian, looking again at the letter, holding it as if it were some token.

Has any botanist discovered the seed of love? Has it been written anywhere how many ways this seed may be planted?

The Virginian handed back to Taylor the sheet of notepaper where a girl had talked unlike any woman he had known. If his eyes had ever seen such a maiden, their eyes had not met. Here was a language altogether new to him.

We drove onward, a mile perhaps, and then two. Though the Virginian had lately been full of words, he barely answered me now. A silence fell on both of us. We must have driven all of ten miles before he spoke again.

"Your real spinster don't speak about herself that easy," he remarked. "What would she be doing in Bear Creek?" he next said. He did not know that the seed of love had floated across wide spaces and was biding its time in his heart.

The next morning we reached Sunk Creek. Judge Henry's welcome and his wife's would have reduced to nothing any hardships I had endured, and I had endured none.

For a while I saw little of the Virginian. He lapsed into addressing me occasionally as "seh." I was sorry. I doubt our friendship would ever have deepened if not for a certain personage—I must call her a personage. I am indebted to her for gaining me a friend whose prejudice against me might never have been otherwise overcome. So I shall tell you her little story, and how her misadventures and her fate helped the Virginian and me appreciate one another. Without her, it is likely I should also not have heard so much of the story of the schoolmarm, and how that lady at last came to Bear Creek.

CHAPTER 6

EM'LY

My personage was a hen, and she lived at the Sunk Creek Ranch.

Judge Henry's ranch was notable for several luxuries. He had milk, for example. In those days his brother ranchmen very often had thousands of cattle, but not a drop of milk except the condensed variety. Therefore they had no butter. The Judge had plenty. Next rarest to butter and milk in the cattle country were eggs. But my host had chickens. At Sunk Creek the omelet and the custard were frequent. The passing traveler was glad to tie his horse to the fence here, and sit down at the judge's table. Its fame was as wide as Wyoming. It was an oasis in the Territory's desolate menu.

After the judge married, I have been assured, his wife's influence became visible in and about the house at once. Shade trees were planted, flowers were attempted, and to the chickens was added the much more troublesome turkey. I, the visitor, was pressed into service when I arrived, green from the East. I began building a better chicken house, while the judge was off creating meadowland in his gray and yellow wilderness. When any cowboy was unoccupied, he would lounge over to my neighborhood, and silently regard my carpentering. He was not alone.

There was Honey Wiggin. There was Nebrasky, and Dollar Bill, and Chalkeye. They came from farms and cities, from Maine and from California. American adventure had drawn them all alike to this great playground of young men, and in their courage, their generosity, and their amusement at me, they resembled one another. Each would silently observe my work with the hammer and the chisel. Then he would retire to the bunkhouse for a good laugh.

But this was only in the morning. On many a summer afternoon I would go shooting, or ride up toward the entrance of the canyon and watch the men working on the irrigation ditches. The canyon would fill with a violet light, and the Bow Leg Mountains would become transformed by unimaginable colors. The sun shone in a sky where never a cloud came. Noon was not too warm nor the dark too cool. And so for two months I went through these pleasant uneventful days. In the mornings, I was the object of good-natured cowboy teasing as I made improvements for the chickens. In the afternoons, I lived in the open air, perfectly content.

In those days, I became known simply as "the tenderfoot," a pathetic newcomer. Mrs. Henry tried to shield me from this humiliation. But I constantly revealed my ignorance by asking to be taught about rattlesnakes, prairie dogs, owls, blue and willow grouse, sage hens, how to rope a horse, and how to tighten the front cinch of my saddle. So she let me rush about with my firearms and made no further effort to fend off the ridicule that my blunders inevitably earned from the ranch hands, her own husband, and any chance visitor who stopped for a meal or stayed the night.

My notorious helplessness ended what little good relations I had with the Virginian. When Judge Henry realized that it was my regular practice to saunter out with a gun and in thirty minutes cease to know north from south, he arranged for my protection. He detailed an escort for me, the trustworthy man! The poor Virginian was taken from his work and his comrades and ordered to play nurse for me. And for a while this humiliation ate into his untamed soul. It was his lot in life to accompany me in my rambles, preside over my blunders, and save me from getting killed. He would keep me from wandering into quicksand. He would tie my horse properly. He would recommend I not shoot my rifle at a white-tailed deer at the moment a wagon was passing behind the animal. Every day, it seemed, he had to save me from sudden death or from ridicule, which is worse. He never became impatient, even when he was bringing me back my horse, which had run away because I had again forgotten to throw the reins over his head and let them trail.

"He'll always stand if you do that," the

Virginian would say. "See how my horse stays right quiet yonder."

Playing nursemaid truly vexed the Virginian. For he was still boyishly proud of his wild calling, and wore his leather straps and jingled his spurs with obvious pleasure. In spite of his opinion of me, my liking for him grew. I found his silent company more and more agreeable. I had, however, almost forgotten that he could be quite talkative until I happened to pass by the bunkhouse one evening after dark. Honey Wiggin and my nursemaid and the rest of the cowboys were gathered inside.

That afternoon the Virginian and I had gone duck shooting. I killed two as they sat close together. But they floated against a beaver dam out in water some four feet deep, where the current might carry them down the stream.

Anxious to have those ducks, I dove into the water with all my clothes on. Moments later, I crawled out, a slippery, triumphant heap. The Virginian's eyes rested a moment on this sorry muddy spectacle. But he said nothing, as usual.

"They ain't overly good eatin'," he observed, tying the birds to his saddle. "They're divers."

"Divers!" I exclaimed. "Why didn't they dive?"

"I reckon they was young and hadn't experience."

"Well," I said, attempting to be humorous, "I did the diving myself."

But the Virginian made no comment. He handed me my double-barreled English gun, which I was about to leave on the ground behind me. We rode home in our usual silence, the pitiful looking ducks dangling from his saddle.

In the bunkhouse he took his revenge. Walking by, I overheard his concluding words, "And the hat on his head was the only mark to show he weren't a snappin' turtle."

His tale met with energetic laughter, and I hurried away into the dark.

The next morning I was occupied with the chickens. Two hens fought daily to sit on some eggs that a third was laying. For the third time, I had kicked Em'ly off seven potatoes she was determined to raise into I know not what sort of family. She was shrieking around the henhouse as the Virginian came in. I suspected he came to see what I might be doing now that could be useful for him to mention later in the bunkhouse.

He stood awhile, and at length said, "We lost our best rooster when Mrs. Henry came to live here."

I felt a little riled about the snapping turtle, and showed no interest in what he was saying. My unusual silence seemed to elicit unusual speech from him.

"You see, that rooster he'd always lived round here when the judge was a bachelor. . . . You ain't got rheumatism, seh?"

"Me? No."

"I reckoned maybe you got damp goin' after them little divers—" He paused.

"Oh, no, not in the least."

"You seemed sort of grave this mornin', and I'm certainly glad it ain't them divers."

"The rooster?" I inquired finally.

"He weren't raised around petticoats. Mrs. Henry walked out to view her new home. The rooster was feedin' by the door, and he seen her. He screeched so awful I run out of the bunkhouse. He went over the fence, took down Sunk Creek, and never come back."

"That hen Em'ly over there has no judgment," I said.

"I never knowed her name before," said he. "That runaway rooster, he hated her. And she hated him same as she hates 'em all."

"Does she ever lay eggs?"

The Virginian had not "troubled his head" over the poultry.

"Well, I don't believe she knows how. I think she came near being a rooster."

"She's sure manly lookin'," said the Virginian. We had walked toward the corral, and he was now scrutinizing Em'ly with interest.

Huge and lean, with a great yellow beak, she stood straight and alert. Her tail slanted far to one side, one feather in it twice as long as the rest. The feathers on her breast had been worn entirely off by her habit of sitting on potatoes and other rough objects. Her eye was remarkably bright. Her legs were blue, long, and remarkably stout.

"She'll set on potatoes, you say?"

"She thinks she can hatch out anything. I've found her with onions, and last Tuesday I caught her on two balls of soap."

In the afternoon the tall cowpuncher and I rode out to get an antelope.

After an hour immersed in thought, he said, "I reckon maybe this here lonesome country ain't been healthy for Em'ly to live in."

"Lonesome?" I replied. "There are forty chickens here."

"That's so," said he. "It don't explain her."

He fell silent again, riding beside me, easy in the saddle. A moment later, he sprang to the ground in what seemed an impossible feat. He had seen an antelope where I saw none.

"Take a shot yourself," I urged him, as he motioned me to be quick. "You never shoot when I'm with you."

"I ain't here for that," he answered. "Now you've let him get away on you!"

The antelope had in truth departed.

"Why," he said to my protest, "I can hit them things any day. What's your notion as to Em'ly?"

"I can't account for her," I replied.

The Virginian made no reply. He was gazing over the wide landscape. He invariably saw game before I did, and was crouched among the sage while I was still getting my left foot clear of the stirrup. I did succeed in killing an antelope however, and we rode home with the head and hind quarters.

"No." said he. "It's not the lonesomeness.

How do you like the lonesomeness yourself?"

I told him I liked it.

"I could not live without it now," he said. "This has got into my system. I went back home to see my folks once. Mother was dyin' slow, and she wanted me. I stayed a year. After she was gone, I told my brothers and sisters goodbye. We like each other well enough, but I reckon I'll not go back."

We returned to find Em'ly seated on a collection of green California peaches, which the judge had brought from the railroad.

"I don't mind her anymore," I said. "I'm sorry for her."

"I've been sorry for her right along," said the Virginian. "She does hate the roosters so." And he said that he was making a collection of every kind of object he found her treating as eggs.

But one morning Em'ly's energies were diverted away from eggs. A turkey appeared with twelve children the same day a family of bantam chicks hatched. Em'ly caught sight of the chicks, crossed the corral at a run, and intercepted two that were trailing somewhat behind. These she kidnapped by assuming a superior tone with the bantam, who was smaller, and obliged to retreat with her still numerous family. I interfered, and put matters straight. But in an hour I saw Em'ly busy with two more bantams, taking care of them (in a way, I must admit, that seemed perfectly efficient).

And now came the first incident that made me suspect her to be demented.

She had taken her new children behind the kitchen, where one of the irrigation ditches ran under the fence. On the other side of the ditch were the twelve young turkeys. Em'ly set off after them instantly, leaving her bantams behind. She crossed the ditch with one jump, flew over the grass, and was among the turkeys at once. There she attempted to herd some away. But this other mama was no bantam. She chased Em'ly away in a few moments.

The Virginian and I witnessed this spectacle. Speechless, he went to the bunkhouse by himself. I took the abandoned bantams back to their momma.

I have often wondered what the other fowls thought of all this. It must have made some impression. In any event, the chicken house was in an uproar for several days. Em'ly now disturbed the bantams and the turkeys. Several bantams had died, though I will not go so far as to say this was the result of her misplaced attentions. Nevertheless, I was seriously thinking of locking her up till the broods got a little older. Then another event happened, and all was suddenly at peace.

The judge's setter came in one morning, wagging her tail. She had had her puppies, and she now took us to where they were housed, in between the floor of a building and the hollow ground. Em'ly was seated on the whole litter.

"No," I said to the judge, "I am not surprised. She is capable of anything."

This time the hen had replaced an unworthy parent. The setter was bored by her own puppies.

At certain periods of the day she returned to the puppies and fed them. But she made no quarrel with Em'ly. The two understood each other perfectly. I have never seen among animals any arrangement so civilized and so unnatural. It made Em'ly perfectly happy. She sat all day jealously spreading her wings over the blind puppies. When they became large enough to come out from under the house and toddle about, Em'ly would scratch and cluck and the puppies would run to her. Can you imagine the confusion in their infant minds as to who the setter was?

"I reckon they think she's the wet nurse," said the Virginian.

When the puppies grew too rowdy, I knew Em'ly's mission was approaching its end. Once or twice they knocked her over, upon which she arose and pecked them severely. I think they began to suspect she was only a hen after all. So Em'ly resigned with an indifference that surprised me, until I remembered that any hen would have ceased to look after her chicks by this time.

But here she was again "out of a job," as the Virginian said. "Now she'll be huntin' around for something else useful to do that ain't in her business."

I did not desire any more bantam and turkey performances. So, to avoid confusion, I played a trick on Em'ly. I went down to Sunk Creek and fetched some smooth, oval stones. She was quite satisfied with these, and passed a quiet day with them in a box. This was not fair, the Virginian insisted.

"You ain't going to jus' leave her fooled that a-way?"

I did not see why not.

"Why, she raised them puppies all right. Ain't she showed she knows how to be a mother anyways? Em'ly ain't going to get her time took up for nothing while I'm round here," said the cowpuncher.

He laid a gentle hold of Em'ly and tossed her to the ground. She, of course, rushed out among the corrals in a great state of nerves.

"I don't see what good you do meddling," I protested.

To this he made no reply, but removed the unresponsive stones from the straw.

"Why, if they ain't right warm!" he exclaimed. "It is kind of foolish, I expect, but that hen's goin' to have a real egg to set on." With this he removed one from beneath another hen. "We'll have Em'ly raise this here," said he. And so, on Friday near sundown, Em'ly began sitting on the one egg the Virginian had so carefully provided for her.

Early the next morning my sleep was shattered by an unearthly sound. I bounded out of the house in my pajamas.

There was Em'ly, walking wildly about. Her egg had miraculously hatched within ten hours. The Virginian had taken an egg from a hen that had already been sitting for three weeks. The little lonely yellow ball of down went cheeping along behind, following its mother as best it could.

I dressed in haste, hearing Em'ly's outcry. It steadily sounded, marking her erratic journey back and forth through stables, lanes, and corrals. The shrill disturbance brought all of us out to see the crazed hen, outraged at this overturning of natural law. Behind her, entirely ignored and neglected, trailed the little chick. She never looked at it. The Virginian put out food and water for the hen, but she tasted nothing. I am glad to say that the little chicken did.

The heat went out of the air, and in the canyon the violet light began to show. Many hours had passed, but Em'ly never ceased. Now she suddenly flew up in a tree and sat there with her noise still going, a sound like none I ever heard before or since. Below the tree stood the bewildered little chicken, cheeping, and making tiny jumps to reach its mother.

"Yes," said the Virginian, "it's comical. Even her egg acted different from anybody else's." He paused, and looked at Em'ly in the tree and the yellow chicken. "It ain't so damned funny."

When we came back out from supper, I found the hen lying on the ground, dead. I took the chick to a family in the henhouse.

No, it was not altogether funny anymore. And I did not think less of the Virginian when I came upon him secretly digging a little hole in the field for her.

"I have buried some citizens here and there," said he, "that I have respected less."

And when the time came for me to leave Sunk Creek, my last word to the Virginian was, "Don't forget Em'ly."

"I ain't likely to," responded the cowpuncher.

He had long before dropped the "seh," and all other barriers between us. We were friends, and had exchanged many confidences both of the flesh and of the spirit. He even promised he would write me the Sunk Creek news if I would send him a line now and then. I have many letters from him now. Their spelling came to be faultless.

The judge himself drove me to the railroad by another way—across the Bow Leg Mountains, and south through Balaam's Ranch and Drybone to Rock Creek.

"I'll be very homesick," I told him.

"Come and knock on our door whenever you please," he bade me. I wished that I might! No land ever cast its spell upon a man's heart more than Wyoming had enchanted mine.

CHAPTER
7

THROUGH TWO SNOWS

In the spring, the Virginian wrote me a letter with but a few mistakes:

Dear Friend,

Received your letter. It must be terribel to be sick. That time I was shot at Canada de Oro would have made me sick if it had been a littel lower. You will be well if you take an elk hunt with me about August or September.

Things do not please me here just now. I am going to settel it by vamoosing. But I would be glad to see you. It would be a pleasure not business for me to show you plenty elk and get you strong. I am not crybabying to the judge. He will want me back.

To answer your questions. Yes the Emmily hen might have ate locoweed if hens do. I never saw anything but stock and horses get poisoned with locoweed. No the school is not built yet. No I have not seen Steve. He is around but I am sorry for him. Yes I have been to Medicine Bow. I had the welcom I wanted. Do you remember a man I played poker and he did not like it? He is working on the upper ranch near Ten Sleep. He does not amount to a thing except with weaklings. Uncle Hughey has twins. The boys tease him some about it, but I think they are his. Now that is all I know today and I would like to see you poco presently as they say at Los Cruces. There's no sense in you being sick.

The rest of this letter discussed the best meeting point for us should I decide to join him for a hunt.

We did hunt, for an entire week. The Virginian was then able to explain a little more fully his reason for leaving Sunk Creek Ranch and the judge. Not much was said, to be sure; the Virginian seldom spent many words about himself. Owing to some jealousy on the part of the foreman, he found himself continually doing another man's work. But things were so skillfully arranged that he got neither credit nor pay for it. He would not stoop to telling the judge. Therefore he devised the device of simply going away. He calculated that Judge Henry would make the connection and call the Virginian back at the first opportunity.

He said no more about Steve than he had written. But it was plain that the friendship had ceased.

He would take no money for his services during the hunt, claiming he had not worked enough to earn any. The expedition ended in an isolated corner of Yellowstone Park.

The Virginian had foreseen correctly events at Sunk Creek. The only thing that he had not foreseen was the impression made upon the judge's mind.

Toward the close of that winter, Judge and Mrs. Henry visited the East. Through them a number of things became revealed. The Virginian was back at Sunk Creek.

"And," said Mrs. Henry, "he would never have left if I had had my way, Judge H.!"

The judge laughed. "How cleverly he taught me the value of his services by depriving me of them. I am no longer certain it was safe to take him back."

"Safe!" cried Mrs. Henry.

"Safe, my dear. Because I'm afraid he is as clever as I am. And that's rather dangerous in a hired hand." The judge laughed again. "But the way he handled Steve has made me feel easy."

And then it came out. The Virginian was thought to have discovered that Steve had lost his respect—shall we say—for other men's cattle. Calves had begun to disappear in Cattle Land. Some cows had been found killed. And calves with one brand had been found with mothers that bore a different brand. No one knew for sure who was involved, and Steve was not quite fully suspected yet. What was certain was that the Virginian had parted company with him. And neither man would talk about it.

There was further news. The Bear Creek schoolhouse stood complete. The lady from Bennington, Vermont, had decided to try her hand at educating the new generation.

THE SINCERE SPINSTER

Did you agree with Mr. Taylor's earlier estimate
that Miss Mary Stark Wood of Bennington,
Vermont, was forty years of age? That would be in
error. At the time she wrote the letter to Mrs.
Balaam, previously quoted in these pages, she had
been twenty for eight months.

It is unusual for young ladies of twenty to con-
template any journey of nearly two thousand miles.
A young lady would most certainly not venture out
to a country where Indians and wild animals live
unchained, unless going with a protector or to a
protector's arms. School teaching on Bear Creek is
also an unusual ambition for such young ladies. But
Miss Mary Stark Wood—known as Molly—was an
unusual young lady for two reasons.

First, there was her descent. Had she so wished,
she could have belonged to any number of patriotic
societies. But she had been willing to join none,
although invitations to do so were by no means lack-
ing. I cannot tell you her reason. I do know that her
most precious possession—a treasure which accompanied her even if she went away for only one

night—was a little miniature portrait of her ancestor Molly Stark, painted when she must also have been little more than twenty. Molly Stark, whose husband, Captain John Stark, fought at the Battle of Bunker Hill. That is the same General John Stark who, at the Battle of Bennington, called on the name of his wife. History records that he said, "Yonder are the Redcoats. Tonight, the American flag flies from yonder hill or Molly Stark sleeps a widow."

Each summer our Molly went to Dunbarton, New Hampshire, to visit the last of her relations who bore the name of Stark. What pleased her most about these visits was when a certain great-aunt would take her by the hand, look intently at her, and declare, "My dear, you're getting more like the General's wife every year."

After this annual conversation, Molly would run to her room, and there in privacy consult two objects. These objects, as you have already correctly guessed, were the miniature of the General's wife and the mirror.

The second reason why she was an unusual girl was her character, the result of pride and family pluck in the face of family hardship.

Fortune had turned her back upon the Woods. Their possessions had never been great ones, but they were enough. From generation to generation, the family had gone to school like gentlefolk, dressed like gentlefolk, used the speech and ways of gentlefolk, and as gentlefolk lived and died. And then the mills failed.

Instead of thinking about her first evening dress, Molly found pupils for music lessons. She found handkerchiefs to embroider with initials. And she found fruit to make into preserves.

There were people in Bennington who "wondered how Miss Wood could go from house to house teaching the piano, and she a lady." There always have been such people, I suppose, because the world must always have a garbage heap. These fine folk also declared that "Sam Bannett was good enough for anybody who did fancy embroidery at five cents a letter."

Public opinion was indignant over Molly's conduct. "She could stoop to work for money," they alleged, "yet she holds herself above the most rising young man around because there was a difference in their grandmothers!"

Was this the reason? I cannot be certain, because I have never been a girl myself. Perhaps she thought that work is not stooping, and that marriage may be. Perhaps—but all I really know is that Molly Wood continued cheerfully to embroider handkerchiefs, make the preserves, teach the pupils—and firmly to reject Sam Bannett.

Thus it went on until she was twenty. Then certain members of her family began to tell her how rich Sam was going to be—was, indeed, already. It was at this time that she wrote Mrs. Balaam about migrating to Bear Creek. It was at this time also that her face grew a little paler. Her friends thought she was overworked. Mrs. Flynt feared she was losing her looks. It was at this time, too, that she grew closer to her great-aunt from Dunbarton. From her, Molly received comfort and strength.

"Never!" said the old lady, "especially if you can't love him."

"I do like him," said Molly, "and he is very kind."

"Never!" said the old lady again. "When I die, you'll have something—and that will not be long now."

Molly flung her arms around her aunt, and stopped her words with a kiss. And then one winter afternoon, two years later, came the last straw.

The front door of the old house had shut. Out of it stepped Mr. Bannett, the persistent suitor. Mrs. Flynt watched him drive away in his fancy sleigh.

"That girl is a fool!" she said furiously, watching from her observation post, her bedroom window.

Inside the old house a door had also shut. This was the door of Molly's own room. And there she sat, in floods of tears. She could not bear to hurt a man who loved her with all the power of love that was in him.

It was about twilight when her door opened, and an elderly lady came softly in.

"My dear," she began, "you couldn't—"

"Oh, mother!" cried the girl, "have you come to say that too?"

The next day Miss Wood became relentless. In three weeks she had accepted the position on Bear Creek. In two months she started, with a heavy heart, but with a spirit craving the unknown.

CHAPTER 9

THE SPINSTER
MEETS THE UNKNOWN

On a Monday at noon, a small company of horse-men strung out along the trail from Sunk Creek to gather cattle out on the range. Spring was slow in arriving, and so they cheerily cursed a cold week's work and sometimes sang. The Virginian, as usual, looked quite serious and rarely spoke, but he kept a song going—for seventy-nine verses. Seventy-eight were quite unprintable and amused his brother cowpunchers monstrously. They never pressed him to begin the song, afraid he might tire of the lyrics. But after a day of silence, he finally lifted up his gen-tle voice and began:

> If you go to monkey with my Lulu girl,
> I'll tell you what I'll do:
> I'll carve your heart out with my razor *and*
> I'll shoot you with my pistol, too.

With each verse, the other cowboys loudly repeated each last line, three, four, ten times, kick-ing holes in the ground to the beat.

By Bear Creek they came upon the school-house, roofed and ready. It symbolized the dawn of a neighborhood. The feel of it struck cold on the free spirits of the cowpunchers. They told each other that, what with women and children and wire fences, this country would not long be a country for men. They stopped for a meal at an old comrade's. They looked over his gate, and there he was puttering in the garden.

"Pickin' bouquets?" inquired the Virginian.

"You only recognize potatoes when they're in a dish?" his old comrade shot back. But he grinned sheepishly at the same time because they knew he had not always lived in a garden. Then he took them into his house. There, an infant was crawling across the floor with a handful of matches. He began to remove the matches, but stopped in alarm at the babe's noisy refusal. His wife, looking in from the kitchen, warned him against spoiling little Christopher.

When she spotted the matches she was shocked. But when she saw her baby grow quiet in the arms of the Virginian, she smiled at that cowpuncher and returned to her kitchen.

Then the Virginian slowly spoke again, "How many little strangers have you got, James?"

"Only two."

"My! Ain't it most three years since you married? Mustn't let time creep ahead of you, James."

The father once more grinned at his guests, who themselves turned sheepish and polite. Mrs. Westfall came in. brisk and hearty, and set the meat on the table. After that, it was she who talked. The guests ate scrupulously, muttering, "Yes, ma'am" and "No, ma'am" in their plates. Their hostess told them all about the new families of Bear Creek, and the expected schoolteacher, and little Alfred's early teething, and how it was time for all of them to become husbands like James. The bachelors of the saddle listened, but ate heartily to the end. Soon after, they rode away.

The wives of Bear Creek were few as yet. Homes were scattered here and there. The schoolhouse was only a speck in a vast world of elk and bear and uncertain Indians.

That night, the Virginian recited to his cowpunchers a new verse about takin' his Lulu girl to the schoolhouse to learn her ABC's. Needless to say, the words were quite original and completely unprintable.

On another Monday, likewise at noon, some tearful women waved handkerchiefs at a train leaving Bennington, Vermont. A girl's face smiled back, then withdrew. They must not see the smile die away.

She had a little money, a few clothes, and a rigid determination not to be a burden to her mother and not to give in to that mother's desires. (Absence alone would enable her to carry out this determination.) She also brought along some spelling books and that craving for the unknown previously mentioned. Bold Grandmother Stark ruled Molly's spirit this Monday.

At Hoosic Junction, she passed the train bound back to her home. Seeing the engineer and the conductor—faces she knew well—her courage nearly failed her. She shut her eyes against this glimpse of the things she was leaving behind. To keep herself steady she gripped tightly a little bunch of flowers in her hand.

After Rotterdam Junction, some forty minutes farther, Molly Wood sat up bravely. She would soon be entering the unknown. On Thursday, she wrote a long letter to Bennington. She had seen a black pig on a white pile of buffalo bones, catching drops of water in the air as they fell from the railroad tank. Trees were becoming scarce. By the time she left the train at Rock Creek, late on the fourth night, she had really reached the unknown. She sent an expensive telegram to say that she was quite well.

At six the next morning, she got on a stagecoach. It drove away into the sagebrush, with her as its only passenger. By sundown she had already experienced the perils of this new world. Shortly after a new team of horses was hitched up, they tried to throw off their harnesses. They took the stage down to the bottom of a gully, while Miss Wood sat silent and unflinching beside the driver. When it was over, and they got on the proper road again, he invited her—more than once during the next fifteen miles—to be his wife. He told her of his snug cabin and his horses and his mine. He was a sincere boy, who had paid her the highest compliment. But, as soon as she could excuse herself politely, she got down and rode inside the coach.

The proposal of the first driver was banished from her mind when she met the second driver. He was not a sincere boy. He was a whiskey drinking man. All night long he drank. His passenger, helpless and sleepless inside the lurching stage, sat as upright as she possibly could. Sunrise found the stage still lurching violently from side to side. The driver sat up top with a bottle. A pale girl sat beneath, staring out at the plains, knotting in her handkerchief some utterly dead flowers. They came to a river where the man bungled the crossing. Two wheels sank down into the riverbank. Water quickly reached the upper spokes of the wheels. She put out her head and nervously asked if anything was wrong. But the driver was addressing his team with harsh language and his whip.

A tall rider appeared as if from nowhere. He took her out of the stage onto his horse so suddenly that she screamed. She felt splashes, saw the river, and found herself lifted down to the shore. The rider said something about cheering up and its being all right, but she no longer had her wits about her. She did not speak. She did not thank him. After four days of train and thirty hours of stage, she had faced a little too much of the unknown all at once. The tall man withdrew, leaving her to become herself again. She limply gazed at the river pouring around the slanted stage. Horsemen with ropes righted the vehicle, got it quickly to dry land, and disappeared at once with a herd of cattle, uttering lusty yells.

She saw the tall one delay beside the driver. He spoke so quietly that not a word reached her, until all of a sudden the driver began protesting loudly. The man had thrown something, which turned out to be a bottle. It twisted high in the air and dived into the stream. The cowboy put his hand on his saddle horn. For a moment, he looked half-lingeringly at the passenger on the bank. But when she glanced his way, he dropped his eyes. Swinging up on his horse, he was gone. At the same instant, the passenger opened her mouth and with inefficient voice murmured, "Oh, thank you!" at his departing back.

The driver drove up now, a humbled creature. He helped Miss Wood in, and inquired after her welfare with a hanging head. Then, meek as his own drenched horses, he climbed back to his reins, and nursed the stage on toward the Bow Leg Mountains as if it were a baby carriage.

Miss Wood sat recovering. She wondered what the man on the horse must think of her. She was not ungrateful. Had he given her the opportunity she would have explained herself. Did he suppose that she did not appreciate his act? Then, in the midst of these thoughts came a sudden memory that she had screamed. She could not be sure when.

She recounted the adventure from the beginning, and found one or two further uncertainties. How had it all been while she was on the horse, for instance? What had she done with her arms? She knew where one of his arms had been. And the handkerchief with the flowers was gone. She made a few rapid dives in search of it. Had she, or had she not, seen him putting something in his pocket? And why had she behaved so unlike herself? By the time the stage had traveled a few miles, Miss Wood had entertained thoughts of maidenly resentment toward her rescuer and of maidenly hope to see him again.

She could not know that the tall man would come to that river crossing again, alone, when the days were growing short. By then, the crossing was dry sand, and the stream a trickle. He found a pool—pools always survive the year round in this stream—and having watered his pony, he lunched near the spot to which he had carried the frightened passenger that day. Where the flowing current had been he sat, regarding the now safe channel.

"She certainly wouldn't need to grip me so close this mornin'," he said. "I reckon it will mightily astonish her when I tell her how harmless the torrent is lookin' now." He held out to his pony a slice of bread matted with sardines, which the pony expertly accepted. "Monte," he continued as the horse rubbed his nose on his master's shoulder, "I wouldn't trust you with berries and cream. No, seh. Even though you did rescue a drownin' lady."

Presently the tall man tightened the forward cinch and got in the saddle. The pony fell into a steady jog. The pony had come a long way and was going a long way, and he knew this as well as the man did.

To use the language of Cattle Land, steers had "jumped to seventy-five." This was a great increase in their value. Those who lived through that golden time are not, as I write this, even middle-aged. But it is Wyoming mythology already. On the strength of this vigorous price of seventy-five, the Swinton Brothers were giving a barbecue. Of course the whole neighborhood was invited. Everyone within forty miles would come. Some would come further—the Virginian was coming a hundred and eighteen. This was his opportunity to see how they were getting along up there on Bear Creek. "They" was how he put it to his acquaintances. His acquaintances did not know that he had bought himself a pair of trousers and a scarf finer than was needed for such a visit. They did not know that in the spring, two days after the adventure with the stage, he had learned accidentally who the lady in the stage was. This he had kept to himself. No one in the camp noticed that he no longer sang that eightieth stanza, the one about the ABC's.

All spring he had ridden trail. Summer, he had worked at ditches. Now he had just finished the roundup. Only yesterday, a traveler from the north gossiped of Bear Creek, and the fences up there, and the farm crops, and the young schoolmarm from Vermont, for whom the Taylors had built a cabin next door to theirs. The traveler had not seen her, but Mrs. Taylor and all the ladies thought the world of her. She would have plenty of partners at this Swinton barbecue.

The Virginian heard, but asked no questions. He left town in an hour, with the scarf and trousers tied in his slicker behind his saddle. After looking at the ford again, even though it was dry and not at all the same place, he journeyed inattentively. When you have been hard at work for months with no time to think, of course you think a great deal during your first empty days. "Step along, you Monte horse!" he said, rousing after some while. He disciplined Monte, who flattened his ears and snorted. "Why, you surely ain' thinkin' of yourself as a hero? She wasn't really a-drownin', you pie-biter. She's not likely to have forgot that day, though. I guess I'll not remind her about grippin' me, and all that. She's not the kind a man ought to josh about such things. She has a right clear eye." Thus, tall and loose in the saddle, he jogged along the sixty miles which still lay between him and the dance.

WHERE FANCY WAS BRED

Two nights of camping in the open, and the Virginian's Monte horse, untired, brought him to the Swintons' in time for the barbecue. The horse received good food, while his rider was welcomed with good whiskey. *Good* whiskey—for had not steers jumped to seventy-five?

Inside the kitchen of the Goose Egg Ranch many small delicacies were being prepared, while a whole steer roasted outside. The bed of flame under it showed steadily brighter against the dusk. The busy hosts went and came, while men stood and men lay near the fire's glow. Chalkeye was there, and Nebrasky, and Trampas, and Honey Wiggin, and others, enjoying the occasion. Honey Wiggin was especially enjoying himself.

"Hello!" he said, noticing the Virginian. "So you've dropped in for your turn! Number six, ain't he, boys?"

"Depends who's countin'," said the Virginian, who stretched himself down among the audience.

"Well, boys," said Wiggin, "I expect it will be Miss Schoolmarm says who's number one tonight."

"So she's arrived?" observed the Virginian, very casually.

"Arrived!" said Trampas again. "Where have you been grazing lately?"

"A right smart way from the mules."

"Say, Nebrasky, what happened to that canary you offered the schoolmarm?" asked Wiggin.

Nebrasky grinned wretchedly.

"Well, she's a lady, and she wouldn't be takin' a man's gift when she don't take the man. But you ought to get back all them letters you wrote her."

"Pshaw, Honey!" protested the youth. It was well known he could not write his name.

"Why, if it ain't Bokay Baldy!" cried Wiggin, seeking fresh prey. "Baldy can stay on a tame horse almost as well as the schoolmarm. But you give him a pair of knittin' needles! He made an elegant pair of slippers with pink cabbages on 'em for Miss Wood."

"I bought 'em at Medicine Bow," blundered Baldy.

"Baldy bought 'em. Then, on the road to her cabin there at the Taylors' he got thinkin' they might be too big. And he fixes to tell her about his not bein' sure of the size, but when he got right near her door, why, he couldn't find his courage. So he slips the parcel under the fence and starts serenadin' her. But she ain't inside her cabin at all. She's at supper next door with the Taylors while Baldy's singin' to an empty house. Just then, Lin McLean was comin' up by Taylor's corral, where Taylor's

Texas bull was. Well, it was terrible sad. Baldy's pants got tore and he fell inside the fence. Lin drove the bull back and somebody stole them Medicine Bow slippers. Are you goin' to knit her some more, Bokay?"

"About half that ain't true," Baldy commented, with mildness.

"The half that was tore off yer pants? Well, never mind, Baldy. Lin will get left too, same as all of you."

"Is there many?" inquired the Virginian. He was still stretched on his back, looking up at the sky.

"I don't know how many she's been used to where she was raised," Wiggin answered. "A kid stage driver come from Point of Rocks one day and went back the next. Then the foreman of the 76 outfit, and the horse-wrangler from the Bar-Circle-L, and two deputy marshals. Old Judge Burrage from Cheyenne come up in August for a hunt and stayed round here and never hunted at all. There was that horse thief—awful good-lookin'. Taylor wanted to warn her about him, but Mrs. Taylor said she'd look after her if it was needed. Mr. Horse Thief gave it up quicker than most. And the school-marm couldn't have knowed he had a Mrs. Horse Thief back home."

"Bah!" said Trampas.

The Virginian stopped looking at the sky, and watched Trampas instead.

"I think she encourages a man some," said poor Nebrasky.

"Encourages? Because she lets you teach her how to shoot?" said Wiggin. "The only folks I'd say she encourages is the school kids. She kisses them."

"Riding and shooting and kissing the kids," sneered Trampas. "That's a heap too dainty for me."

They laughed. The sagebrush audience is enthusiastically cynical.

Trampas went on. "She leaves Baldy sittin' on the fence while she and Lin McLean—"

They laughed loudly at the offensive picture he drew, until the laugh stopped short. The Virginian stood over Trampas.

"You can rise up now, and tell them you lie," he said.

The man was still for a moment in the dead silence. "I thought you claimed you and her wasn't acquainted."

"Stand up, you polecat, and say you're a liar!"

Trampas's hand moved behind him.

"Quit that," said the Southerner, "or I'll break your neck!"

The eyes of a man are the deadliest of weapons. Trampas looked in the Virginian's, and slowly rose. "I didn't mean—" he began, and paused, his face poisonously bloated.

"Well, I'll call that sufficient. Keep a-standin' still. I ain' going to trouble you long. In admittin' yourself to be a liar you have spoke God's truth for once. We ain' what you'd call a Christian outfit and maybe we have most forgotten what decency feels like. But I reckon we haven't forgot what it means. You can sit down now, if you want."

The liar stood and sneered. He looked around. Public opinion was no longer with him. "That's so" and "She's a lady" and other such moral comments were all he heard. So he held his peace. When, however, the Virginian had departed, Trampas sat down and tried again.

"Shut your rank mouth," said Wiggin to him, amiably. "I don't care whether he knows her or if he done it on principle. I'll accept the roundin' up he gave us! You'll swallow your dose, too! Us boys'll stand with him."

So Trampas swallowed. And what of the Virginian?

He had championed the feeble, and spoken honorably, but he had given them a peep through the keyhole at his inner man. As he prowled away he felt vicious rather than virtuous. So Lin McLean was hanging round that schoolmarm! Yet he joined Ben Swinton in seemingly fine spirits. The Virginian took some whiskey and praised the size of the barrel, speaking to his host. "There certainly ain't goin' to be trouble about a second helpin'."

"Hope not. We'd ought to have more trimmings, though. We're shy on ducks."

"But you have a barrelful. Has Lin McLean seen that?"

"No. We tried for ducks. A real barbecue—"

"There's large thirsts on Bear Creek. Lin McLean will pass on ducks."

"Lin's not thirsty this month."

"Signed for one month, has he?"

"Signed! He's courting our schoolmarm!"

"They claim she's a right sweet-faced girl."

"Yes, awfully agreeable. And next thing you're fooled clean through."

"You don't say!"

"She keeps a-teaching the darned kids, and it seems like no good growed-up man can interest her."

"*You don't say!*"

"There used to be all the ducks you wanted at the Laparel Ranch, but their fool cook's dead stuck on raising turkeys this year."

"That must have been mighty close to a drownin' the schoolmarm got at South Fork."

"Why, I guess not. When? She's never spoken of any such thing—that I've heard."

"Most likely the stage driver got it wrong, then."

"That's her ridin' the horse. Hey, where you runnin' to?"

"To fix up. Got any soap 'round here?"

"Yes," shouted Swinton, for the Virginian was now some distance away, "towels and everything in the dugout." And he went to welcome his first formal guests.

The Virginian reached his saddle under a shed. "So she's never mentioned it," said he, untying his slicker for the trousers and scarf. "I didn't notice Lin anywheres around her." He was over in the dugout now, whipping off his overalls. Soon he was excellently clean and ready, except for the tie in his scarf and the part in his hair. "I'd have knowed her in Greenland," he remarked. He held the candle up and down at the mirror and the mirror up and down at his head. "It's mighty strange why she ain't mentioned that." He tightened the scarf a fold or two further and, a trifle more than satisfied with his appearance, he proceeded most calmly toward the sound of fiddles.

"Why, Lin ain't here yet!" said the Virginian, looking in upon the people. There was Miss Wood, standing up for the next dance. "I didn't remember her hair was that pretty," said he. "But ain't she a little, little girl!"

In truth, she was five foot three, but he could look down on the top of her head.

"Salute your honey!" called the first fiddler. All partners bowed to each other, and as she turned, Miss Wood saw the man in the doorway. Again, as it had been at South Fork that day, his eyes dropped from hers. She knew instantly why he had come after half a year, thought of the handkerchief and of that scream of hers in the river, and became filled with heartlessness and anticipation. He was fine to look upon. She danced away, carefully unaware of his existence.

"First lady, center!" said her partner, reminding her of her turn. "Have you forgotten how it goes since last time?"

Molly Wood did not forget again, but danced

with the most sprightly devotion.

"I see some new faces tonight," said she, presently.

"You always do forget our poor faces," said her partner.

"Oh, no! There's a stranger now. Who is that dark-haired man?"

"Well—he's from Virginia."

"He's a tenderfoot, I suppose?"

"Ha, ha, ha! That's rich!" without knowing it, the simple partner had explained a great deal about the Virginian to Molly Wood. At the end of the set she saw the man by the door take a step in her direction.

"Oh," said she, quickly, to the partner, "how warm it is! I must see how those babies are doing." And she passed the Virginian in a breeze of unconcern.

His eyes gravely lingered where she had gone. "She knowed me right away," said he. He looked for a moment, then leaned against the door. "'How warm it is!' said she. And as for checkin' the babies when the natural mothers are dancin'—" He broke off and looked again at where she had gone. And then Miss Wood passed him brightly again, and was dancing almost immediately. "Oh, yes, she knows me," the cowpuncher considered. "She's taking the trouble not to see me. Hello!"

"Hello!" returned Lin McLean.

"Not dancin'?" the Southerner inquired.

"Don't know how."

"Had scarlet fever and forgot your past life?"

Lin grinned.

"Better persuade the schoolmarm to learn it. She's goin' to give me instruction."

"Huh!" went Mr. McLean, and skulked out to the barrel.

"Why, they claimed you weren't drinkin' this month!" said his friend, following.

"Well, I am. Here's luck!" The two pledged in tin cups. "But I'm not waltzin' with her," blurted Mr. McLean bitterly. "She called me an exception."

"Waltzin'," repeated the Virginian quickly, and hearing the fiddles he hurried away.

Few in the Bear Creek Country could waltz. The Southerner was determined to profit from his skill. He entered the room. His lady saw him coming and her thoughts grew a little hurried.

"Will you try a turn, ma'am?"

"I beg your pardon?" It was with a cold, well-schooled eye that she looked at him now.

"If you like a waltz, ma'am, will you waltz with me?"

"You're from Virginia, I understand?" said Molly Wood, regarding him politely, but not rising. One gains authority immensely by keeping one's seat. All good teachers know this.

"Yes, ma'am, from Virginia."

"I've heard that Southerners have such good manners."

"That's correct." The cowpuncher flushed, but spoke in his unvaryingly gentle voice.

"In New England, you know," continued Miss Molly—noting his scarf and clean-shaven chin, and then again steadily meeting his eye— "gentlemen ask to be presented to ladies before they ask them to waltz."

He stood a moment before her, deeper and deeper scarlet. The more she saw his handsome face, the more rose her excitement. She waited for him to speak of the river. Then she would be surprised, and gradually remember, and finally be very nice to him. But he did not wait. "I ask your pardon, lady," said he, and bowing, walked off, leaving her at once afraid that he might not come back. But she had altogether mistaken her man. Back he came with Mr. Taylor, and was duly presented to her.

It can never be known what the cowpuncher was going to say next. Uncle Hughey stepped up with a glass of water which he had left Miss Wood to bring, and asking for a turn, most graciously received it. She danced away from a situation where she began to feel herself getting the worst of it. One moment the Virginian stared at his lady as she lightly circulated, and then he went out to the barrel.

Leave him for Uncle Hughey! Jealousy is deep and delicate. It works its spite in many ways. The Virginian had been ready to look at Lin McLean with a hostile eye. Finding him now beside the barrel, he felt a brotherhood between himself and Lin.

"Here's how!" said he to McLean. And they drank to each other in the tin cups.

"Been gettin' them instructions?" said Mr.

McLean, grinning. "I thought I saw you learnin' your steps."

"Here's to your good health," said the Southerner. Once more they pledged each other handsomely.

"Did she call you an exception, or anything?" said Lin.

"Well, something right close in that neighborhood."

"She told me I was the first exception she'd struck."

"What rule were you provin' at the time, Lin?"

"Well, you see, I started to kiss her."

"You didn't!"

"Shucks! I didn't mean nothin'."

"I reckon you stopped mighty sudden?"

"Why, I'd been ridin'—ridin' to school, ridin' from school, and she chattin' cheerful and askin' me a heap of questions all about myself every day, and I not lyin' much neither. And so I figured she wouldn't mind. Lots of 'em like it. But she didn't, you bet!"

"No," said the Virginian, deeply proud of his lady who had slighted him. But he muttered, "Plumb ridiculous!" as her injustice struck him again, while the outraged McLean told his tale.

"We was startin' to come here. The Taylors were ahead in the buggy, and I was holdin' her horse, and helpin' her up in the saddle, like I done for days and days. Who was there to see us? And I figured she'd not mind, and she calls me an exception! You ought to've just heard her go on about

Western men respectin' women. That's the last word we've spoke. We come twenty-five miles then, her horse kickin' the sand in my face. Mrs. Taylor, she guessed something was up, but she didn't tell."

"Miss Wood did not tell?"

"Not she! She'll never open her head. She can take care of herself, you bet! There she goes," said Lin.

"With Uncle Hughey again," said the Virginian, sourly. "You might suppose he didn't have a wife and twins, to see the way he's kickin' up his heels."

"Westfall is takin' a turn with her now," said McLean.

"James!" exclaimed the Virginian. "He's another with a wife and family, and he gets the dancin', too."

"There she goes with Taylor," said Lin, presently.

"Another married man!" the Southerner commented. They prowled round to the storeroom, passed through the kitchen, and found themselves standing in that place set apart for the sleeping children. Just at this moment one of two babies stowed beneath a chair uttered a drowsy sound. A much louder cry would have been needed to reach the ears of the parents in the room beyond, such was the noise of the dance. But in this quiet place the light sound caught Mr. McLean's attention, and he turned to see if anything were wrong. But both babies were sleeping peacefully.

"Them's Uncle Hughey's twins," he said.

"How do you happen to know that?" inquired the Virginian, suddenly interested.

"Saw his wife put 'em under the chair so she could find 'em right off when she come to go home."

"Oh," said the Virginian, thoughtfully. "Oh, find 'em right off. Yes. Uncle Hughey's twins." He walked to a spot from which he could view the dance. "Well," he continued, returning, "the schoolmarm must have taken quite a notion to Uncle Hughey. He has got her for this dance, too." The Virginian was now speaking without bitterness; but his words came with slightly more drawl. With him, this was often a bad omen. He now turned his eyes to the collected babies wrapped in various colored shawls and knitted work. "Nine, ten, eleven, beautiful sleepin' strangers," he counted, in a sweet voice. "Any of 'em yours, Lin?"

"Not that I know of," grinned Mr. McLean.

"Eleven, twelve. This here is little Christopher in the blue-stripe quilt—or maybe that other yellow-head is him. The angels have commenced to drop in on us right smart along Bear Creek, Lin."

"What trash are you talkin' anyway?"

"If they look so awful alike in the heavenly garden," the gentle Southerner continued, "I'd just hate to be the folks that has to cut 'em out of the herd," he added softly. "Them under the chair are Uncle Hughey's, didn't you tell me?" And stooping, he lifted the sleepy babies and placed them beneath a table. "No, that ain't thorough," he murmured. With wonderful dexterity and care for their welfare, he removed the loose wrap from around them. This soon led to an intricate process of exchange. For a moment Mr. McLean had been staring at the Virginian, puzzled. Then, with a joyful yelp, he sprang to his aid.

And while both busied themselves with the shawls and quilts, the unconscious parents went on dancing. The small, occasional cries of their offspring did not reach them.

CHAPTER 11

"YOU'RE GOING TO LOVE ME BEFORE WE GET THROUGH"

The Swinton barbecue was over. The fiddles were silent, the steer was eaten, the barrel almost emptied, and the candles snuffed out. Round the house, all was quiet. The families had departed long ago. After the hospitable turbulence of the festivities, the Swintons slept.

Mr. and Mrs. Westfall drove through the night. As they neared their cabin, a still, small voice came from the bundled wraps.

"Jim," said his wife, "I said Alfred would catch cold."

"Lizzie, don't you fret. He's a little more than a yearlin'. Of course he'll snuffle."

"How you can speak of Alfred that way, as if he was a calf? And he's just as much your child as mine!"

"Why, what under the sun do you mean?"

"There he goes again! Do hurry up home, Jim. He's got a real strange cough."

So they hurried home. Soon the nine miles were finished. James was unhitching the wagon by his stable lantern. His wife hurried in the house to deliver their offspring to bed. The horses were nearly unbuckled when James heard himself called. Indeed, something in his wife's voice made him jerk out his pistol as he ran. But it was no bear or Indian—only two strange children on the bed. His wife was glaring at them.

He sighed with relief and laid down the pistol.

"Put that on again, James Westfall. You'll need it. Look here!"

"Well, they won't bite. Whose are they? Where have you stowed ours?"

"Where have I—" Words failed this mother for a moment. "Ask Lin McLean, the one who sets bulls on folks and steals slippers. What's he done with our innocent lambs? Mixing them up with other people's coughing, unhealthy brats! That's Charlie Taylor in Alfred's clothes, and I knew Alfred didn't cough like that. The other one that's been put in Christopher's new quilts is not even a b—b—boy!"

When the nature of the crime became clear to James Westfall, he sat down. Unmindful of his wife's tears and his exchanged children, he broke into unremorseful laughter. Doubtless after his sharp alarm about the bear, he was unstrung. His lady, however, promptly restrung him. By the time they had repacked the no longer peaceful changelings, and were on their way back to the Taylors', he began to share her outrage. Then they reached the Taylors'. There he learned from Miss

Wood that a child had been unwrapped at this house that nobody could identify. Mr. and Mrs. Taylor were already on the road to the Swintons'. Now James Westfall had grown almost as thirsty for revenge as his wife.

Back where the steer had been roasted, Lin McLean sat up cautiously among the outdoor slumberers and waked his neighbor.

"We better hightail it out of here," Lin whispered. "I never before thought you had that much of the devil in you. I tell you we must skip."

"Skip, then, and keep yourself mighty scarce till they can appreciate our frolic," the Virginian murmured from the warmth of his blankets.

The Southerner withdrew deeper into his bed. Mr. McLean informed him he was a fool and saddled his horse. He brought a parcel out from his saddlebag, lay it down beside Bokay Baldy, and was gone. When Baldy awoke later, he found the pair of flowery slippers.

Though he thought the Virginian a fool, Mr. McLean was scarcely wise. The absent are always guilty.

Before Lin had retreated a mile, the rattle of the Taylor's wagon wheels roused the sleepers. Soon, other wheels sounded. Here were Mr. and Mrs. Carmody, and Uncle Hughey with his wife. Close after them came Mr. Dow, alone, who told how his wife had gone into one of her fits. (Dr. Barker had advised her to avoid all excitement.) Voices of women and children began to be lifted. The Westfalls arrived, and the Thomases. By sunrise, what with fathers and mothers and spectators and loud offspring, there was gathered such a meeting as has seldom been witnessed before. Today you can still hear legends of it from Texas to Montana. But I am providing the little known details.

Of course they blamed poor Lin. Here was the Virginian holding horses and helping ladies descend, while the name of McLean began to be muttered with threats. Soon a party led by Mr. Dow set out in search of him. The Southerner debated for a moment if he should put them on the wrong track. But he concluded that it was safe to let them search.

Mrs. Westfall found Christopher at once in the green shawl of Anna Maria Dow, but everything was not put right that swiftly. Mr. McLean had, as James Westfall pointed out, not merely "swapped the duds, he had shuffled the whole doggone deck." The fathers were of little assistance. The mothers did the heavy work. By ten o'clock some unsolved problems grew so delicate that a ladies' committee was organized in a private room. Men were not admitted. What was done there I can only surmise.

The search party returned. It had not found Mr. McLean. It had found a tree with a notice pegged upon it, reading, "God bless our home!" This was captured.

But the women's meeting had met with success. Each mother emerged, satisfied that she had received her own. After the fire of righteous slaughter has raged in a heart, the flame will eventually burn itself out. The children had been identified. None had taken hurt. The thing was over. The day was beautiful. A tempting feast remained from the barbecue. The Bear Creek fathers could not stay at red heat. Most of them began to see the mirthful side of the adventure. They ceased to feel very severely toward Lin McLean.

Not so the women. They cried for vengeance. But they cried in vain, and were met with smiles.

Mrs. Westfall argued long for punishment. "Anyway," she persisted, "it was real defiant of him putting that sign up on the tree. I might forgive him but for that."

"Yes," spoke the Virginian in their midst, "that wasn't right. Especially as I am the man you're huntin'."

They were dumbstruck.

"Come and kill me," he continued. "I'll not resist."

But they could not resist the way he looked at them. He had chosen the right moment for his confession. He was scolded some. The worst came from the mothers. And all that he could say for himself was, "I am getting off too easy."

"But what was your point?" said Westfall.

"Blamed if I know any more. I expect it must have been the whiskey."

"I would mind it less," said Mrs. Westfall, "if you looked a bit sorry or ashamed."

The Virginian shook his head at her humbly. "I'm tryin' to," he said.

And thus he sat disarming his accusers until they began to lunch on the remnants of the barbecue. He did not join them. In giving you the impression that Mrs. Dow was the only lady absent this historic morning, I was guilty of an unintended omission. There was one other.

The Virginian coolly rode away. As he went, he asked his horse Monte a question. "Do you reckon she'll have forgotten you too, you pie-biter?" Instead of his new trousers, the cowpuncher wore leather chaps. But he had the new scarf knotted at his neck. Most men would gladly have equaled him in appearance. "Monte," said he, "will she be at home?"

It was Sunday, and no school day. He found her in her cabin next to the Taylors' house. Her eyes were very bright.

"I'd thought I'd just call," said he.

"Why, that's such a pity! Mr. and Mrs. Taylor are away."

"Yes, they've been right busy. That's why I thought I'd call. Will you come for a ride, ma'am?"

"Dear me! I—"

"You can ride my horse. He's gentle."

"What! And you walk?"

"No, ma'am. Nor the two of us ride him *this* time, either." At this she turned entirely pink. Noticing, he went on quietly, "I'll catch one of Taylor's horses. Taylor knows me."

"No. I don't really think I could do that. But thank you. Thank you very much. I must go now and see how Mrs. Taylor's fire is."

"I'll look after that, ma'am. I'd very much like to go ridin' with you. You have no babies to be

worrying after this mornin'."

At this reasoning, Grandmother Stark awakened in her, and she made a declaration of war. "I don't know what you mean, sir."

It would be easy now to resort to sassiness and ask her why she changed her tone so abruptly. Any rudeness would have lost him the battle. But the Virginian was not the man to lose such a battle in such a way. She thought he referred to those babies about whom she had shown such excessive concern last night. He now knew she had a guilty conscience about using them as an excuse.

"Why, I mean," said he, easily, sitting down near the door, "that it's Sunday. School won't stop you from enjoyin' a ride today. You'll teach the kids all the better for it tomorrow, ma'am. It's your duty." And he smiled at her.

"My duty! It's quite novel to have strangers—"

"Am I a stranger?" he cut in. "I was introduced, ma'am," he continued, noting how she had flushed again. "And I would not be oversteppin' for the world. I'll go away if you want." He quietly rose, standing hat in hand.

Molly was flustered. She did not at all want him to go. None of her admirers had ever been like this creature. The fringed leather chaps, the cartridge belt, the flannel shirt, the knotted scarf at the neck— these things were now an old story to her. Since her arrival she had seen young men and old dressed like this. But worn by this man now standing at her door, they seemed to radiate romance. She did not want him to go—and she wished to win her battle. And now in her agitation she suddenly became ruthless. He needs a punishment to remember!

"You call yourself a man, I suppose," she said.

But he did not tremble in the least. Her fierceness filled him with delight.

"A grown-up, responsible man," she repeated.

"Yes, ma'am. I think so." He now sat down again.

"And you let them think that—that Mr. McLean—You dare not look me in the face and say that Mr. McLean did that last night!"

"I reckon I can't."

"There! I knew it! I said so from the first!"

"And me a stranger to you!" he murmured.

This second comment left her at a disadvantage. She was silent.

"Who did you mention it to, ma'am?"

She hoped she had him. "Why, are you afraid?" And she laughed lightly.

"I told them myself. And their astonishment seemed so genuine I'd just hate to think they had fooled me that thorough when they knowed it all along from you seeing me."

"I did not see you. I knew it must—of course I did not tell anyone. I said so from the first. I meant—you can understand perfectly what I meant."

"Yes, ma'am."

"And what sort of a trick," she rushed on, "was that to play? Do you call it a manly thing to frighten and distress women—for no reason at all? I should never have imagined it could be the act of a person who wears a big pistol and rides a big horse. I should be afraid to go riding with such an immature protector."

"Yes, that was awful childish. Your words do cut a little. I certainly acted foolish when I forgot to be introduced before I spoke to you last night. Because why? You've found me out in one thing. Won't you take a guess at this too?"

"I cannot sit guessing why people do not behave themselves—who seem to know better."

"Well, ma'am, I've played square with you. And that's not what you're doin' by me. I ask your pardon for saying what I have a right to say in language not as good as I'd like when I talk to you. But at South Fork Crossin' who did any introducin'? Did you complain I was a stranger then?"

"I—no!" she flashed out. Then, quite sweetly she added, "The driver told me it wasn't *really* so dangerous there, you know."

"That's not the point I'm makin'. You are a grown-up woman, a responsible woman. You've come so far, all alone, to a rough country to instruct young children that plays games. Don't you think pretendin' you don't know a man who helped you when help was needed is mighty close to the hide-and-seek them children plays? I ain't so sure there's not a pair of children in this here room."

Molly Wood was regarding him saucily. "I don't think I like you," said she.

"Fair enough. But you're goin' to love me before we get through. I wish you'd come ridin', ma'am."

"Dear, dear, dear! So I'm going to love you? How will you do it? I know men think that they only need to sit and look strong and make chests at a girl—"

"Goodness gracious! I ain't makin' any chests at you!" Laughter overcame him for a moment, and Miss Wood liked his laugh very much. "Please come a-ridin'," he urged. "It's the prettiest kind of a day."

She looked at him frankly, and there was a pause. "I will take back two things that I said to you. I believe that I do like you. And I know that if I went riding with you, I should not have an immature protector." And then, with a final gesture of acknowledgment, she held out her hand to him. "And I have always wanted," she said, "to thank you for what you did at the river."

He took her hand, and his heart bounded. "You're a gentleman!" he exclaimed.

It was now her turn to be overcome with merriment. "I've always wanted to be a man," she said.

"I am mighty glad you ain't," said he, looking at her.

"Where did you learn to make such pretty speeches?" she asked. "Well, never mind that. I gather you have had plenty of practice for one so young."

"I am twenty-seven," blurted the Virginian, and he knew instantly that he had spoken like a fool.

"Who would have dreamed it!" said Molly, with well-measured mockery. She knew that she had scored at last, and that this day was hers.

"Don't be too sure you are glad I'm not a man," she now told him. There was something like a challenge in her voice.

"I'll risk it," he remarked.

"For I am almost twenty-three myself," she concluded. And she gave him a look on her own account.

"And you'll not come ridin'?" he persisted.

"No," she answered him. And he knew that he could not make her.

"Then I will tell you goodbye," said he. "But I am comin' again. And next time I'll have along a gentle horse for you."

"Next time! Next time! Well, perhaps I will go with you. Do you live far?"

"I live on Judge Henry's ranch, over yonder." He pointed across the mountains. "It's on Sunk Creek. A pretty rough trail; but I can come here to see you in a day, I reckon. Well, I hope you'll enjoy good health in the meanwhile, ma'am."

"Oh, there's one thing!" said Molly Wood, calling after him rather quickly. "I—I'm not at all afraid of horses. You needn't bring such a gentle one. I—was very tired that day, and—and I don't scream as a rule."

He turned and looked at her so that she could not meet his glance. "Bless your heart!" said he. "Will you give me one of those flowers?"

"Oh, certainly! I'm always so glad when people like them."

"They're pretty near the color of your eyes."

"Never mind my eyes."

"Can't help it, ma'am. Not since South Fork."

He put the flower in the leather band of his hat, and rode away on his Monte horse. Miss Wood lingered a moment, then made some steps toward her gate, from which he could still be seen. Then, with a toss of her head, she went in and shut her door.

Later in the day the Virginian met Mr. McLean, who looked at his hat and innocently quoted: "'My Lulu picked a daisy.'"

"Don't, Lin," said the Southerner.

"Then I won't," said Lin.

Thus, for this occasion, did the Virginian part from his lady—with nothing said one way or another about the handkerchief that had disappeared during the South Fork incident.

As we fall asleep at night, our thoughts will often ramble back and forth between the two worlds.

"What color were his eyes?" wondered Molly on her pillow. The fire in the great stone chimney of her cabin flickered quietly, its gleams now and again lighting the miniature of Grandmother Stark upon the wall.

Camped on the Sunk Creek trail, the Virginian was telling himself in his blankets, "I ain't too old for education. I'll watch her ways and learn. Maybe she will lend me books."

And then the Virginian was fast asleep.

QUALITY AND EQUALITY

In Bennington, a letter from Bear Creek was always a welcome invitation to gather and hear of doings very strange to Vermont. And when the tale of the changed babies arrived, it created a more than usual sensation. "I hate her to be where such things can happen," said Mrs. Wood.

"I wish I could have been there," said her son-in-law, Andrew Bell.

"She does not mention who played the trick," said Mrs. Andrew Bell.

"We shouldn't be any wiser if she did," said Mrs. Wood.

"I'd like to meet the perpetrator," said Andrew.

"Oh, no!" said Mrs. Wood. "They're all horrible."

And she wrote at once, begging her daughter to take good care of herself, and to see as much of Mrs. Balaam as possible. "And of any other ladies that are near you. For you seem to me to be in a community of roughs. I wish you would give it all up. Did you expect me to laugh about the babies?"

Mrs. Wood was considerably relieved when the

next letter arrived. It contained nothing horrible about barbecues or babies. It mentioned the great beauty of the weather, and how well and strong the fine air was making the writer feel. And it asked that books might be sent, many books of all sorts—novels, poetry, all the good old books and any good new ones that could be spared. Cheap editions, of course.

"Indeed she shall have them!" said Mrs. Wood. "How her mind must be starving in that dreadful place!" The letter was not a long one, and, besides the books, spoke of little else except the fine weather and the chances for outdoor exercise that this gave. "You have no idea," it said, "how delightful it is to ride, especially on a spirited horse, which I can do now quite well."

"How nice that is!" said Mrs. Wood, putting down the letter. "I hope the horse is not too spirited."

"Who does she go riding with?" asked Mrs. Bell.

"She doesn't say, Sarah. Why?"

"Nothing. She has a way of not mentioning certain things, now and then."

"Sarah!" exclaimed Mrs. Wood. "Oh, well, mother, you know just as well as I do that she can be very independent and unconventional."

"Yes, but not in that way. She wouldn't ride with poor Sam Bannett, and after all he is a suitable person."

Nevertheless, in her next letter, Mrs. Wood

cautioned her daughter about trusting herself with anyone of whom Mrs. Balaam did not thoroughly approve. The good lady could never grasp that Mrs. Balaam lived a long day's journey from Bear Creek, and that Molly saw her about once every three months. "We have sent your books," the mother wrote. "Everybody has contributed from their store: Shakespeare, Longfellow, a number of novels by Scott, George Eliot, Hawthorne, and lesser writers, and Jane Austen complete, because you admire her so."

The literature reached Bear Creek about a week before Christmas time. By New Year's Day, the Virginian had begun his education.

"Well, I have managed to get through 'em," he said, as he entered Molly's cabin in February. And he laid two volumes upon her table.

"And what do you think of them?" she inquired.

"I think that I've certainly earned a good long ride today."

"Did you like them?"

"No. Not much. If I'd knowed that one was a detective story, I'd have got you to try something else on me. Can you guess the murderer, or is the author too smart for you? That's all they amount to. Well, he was too smart for me this time, but that didn't distress me any. That other book talks too much."

Molly was scandalized, and she told him it was a great work.

"Oh, yes, yes. But it will keep up its talkin'."

"Didn't you feel sorry for poor Maggie Tulliver?"

"Hmp. Yes. Sorry for her, and for Tommy, too. But the man did right to drown 'em both."

"It wasn't a man. A woman wrote *The Mill on the Floss.*"

"A woman did! Well, then, of course she talks too much."

"I'll not go riding with you!" shrieked Molly.

But she did. And he returned to Sunk Creek, not with a detective story, but this time with a Russian novel.

It was almost April when he brought it back to her—and a heavy sleet storm lost them their ride. So he spent his time indoors with her, not speaking a syllable of love. When he came to take his departure, he asked her for some other book by this same Russian. But she had no more.

"I wish you had," he said. "I never saw a book could tell the truth like that one does."

"Why, what do you like about it?" she exclaimed. To her it had been distasteful.

"Everything," he answered. "That young man and his family that can't understand him—" The Virginian looked at Molly a moment almost shyly. "Do you know," he said, and a blush spread over his face, "I pretty near cried when he was dyin' and said about himself, 'I was a giant.' Life made him a go-getter you see, and then took his chance away."

Molly liked the Virginian for his blush. It made

him very handsome. But she thought that it came from his confession about "pretty near crying." The deeper cause she failed to discover. Like the dying hero in the novel, he felt himself to be a giant whom life had made a "go-getter," and denied opportunity.

He took away with him a volume of Shakespeare. "I've saw good plays of his," he remarked.

Kind Mrs. Taylor in her cabin next door watched him ride off in the sleet, bound for the lonely mountain trail.

"If that girl don't get ready to take him pretty soon," she observed to her husband, "I'll give her a piece of my mind."

Taylor was astonished. "Is he thinking of her?" he inquired.

"Lord, Mr. Taylor, and why shouldn't he?"

Mr. Taylor scratched his head and returned to his newspaper.

It was warm and beautiful at Bear Creek. Snow shone upon the peaks of the Bow Leg range. Lower on their slopes the pines were stirring with a gentle song. Flowers bloomed across the wide plains at their feet.

Molly and her Virginian sat at a certain spring where they had often ridden. He was bidding her farewell before undertaking the most important trust Judge Henry had as yet given him. For this journey she had provided him with Sir Walter Scott's novel *Kenilworth*. Shakespeare he had returned and even bought a volume for himself. "As soon as I got used to readin' it," he had told her, "I knowed for certain that I liked readin' for enjoyment."

But it was not of books that he had spoken much today. He had spoken very little. He had asked her to listen to the meadowlark, when its song fell upon the silence like beaded drops of music. He had showed her where a covey of young willow grouse were hiding. Now, without warning, as they sat by the spring, he had spoken powerfully of his love.

She did not interrupt him. She waited until he was finished.

"I am not the sort of wife you want."

He answered roughly, "I am the judge of that." His roughness was a pleasure to her, yet it made her afraid of herself. When he was away from her, she could sit in her cabin and look at Grandmother Stark. She could read letters from home. She could imagine herself as his guide and companion. But when he was by her side, that part became a difficult one. A force unknown to her before shook her fortress of determination. No man could look as this man could look, when his eyes grew hot with internal fire. What color they were baffled her still. "Can it possibly change?" she wondered. It seemed to her that she had seen this color before, looking from a rock straight down into clear seawater. "Is it green, or is it gray?" she asked herself, but did not turn just now to see. She kept her face toward the landscape.

"All men are born equal," he now remarked slowly.

"Yes," she quickly answered, with a combative flash. "Well?"

"Maybe that don't include women?" he suggested.

"I think it does."

"Do you tell the kids so?"

"Of course I teach them what I believe!"

He pondered. "I used to have to learn about the Declaration of Independence. I hated books when I was a kid."

"But you don't anymore."

"No. I certainly don't. But I used to get kept in at recess for bein' so dumb. I was most always at the tail end of the class. My brother, he'd be head sometimes."

"Little George Taylor is my prize scholar," said Molly. "But poor Bob Carmody. I spend more time on him than on all the rest put together."

"My!" said the Virginian. "Ain't that strange! Well, it is mighty confusin'. George Taylor, he's your best scholar, and poor Bob, he's your worst, and there's a lot in the middle—and you tell me we're all born equal!"

Molly could only sit giggling in this trap he had so ingeniously laid for her.

"I'll tell you what," pursued the cowpuncher, with slow and growing intensity, "equality is a great big bluff."

"I didn't mean—" began Molly.

"Wait, and let me say what I mean. I know a man that mostly wins at cards. I know a man that mostly loses. He says it is his luck. All right. Call it his luck. I know a man that works hard and he's gettin' rich, and I know another that works hard and is gettin' poor. He says it is his luck. All right. Call it his luck. I look around and I see folks movin' up or movin' down, winners or losers everywhere. All luck, of course. But since folks can be born that different in their luck, where's your equality? No, seh! A man has got to prove himself my equal before I'll believe him."

Molly sat gazing at him, silent.

"I know what you meant," he told her now, "by sayin' you're not the wife I'd want. But I am the kind that moves up. I am goin' to be your best scholar." He turned toward her, and that fortress within her began to shake.

"Don't," she murmured. "Don't, please."

"Don't what?"

"Spoil this."

"Spoil it?"

"These rides—I don't love you—I can't—but these rides are—"

"What are they?"

"My greatest pleasure. There! And, please, I want them to go on so."

"Go on so! I don't reckon you know what you're sayin'. You might as well ask fruit to stay green. If the way we are now can keep bein' enough for you, it can't for me. A pleasure to you, is it?

Well, to me it is—I don't know what to call it. I come to you and I hate it, and I come again and I hate it, and I ache and grieve all over when I go. No! You will have to think of some other way than just invitin' me to keep green."

"If I am to see you—" began the girl.

"You're not to see me. Not like this. I can stay away easier than what I am doin'."

"Will you do me a favor, a great one?" said she, now.

"Make it as impossible as you please!" he cried. He thought it was to be some action.

"Go on coming. But don't talk to me about— don't talk in that way—if you can help it."

He laughed out, not permitting himself to swear.

"But," she continued, "if you can't help talking that way—sometimes—I promise I will listen. That is the only promise I make."

"That is a bargain," he said.

Then he helped her mount her horse, restraining himself from taking her in his arms, and they rode home to her cabin.

"You have made it pretty near impossible," he said, as he took his leave. "But you've been square today, and I'll show you I can be square when I come back. I'll not do more than ask you if your mind's the same. And now I'll not see you for quite a while. I am going a long way. But I'll be very busy. And bein' busy always keeps me from grievin' too much about you."

She would rather have heard some other last remark than this. "Oh, very well!" she said. "I'll not miss you either."

He smiled at her. "I doubt if you can help missin' me," he remarked. And he was gone at once, galloping on his Monte horse.

Which of the two won a victory this day?

THE GAME AND THE NATION
ACT FIRST

America is divided into two classes: the quality and the equality.

We decreed that every man should henceforth have equal liberty to find his own level. By this very decree we said, "Let the best man win, whoever he is." Let the best man win! That is America's word. That is true democracy. And true democracy and true aristocracy are one and the same thing. If anybody cannot see this, so much the worse for his eyesight.

The above reflections occurred to me before reaching Billings, Montana, some three weeks after I had unexpectedly met the Virginian at Omaha, Nebraska. I had not known of the mission entrusted to him by Judge Henry, which was taking him East. Looking to ride with him among the clean hills of Sunk Creek, I supposed he was there. But instead, I came upon him one morning in Colonel Cyrus Jones's Eating Palace.

Did you know the Palace? It stood in Omaha, near the trains, and it was ten years old (which was middle-aged in Omaha) when I first saw it. It was a shell of wood, painted with golden symbols: the steamboat, the eagle, the Yosemite. A live bear ate handouts at its entrance. It has gone the way of the Indian and the buffalo, for the West is growing old. You should have seen the Palace and sat there. In front of you passed a rainbow of humanity: Chinese, Indian chiefs, Africans, younger sons, Austrian nobility, wide females in pink.

So I passed that way when the language of Colonel Cyrus Jones came out to me. I had never before seen the actual colonel. He stood at the rear of his Palace with a gray flowery mustache and a Confederate uniform, telling the wishes of his guests to the cook through a hole. People living near the Missouri in those days had their own way of speaking. The colonel's voice refreshed me like a breeze off the plains. I went in to be fanned by it, and there sat the Virginian at a table, alone.

To me he remarked, "I'm right glad to see somebody," which was a good deal to say. "Them that comes here," he observed next, "don't eat. They feed. How do they digest anything in this swallow-and-get-out feeding trough?"

"What are you doing here, then?" said I.

"When you can't have what you choose, you just choose what you have." And he took the menu. I began to realize that he had something on his mind, so I did not trouble him further.

Meanwhile, he sat studying the menu.

"Ever heard of them?" he inquired, shoving the food-stained document toward me.

Canapés and other improbable dishes were listed there, all spelled perfectly. It was the old trick of copying some big city menu to catch innocent travelers. Whenever this is done, the food is wickedly awful and the cowpuncher knew that as well as anybody.

"What about them?" His finger was at a special item: Frogs' Legs a la Delmonico. "Do they truly serve those anywhere?" he asked. And I told him, certainly. I also explained to him about elegant eateries like Delmonico of New York.

"There's not a little bit of use in lyin' to me this mornin'," he said, with a smile. "I ain't goin' to order anything's legs."

I remembered the odd Texas legend about a traveler ordering from the menu. He calls for a vol-au-vent, the finest French pastry. The proprietor looks at the traveler, puts a pistol to his ear and says, "You'll take hash." I was thinking of this and wondering what would happen to me. So I placed the order.

"Wants frogs' legs, does he?" shouted Colonel Cyrus Jones. He fixed one eye on me, and it narrowed to a slit. "Missionary ate the last leg off me just now," said he. "Brown the wheat!" he commanded, through the hole to the cook. Someone had ordered hot cakes.

"I'll have fried eggs," said the Virginian. "Cooked both sides."

"White wings!" sang the colonel through the hole. "Let 'em fly up and down."

"Coffee an' no milk," said the Virginian.

"Draw one in the dark!" the colonel roared.

"And beefsteak, rare."

"One slaughter in the pan, and let the blood drip!"

"I should like a glass of water, please," said I. The colonel threw me a look of pity.

"One Missouri and ice for the professor!" he said.

"That fellow's a right lively man," commented the Virginian. But he seemed thoughtful. Presently he inquired, "You say he was a foreigner, and learned fancy cookin' in New Yawk?"

That was this cowpuncher's way. He'd never drop a new thing until he had all the information. So I told him the history of Lorenzo Delmonico, as much as I knew, and the Southerner listened intently.

"Mighty interestin'," he said. "He could just take little old ornery frogs, and dandy 'em up. I expect his cookin' would give an outraged stomach to a plain-raised man."

"If you want to follow it up," said I, by way of a sudden experiment, "Miss Molly Wood might have some book about French dishes."

But the Virginian did not turn a hair. "I reckon she wouldn't," he answered. "She was raised in Vermont. They don't bother overly about their eatin' up in Vermont. Here's what Miss Wood recommended the last time I was seein' her," the cowpuncher added, bringing *Kenilworth* from his pocket. "Right fine story. That Queen Elizabeth must have certainly been a competent woman."

"She was," said I. But talk came to an end here. A dusty crew of men now entered and drifted to a table. Each man of them gave the Virginian about a quarter of a slouchy nod. His greeting to them was very calm. *Kenilworth* went back into his pocket, and he breakfasted in silence. Among those who had greeted him I now recognized a face.

"Why, that's the man you played cards with at Medicine Bow!" I said.

"Yes, Trampas. He's got a job at the ranch now." The Virginian said no more, but went on with his breakfast.

The Virginian had changed. Aged I would say. He no longer looked young. The boy was altogether gone from his face—the boy who turned Medicine Bow upside down, whose baby trading had outraged Bear Creek, who loved to jingle his spurs. But manhood had only reined in, not broken his youth.

Presently we went together to the railway yard. There he showed me the judge's first shipment of beef by train. He began telling me about it very casually indeed, so I knew this was important. "The whole lot's shipped through to Chicago in two sections over the Burlington Railroad." Two trains, twenty cars, each car packed with huddled, round-eyed steers.

"They ain't ate or drank anything to speak of," he said. "You might suppose they know what they're travelin' to Chicago for." And casually, always casually, he told me the rest. Judge Henry could not spare his foreman. Instead, the Virginian was put in charge of these twenty train cars and a double crew of cowboys. After Chicago, he was to return by St. Paul over the Northern Pacific Railroad. Along the way he was to negotiate favorable rates for the Sunk Creek outfit from the railroad directors. This was all the Virginian told me and all there was to tell, to be sure.

"So you're acting foreman," said I.

"Why, somebody has to have the say, I reckon."

"And of course you hated the promotion?"

"I don't know about promotion," he replied. "The boys have been used to seein' me one of themselves. You ought to come along with us far as Plattsmouth." Thus he shifted the subject from himself. But he could not hide the judge's show of confidence in him. The Virginian had the care of several thousand perishable dollars and the control of men. There were more steers than men to be responsible for. But none of the steers had been suddenly picked from the herd and set above his fellows. Even worse, the new deputy foreman had to keep those six restless fellow cowboys away from towns. The judge needed their services back at the ranch.

While the cowpunchers absorbed themselves in a deep but harmless game of poker, the Virginian and I sat on the top of a car, contemplating the sandy shallows of the Platte River.

"I should think you'd play," said I.

"Poker? With them? When I play, I want it to

be interestin'." He took out Sir Walter's *Kenilworth* once more, and turned the volume over and over slowly without opening it. Perhaps, in spirit, he was wandering on Bear Creek with the girl whose book it was. "Queen Elizabeth would have played a mighty powerful game," was his next remark.

"Poker?" said I.

"Yes, seh. Do you expect Europe has got any queen equal to her at present?"

I doubted it.

"Say, do you remember Shakespeare's fat man?"

"Falstaff? Oh, yes, indeed."

"Ain't that grand? Why, Shakespeare sure makes men talk the way they do in life. I reckon he couldn't get printed today. It's a shame Shakespeare couldn't know about poker. He'd have had Falstaff playing all day and the prince beating him."

"The prince had the brains," said I.

"Did he? A game like whist you play with brains and cards. Falstaff could have played whist. But they're only part of poker playin' in this here world. A man like that prince will play winnin' poker with whatever hand he's holdin'."

"Then I'd be grateful for your definition of poker," said I.

Before I had any reply, I had to jump off the train. "Tell the judge the steers was all right this far," said the Virginian.

That was the last I saw of the deputy foreman for a while.

BETWEEN THE ACTS

My road to Sunk Creek was a crooked one. By rail I traveled northwest to Fort Meade. From there, I made my way on horseback. Riding through the Black Hills, it rained most unpleasantly. The horse and I could not enjoy the country. When I finally changed from the saddle into a stagecoach, I caught a thankful expression on the animal's face, and returned the same.

"Six legs inside this carriage tonight?" said somebody, as I climbed the wheel. "Give thanks for not havin' eight," he added cheerfully. "Clamp your mind on to that, Shorty." And he slapped the shoulder of his neighbor. Naturally I took these two for old companions. But we were all total strangers. They told me of the new gold excitement at Rawhide, and supposed it would bring the Northern Pacific Railroad. We spoke of all sorts of things. And when there was silence, I anticipated the autumn holiday promised me by Judge Henry. His last letter had said that an outfit would be starting for his ranch from Billings on the seventh, and he would have a horse for me. This was the fifth.

The man who had slapped Shorty soon introduced himself. "Scipio le Moyne, from Gallipolice, Ohio," he said. "Scipio. It's French. But us folks have been Americans for a hundred years." Cattle was his business, as a rule, but of late he had been "looking around some," and the rumored gold in Rawhide seemed much on his brain. Shorty struck me as "looking around" also. He was quite short, indeed, and got tossed around every time the wagon jerked. He was light haired and mild. Think of a lost yellow dog that imagines each newcomer is going to turn out to be his master, and you will have Shorty.

As we neared Medora, something roused me from sleep. Scipio and Shorty were rushing from the wagon. The Northern Pacific had changed its schedule. Running with our satchels was difficult enough but then we found our way blocked by sand and wood piles. A piece of stray wire caught on my ankle. Two of us waved hats, and all of us screeched. Making the train meant twenty-four hours to us.

As it moved off in our faces, smooth and easy and insulting, Scipio dropped instantly to a walk. We two others passed him, only to reach an empty track. There went the train. I kicked my valise, and then sat on it, dumbfounded.

Shorty walked aimlessly around, bemoaning his fate. He had lost his job and lost at cards. He had sold his horse and saddle to catch a friend on this train. He threw out a string of grievances to the air, as if the air understood him.

Meanwhile, Scipio arrived at his leisure. He watched the rear car ooze away westward among the hills. Then Scipio spoke to it. "Leave me behind you plush-lined, nickel-plated, whistlin' washroom? No, I'm stayin' right here because it suits me, you dude-inhabited hot-box!" From that point, his speech appalled me and held me spellbound. But it's not for me to relate it to you. Then he calmed down a bit, finishing with expressions of sympathy for the train because it could never have known a father.

"What did you expect?" inquired a slow voice behind us. I jumped round, and there was the Virginian. "I got them steers through all right," he added to me. "Sorry to see you get so out of breath runnin' after the train. Is your valise sufferin' any?"

"Who's he?" inquired Scipio, curiously, turning to me.

The Southerner sat with a newspaper on the rear platform of a caboose. The caboose stood hitched behind a mile or so of freight train headed west. So here was the deputy foreman, his steers delivered in Chicago, his men (I could hear them) safe in the caboose, his legs dangling at ease over the railing. He wore the look of a man for whom things are going smooth. And for me the way to Billings was smooth now, also.

"Who's he?" Scipio repeated.

From inside the caboose loud laughter and noise broke on us. Someone was reciting "And It's My Night to Howl."

"We'll all howl when we get to Rawhide," said another and they all howled now.

"Some men's words travel faster than they do," said the Virginian to Scipio. Of Shorty he took no more notice than he did of the cowboys in the caboose.

"So you heard me speakin' to the express," said Scipio. "Well, I guess, sometimes I—See here," he exclaimed, "I may have talked some, but I walked a whole lot. You must have noticed—"

"I noticed," said the Virginian, "that thinkin' came quicker to you than runnin'."

I was glad I was not Scipio, judged merely on my way of missing a train. And of course I was sorry that I had kicked my valise.

"Oh, I'm glad you enjoyed our misfortune!" said Scipio. "Observin' somebody else's trouble always kind of refreshes me too. You must be a philosopher."

Approval now grew plain upon the face of the

Virginian. "By your legs," said he, "you are used to the saddle."

"I'd be called used to it, I expect."

"By your hands," said the Southerner, again, "you ain't roped many steers lately. Been cookin' or something?"

"Say," retorted Scipio, "tell my future some now."

"I'm right distressed," answered the gentle Southerner, "we've not a drop to drink in this outfit."

"Step down, now. Scipio le Moyne's my name. And it ain't a bit far to whiskey from here!" urged Scipio. "Step down. I've got a forty-dollar thirst."

Just then the singing from the caboose resumed:

> I'm wild, and woolly, and full of peas;
> I'm hard to curry above the knees;
> I'm a she-wolf from Bitter Creek, and
> It's my night to ho-o-wl—

And as they howled and stamped, the wheels of the caboose began to turn gently and to murmur.

The Virginian rose suddenly. "Will you save that thirst and take a forty-dollar job?"

"Doin' what? Missin' trains, shouting profanity, or what?" said Scipio.

"I'll tell you soon as I'm sure."

At this Scipio looked hard at the Virginian. "Why, you're talkin' business!" said he, and leaped on the caboose, where I was already. "I *was* thinkin' of Rawhide," he added, "but I ain't anymore."

"Well, good luck!" said Shorty, on the track behind us.

"Oh, say!" said Scipio, "he wanted to go on that train, just like me."

"Get on," called the Virginian. "But as to getting a job, he ain't just like you." So Shorty came, like a lost dog when you whistle to him.

Our wheels clicked as our train crossed onto the main track. A train hand threw the switch shut after us, jumped aboard, and returned forward over the roofs. Inside the caboose they had reached the third howling of their she-wolf song.

"Friends of yours?" said Scipio.

"My outfit," drawled the Virginian.

"Do you always travel outside?" inquired Scipio.

"It's lonesome in there," returned the deputy foreman. And here one of them came out, slamming the door.

"Hell!" he said, at sight of the distant town. Then, ill-tempered, he addressed the Virginian, "I told you I was going to get a bottle here."

"Have your bottle, then," said the deputy foreman, and kicked him off into Dakota. (It was not North Dakota yet; they had not divided it.) At the same time, the Virginian had retrieved a pistol from his boot. Therefore the man sat in Dakota quietly, watching us go away into Montana, offering no objections. Just before he became too small to make out, we saw him rise and head back toward the saloons.

CHAPTER 15

THE GAME AND THE NATION
ACT SECOND

"That is the only harsh step I have had to take this whole trip," said the Virginian. He holstered his pistol with a jerk. "I have been fearing he would force it on me." And he looked at empty, receding Dakota with disgust. "So near to home!" he muttered.

"Known your friend long?" whispered Scipio to me.

"Fairly," I answered.

"I've had these cowboys almost three thousand miles," said the Virginian, tilting his head toward the noise in the caboose. "And I've attempted to deliver them back as I received them. The whole lot. And I would have. But he has spoiled my hopes." The deputy foreman looked again at Dakota. "It's a disappointment," he added. "You may know what I mean."

I had known a little, but not to the depth of this man's pride. Scipio gave him sympathy. "There must be quite a balance of 'em left with you yet," said Scipio, cheeringly.

"I had the boys plumb contented," continued the deputy foreman, hurt into openly talking about himself. "By the time we got to St. Paul I had them reconciled to my authority. Then this news about gold had to strike us."

"And they're dreamin' nuggets," suggested Scipio.

The Virginian smiled gratefully at him. "Fortune is shinin' bright and blindin' their delicate young eyes," he said, regaining his usual self.

We all listened a moment to the rejoicings within.

"Energetic, ain't they?" said the Southerner. "Though they're strainin' mighty hard not to be tame, they're goin' back to Sunk Creek with me accordin' to the judge's orders. Not one of them will desert to Rawhide, for all their dangerousness. And I ain't goin' to have to fuss over it. Only one is left now that don't sing. Maybe I will have to make some arrangements about him. The man I have parted with," he said, with another glance at Dakota, "was our cook, and I will ask you to replace him, Colonel."

Scipio gaped wide. "Colonel! Say!" He stared at the Virginian. "Did I meet you at the Palace?"

"Not exactly meet," replied the Southerner. "I was present one mornin' last month when this gentleman ordered frogs' legs."

"Sakes and saints, but that was a terrible position, havin' to say something to anybody who came in any time of day," burst out Scipio. "I told them they could hire some fresh man, for I was goin' back to punch cattle or fight Indians, or take a rest somehow. I didn't propose to get weary of the world at twenty-five. There ain't no regular Colonel Cyrus Jones any more, you know. He's dead and buried. But his Palace was doin' big business, and he had been a kind of attraction. Now, they always keep a live bear outside, and some poor fellow fixed up like the colonel inside. Course I'll cook for you. You've got a dandy memory for faces!"

"I wasn't right convinced till I kicked him off and you gave that shut to your eyes again," said the Virginian.

Once more the door opened. A man with slim black eyebrows, slim black mustache, and a black shirt tied with a white handkerchief was looking steadily from one to the other of us.

"Good day!" he remarked generally. Then, to the Virginian, "Where's Schoffner?"

"I expect he'll have got his bottle by now, Trampas."

Trampas looked from one to the other of us again. "Didn't he say he was coming back?"

"He reminded me he was going for a bottle, and after that he didn't wait to say a thing."

Trampas looked at the platform and the railing and the steps. "He told me he was coming back."

"I don't reckon he has come, not unless he climbed up somewhere ahead of this car. I must say, when he got off he didn't look like a man does when he has the intention of returnin'."

For a moment Trampas's thoughts seemed troubled. Then he commented, "This seems to have become a passenger train," and returned abruptly inside the caboose.

"Is he the member who don't sing?" asked Scipio.

"That's the specimen," replied the Southerner.

The noise inside the caboose had dropped quickly to stillness. You could scarcely catch the sound of talk. Our caboose was clicking comfortably westward, rail after rail, mile upon mile. Night was beginning to rise.

"I think I'll maybe join their meeting," said the Virginian. He opened the door. "Kind of dark here, ain't it?" said he. And lighting the lantern, he shut us out.

"What do you think?" said Scipio to me. "Will he take them to Sunk Creek?"

"He evidently thinks he will," said I. "He says he will, and he has the courage of his convictions."

"That ain't near enough courage to have!" Scipio exclaimed. "There's times in life when a man has got to have courage *without* convictions."

"If there's to be any gunplay," put in the excellent Shorty, "I'll stand with him."

"Ah, go to bed with your gunplay!" responded Scipio, entirely good-humored. "Is the judge paying for a carload of dead punchers to gather his beef for him? And this ain't a proposition worth a man's gettin' hurt for himself, anyway."

Scipio had said his piece. He lighted a cigarette, and no more wisdom came from him. The night was established. The rolling badlands sank away in it. A chill wind came blowing, bringing with it the feel of the distant mountains.

"That's Montana!" said Scipio. "I am glad to have it inside my lungs again."

"Ain't you getting cool out there?" said the Virginian's voice. "Plenty room inside."

Perhaps he had expected us to follow him. Perhaps he had meant us to delay long enough not to seem like reinforcements. "These gentlemen missed the express at Medora," he explained to his men.

I cannot say who they took us for or what they believed. The atmosphere of the caboose was charged with voiceless currents of thought. By way of a friendly beginning to the three hundred miles of caboose we were now to share, I reminded them who I was. "I am so lucky to have caught you again," I finished. "I was afraid my last chance of reaching the judge's had gone."

They met my small talk with the smallest talk you can have. I suppose we had made twenty miles before one of them asked his neighbor had he ever seen New York.

"No," said the other. "Flooded with dudes, ain't it?"

"Swimmin'," said the first.

"Leakin', too," said a third.

"Well, my gracious!" said a fourth, and beat his knee in private delight. None of them ever looked at me. For some reason I felt very ill at ease.

"Good clothes in New York," said the third.

"Rich food," said the first.

"Fresh eggs, too," said the third.

"Well, my gracious!" said the fourth, beating his knee.

"Why, yes," observed the Virginian, unexpectedly, "they tell me that eggs there ain't liable to be as rotten as what you'll find in this country."

None of them had a reply for this, and New York was abandoned. For some reason I felt much better.

They started a new subject next, led off by Trampas.

"Going to the excitement?" he inquired, selecting Shorty.

"Excitement?" said Shorty, looking up.

"Going to Rawhide?" Trampas repeated. And all watched Shorty.

"Why, I'm all adrift after missin' that express," said Shorty.

"Maybe I can give you employment," suggested the Virginian.

"You'll find most folks going to Rawhide, if you're looking for company," pursued Trampas, fishing for a recruit.

"How about Rawhide, anyway?" said Scipio. "Are they taking much mineral out? Have you seen any of the rock?"

"Rock?" broke in the enthusiast who had beaten his knee. "There!" And he brought some from his pocket.

"You're always showing your rock," said Trampas, sulking, for Scipio now led the conversation, and

Shorty returned safely to his dozing.

"Hmm!" went Scipio at the rock. He turned it back and forth in his hand, looking it over. He tossed it, caught it in the air, and handed it back. "Got some feldspar in there, I see." That was his only word about it. He said it cheerily. He left no room for discussion. You could not damn a thing worse. "Ever been in Santa Rita?" pursued Scipio, while the rock got pushed back into a pocket. "That's down in New Mexico. Ever been to Globe, Arizona?" And Scipio talked away about the mines he had known.

There was no getting at Shorty any more that evening. Trampas was foiled of his fish, or of learning where the fish's heart lay. I too escaped for the rest of this night. At Glendive we had a dim supper. I bought some blankets. It was late, and sleep occupied the attention of us all.

We lay along the shelves of the caboose, a peaceful sight I should think. I slept almost immediately, so tired that not even our stops or anything else waked me, except once. Suddenly, the air I was breathing grew pure, and I roused. Sitting in the door was the lonely figure of the Virginian. He leaned in silent contemplation of the occasional moon. On the caboose shelves the others slept sound and still. They were not untrustworthy to look at, it seemed to me—except Trampas. The others were average rough male blood, merely needing to be told the proper things at the right time. There was a light sound by the door, and I found the Virginian's eye on me. Finding who it was, he nodded and motioned with his hand to go to sleep. And this I did with him in my sight, still leaning in the open door, through which came the interrupted moon and the sound of the rippling Yellowstone River.

CHAPTER 16

THE GAME AND THE NATION
LAST ACT

Everyone has experienced awakening in the morning and wondering where on earth you are. So it was with me as I awoke in the caboose, hearing voices, but not the actual words at first.

I heard, "Hathaway!" and then more clearly, "Portland 1291!"

This meant nothing to me, and I drowsed off again to the rhythm of the wheels. Next, the shock of stopping brought me to. When we were again in motion, I heard, "Rosebud! Portland 1279!" These figures jarred me awake. I said, "It was 1291 before," and sat up in my blankets.

They were counting the lessening distance westward. We were drawing near the Rawhide Station—the point where you leave the railway for the new mines. Rawhide Station lies this side of Billings. Here desertion would be easy. The more difficult choice—duty and Sunk Creek—was still some fifty miles away. Here was Trampas's best chance. He could just lie low. With temptation right in front of the men, Trampas might win his battle over the deputy foreman without making a move. Untroubled, the Virginian seemed to find only enjoyment in this sunny September morning, and ate his breakfast peacefully.

The mutineers just sat, digesting. "What's your scar?" one asked after inspecting the neck of his neighbor.

"Foolishness," the other answered. "One day last summer we come on a big snake by Torrey Creek Corral. The boys got to betting that I wouldn't make good on my word that I could deal with snakes. So I looped my rope and catched him up by the tail. I cracked him like a whip, and snapped his head off. You've saw it done?" he said to the audience.

The audience nodded wearily.

"But the loose head flew agin me, and the fangs caught. I was pretty sick for a while."

"It don't pay to be clumsy," said the first man. "If you'd snapped the snake away from you instead of toward you, its head would have whirled off into the brush, same as they do with me."

"That's odd," I said. "Your scar looks like a knife cut."

"Don't it?" said the snake-snapper. "There's many that gets fooled by it."

"An antelope knows a snake is his enemy," said another to me. "Ever seen a buck circling round and round a rattler?"

"I have always wanted to see that," said I. This I knew to be a respectable piece of truth.

"It's worth seeing," the man went on. "After

the buck gets close in, he gives an almighty jump up in the air, and down comes his four hoofs in a bunch right on top of Mr. Snake. Cuts him all to hash. Now you tell me how the buck knows that."

Of course I could not tell him. And again we sat in silence for a while—friendlier silence, I thought.

"Speakin' of bites," spoke up a new man, "how's that?" He held up his thumb.

"My!" breathed Scipio. "Must have been a lion."

The man wore a wounded look. "I was huntin' owl eggs for a botanist from Boston," he explained to me.

"Chiropodist, weren't he?" said Scipio. "Or maybe a sonnabulator?"

"No, honest," protested the man with the thumb, so that I was sorry for him and begged him to go on.

And I wondered why this politeness of mine should throw one or two of them into stifled laughing. Scipio, on the other hand, gave me a disgusted look and sat back sullenly for a moment, and then took himself out on the platform, where the Virginian was lounging.

"The young feller wore knee-pants and thick spectacles," resumed the narrator, "and he carried a tin box strung on a strap. I took it for his lunch till it flew open and a horned toad hustled out. Then I was sure he was a botanist—or whatever you call 'em. Well, he was after owl eggs—eggs of them little prairie owls that some claim can turn their head clean around and keep a-watchin' you. We was ridin' through that prairie-dog town, used to be on the flat just after you cross the south fork of Powder River. I said I'd dig an owl nest out for him if he was willing to camp till I'd dug it. So while the botanist went glarin' around the town with his glasses to see if he could spot a prairie dog and an owl usin' the same hole, I was diggin' in a hole I'd seen an owl run down. And that's what I got." He held up his thumb again.

"The snake!" I exclaimed.

"Yes, sir. Mr. Rattler was keepin' house that day. Took me right there. I hauled him out of the hole hangin' on to me. Eight rattles."

"Eight!" said I. "A big one."

"Yes, sir. Thought I was dead. But the woman—"

"The woman?" said I.

"Yes, woman. Didn't I tell you the botanist had his wife along? She acted better than the man. He was shoutin' that he had no whiskey, and that his knife wasn't sharp enough to amputate my thumb and the doctor was twenty miles away. He was screeching out 'most everything he knew in the world. But she just clawed his pocket and burrowed and kep' yelling, 'Give him the stone, Augustus!' And she whipped out one of them Injun medicine stones—first one I ever seen—and she clapped it on to my thumb, and it started in right away."

"What did it do?" said I.

"Sucked. Like blotting-paper. Soft and funny it was, and gray. They get 'em from elks' stomachs, you know. And when it had sucked the poison out of the wound, it falls off my thumb by itself! And I thanked the woman for saving my life and keeping her head that cool. I never knowed how excited she had been till afterward. She was awful shocked."

"I suppose she started to talk when the danger was over," said I, with deep silence around me.

"No, she didn't say nothing to me. But when her next child was born, it had eight rattles."

Wild commotion in the caboose was the response to this conclusion. And I joined them. Who could help it? Fact and falsehood blended with such perfect art, with a conclusion so new, but made with such old material! I cared nothing that I was the victim, and I joined them. Then suddenly I felt a chill. It was in their laughter. The loudness was too loud. I caught the eyes of Trampas fixed on the Virginian with malevolence. Scipio's disgusted glance was on me from the door.

Dazed by these signs, I went out on the platform to get away from the noise. There the Virginian said to me, "Cheer up! You'll not be so easy for 'em that-a-way next season."

He said no more; and with his legs dangled over the railing, appeared to resume his newspaper.

"What's the matter?" said I to Scipio.

Scipio answered. "Couldn't you see? You kept hinderin' me with askin' those urgent questions of yours! You don't understand. You ain't a common tenderfoot this trip. You're the foreman's friend. They've hit him through you. That's the way they count it. It's encouraged them. Can't you see that?"

Scipio had stated it plainly. And as we ran by the next station, "Howard!" they harshly yelled. "Portland 1256!"

We had been passing gangs of workmen on the track. And at that last yell the Virginian rose. "I reckon I'll join the meeting again," he said. "This filling and repairing makes it look like all those stories about a washout might have been true."

"Washout?" said Scipio.

"Bighorn Bridge, they say—four days ago."

"Then I wish it came this side of Rawhide Station."

"Do you?" drawled the Virginian. And smiling at Scipio, he lounged in through the open door.

"He beats me," said Scipio, shaking his head. "His trail is terrible hard to anticipate."

We listened.

"Work bein' done on the road, I see," the Virginian was saying, very friendly and conversational.

"We see it too," said the voice of Trampas.

"Seem to be easin' their grades some."

"Grading! Can't you tell when a flood's been eating the banks?"

"Why, yes," said the Virginian, sweet as honey. "But 'ain't you heard of the improvements west of Big Timber, all the way to Missoula, this season? I'm talkin' about them."

"Yes, I've heard."

"Good money-savin' scheme, ain't it?" said the Virginian. "Lettin' a freight run down one hill and up the next as far as she'll go without steam, and shavin' the hill down to that point." Now this was an honest engineering fact. "Better than dudes squintin' through telescopes," the Southerner commented.

"It's common sense," assented Trampas. "Have you heard the new scheme about the water-tanks?"

"I ain't right certain," said the Southerner.

"I must watch this," said Scipio, "or I shall bust." He went in, and so did I.

"They used to put all their tanks at the bottom of their grades," said Trampas.

"Why, you get the water easier at the bottom."

"You can pump it to the top, though," said Trampas, growing superior. "And it's cheaper."

"That gets me," said the Virginian, interested.

"Trains after watering can start down hill now and get the benefit of the gravity. It'll cut down operating expenses a heap."

"That's certainly common sense!" exclaimed the Virginian, absorbed. "But ain't it kind of late for that?"

"Live and learn. So they gained speed, too. High speed on half the coal this season, until the accident."

"Accident!" said the Virginian, instantly.

"Yellowstone Limited. Man fired a pistol at the engineer. Train was flying past so quick the bullet broke every window and killed a passenger on the back platform," finished Trampas, and turned on his heel.

Someone began to laugh, but his neighbor gripped him to silence. This was a triumph too serious for noise. Not a mutineer moved. I felt cold.

"Trampas," said the Virginian, "I thought you'd be afeared to try it on me."

Trampas whirled round. His hand was at his belt. "Afraid!" he sneered.

"Shorty!" said Scipio, sternly, and leaping upon that youth, took his half-drawn pistol from him.

"I'm obliged to you," said the Virginian to Scipio. Trampas's hand left his belt. He threw a slight, easy look at his men, and keeping his back to the Virginian, walked out on the platform and sat on the chair where the Virginian had sat so much.

"Don't you comprehend," said the Virginian to Shorty, amiably, "that this here question has been discussed peaceable by civilized citizens? Now you sit down and be good, and Mr. le Moyne will return your gun when we're across that broken bridge, if they have got it fixed for heavy trains yet."

"This train will be lighter when it gets to that bridge," spoke Trampas, out on his chair.

"Why, that's true, too!" said the Virginian. "Maybe none of us are crossin' that Bighorn Bridge now, except me. Funny if you would end up persuadin' me to quit and go to Rawhide myself! But I reckon I'll not. I reckon I'll worry along to Sunk Creek, somehow."

"Don't forget I'm cookin' for you," said Scipio, gruffly.

"I'm obliged to you," said the Southerner.

"You were speaking of a job for me," said Shorty.

"I'm right obliged. But you see—I ain't exactly foreman the way this comes out, and my promises might not bind Judge Henry to pay salaries."

The train began slowing for the Rawhide Station, and all began to be busy and to talk. "Going up to the mines today?" "Oh, let's grub first." "Guess it's too late, anyway." And so forth. They rolled and roped their bedding, put on their coats with a good deal of elbow motion, and otherwise showed off. It was wasted. The Virginian did not know what was going on in the caboose. He was leaning and looking out ahead, and Scipio's puzzled eye never left him. And as we halted for the water-tank, the Southerner exclaimed, "They ain't got away yet!" as if it were good news to him.

He meant the delayed trains. Four stalled expresses were in front of us, besides several freights. And two hours more at least before the bridge would be ready.

Travelers stood and sat about unhappily, near the cars, out in the sagebrush, anywhere. People in hats and spurs watched them, and Indian chiefs offered them painted bows and arrows and shiny horns.

"I reckon them passengers would prefer a leg of mutton," said the Virginian to a man loafing near the caboose.

"Bet your life!" said the man. "First bunch of 'em has been stuck here four days."

"Plumb starved, ain't they?" inquired the Virginian.

"Bet your life! They've eat up their dining cars and they've eat up this town. Fine business here if we'd only been ready," he continued. "Indians come over from the reservation bringin' some beef and game and fish. Big money in it, bet your life! Them Eastern passengers has just been robbed. I wisht I had somethin' to sell!"

"Anything starting for Rawhide this afternoon?" said Trampas, out of the caboose door.

"Not until morning," said the man. "You going to the mines?" he resumed to the Virginian.

"Why," answered the Southerner, slowly and casually, and addressing himself strictly to the man, while Trampas, on his side, paid obvious inattention, "this here delay may unsettle our plans some. But it'll be one of two ways. Either we're all goin' to Rawhide, or we're all goin' to Billings. We're all one party, you see."

Trampas laughed audibly inside the door as he rejoined his men. "Let him keep up appearances," I heard him tell them. "It don't hurt us what he says to strangers."

"But I'm goin' to eat hearty either way," continued the Virginian. "And I ain't goin' to be robbed. I've been promisin' myself a treat if we stopped here."

"Town's cleaned out," said the man.

"So you tell me. But all you folks has forgot one source of revenue that you have right close by, mighty handy. If you have got a gunny sack, I'll show you how to make some money."

"Bet your life!" said the man.

"Mr. le Moyne," said the Virginian, "the outfit's cookin' stuff is aboard, and if you'll get the fire ready, we'll see how frogs' legs go fried." He walked off at once, the man following like a dog. Inside the caboose rose a gust of laughter.

"Frogs!" muttered Scipio. And then turning a blank face to me, "Frogs?"

"Colonel Cyrus Jones had them on his bill of fare," I said. "'Frogs' Legs a la Delmonico.'"

"Shoo! They had it when I came. Never looked at it. Frogs?" He went down the steps very slowly, with a long frown. Reaching the ground, he shook his head. "That man's trail is surely hard to anticipate," he said. "But I must hurry up that fire. For his appearance has given me encouragement," Scipio concluded, and became brisk. Shorty helped him, and I brought wood. Trampas and the other people strolled off to the station, a compact band.

Our little fire was built beside the caboose, so the cooking things might be easily reached and put back. You would scarcely think such operations held any interest, even for the hungry, when there seemed to be nothing to cook. A few sticks of wood blazed tamely in the dust. Three silent men attended a frying pan, half a tin bucket of lard, some water, and barren plates and knives and forks. That was all. But the travelers came to see. They drew near, and stood, a sad, lonely, shifting audience. Four to begin with; and then two wandered away. Soon, one of these came back, finding it worse elsewhere. "Supper, boys?" said he.

"Breakfast," said Scipio, crossly. And no more of them addressed us. I heard them joylessly mention Wall Street to each other, and Saratoga. I even heard the name Bryn Mawr, which is near Philadelphia. But these fragments of home dropped in the Montana wilderness were of no interest to me now.

"See them marshy slogs full of weeds?" said Scipio. We took a little turn and had a sight of the Virginian quite active among the ponds. "Hush! I'm getting some thoughts," continued Scipio. "He wasn't sorry enough. Don't interrupt me."

Presently Scipio swore loud and brilliantly. "What did he say to Trampas after that play they exchanged over railroad improvements and Trampas put the josh on him? Didn't he say, 'Trampas, I thought you'd be afraid to do it?' Well, sir, Trampas had better have been afraid. Course he wasn't sorry. I guess he had the hardest kind of work to look as sorry as he did. You wait."

"Wait? What for? Go on, man! What for?"

"I don't know! I don't know! Whatever hand he's been holdin' up, this is the showdown, here before the caboose gets off the bridge. Supper's in sight, Shorty. Food for reflection."

"None for the stomach?" asked the passenger who had spoken once before.

"We're figuring on that too," said Scipio. His crossness had melted entirely away.

"Why, they're cowboys!" exclaimed another passenger; and he moved nearer.

Trampas now came back from the station, his herd following behind. They had found hunger, and no hope of supplies until the next train from the East. This was no fault of Trampas, but they were following him less compactly. They carried one piece of cheese, the size of a fist, the weight of a brick, the color of a corpse. And the passengers, seeing it, exclaimed, "There's Old Faithful again!" and took off their hats.

"You gentlemen met that cheese before, then?" said Scipio, delighted.

"It's been offered me three times a day for four days," said the passenger. "Did he want a dollar or a dollar and a half?"

"Two dollars!" said the enthusiast, the one who earlier had slapped his knee. And all of us save Trampas fell into fits of idiotic laughter.

"Here comes our grub, anyway," said Scipio, looking off toward the marshes. And his hilarity sobered away in a moment.

"Well, the train will be in soon," stated Trampas. "I guess we'll get a decent supper without frogs."

All interest settled now upon the Virginian. He was coming with his man and his gunny sack, and the gunny sack hung from his shoulder heavily, as a full sack should. He took no notice of the gathering, but sat down and partly emptied the sack. "There," said he, very businesslike, to his assistant, "that's all we'll want. I think you'll find a ready market for the rest."

"Well, my gracious! What fool eats a frog?"

"Oh, I'm fool enough for a tadpole!" cried the passenger. And they began to take out their pocketbooks.

"You can cook yours right here, gentlemen," said the Virginian, with his slow Southern courtesy.

"How much will you sell a couple for?" inquired the enthusiast.

The Virginian looked at him with friendly surprise. "Why, help yourself! We're all together yet awhile. Help yourselves," he repeated, to Trampas and his followers. They hung back a moment, then, with a slinking motion, set the cheese upon the earth and came forward to receive some supper.

Scipio's frying pan got busy, and prosperous odors rose from it.

"Run for a bucket of fresh water, Shorty," the Virginian continued, beginning his meal. "Colonel, you cook pretty near good. If you had sold 'em as advertised, you'd have certainly made a name for yourself."

Several were now eating with satisfaction, but not Scipio. It was all that he could do to cook without laughing. The whole man seemed to glisten. His eye was shut to a slit once more, while the innocent passengers thankfully swallowed.

"Now, you see, you have made some money,"

began the Virginian to the local who had helped him get the frogs.

"Bet your life!" exclaimed the man. "Take your share, won't you?" And he held out half his gains.

"Keep 'em," returned the Southerner. "I reckon we're even. But I expect they'll not equal Delmonico's, seh?" he said to a passenger.

"Don't trust the judgment of a man as hungry as I am!" exclaimed the traveler, with a laugh. And he turned to his fellow travelers. "Did you ever enjoy supper at Delmonico's more than this?"

"Never!" they sighed.

"Why, look here," said the traveler, "what fools the people of this town are! Here we've been all these starving days, and you come and get ahead of them!"

"That's right easy explained," said the Virginian. "I've been where there was big money in frogs, and they 'ain't been. They're all cattle here. They talk cattle, think cattle, and they're bankrupt in consequence. Ain't that so?" he inquired of the native.

"That's about the way," said the man.

"It's mighty hard to do what your neighbors ain't doin'," pursued the Virginian. "Montana is all cattle. Nobody noticed the country right here is too small and too swampy for a range. It's just waitin' to be a frog ranch."

At this, those who understood what the Virginian was doing all put on serious faces.

"Travelin' learns a man many customs," said

the Virginian to his assistant. "Course, you'll never do here the business they done at Tulare, California, north side of the lake. They certainly utilized them hopeless swamps splendid. Of course they put up big capital and went into it scientific. They got advice from the government Fish Commission, and such like knowledge. You see, they had big markets for their frogs: San Francisco, Los Angeles, and clear to New York after the Southern Pacific was through. Up here you could sell to passengers every day like you done this day. They would get to know you. Competing swamps are scarce. The dining cars would take your frogs, and you would have the Yellowstone Park for four months in the year. Them hotels are anxious to please. They would buy off you whatever their Eastern patrons consider fine eatin'. And you folks would be sellin' something instead of nothin'."

"That's a practical idea," said a traveler. "At little cost."

"At little cost," said the Virginian.

"Would Eastern people eat frogs?" inquired the man.

"Look at us!" said the traveler.

"Delmonico doesn't give you such a treat!" said the Virginian.

"Not exactly!" the traveler exclaimed.

"How much would be paid for frogs?" said Trampas. And I saw Scipio bend closer to his cooking.

"Oh, I don't know," said the traveler. "We've paid pretty well, you see."

"You're late for Tulare, Trampas," said the Virginian.

"I was not thinking of Tulare," Trampas retorted. Scipio's nose was in the frying pan.

"To hear 'em talk frogs at Tulare!" said the Virginian, looking round upon the whole company. Lost in memory for a moment, he allowed himself a broad smile. "Same as other folks talks horses or steers or whatever they're raising to sell."

"And it paid good?"

"The only money in the county was right there," answered the Virginian. "It was a dead county, and only frogs was sellin'. All the men had been cattlemen at one time or another. It would give almost anybody a shock to hear 'em speak about herdin' the bullfrogs in a pasture by themselves." The Virginian allowed himself another smile, but became serious again.

"That was their policy," he explained. "Except at certain times they kept the bulls separate. The Fish Commission told 'em they'd better, and it worked mighty well. There was millions. And the money rolled in! It was a gold mine for the owners. Forty percent they netted some years. And they paid generous wages. They sold to all them French restaurants in San Francisco. The Palace Hotel made it a specialty. Only in Sacramento frogs was dull. I expect the California legislature was too ornery for such fine luxuries. They tell of a senator that raked a million out of Los Angeles real estate, and started in for a bang-up meal with champagne.

Wanted to scatter his new gold thick and quick. But he got astray among all the fancy dishes, and just yelled right out before the ladies, 'Damn it! Bring me forty dollars' worth of ham and eggs.' He was a funny senator, now."

The Virginian paused, and finished eating a leg. And then with diabolic art he made as if to steer into a different subject. "Talkin' of senators," he resumed, "Senator Wise—"

"How much did you say wages were at Tulare?" inquired one of Trampas's group.

"How much? Why, I never knew what the fore-man got. The regular hands got a hundred. Senator Wise—"

"A hundred a *month*?"

"Why, it was wet and muddy work. A man risked gettin' rheumatism. But I was going to tell about Senator Wise. When Senator Wise was speaking of his visit to Alaska—"

"Forty percent, was it?" said Trampas.

"Oh, I must call my wife," said the traveler behind me. "This is what I came West for." And he hurried away.

"Not forty percent the bad years," replied the Virginian. "The frogs had enemies, same as cattle. I remember when a pelican got in the spring pasture, and the herd broke through the fence—"

"Fence?" said a passenger.

"Wire net. Every pasture was a square swamp with a ditch around, and a wire net. You've heard the mournful, mixed-up sound a big bunch of cattle will make? Well, seh, as you drove from the railroad to the Tulare frog ranch you could hear 'em a mile away. But in a bad year it might only be twenty per-cent."

"Well, twenty percent is good enough for me," said Trampas, "if Rawhide don't suit me."

"A hundred a month!" said the local man. And busy calculations began to arise among them.

"It went to fifty percent," pursued the Virginian, "when New York and Philadelphia got to biddin' against each other. Both cities had signs all over 'em claiming to furnish the true Tulare frog. And both had 'em all right. Same as cattle trains, you'd see frog trains tearing across Arizona—big glass tanks with wire over 'em—through to New York, with the frogs starin' out."

"Why, George," whispered a woman's voice behind me, "he's merely deceiving them! He's merely making that stuff up out of his head."

"Yes, my dear, that's merely what he's doing."

"Well, I don't see why you imagined I should care for this. I think I'll go back."

"Better see it out, Daisy. This beats the geysers or anything we're likely to find in the Yellowstone."

"Then I wish we had gone to Bar Harbor as usual," said the lady, and she returned to her Pullman.

But her husband stayed. Indeed, the crowd had grown. The men edged close, drawn by a common tie. Those who understood did not know his motive. Those with gold fever were taken in. They were counting the money they'd make. Had any man given a sign to warn them, I think he would have been lynched. Even the Indian chiefs had come to see. They naturally understood nothing of it, yet instinctively recognized that the Virginian was a great man. They watched him with approval.

Trampas declared that tickets to California would be expensive so Rawhide had better come first. That was just what the Southerner needed to inspire his heaven-born imagination.

"There's a better reason for Rawhide than tickets, Trampas," said he. "I said it was too late for Tulare."

"I heard you," said Trampas. "Opinions may differ. You and I don't think alike on several points."

"Do you reckon I'd be rotting here on forty dollars if Tulare was like it used to be? Tulare is broke."

"What broke it? Your leaving?"

"Revenge broke it, and disease," said the Virginian, striking the empty frying pan on his knee. At those lurid words the crowd seemed to lean nearer.

"Yes, it was a case of revenge," resumed the Virginian, "and disease. A man named Saint Augustine came to Philadelphia, dead broke. He saw Philadelphia was full of Quakers that dressed plain and ate humdrum. So he started cooking for 'em, anythin' but humdrum: turtle, bird, and a broth called consommé he made from forty chickens. It caught right on. He got rich, and Philadelphia got well known, and Delmonico in New York got jealous. Lorenzo was his front name. He was the cook that had the say-so in New York.

"He aimed to cut away the trade from Saint Augustine and put Philadelphia back where he thought she belonged. Frogs was the fashion rage then. These foreign cooks set the fashion in eatin', same as foreign dressmakers do women's clothes. Both cities was catchin' and swallowin' all the frogs Tulare could throw at 'em. So he—"

"Lorenzo?" inquired a fascinated mutineer.

"Yes, Lorenzo Delmonico. He bid a dollar a tank higher. Saint Augustine raised him fifty cents. And Lorenzo raised him a dollar. And Saint Augustine shoved her up three. Quite sudden, Lorenzo starts for Tulare. He buys tickets over the Santa Fe. But, gentlemen, hush! The very same day, Saint Augustine tears out of Philadelphia. He travels by way of Washington. Of course Tulare didn't know nothin' of this. All it knowed was how the frog market was soarin'. Then the two chefs arrived, breathless, and started in to screechin' what they'd pay for the frog monopoly. Them unsuspectin' Tulare boys got a little too amused at 'em. Well, them two cooks quit that ranch without disclosin' their identity. Then, soon as they got to a safe distance they swore eternal friendship. And they went home over the Union Pacific, sharing the same car. Their revenge killed frogs. The disease—"

"How did it kill frogs?" demanded Trampas.

"Just killed 'em. Delmonico and Saint Augustine wiped frogs off the plate of fashion. Not a banker in Fifth Avenue'll touch one now if another banker's around watchin' him. As for the disease . . . if ever you see a man that hides his feet and won't take off his socks in company, he has worked in them Tulare swamps and got the disease. Catch him wadin', and you'll find he's web-footed. The frogs are dead, Trampas . . . and so are you."

"Rise up, liars, and salute your king!" yelled Scipio. And he threw his arms round the Virginian.

"Let me shake hands with you," said the traveler who had failed to interest his wife in these things. "I wish I was going to have more of your company."

"Thank you, seh," said the Virginian.

Other passengers greeted him, and the Indian chiefs came, saying, "How!" because they followed their feelings without understanding.

"Don't feel so humbled, boys," said the deputy foreman to his most sheepish crew. "These gentlemen from the East have been enjoying you some, I know. But think what a weary wait they have had here. Didn't I have it to do? And I'll tell you one thing for your consolation. When I got to the middle of the frogs, I almost believed it myself." And he laughed out the first laugh I ever heard him give.

One man shook his hands. That started it off. The rest followed, with Trampas at the end. The tide was too strong for him. He was not a graceful loser, but he got through this.

Word came that the bridge was open. The

trains, with noise and triumph, began to move westward at last. Everyone waved farewell to everyone, craning from steps and windows. In twenty minutes the trains in front had moved, and our turn came.

"Last chance for Rawhide," said the Virginian.

"Last chance for Sunk Creek," said a reformed mutineer, and everyone sprang aboard. There was no question who had won his spurs now.

Our caboose trundled on to Billings along the cotton-wooded Yellowstone. The plains and bluffs and the distant snow began to grow familiar, even to me. We turned to our baggage that was to come off, since camp would begin in the morning. I saw the Virginian carefully rewrapping *Kenilworth*, that he might bring it to its owner unharmed. I said, "Don't you think you could have played poker with Queen Elizabeth?"

"No. I expect she'd have beat me," he replied. "She was a lady."

It was at Billings, on this day, that I made my reflections about equality. The Virginian had been equal to the occasion. That is the only kind of equality I recognize.

CHAPTER 17

SCIPIO MORALIZES

What mood did the Virginian fall into now? Being less busy, was he "grieving" for the girl on Bear Creek? I only know that after talking so lengthily he fell into a nine days' silence.

Only official words came from him as we rode southward from the railroad, gathering the judge's stray cattle. During the many weeks since the spring roundup, some of these animals had as usual got very far off their range. Getting them on again became the present business of our party.

Directions and commands he duly gave. But routine has never at any time of the world passed for conversation. Utterances such as "We'll work Willow Creek tomorrow mornin'" I did not consider a breaking of the man's true silence. Seeming to keep easy company with the camp, he yet kept altogether to himself. That final pitched battle of wits had made the men his captives and admirers—all but Trampas. Of him the Virginian did not seem to be aware.

But Scipio le Moyne would say to me now and then, "If I was Trampas, I'd pull my freight."

"Yes, he ought to be leavin'," our friend Shorty murmured. Then, with his eye upon the quiet Virginian, he added, "He's sure studying his revenge."

"He ain't studying. He knows what he'll do," said Scipio. "The time ain't arrived." This was the way they felt about it. And, not unexpectedly, this was the way they made me feel about it. That Trampas also felt something was easy to know. One spot of sulkiness in camp will spread its dull flavor through anyone that sits near it. We had to sit near Trampas at meals for nine days.

Trampas's thoughts could not have been pleasant. His supporters had forsaken him and gone over to the enemy. Why then did he not simply take off—"pull his freight," as Scipio said? Pay was due him—"time" as it was called in cow land. To have this money, he must stay under the Virginian's command until they reached the judge's ranch on Sunk

Creek. Meanwhile, each day's work added to the wages in store for him. And, once at Sunk Creek, it would no longer be the Virginian who commanded him. It would be the real ranch foreman. At the ranch he would be the Virginian's equal again.

Shorty's word about "revenge" seemed backward to me. Revenge, as I told Scipio, was what I should be thinking about if I were Trampas.

"He dare not," was Scipio's immediate response. "Not till he's strong again. He got laughed plumb sick by the bystanders. Whatever spirit he had was broke in the presence of us all. He'll have to recuperate." Scipio then spoke of the Virginian's attitude. "Maybe revenge ain't just the right word for where this affair has got to now for him. When you beat another man at his own game—like he done to Trampas—you've had all the revenge you can want, unless you're a hog. And he's no hog. But if a man acted that spiteful to you, would you quit thinkin' about him just because you'd headed him off? He's got to deal with Trampas somehow—man to man. Trampas and him can't stay this way when they get back and go workin' same as they worked before. No, sir! He's goin' to reckon to a finish."

On the afternoon following this talk, I invited Scipio to tell me what sort of "finish" he expected, after the finishing Trampas had already been dealt. Scipio rose, and, with the frying pan he had been washing, walked slowly at me.

"I do believe you oughtn't be let to travel alone

the way you do." He put his face close to mine. "What has come and gone between them has only settled one point. He was appointed boss of this outfit in the absence of the regular foreman. Since then all he has been playin' for is to hand back the men in as good shape as they'd been handed to him, without losing any on the road through desertion or shooting or what not. He had to kick his cook off the train that day, and the loss made him sorrowful. But once he'd jumped me into the vacancy, I expect he felt some consolation. As boss of the outfit he beat Trampas who was settin' himself up as opposition boss. The outfit is better than satisfied it come out that way, and they're stayin' with him. He'll hand them all back in good condition, barrin' that lost cook. So for the present his point is made, you see. But look ahead a little. We get back to the ranch. He's not boss there any more. He is just one of us again, taking orders from a foreman they tell me has showed partiality to Trampas more'n a few times. That's what Trampas is plainly trusting to. Trusting it will fix him all right and fix his enemy all wrong. He'd not otherwise dare to stay sour like he's been."

Scipio looked across a little creek to where the Virginian was helping throw down the gathered cattle. "He's got to remember Mr. Trampas and his spite-work," he said, pointing the frying pan at the Southerner. "And I am goin' to advise your folks," ended the complete Scipio, "not to leave you travel so much alone—not till you've learned more."

He had convinced me of my inexperience. During the final days of our journey I no longer sought his advice on this special topic: What would the Virginian do to Trampas? Would it be another intellectual crushing of him, like the frog story? Or this time, would there be something more concrete—muscle or gunpowder—in it?

After several years, the Virginian still remained utterly beyond me. Scipio's experience was not yet three weeks long. So I let him alone about all this, though we continued discussing most other things good and evil in the world. Scipio's twenty odd years were indeed a library of life. I have never met a better heart, a shrewder wit, looser morals, or a more hard and fast sense of decency and duty.

All the time I was wondering about the Virginian, we were spending many hours together: eating, sleeping, and riding.

I made attempts at conversation—and failed. Once after a sudden storm of hail had chilled the earth numb and white, we sat drying and warming ourselves by a fire. I brought up the subject of equality about which I knew he held strong opinions. "Oh," he would reply, and "Certainly." When I asked him what it was that made a man a leader of men, he shook his head and puffed his pipe. Then, noticing how the sun had restored the earth to summer in half an hour, I spoke of our American climate.

"Yes," said he, wiping the damp from his Winchester rifle.

Our American climate, I said, had worked remarkable changes, at least.

"Yes," he said. And I could not tell whether he heard. So I decided to test his attention.

"It has, for example, changed all of us into poker players—"

Bang went his Winchester. The bullet struck close to my left. I sat up angrily.

"That's the first foolish thing I ever saw you do!" I said.

"Yes," he drawled slowly, "I'd ought to have done it sooner. He was pretty near lively again." And then he picked up a rattlesnake six feet behind me. It had been numbed by the hail and then partly revived by the sun. He had shot its head off.

CHAPTER
18

"WOULD YOU LIKE TO
BE A PARSON?"

After this I gave up my experiments in conversation. By the final afternoon of our journey, with Sunk Creek actually in sight, my speculating had risen to a fever pitch. Soon the Virginian and Trampas would be "man to man."

And at that very time, the talking part of the Virginian awoke after nine days asleep. He suddenly asked me, "Would you be a parson?"

I was mentally so far away that I couldn't get back in time to understand or answer before he repeated, "What would it take for you to become a parson?"

He drawled it out in his gentle way, as if it had not been nine days since our last talk.

"Take?" I still felt rather distant. "How?"

His next question brought me home.

"I expect the pope's the biggest of them parson jobs?"

"Well, yes—decidedly the biggest."

"Beats the English one? Archbishop—ain't it? Of Canterbury? The pope comes ahead of him?"

"His Holiness would say so if his Grace did not."

The Virginian turned half in his saddle and I saw the gleam of his teeth beneath his mustache. It was seldom I could make him smile, even slightly. But with his next words, his eyes grew distant.

"His Holiness and His Grace. Now if I was to hear 'em namin' me that-a-way every mornin', I'd have trouble getting' down to business."

"Oh, you'd get used to the pride of it."

"It isn't the pride. The laugh is what would ruin me. Keepin' a straight face would take 'most all of my attention. The archbishop"—here he took one of his wide mental turns—"is apt to be a big man in them Shakespeare plays. Kings take talk from him they'd not stand from anybody else, and he talks fine, frequently. About the bees, for instance, when Henry is going to fight France. He tells him a beehive is similar to a kingdom. I learned that piece." The Virginian could not have expected to blush at uttering these last words. He knew that his sudden color must tell me in whose book it was he had learned the piece. Was not her copy of *Kenilworth* even now in his pocket? So to cover his blush, he now very deliberately asked me a question.

"How many religions are there?"

"All over the earth?"

"Begin with ourselves. Right here at home. You do the countin'."

I accordingly did. "Anyhow, there are at least fifteen."

"Fifteen." He held this fact a moment. "And

they don't worship a whole heap of different gods like the ancients did?"

"Oh, no!"

"It's just the same one?"

"The same one."

The Virginian folded his hands over the saddle horn, and leaned forward in contemplation of the wide, beautiful landscape.

"One God and fifteen religions," was his reflection. "That's right many religions for just one God."

"Do you think there are fifteen varieties of good people?" Though his voice now had an edge that could cut glass, it was still not raised. "There ain't fifteen. There ain't two. There's one kind. And when I meet it, I respect it. Neither praying nor preaching has ever made me ashamed of myself. That's come from one or two people I have knowed that never said a superior word to me. They thought more of me than I deserved, and that made me behave better than I naturally wanted to."

He had looked away again to the hills behind Sunk Creek Ranch, to which our walking horses had now almost brought us.

"I reckon some parsons have a right to tell you to be good. The bishop of this here Territory has a right. But I'll tell you: a middlin' doctor is a poor thing, and a middlin' lawyer is a poor thing; but keep me from a middlin' man of God."

Once again he had reduced matters to their essentials, but I did not laugh this time. I agreed that there should be a heavy price for malpractice on human souls.

"What do you make of that proposition yonder?" As he pointed to the cause of this question he had become again his regular, engaging self. I saw over in a fenced meadow, to which we were now close, what he called "the proposition." It meant a stranger clad in black, who would have been visible to a watchful eye for a mile or two.

"I reckoned you hadn't noticed him. He set me goin' on the subject of parsons a while back. I expect he is another missionary to us poor cowboys."

I seemed to feel the stranger's forceful personality from a hundred yards. It was in his walk—I should better say stalk—as he strolled along the creek. His hands were behind his back, and there was a sense of displeased waiting in his movements.

"Yes, he's a missionary all right," said the Virginian, conclusively. He took to singing, or rather to whining, with his head tilted at an absurd angle upward at the sky:

> Great big fool, he hasn't any knowledge.
> Gosh! How could he, when he's never been to college?
> Neither has I. But I've come mighty near.
> I peaked through the door once last year.

He was beginning the next stanza, but stopped short. A horse had neighed close behind us.

"Trampas," said he, without turning his head, "we are home."

"It looks that way." Some ten yards were between us and Trampas.

"And I'll trouble you for my rope you took this mornin' instead of your own."

"I don't know if it's your rope I've got." Trampas skillfully spoke such that the opposite meaning flowed from his words.

If it was discussion he tried for, he failed. The Virginian's hand moved, and for one thick, flashing moment I evidently had the same thoughts as Trampas. But the Virginian only held out to Trampas the rope which he had detached from his saddle.

"Take your hand off your gun, Trampas. If I had wanted to kill you you'd be lying dead nine days back. Here's your rope. Did you expect I wouldn't know it? It's the only one in camp that's stiff. Maybe you expected me to notice, and not take notice?"

"I don't spend my time in expectations about you. If—"

The Virginian wheeled his horse across the road. "You're talkin' too soon after reachin' safety, Trampas. I didn't tell you to hand me that rope this mornin', because I was busy. I ain't foreman now. And I want that rope."

Trampas produced a smile as skillful as his voice. "I guess your having mine proves this one is yours." He rode up and took the coil the Virginian held out, while unloosing the disputed one on his saddle. No small insult in cattle land is more offensive than taking another man's rope. And it is the small insults which lead to the big bullets. Trampas put a smooth coating of plausibility over the whole transaction. "After the rope corral we had to make this morning"—his voice had a tone of mockery—"the ropes was all strewed round camp, and in the hustle I—"

"Pardon me," said a deep voice behind us, "do you happen to have seen Judge Henry?" It was the reverend, now standing by the fence. As we turned round, he spoke on with an outward show of great authority. "From his answer to my letter, Judge Henry undoubtedly expects me here. I have arrived to find that he has been absent all day—absent the whole day."

The Virginian sat sidewise to talk. One long, straight leg supported him on one stirrup. The other bent at ease, the boot half-lifted from its dangling stirrup. He made himself the perfection of courtesy. "The judge is frequently absent all night, seh."

"Not tonight, I should think. I thought you might know something about him."

"I have been absent myself, seh."

"Ah! On a vacation, perhaps?" His strong glance was straight and frank and fearless. But his smile reminded me of my school days. When we would return to school from the Christmas holidays, the masters would shake our hands and welcome us with, "Robert, John, Edward, glad to see you all looking so well! Rested, and ready for hard work, I'm sure!"

That smile does not really please even good, tame little boys. The Virginian was nearing thirty.

"It has not been a vacation this trip, seh," said he, settling straight in his saddle. "There's the judge driving in now, in time for all questions you have to ask him."

His horse took a step, but was stopped short. There lay the Virginian's rope on the ground. I had looked upon Trampas's departure as quite proper. And, as he was leaving, I was aware of his placing the coil across the back of the Virginian's saddle. Had Trampas intended it to fall? If so, the sly maneuver succeeded, supposing he meant to nag the owner of the rope. A few hundred yards ahead of us Trampas was now shouting loud cowboy shouts. Were they to announce his return or his disrespect? The Virginian leaned, keeping his seat. He swung down his arm, caught up the rope, and hung it on his saddle. Rage spread over his face.

From his fence the reverend spoke with another strong, cheerless smile. "You pick up that rope as if you were well trained to it."

"It's part of our business, seh, and we try to mind it like the rest." He answered in a gentle drawl. But his words could not pierce the missionary's armor, his air of superiority. You could take the reverend for nothing more than a vigorous, sincere, dominating man, full of the highest purpose. I admired him for coming all this way with his clean, short, gray whiskers and his black, well-brushed suit. But whatever his faith, I already doubted he was the right one to make it grow in these new, wild fields.

Meanwhile, the Virginian rode beside me. He sat silent in a volcanic wrath I failed to notice. The missionary coming on top of Trampas had been more than he could stand. But I did not know, and I spoke with innocent cheeriness.

"Is the parson going to save us?" I asked and I fairly jumped at his answering voice.

"Don't talk so much!" he burst out.

"Who's been talking?" I screeched back. "I'm not trying to save you. I didn't take your rope." And having poured this out, I whipped up my pony.

But he spurred his own alongside of me. Glancing at him, I saw that his mood had reversed itself. Suddenly he was having trouble containing his laughter.

"I'm right obliged to you," he laid his hand on my horse's mane as he spoke, "for bringing me back out of my nonsense," he confessed. "A grown man ought to own a big lot of temper. But like all his valuable possessions, he ought to keep it and not lose any." This was his full apology.

I had half a mind to speak to the judge about Trampas, only it seemed beyond a visitor's business. Our missionary was at this moment speaking to Judge Henry at the door of the ranch.

"I reckon he's explaining he has been a-waiting."

The Virginian said, throwing his saddle. "And the judge don't look hopelessly distressed."

The judge had just returned from a day's excursion with a wagonful of guests. He waved me a welcome, which I waved back. "He's got Miss Molly Wood there!" I exclaimed.

"Yes." The Virginian was brief about this fact. "I'll look after your saddle. You go and get acquainted with the company."

This favor was his way of saying he hoped—after our recent boiling over—that all was now more than right between us. So for the moment, I left him to his horses, and his corrals, and his Trampas, and his foreman, and his imminent problem.

CHAPTER 19

DR. MACBRIDE BEGS PARDON

Judge and Mrs. Henry, Molly Wood, and two strangers, a lady and a gentleman, had gone driving in the large three-seated wagon. They seemed a merry party. But as I came close enough to hear, the minister's stern voice reached me first. He was ending a sentence with "...more opportunity for them to have the benefit of hearing frequent sermons.".

"Yes, to be sure, sir." The judge turned and gave me an especially warm welcome. Perhaps he was relieved that my timely arrival had put a stop to the previous conversation. "Let me introduce you to the Reverend Dr. Alexander MacBride. Doctor, another guest we have been hoping for about this time" was my introduction. I made my final bows to the gentleman and wife from New York. But I had not ended all discussion.

"We may be said to have met already." Dr. MacBride addressed me. It occurred to me that if they had policemen in heaven, he would be at least a captain. He did not mean to be unpleasant. His mind, filled with weighty matters, simply had no room left for pleasure. "I was saying to Judge

Henry," he continued, "I wish horsemen as skillful as your friend might ride to a church on the Sabbath. A church where they would have opportunity to hear frequent sermons."

"Yes," said Judge Henry, "yes. It would be a good thing."

Mrs. Henry murmured something about the kitchen and went into the house.

"I was informed before undertaking my journey," Dr. MacBride continued again, "that I should find this a bleak and godless country. But to ride three hundred miles from Medicine Bow without passing a church of any faith!"

The judge explained that there had been a few a long way to the right and left of him. "Still," he admitted, "you are quite right. But don't forget that this is the newest part of a new world."

"Judge," said his wife, reappearing at the door, "you're keeping everyone standing in the dust with your talking."

This finally did end the discussion. As our little party entered the house, the judge kept me behind long enough to whisper sorrowfully, "He's going to stay a whole week."

I had hopes he would not stay a whole week when our hosts apologized for the crowded arrangements. They were delighted to have us, but hadn't expected everyone to arrive at the same time. The foreman's house had been prepared for two of us, and did we mind? The two of us were Dr. MacBride and myself. I expected him to mind. But

I was wrong. He had tried straw in a stable several times, he assured Mrs. Henry, and this was better than that. How the foreman and his wife liked being turned out for a missionary and myself was not my concern. It must have been hard on them. The room with its two cots and furniture was as nice as possible. We closed the door on the adjoining room, though it seemed empty.

Mrs. Henry gave us a meal so good that I still remember it. The judge tried his best to keep the mealtime merry. He poured out anecdotes like wine. They warmed all of us except Dr. MacBride. Perhaps he was thinking about his sermon. I told Miss Wood about the many I had seen him pull from his case. "Goodness!" said she. "Are we to hear one every evening?" This I doubted. He was probably trying to pick the most suitable one for the occasion. Her tone grew delightfully sharp. "Do you know, when I first heard him I thought his voice was enthusiastic. But if you listen, you'll find it's merely militant. He never really meets you with it. He's off on his hill watching the battlefield the whole time."

"He will find at least one hard-edged doubter here."

"Judge Henry?"

"Oh, no! The wild man you're taming."

She was smooth. "Oh, as if anyone could tame him! But don't you find him intelligent?"

Suddenly I somehow knew that she didn't want to tame him. But what did she want to do? The thought of her had made him blush this afternoon. No thought of him made her blush this evening.

A great laugh from the other guests made me aware that the judge must have just completed his tale of the "Sole Survivor."

"And so," he finished, "they all went off mad because it hadn't been a massacre." Mr. and Mrs. Ogden—they were the New Yorkers—gave this story much applause, and Dr. MacBride half a minute later laid his "ha-ha," like a heavy stone, upon the party.

"Talking of massacres," I now quickly addressed the table, "I have recently escaped one myself."

The judge had told the last of his stories. "Oh, tell us!" he implored.

"Seriously, sir, I think we came close to tragedy. But your extraordinary man brought us out into comedy safe and dry."

This gave me their attention. I then related the whole tale of my experience from that afternoon in Dakota when I first stepped aboard the caboose.

They followed my narrative intently. The New Yorkers were fascinated because such events do not happen on Manhattan Island. Mrs. Henry was attentive because she was my hostess. Miss Wood followed for whatever her reasons were—I couldn't see her eyes. But the judge and the missionary were gripped the most. When I finished, they voiced their quite dissimilar opinions.

Judge Henry struck the table lightly with his

fist. "I knew it!" And he leaned back in his chair with a face of contentment. He had trusted his man, and his man had proved worthy.

"Pardon me." Dr. MacBride had a manner of saying "pardon me" which made forgiveness impossible. "Am I to understand that these cowboys abandoned their mutiny because they were less skillful at lying than the man they had plotted against?"

I began an answer. "It was other qualities, sir, that were revealed in what you call his lying that—"

"And what am I to call it, if it is not lying? A competition in deceit in which, I admit, he outdid them."

"It's their way to—"

"Pardon me. Their way to lie? They bow down to the greatest in this?"

"Oh," said Miss Wood in my ear, "give him up."

The judge took a turn. "We-ell, Doctor..." He seemed to stick here.

Mr. Ogden helped him. "You've said the word yourself, Doctor. It's the competition, don't you see? The trial of strength by no matter what test."

"Yes," said Miss Wood, unexpectedly. "And it wasn't that George Washington couldn't tell a lie. He just wouldn't. I'm sure if he'd attempted it he'd have told a much better one than General Cornwall."

Dr. MacBride now adopted his deepest tone of voice. "Pardon me. I cannot accept such a view, sir.

No matter how you try to put it, in the end we have a struggle between men where lying decides the survival of the fittest. Better, far better, if it was to come, that they had shot honest bullets. There are worse evils than war."

The doctor's eye glared righteously about him. Mrs. Henry at once introduced the subject of trout fishing. Dr. MacBride had brought his rod. We assured him that the streams on the west slope of the Bow Leg Mountains would afford him fine sport. Thus we ended our meal in harmony.

CHAPTER 20

THE JUDGE IGNORES PARTICULARS

"Do you often have visits from missionaries?" Ogden inquired of Judge Henry. All but one of the male dinner guests had gone to the judge's office. Dr. MacBride had retired to his quarters in the foreman's house to prepare for the service he would soon be holding.

The judge laughed. "They come now and then. I would like the bishop to come. And the men always like it. But I fear our friend will scarcely please them so well."

"You don't mean they'll—"

"Oh, no. They'll keep quiet. The fact is, they have a good deal better manners than he has, if he only knew it. But as for any good he'll do—"

There was a somewhat heavy knock at the office door, and I think we all feared it was Dr. MacBride. But when the judge opened, the Virginian was standing there in the darkness.

"So!" The judge opened the door wide. He was very hearty to the man he had trusted. "You're back at last."

"I came to report."

While they shook hands, Ogden nudged me. "That the fellow?" I nodded. "Fellow who kicked the cook off the train?" I again nodded, and he looked the Virginian over.

Judge Henry introduced him to Ogden.

The New Yorker, meaning well, said, "You're the man I've been hearing such a lot about."

"Then I expect you have the advantage of me, seh," said the Virginian, very politely. "Shall I report tomorrow?" His eyes were on the judge again.

"Yes, yes—I'll want to hear about the cattle tomorrow. But step inside a moment now. There's a matter..." The Virginian stepped inside, and took off his hat. "Sit down. You had trouble—I've heard something about it," the judge went on.

The Virginian sat down, grave and graceful. But he held the brim of his hat all the while. He looked at Ogden and me, and then back at his employer. There was reluctance in his eye. I wondered if his employer was going to make him tell his own exploits in the presence of us outsiders.

"You had some trouble," repeated the judge.

"Well, there was a time when they had some notions. They're good boys." And he smiled a very little.

Contentment increased in the judge's face. "Trampas a good boy too?"

But this time he did not smile. He sat with his eyes fixed firmly on his employer.

The judge passed rather quickly on to his next

point. "You've brought them all back, though, I understand, safe and sound, without a scratch?"

The Virginian looked down at his hat, then up again at the judge, mildly. "I had to part with my cook."

There was no use. Ogden and myself exploded in laughter. Even on the embarrassed Virginian a large grin slowly forced itself. "I guess you know about it," he murmured. And he looked at me accusingly. He knew I had told the tale.

"I only want to say," said Ogden, "that I know I couldn't have handled those men."

The Virginian relented. "You never tried, seh."

The judge had remained serious, but plainly he felt contented. "Quite right," he said. "You had to part with your cook. When I put a man in charge, I put him in charge. I don't make particulars my business. Do you understand?"

"Thank you." The Virginian understood that his employer was praising his management of the expedition. But I don't think he realized that his employer had just been putting him to a further test. Some men would have taken the opportunity to complain about their fellow workman and to seek praise on their own deeds. The judge was delighted with the Virginian's modesty. The tall man made a move as if to rise.

"I haven't finished," said the judge. "I was coming to the matter. I fancy Trampas has learned something he didn't expect."

This time the Virginian evidently did not

understand, any more than I did.

The judge explained. "I mean about Roberts."

A pulse of triumph shot over the Southerner's face. He understood now, and was unable to suppress his mild reaction. But he was silent.

"You see," the judge explained to me, "I was obliged to let Roberts, my old foreman, go last week. His wife could not have stood another winter here, and a good position was offered to him near Los Angeles."

I did see. I saw a number of things. I saw why the foreman's house had been empty to receive Dr. MacBride and me. And I saw that the judge had been very clever indeed. Though I had not revealed anything about the current feelings between Trampas and the Virginian, he had understood. He knew that in Roberts, Trampas had lost a powerful friend. He and the Virginian now stood man to man.

"And so," the judge continued speaking to me, "here I am at a very inconvenient time without a foreman. Unless"—I caught the twinkle in his eyes before he turned to the Virginian— "unless you're willing to take the position yourself. Will you?"

I saw the Southerner's hand grip his hat as he was turning it round. He held it still now. His other hand found it and gradually crumpled the soft crown. It meant everything to him: recognition, higher station, better fortune, a separate house of his own, and—perhaps—one step nearer to the woman he wanted. I don't know what he might have said to the judge had they been alone, but the judge had chosen to do it in our presence. Sweat came out on the Virginian's forehead, and his eyes dropped from his employer's.

"Thank you," was all he managed to say.

"Well, now, I'm greatly relieved!" exclaimed the judge, rising at once. "I was in something of a hole," he said to Ogden and me, "and this gives me one thing less to think about. Saves me a lot of particulars," he lightheartedly added to the Virginian, who was now also standing up. "Begin right off. Leave the bunkhouse. The gentlemen won't mind your sleeping in your own house."

Thus he dismissed his new foreman. But the new foreman, when he got outside, turned back for one gruff word, "I'll try to please you." That was all. He was gone in the darkness. But there was light enough for me, looking after him, to see him lay his hand on a shoulder-high gate and vault it. Sounds of cheering came to us a few moments later from the bunkhouse. Evidently he had "begun right away," as the judge had directed. He had told his good fortune to his brother cowpunchers, and this was their answer.

"I wonder if Trampas is shouting too?" inquired Ogden.

"Hm!" said the judge. "That is one of the particulars I wash my hands of."

I knew that he meant it completely. I knew, once he had decided to appoint the Virginian as his lieutenant, that, like a wise commander-in-chief, he would trust his lieutenant to take care of his own business.

"Well," Ogden pursued with interest, "haven't you landed Trampas completely at his mercy?"

The phrase tickled the judge. "That is where I've landed him!" he declared. "And here is Dr. MacBride."

CHAPTER 21

IN A STATE OF SIN

Thunderclouds brewed on the missionary's brow. Here the storm would presently break upon the congregation. The tables in the hall had been pushed back and the chairs gathered. "Eight-thirty?" he inquired.

It was only twenty minutes away. We threw the unsmoked portions of our cigars away, and returned to offer our services to the ladies. This amused the ladies. They had done without us. All was ready in the hall.

"Has Dr. MacBride announced his text yet? I've got one for him," said Molly Wood, joining us. She stood on tiptoe and spoke it comically in our ears. "All men are liars." This made us merry as we stood among the chairs in the congested hall.

I left the ladies, and sought the bunkhouse. I had heard the cheers, but I was curious also to see the men, and how they were taking it. There was little to see in the room but a great deal to hear. Amid much talking they were getting ready to come to church: brushing their hair, shaving, and making themselves clean. Their words were occasionally offensive and always entertaining.

"I'm a Mohammedan," one declared. "I hope I ain't goin' to hear nothin' to shock me."

And they went on with their joking. But Trampas was out of the joking. He lay on his bed reading a newspaper, making no attempt to look pleasant. My eyes were considering him when Scipio came in.

"Don't look so bashful," said he. "There's only us girls here."

He had been helping the Virginian move his belongings from the bunkhouse over to the foreman's cabin. He was to occupy the Virginian's old bed here. "And I hope sleepin' in it will bring me some of his luck," said Scipio. "You'd ought to have seen it when he told us in his quiet way. Well," Scipio sighed a little, "it must feel good to have your friends glad about you."

"Especially Trampas," said I. "The judge knows about that," I added.

"Knows, does he? What's he say?" Scipio drew me quickly out of the bunkhouse.

"Said he didn't want to know and didn't care."

"How did he happen to hear about it?" snapped Scipio. "You told him!" he immediately guessed. Scipio jerked his thumb at the Virginian, who appeared for a moment in the lighted window of the new quarters he was arranging. "He never would tell."

"Has something happened?" I was as curious as Scipio had been.

"No, not yet. But there will."

"Great Heavens, man! When?"

"As soon as Trampas makes the first move," Scipio replied easily.

I became dignified. Scipio had evidently been told things by the Virginian.

"I up and asked him plumb out," Scipio answered. "I was liftin' his trunk in at the door, and I couldn't stand it no longer. 'You've sure got Trampas where you want him.' That's what I said. And he up and answered and told me. So I know." At this point Scipio stopped. I was not to know.

Scipio became serious. "It's too blamed grand to tell you. I'll leave you to see it happen. Keep around, that's all. Keep around. I pretty near wish I didn't know it myself."

What with my feelings dependent on Scipio's judgment, and my human curiosity, I was not in the mood for a sermon. Dr. MacBride could read Scripture without my being conscious of a word that he had uttered. When I saw him opening the manuscript of his sermon, I suddenly remembered I was sitting—so to speak—in church. Our chairs were in the front line, of course; but, being next to the wall, I could easily see the cowboys behind me. They were perfectly well mannered. If Mrs. Ogden were looking for pistols, daredevil attitudes, and so forth, she must have been greatly disappointed. Except for their weather-beaten cheeks and eyes, they were simply American young men with mustaches. They could have been sitting, say, in

Danbury, Connecticut. Even Trampas gave in to the general calm. Only the Virginian did not look like Danbury, but he politely fixed his eyes on Dr. MacBride.

Our missionary did not choose Miss Wood's text. He made his selection from a different Psalm. After he began, I dared not even look at anybody else. "They have altogether become filthy. There is none of them that doeth good, no, not one," he droned. His eye showed us he included those seated before him in his remarks. He repeated the text once more. Then, he launched into his speech. He left no one with even a ray of hope.

I had heard it all often before; but preached to cowboys it became even more excessive. The cowboys were told not only that they could do no good, but that if they did manage to do good, it would not help them. He killed his chance to be useful. I must admit, however, that his words disturbed me more than they disturbed the cowpunchers. Their attention merely wandered.

I said their attention wandered, but I forgot the Virginian. At first his attitude might have been mere good manners. One can look respectfully at a preacher and be internally breaking all the commandments. But I saw real attention light in the Virginian's eye. And keeping track of the concentration that grew on him with each minute made the sermon short for me. By the end, his gaze at the preacher was unswerving.

When it was over, the preacher spoke of having

broken ground for the lessons to follow. For a while, he discussed trout fishing and rumors about hostile Indians northward where he was going. It was plain he never gave a thought to his personal safety. He soon bade us good night.

The Ogdens shrugged their shoulders and were amused. That was their way of taking it. Dr. MacBride weighed too heavily on the judge's shoulders for him to shrug. As a leading citizen in the Territory he kept open house for all newcomers. Policy and good nature made him bid welcome a wide variety of travelers. Even an out-of-work cowboy would get a bed and a meal for himself and his horse. Up till now, missionaries had always been well received at Sunk Creek Ranch.

"I suppose I'll have to take him fishing," said the judge, regretfully.

"Yes, my dear," said his wife, "you will. And I shall have to make his tea for six days."

"Otherwise," Ogden suggested, "it might be reported that you were enemies of religion."

"That's about it," said the judge. "I can get on with most people. But elephants depress me."

So we named the Doctor "Jumbo," and I departed to my quarters.

At the bunkhouse, the comments were similar but more highly salted. They had not liked to be told that they were "altogether become filthy." It was easy to call names. They could do that themselves. One fellow especially found the right words, "If I ever learned what I was predestinated to do,

I'd do the other thing, just to show 'em!"

And Trampas? And the Virginian? They were out of it. The Virginian had gone straight to his new home. Trampas lay awake, sullen as ever.

No light burned in the cabin as I approached its door. The Virginian's room was quiet. Dr. MacBride slumbered loudly. Go fishing with him! I selfishly decided the judge could have this privilege entirely to himself. Sleep came to me fairly soon, in spite of the doctor. I was wakened from it by my bed being jolted—not a pleasant thing that night. It was the quiet voice of the Virginian that told me he was sorry to have accidentally disturbed me. This disturbed me a good deal more. But his steps did not go to the bunkhouse, as my sensational mind had suggested. He was not wearing much, and in the dimness he seemed taller. I next made out that he was bending over Dr. MacBride who sprang upright at last.

"I am armed," he said. "Take care. Who are you?"

"You can lay down your gun, seh. I feel like my spirit is in need of enlightening."

He was using some of the missionary's own language. How baffling! The doctor got out of bed, lighted his lamp, and found a book. The two retired into the Virginian's room, from which came the sounds of the reverend's questionable wisdom. In time the doctor returned, blew out his lamp, and settled himself. Though I had been very much awake, I had nearly fallen sleep again, when the door creaked and the Virginian stood by the doctor's side.

"Are you awake, seh?"

"What? What's that? What is it?"

"Excuse me, seh. The enemy is winning on me. I'm feeling less inward opposition to sin."

The lamp was lighted, and I listened to some further sounds. They must have taken half an hour. When the doctor was in bed again, I thought I heard him sigh. Soon he was snoring again. I envied his ability to fall sleep. I dropped off myself until lamplight in my eyes awakened me as he came back for the third time from the Virginian's room. Before blowing the light out he looked at his watch. I asked the time.

"Three," said he.

I could not sleep anymore now, and I lay watching the darkness.

"I'm afeared to be alone!" said the Virginian's voice presently in the next room. "I'm afeared." There was a short pause, and then he shouted very loud, "I'm losin' my desire after the sincere milk of the Word!"

"What? What's that? What?" The doctor's cot gave a great crack as he started up listening. I put my face deep in the pillow.

"I'm afeared! I'm afeared! Sin has quit being bitter in my belly."

"Courage, my good man." The doctor was out of bed with his lamp again, and the door shut behind him. Between them they made it long this time. I saw the window become gray. Outside, a chorus of blackbirds began to fill the dawn. But the doctor continued working hard over his patient in the next room. Only a word here and there was distinct; but it was plain from the Virginian's fewer remarks that the sin in his belly was alarming him less. Yes, it took them a long time. And it proved to be the last time.

I looked at my own watch, and it was six. I had been in my bed about seven hours. The doctor had been out of his for seven. The door opened, and he came in with his book and lamp. He seemed to be shivering a little, and I saw him cast a longing eye at his couch. But the Virginian followed him.

"You'll be going to breakfast and the ladies, seh, pretty soon," said the Virginian, with a subdued voice. "But I'll worry through the day somehow without you. Tonight you can turn your wolf loose on me again."

It was no use. My face was deep in my pillow, but I still sounded like a hen who has laid an egg. The truth broke over the doctor that instant.

He tried to speak calmly. "This is a disgrace. An infamous disgrace. Never in my life have I . . ." Words failed him, and his face grew redder. "Never in my life..." He stopped again, because, at the sight of him being dignified in his red drawers, I was making the noise of a dozen hens. It was suddenly too much for the Virginian. He hastened into his room, and there sank on the floor with his head in his hands. The doctor immediately slammed the door upon him, and this rendered me easily fit for a lunatic asylum. I cried into my pillow, and wondered if the doctor would come and kill me. But he took no notice of me whatever. I could hear the Virginian's convulsions through the door. I could also hear the doctor furiously dressing within three feet of my head. I lay quite still with my face the other way, for I was really afraid to look at him. When I heard him walk to the door in his boots, I ventured to peep. There he was, going out with his bag in his hand. As I still continued to lie, weak and sore, the Virginian's door opened. He was clean and dressed and decent, but the devil still sported in his eye. I have never seen a creature more handsome.

Then my mind worked again. "You've gone and done it," said I. "He's packed his valise. He'll not sleep here tonight."

The Virginian looked quickly out of the door. "Why, he's leavin' us!" he exclaimed. "Drivin' away right now in his little old buggy!" He turned to me, and our eyes met solemnly over this large fact. I thought I perceived the faintest hint of dismay in the features of Judge Henry's new, responsible, trusty foreman. Once again he looked out at the departing missionary. "Well," he declared spitefully, "I certainly ain't goin' to run after him." And he looked at me again.

"Do you suppose the judge knows?" I inquired.

He shook his head. "The window shades is all

down over yonder." He paused. "I don't care," he stated, quite as if he had been ten years old. Then he grinned guiltily. "I was mighty respectful to him all night."

"Oh, yes, respectful! Especially when you invited him to turn his wolf loose."

The Virginian gave a joyous gulp. He now came and sat down on the edge of my bed. "I spoke awful good English to him most of the time," said he. "I can, you know, when I tie my attention tight to it. Yes, I certainly spoke a lot of good English. I didn't understand some of it myself!"

He was now growing even more pleased with his exploit. Then he began to give me his real heart. "I never set up for being better than others. Not even to myself. But to have to sit like a dumb lamb and let a stranger tell you for an hour that you're a hog and a swine, just after you have acted in a way which them that know the facts would call honorable—"

"Trampas!" I could not help exclaiming.

For there are moments of insight when a guess amounts to knowledge.

"Has Scipio told—"

"No. Not a word. He wouldn't tell me."

"Well, you see, I arrived home this evenin' with several thoughts workin' and stirrin' inside me. And not one of them thoughts was what you'd call Christian. I ain't the least little bit ashamed of 'em. I'm a human. But after the judge—well, you heard him. And so when I went away from that talk and saw how positions was changed—"

A step outside stopped him short. Nothing more could be read in his face, for there was Trampas himself in the open door.

"Good morning," said Trampas, not looking at us. He spoke with the same cool resentment of yesterday.

We returned his greeting.

"I believe I'm late in congratulating you on your promotion," said he.

The Virginian consulted his watch. "It's only half after six," he returned.

"Any man is to be congratulated on getting a promotion, I expect."

This time the Virginian let him have it. "Certainly. And I ain't forgetting how much I owe mine to you."

Trampas would have liked to let himself go. "I've not come here for any forgiveness," he sneered.

"When did you feel you needed any?"

Trampas understood he wasn't getting anywhere. He spoke straight out now. "Oh, I haven't any judge behind me, I know. I heard you'd be paying the boys this morning, and I've come for my time."

"You're thinking of leaving us?" asked the new foreman. "What's your dissatisfaction?"

"Oh, I'm not needing anybody back of me. I'll get along by myself." It was thus he revealed his expectation of being dismissed by his enemy.

This would have knocked any generosity out of my heart. But I was not the Virginian. He shifted his legs, leaned back a little, and laughed. "Go back to your job, Trampas, if that's all your complaint. You're right about me being in luck. But maybe there's two of us in luck."

It was this that Scipio had preferred me to see with my own eyes. The Virginian would not use his official position to crush his subordinate.

Trampas departed with something muttered that I did not hear, and the Virginian closed the conversation by saying, "You'll be late for breakfast." With that he also took himself away. And so did I.

The ladies were rather shocked when I told them what I had witnessed, but not the judge. He brought his fist down on the table—and not lightly. "I'd make him lieutenant general if the ranch offered that position!" he declared.

Miss Molly Wood said nothing at the time. But in the afternoon, by her wish, she went fishing, with the Virginian as her escort. I rode with them, for a while. I was not going to continue a third in that party. The Virginian was too well dressed, and I saw *Kenilworth* peeping out of his pocket. I meant to be fishing by myself when that volume was returned.

But Miss Wood talked with skillful openness as we rode. "I've heard all about you and Dr. MacBride," she said. "How could you do it, when the judge places such confidence in you?"

He looked pleased. "I reckon," he said, "I

couldn't be so good if I wasn't bad once in a while."

"Why, there's a skunk," said I, noticing the pretty little animal trotting in front of us at the edge of the thickets.

"Oh, where is it? Don't let me see it!" screamed Molly. And at this deeply feminine remark, the Virginian looked at her with a smile.

The lady did not notice. Or rather—I had better say—whatever her feelings, she very naturally did not display them. Instead she managed to seem unaware of the expression which had passed over the Virginian's face.

It was later that these few words reached me while I was fishing alone: "Have you anything different to tell me yet?" I heard him say.

"Yes, I have. I wish to say that I have never liked any man better than you. But I expect to!"

He must have drawn small comfort from an answer like that. But he laughed out loud, more determined than ever. "Don't you go betting on any such expectation!" And then their words ceased to be clear. I heard only their two voices wandering among the windings of the stream.

"What Is a Rustler?"

We all know what birds of a feather do. Imagine a bird of one particular feather long unable to see other birds of its kind. Should such birds land in its vicinity it will flock together with them all the more attentively.

The Ogdens were birds of Molly's feather. Their song was a different song from that which the Bear Creek birds sang. The Eastern warblings of the Ogdens sounded doubly sweet to Molly Wood. And Molly, whose Eastern song had been silent in this strange land, began to chirp it again during the visit that she made to the Sunk Creek Ranch.

Thus the Virginian's cause did not prosper at this time. His forces were scattered. Molly's were concentrated. The girl was not at that point where absence makes the heart grow fonder. While the Virginian was laboring through his long, responsible miles in the caboose, delivering the cattle at Chicago, vanquishing Trampas along the Yellowstone, she had regained herself.

That is why she could tell him so easily during those first hours alone together after his return, "I expect to like another man better than you."

And his forces were, as I have said, scattered. His promotion gave him no more time for courting. He was foreman now. He had said to Judge Henry, "I'll try to please you."

He did not understand how much he had already pleased his superior. The judge was delighted with both of his new foreman's first acts. He could not decide which pleased him more: the Virginian's performance with the missionary, or his high-mindedness with Trampas.

The Virginian never saw his sweetheart alone again while she was at the Sunk Creek Ranch. His duties called him away so much there was no chance. Worse still, that habit of birds of a feather brought about an even greater separation. She arranged to go East with the Ogdens. It was a rare opportunity to travel with friends, instead of making the journey alone!

In the schoolhouse, Molly had greatly pleased Bear Creek. She was warmly urged to take a holiday. School could afford to begin a little late. So she departed.

The Virginian hid his sore heart from her during the brief farewell they had.

"No, I'll not want any more books," he said, "till you come back." And then, growing more cheerful, "It's just the other way round!"

"What is the other way round?"

"Why, last time it was me that went traveling, and you that stayed behind."

"So it was!" And here she gave him a last scratch. "But you'll be busier than ever," she said, "no spare time to grieve about me!"

She could wound him, and she knew it. Nobody else could. That is why she did it.

But he gave her something to remember, too.

"Next time," he said, "neither of us will stay behind. We'll both go together."

And with these words he gave her no laughing glance. A look mingled with his words. Now and again in the train, both came back to her. She sat deep in thought, drawing near to Bennington hearing his voice and seeing his eyes.

This girl cried at having to tell Sam Bannett she could not think of him. How is it she could treat the Virginian as she did? I cannot tell you, having never (as I said before) been a woman myself.

Bennington opened its arms to its adventuresome daughter. Much was made of Molly Wood. Old faces and old places welcomed her. And Sam Bannett of course took her out driving more than once.

"I want to see the Hoosic Bridge," she would say. They would reach that well-remembered point. "How lovely it is!" she would remark. And as she gazed at the view up and down the valley, she would grow distant. When they drove up the valley, she said, "I had forgotten it was so nice and lonely. But after all, no woods are so interesting as those where you might possibly see a bear or an elk."

Sam took the opportunity to begin courting Molly again. "I haven't forgotten you," said Sam.

"Do you remember me? Or is it 'out of sight out of mind'?"

She told him that she forgot no one. She would always return, for fear they might forget her.

Over in the house at Dunbarton, the old lady held Molly's hand and looked a long while at her. "You have changed very much," she said finally.

"I am a year older," said the girl.

"Pshaw, my dear!" said the great-aunt. "Who is he?"

"Nobody!" cried Molly, with indignation.

"Then you shouldn't answer so loud," said the great-aunt.

The girl suddenly hid her face. "I don't believe I can love anyone," she said, "except myself."

And then that old lady began to stroke her niece's buried head, because she more than half understood. Understanding this much, she asked no prying questions. Instead, she recalled the days of her own youth and spoke only of love to encourage Molly.

"I am an old, old woman," she said. "But I haven't forgotten about love. They objected to him because he had no fortune. But he was brave and handsome, and I loved him, my dear. Only I ought to have loved him more. I gave him my promise to think about it. And he and his ship were lost." The great-aunt's voice had become very soft and low, and she spoke with many pauses. "So long as you can help it, do not marry! But when you cannot help it a moment longer, then listen to nothing but that. I know, dear, your choice will be worthy of the Starks. And now—let me see his picture."

"Why, aunty!" said Molly.

"Well, I won't pretend to be supernatural," said the aunt, "but I thought you kept one back when you were showing us those Western views last night."

Now this was the precise truth. Molly had brought a number of photographs from Wyoming to show to her friends at home. These, however, with one exception, were not portraits. They were views of landscapes, cattle roundups, and other scenes characteristic of ranch life. She did have several photographs of young men. All but one of these she had left behind. Her aunt's shrewdness mesmerized the girl. She rose obediently and sought that picture of the Virginian. It was full length, displaying him in all his cowboy trappings: leather chaps, belt and pistol, and—in his hand—a coil of rope.

Not one of her family had seen it, or suspected its existence. She now brought it downstairs and placed it in her aunt's hand.

"Mercy!" cried the old lady.

Molly was silent, but her eyes grew defiant.

"Mercy!" the aunt murmured, staring at the picture.

Molly remained silent.

Her aunt looked slowly up at her. "Has a man like that presumed—"

"He's not a bit like that. Yes, he's exactly like

that," said Molly. And she would have snatched the photograph away, but her aunt held on to it.

"Well," she said, "I suppose there are days when he does not kill people."

"He never killed anybody!" And Molly laughed.

"Are you seriously—" said the old lady.

"I almost might—at times. He is perfectly splendid."

"My dear, you have fallen in love with his clothes."

"It's not his clothes. And I'm not in love. He often wears others. He wears a white collar like anybody."

"Then that would be a more suitable way to be photographed, I think. He couldn't go round like that here. I could not receive him myself."

"He'd never think of such a thing. Why, you talk as if he were a savage."

The old lady studied the picture closely for a minute. "I think it is a good face," she finally remarked. "Is the fellow as handsome as that, my dear?"

More so, Molly thought.

"Who is he?" and "What are his prospects?" were the aunt's next questions. She shook her head at the answers. She also shook her head over her niece's forceful denial that her heart was lost to this man. But when their parting came, the old lady said, "God bless you and keep you, my dear. I'll not try to manage you. They managed me—" A sigh spoke the rest of this sentence. "But I'm not worried about you—at least, not very much. You have never done anything that was not worthy of the Starks. And if you're going to take him, do it before I die so that I can bid him welcome for your sake. God bless you, my dear."

And after the girl had gone back to Bennington, the great-aunt thought, "She is like all of the Stark women. She wants a man that is a man." Nor did the old lady disclose anything to any member of the family. She remained loyal. Molly's trust was sacred to her.

"Besides," she reflected, "if even I can do nothing with her, what a mess *they'd* make of it! She would elope."

So Molly's immediate family never saw that photograph, and never heard a word from her upon this subject. But on the day she left for Bear Creek, they sat missing her and discussing her visit.

"I never saw her better, Sarah. That horrible place seems to agree with her."

"Oh, yes, agree. It seemed to me—"

"Well?"

"Oh, just somehow that she was thinking."

"Thinking?"

"Well, I believe she has something on her mind."

"You mean a man," said Andrew Bell.

"A man, Andrew?"

"Yes, Mrs. Wood, that's what Sarah always means."

Sarah's conclusions did not contribute to her mother's happiness. Even worse, a rumor circulated. With it came a vague and dreadful word. Somebody told Andrew Bell that they heard Miss Molly Wood was engaged to marry a *rustler*.

"Heavens, Andrew!" said his wife. "What is a rustler?"

It was not in any dictionary. A man at Hoosic Falls said that he had passed through Cheyenne. There, he insisted, the term was a compliment, referring to people who were alive and pushing. Another man had always supposed it meant some kind of horse. But the most alarming version of all was that a rustler was a cattle thief. In a very few days, gossip had it that Molly was engaged to a gambler, a gold miner, an escaped stage robber, and a Mexican bandit.

Along Bear Creek, however, Molly and her "rustler" took a ride soon after her return. They were neither married nor engaged, and she was telling him about Vermont.

"I never was there," said he. "Never happened to strike in that direction."

"What decided your direction?"

"Oh, looking for chances. I reckon I must have been more ambitious than my brothers—or more restless. They stayed around on farms. But I got out. When I went back again six years afterward, I was twenty. They was talking about the same old things. I told my mother about what I'd seen here and there, and she liked it. But the others—their whole world was hogs and turkeys. I put on my hat one mornin' and told 'em maybe when I was fifty I'd look in on 'em again to see if they'd got any new subjects. But they'll never. My brothers don't seem to want chances."

"You have lost a good many yourself," said Molly.

"That's correct."

"And yet," said she, "sometimes I think you know a great deal more than I ever shall."

"Why, of course I do," said he, quite simply. "I have earned my living since I was fourteen. And that's from old Mexico to British Columbia. I have never stolen or begged a cent. I'd not want you to know what I know."

She was looking at him, half-listening and half-thinking of her great-aunt.

"I am not losing chances any more," he continued. "And you are the best I've got."

She was not sorry to have Georgie Taylor come galloping along at this moment to join them. But the Virginian swore under his breath. And on this ride nothing more happened.

VARIOUS POINTS

Love had been snowbound for many weeks. Winter prevented the Virginian's visits to Bear Creek. On the ranch, there was little work or responsibility to fill his thoughts and blood with action. So he set himself a task much lighter. Schoolbooks lay open on his cabin table. Penmanship and spelling helped the hours pass. He filled many sheets of paper with various exercises. Mrs. Henry gave him her assistance in advice and corrections.

"I shall presently be in love with him myself," she told the judge. "And it's time for you to be worried."

"I am perfectly safe," he replied. "There's only one woman for him anymore."

"She is not good enough for him," declared Mrs. Henry. "But he'll never see that."

So the snow fell, the world froze, and the spelling books and exercises went on. But this was not the only case of education which was progressing at the Sunk Creek Ranch while love was snowbound.

One morning Scipio le Moyne entered the Virginian's sitting room to find him looking intently out the window. Scipio went to the window to see for himself. "Well," he said, having seen, "when is he going to leave us?"

The foreman continued looking at two horsemen riding together. Their shapes, small in the distance, showed black against the universal whiteness.

"When do you figure he'll leave us?" repeated Scipio.

"He," murmured the Virginian, always watching the distant horsemen. And again, "he."

Scipio and the Virginian had come to know each other very well. The Virginian often talked to Scipio quite openly. Consequently, Scipio now understood precisely what the Virginian meant.

"Hm," Scipio remarked. "Well, one will be a gain, and the other won't be no loss."

"Poor Shorty!" said the Virginian. "Poor fool!"

Scipio was less compassionate. "No," he persisted, "I ain't sorry for him. Any man old enough to have hair on his face ought to see through Trampas."

The Virginian looked out the window again, and watched Shorty and Trampas as they rode in the distance. "Shorty is kind to animals," he said. "He has gentled that horse Pedro he bought with his first money. Gentled him wonderful. When a man is kind to dumb animals, I always say he had got some good in him."

"Yes," Scipio reluctantly admitted. "Yes. But I always did hate a fool."

"This here is a mighty cruel country," pursued the Virginian. "To animals that is. Think what we do to hundreds and thousands of little calves! Throw 'em down, brand 'em, cut 'em, ear mark 'em, turn 'em loose, and then go on to the next. I say this. If a man can go jammin' hot irons on to little calves and still keep a kindness for animals in his heart, he has got some good in him. And that's what Shorty has got. But he is lettin' Trampas get hold of him, and both of them will leave us." And the Virginian looked out across the huge winter whiteness again. But the riders had now vanished behind some foothills.

Scipio sat silent. He had never put these thoughts about men and animals to himself, and when they were put to him, he saw that they were true.

"Strange," he observed finally.

"What?"

"Why, Trampas. He done you dirt. You pass that over. You could have fired him, but you let him stay and keep his job. That's goodness. And badness is resultin' from it, straight. Badness straight from goodness."

"First point: I didn't expect to do Trampas any good by not killin' him, which I came pretty near doin' three times. Nor did I expect to do Trampas any good by lettin' him keep his job. But I am foreman of this ranch. And I can sit and tell all men to their face, 'I was above that meanness.' Point two: It ain't from *goodness*, it is from *Trampas* that badness has resulted. Put him anywhere and it will be the same. Put him under my eye, and I can follow his moves a little, anyway. Remember when you and I run on to that dead polled Angus cow, that was still warm when we got to her? Since then we have found no more cows dead of sudden death. We came mighty close to catchin' whoever it was that killed that cow and ran her calf off to his own bunch. He wasn't ten minutes ahead of us. We can prove nothin' and he knows that just as well as we do. But our cows have all quit dyin' of sudden death. And Trampas? He's gettin' ready for a change of residence. As soon as all the outfits begin hirin' new hands in the spring, Trampas will leave us and take a job with one of them. And maybe our cows'll commence gettin' killed again. And maybe we'll have to take steps that will be more emphatic—maybe."

Scipio meditated. "I wonder what killin' a man feels like?" he said.

"Why, nothing to bother you—when he'd ought to have been killed. Next point: Trampas'll take Shorty with him, which is certainly bad for Shorty. But it's me that has kept Shorty out of harm's way this long. If I had fired Trampas, he'd have worked Shorty into dissatisfaction that much sooner."

Scipio meditated again. "I knowed Trampas would leave," he said. "But I didn't think of Shorty. What makes you think it?"

"He asked me for a raise."

"He ain't worth the pay he's getting now."

"Trampas has told him different."

"When a man ain't got no ideas of his own," said Scipio, "he ought to be kind of careful who he borrows 'em from."

"That's mighty correct," said the Virginian. "Poor Shorty! He has told me about his life. It is sorrowful. And he will never get wise. It was too late for him to get wise when he was born. D' you know why he's after higher wages? He sends 'most all his money east."

"I don't see what Trampas wants him for," said Scipio.

"Oh, a handy tool someday."

"Not very handy," said Scipio.

"Well, Trampas is aimin' to train him. Supposin' you were figuring to turn professional thief—you'd be wantin' a young trustful accomplice to take all the punishment and let you take the rest."

"No such thing!" cried Scipio, angrily. "I'm no shirker." And then, perceiving the Virginian's expression, he broke out laughing. "Well," he exclaimed, "you fooled me that time."

"Looks that way. But I mean it about Trampas."

Presently Scipio rose, and noticed the half-finished exercise upon the Virginian's desk. "Trampas is a rolling stone," he said.

"A rolling piece of mud," corrected the Virginian.

"Mud! That's right. I'm a rolling stone. Sometimes I'd most like to quit being so."

"That's easy done," said the Virginian.

"No doubt, when you've found the moss you want to gather." As Scipio glanced at the schoolbooks again, a sparkle lurked in his bleached blue eyes. "I can write some," he said. "But I expect I've got my own notions about spelling."

"I retain a few private ideas that way myself," remarked the Virginian, innocently. Scipio sparkled more brightly.

"As to my geography," he pursued, "that's away out loose in the brush. Is Bennington the capital of Vermont? And how do you spell bridegroom?"

"Last point!" shouted the Virginian, letting a book fly after him.

But Scipio had dodged the book, and was gone. As he went his way, he said to himself, "All the same, it must pay to fall regular in love."

In the evening, the Virginian brought Shorty into his room. He usually knew what he had to say, usually found it easy to arrange his thoughts. But as he looked at Shorty, this did not happen to him. There was neither a line of badness in the face nor a line of strength. Hopelessness filled the Virginian as he looked at this lost dog, and his dull, wistful eyes.

But some beginning must be made.

"I wonder what the thermometer has got to be," he said. "You can see it, if you'll hold the lamp to that right side of the window."

Shorty held the lamp. "I never used any," he said, looking out at the instrument.

The Virginian had forgotten that Shorty could not read. So he looked out of the window himself, and found that it was twenty-two below zero. "This is pretty good tobacco," he remarked. Shorty helped himself, and filled his pipe.

"I had to rub my left ear with snow today," said he. "I was just in time."

"I thought it looked pretty freezy out where you was riding," said the foreman.

The lost dog's eyes showed plain astonishment. "We didn't see you out there," said he.

"Well," said the foreman, "it'll soon not be freezing anymore. Then we'll all be warm enough with work. Everybody will be working all over the range. And I wish I knew somebody that had a lot of stable work to be attended to. I certainly do for your sake."

"Why?" said Shorty.

"Because it's the right kind of a job for you."

"I can make more—" began Shorty, and stopped.

"There is a time coming," said the Virginian, "when I'll want somebody that knows how to get the friendship of horses. I'll want him to handle some special horses the judge has plans about. Judge Henry would pay fifty a month for that."

"I can make more," said Shorty, this time with stubbornness.

"Well, yes. Sometimes a man can—when he's not worth it, I mean. But it don't generally last."

Shorty was silent. "I used to make more myself," said the Virginian.

"You're making a lot more now," said Shorty.

"Oh, yes. But I mean when I was fooling around the earth, jumping from job to job, and helling all over town. I was not worth fifty a month then, not even twenty-five. But there was nights I made a heap more at cards."

Shorty's eyes grew large.

"And then, bang! It was gone with treatin' the men and the girls."

"I don't always—" said Shorty, and stopped again.

The Virginian knew that he was thinking about the money he sent east. "After a while," he continued, "I noticed a right strange fact. The money I made easy that I *wasn't* worth, it went like it came. I strained myself none gettin' or spendin' it. But the money I made hard that I *was* worth, why I began to feel right careful about that. And now I have got savings stowed away. If once you could know how good that feels—"

"So I would know," said Shorty, "with your luck."

"What's my luck?" said the Virginian, sternly.

"Well, if I had took up land along a creek that never goes dry and improved upon it like you have, and if I had saw that land raise its value on me with me lifting no finger—"

"Why did you lift no finger?" cut in the Virginian. "Who stopped you taking up land? It stretches in front, behind, and all around you, the biggest, baldest opportunity in sight. I lifted my finger, but you didn't."

Shorty stood stubborn.

"But never mind that," said the Virginian. "Take my land away tomorrow, and I'd still have my savings in bank. I found out what I could do, and I settled down and did it. Now you can do that too. The only tough part is the finding out what you're good for. And for you, that is found. If you'll just decide to work at this thing you can do, and gentle those horses for the judge, you'll be having savings in a bank yourself."

"I can make more," said the lost dog.

The Virginian was on the point of saying, "Then get out!" But instead, he spoke kindness to the end. "The weather is freezing yet," he said, "and it will be for a good long while. Take your time, and tell me if you change your mind."

Shorty returned to the bunkhouse. The

Virginian knew the boy had thoroughly learned his lesson of discontent from Trampas. Since that first moment in the Medicine Bow saloon when the Virginian had shut the mouth of Trampas, the man had been trying to get even. With each successive clash with the Virginian, he had merely met another public humiliation. Now, at the Sunk Creek Ranch in these cold white days, he knew that by poisoning Shorty's mind he had some sort of revenge.

In the springtime, it happened as the Virginian had predicted. Trampas departed to a "better job," as he took pains to say. With him rode the meek Shorty on his horse Pedro.

In time, love was no longer snowbound. The mountain trails were open enough for the sure feet of love's steed—that horse called Monte. But duty blocked the path of love. Instead of turning his face to Bear Creek, the foreman had other journeys to make, full of heavy work, watchfulness, and councils with the judge. The cattle thieves were growing bold, and winter had scattered the cattle widely over the range. Therefore the Virginian, instead of going to see her, wrote a letter to his sweetheart. It was his first.

CHAPTER 24

A LETTER WITH A MORAL

The letter the Virginian wrote to Molly Wood was the first he had ever addressed to her. It was not written with ease. It would have to be called a literary *effort*. It was completed in pencil before it was copied in ink. The first draft of it in pencil was nearly illegible with erasures and changes.

In the midst of the writing, Scipio put his head in. "You coming to dinner?" he inquired.

"You go to hell," replied the Virginian.

Scipio shut the door without further remark.

To tell the truth, I doubt if this letter would ever have been begun, let alone completed and sent if not for the Virginian's disappointment. All winter long he had looked to that day when he should knock at the girl's door, and hear her voice. All winter long he had been choosing the ride he would take her. He had imagined a sunny afternoon, a hidden grove, and some words of his that should conquer her at last and leave his lips upon hers. And with this controlled fire pent up within him, he had counted the days, scratching them off his calendar so briskly that once or twice he broke the pen.

Then, though the trail stood open, the meeting was put off again. He could not tell for how long. So, gripping his pencil, he consoled himself as best he could by writing her.

By the time the letter reached its destination, it was some twenty days old. It had first been carried by hand. Then it had taken the stagecoach, become late, reached a point of transfer, and waited there for the postmaster to begin, continue, end, and recover from a game of poker mixed with whiskey. Then it once more proceeded, was dropped at the right way point, and carried by private hand to Bear Creek. The experience of this letter, however, was not at all unusual at that time in Wyoming.

Molly Wood looked at the envelope. She had never before seen the Virginian's handwriting. She knew it instantly. She closed her door and sat down to read it with a beating heart.

Sunk Creek Ranch, May 5

My Dear Miss Wood:

I am sorry about this. My plan was to get over for a ride with you about now or sooner. This year Spring is early. The snow is off the flats this side the range. Where the sun gets a chance to hit the earth strong all day it is green and has flowers too, a good many. I had planned to take a look at this with you and that was a better plan than what I have got to do. The water is high but I could have got over. As for the snow on top of the mountain a man told me nobody could cross it for a week yet, because he had just done it himself. Was not he a funny man? You ought to see how the birds have streamed across the sky while Spring was coming. But I can't come now Miss Wood. There is a lot for me to do that has to be done and Judge Henry needs more than two eyes just now. I could not think much of myself if I left him for my own wishes.

But the days will be warmer when I come. We will not have to quit by five, and we can get off and sit too. We could not sit now unless for a very short while. If I know when I can come I will try to let you know, but I think it will be this way. I think you will just see me coming for I have a good number of things to do of an unsure nature. Do not believe reports about Indians. They are started by editors to keep the soldiers here. The friends of the editors get the hay and beef contracts. Indians do not come to settled parts like Bear Creek, only editors and politicians.

Nothing has happened worth telling you. I have read that play *Othello*. No man should write down such a thing. Do you know if it is true? I have seen one worse affair down in Arizona. He killed his little child as well as his wife but such things should not be put down in fine language for the public. I have read *Romeo and Juliet*. That is beautiful language but Romeo is no man. I like his friend Mercutio that gets killed. He is a man.

If he had got Juliet there would have been no foolishness and trouble.

Well Miss Wood I would like to see you today. Do you know what I think Monte would do if I rode him out with the reins slack? He would come straight to your gate for he is a horse of great judgement.

"That's the first word he has misspelled," said Molly.

There is no news here. Only calves and cows and the hens laying now which is not news to a hen every time she does it. Did I ever tell you about a hen Emily we had here? She was adventuresome, but had poor judgement and would make no family ties. She tried taking charge of little chicks and bantams and turkeys and puppies one time, and she thought most anything was an egg. I will tell you about her sometime. She died without family ties one day while I was building a house for her to teach school in.

"The outrageous wretch!" cried Molly! And her cheeks turned deep pink as she sat alone with her lover's letter.

I am coming the first day I am free. I will be a hundred miles from you most of the time when I am not more. When I can, I will ride a hundred miles in one hour to see you. Monte is up to that.

After never seeing you for so long I will make one hour do if I have to. Here is a flower I have just been out and picked. I have kissed it now. That is the best I can do yet.

Molly laid the letter in her lap and looked at the flower. Then suddenly she jumped up and pressed it to her lips, and after a long moment held it away from her.

"No," she said. "No, no, no." She sat down.

It was some time before she finished the letter. Then once more she got up and put on her hat.

Mrs. Taylor wondered where the girl could be walking so fast. But she was not walking anywhere. In half an hour she returned, rosy with her swift exercise, but with a spirit as upset as when she had set out.

Next morning at six, when she looked out of her window, there was Monte tied to the Taylor's gate. If only he had come the day before. If only he had been there when she returned from that swift walk of hers!

CHAPTER 25

PROGRESS OF THE LOST DOG

The Virginian's visit with his ladylove lasted not even an hour. But he had not come a hundred miles to see her. The necessities of his work had chanced to bring him close enough for a glimpse of her, and this glimpse he took. Then he had to rejoin his company of men at once.

"You got my letter?" he said.

"Yesterday."

"Yesterday! I wrote it three weeks ago. Well, you got it. This cannot be the hour with you that I mentioned. That is coming, and maybe very soon."

She could say nothing. Relief she felt, and yet with it something like a pang.

"Today does not count," he told her, "except that every time I see you counts with me. But this is not the hour that I mentioned."

He returned to her two volumes she had lent him long ago. He left with Taylor a horse he had brought for her to ride. As a goodbye, he put a bunch of flowers in her hand. Then he was gone. As he rode away on Monte, she watched him, half-chilled by reason, half-melted by passion, unresolved.

Therefore, the days that came for her now were all unhappy ones. For him they were filled with work well done, and with changeless longing.

One day it seemed as if a lull was coming, a pause in which he could at last attain that hour with her. He left the camp and turned his face toward Bear Creek. The way led him along Butte Creek. Across the stream lay Balaam's large ranch. On the other bank he saw Balaam himself, and reined in Monte for a moment to watch what Balaam was doing.

"That's what I've heard," he muttered to himself. For Balaam had led some horses to the water, and was lashing them heavily because they would not drink. He watched so intently that he did not see Shorty approaching along the trail.

"Morning," said Shorty to him, with little emotion. But the Virginian gave him a pleasant greeting. "This is for you," said Shorty. He handed his recent foreman a battered letter. It was from the judge. It had not come very gradually, in the pockets of three different cowpunchers. The Virginian glanced over it. When he found a note inside for Balaam, his heart fell. Here were new orders for him, and he could not go to see his sweetheart.

"Hello, Shorty!" said Balaam, from over the creek. To the Virginian he gave a slight nod. He did not know him, although he knew well enough who he was.

"Here's a letter from Judge Henry for you," said the Virginian, crossing the creek.

Many weeks before, Balaam had borrowed two
horses from the judge, promising to return them at
once. But the judge, of course, wrote very politely.
He hoped that "this reminder" might be excused.
As Balaam read the reminder, he wished he had sent
the horses before. The judge was a more important
man than he was in the Territory. So Balaam had no
choice but to excuse the "reminder." But he was
ready to be disagreeable to somebody.

"Well," he said, musing aloud in his annoyance,
"Judge Henry wants them by the thirtieth. This is
the twenty-fourth. There's time enough yet."

"This is the twenty-seventh," said the
Virginian, briefly.

That made a difference! Not so easy to reach
Sunk Creek in good order by the thirtieth! The
horses were not even here at the ranch. Balaam was
ready to be very disagreeable now. Suddenly he perceived the date of the judge's letter. He held it out
to the Virginian, and struck the paper.

"What's your idea in bringing this here two
weeks late?" he said.

Now, when he had struck that paper, Shorty
looked at the Virginian. But nothing happened
beyond a certain change of light in the Southerner's
eyes. And when the Southerner spoke, it was with
his usual gentleness and civility. He explained that
the letter had been put in his hands just now by
Shorty.

"Oh," said Balaam. He looked at Shorty. How
had he come to be a messenger? "You working for

the Sunk Creek outfit again?" said he.

"No," said Shorty.

Balaam turned to the Virginian again. "How do you expect me to get those horses to Sunk Creek by the thirtieth?"

The Virginian leveled a lazy eye on Balaam. "I ain' doin' any expecting," said he. "The judge has friends goin' to arrive from New York for a trip across the Basin," he added. "The horses are for them."

Balaam grunted with displeasure, thinking of the sixty or seventy days since he had told the judge he would return the horses at once. He looked across at Shorty seated in the shade, and noticed what a good pony the youth rode. It was the same animal he had seen once or twice before. But something must be done. The judge's horses were far out on the big range, and must be found and driven in, which would take certainly the rest of this day, possibly part of the next.

Balaam called to one of his men. He gave some sharp orders, emphasizing details, and urging great speed. The Virginian leaned slightly against his horse, with one arm over the saddle, hearing and understanding, but not smiling outwardly. The man departed to saddle up for his search on the big range, and Balaam resumed the unhitching of his team.

"So you're not working for the Sunk Creek outfit now?" he inquired of Shorty. He ignored the Virginian. "Working for the Goose Egg?"

"No," said Shorty.

"Sand Hill outfit, then?"

"No," said Shorty.

Balaam grinned. He noticed how Shorty's yellow hair stuck through a hole in his hat, and how old and battered were Shorty's overalls. Shorty had been glad to accept payment for bearing the letter he had delivered to the Virginian. But even that small sum was no longer in his possession. He had passed through Drybone on his way, and at Drybone there had been a game of poker. Shorty's money was now in the pocket of Trampas. But he had one valuable possession in the world left to him, and that was his horse Pedro.

"Good pony of yours," said Balaam to him now, from across Butte Creek. Then he struck his own horse in the jaw because he held back from coming to the water as the other had done.

"Your trace ain't unhitched," commented the Virginian, pointing.

Balaam loosed the strap he had forgotten, and hit the horse again for consistency's sake. The animal, bewildered, now came down to the water with its head in the air, taking short, nervous steps.

The Virginian looked on, silent and serious. How could he interfere between another man and his own horse? But neither could he condone Balaam's mistreatment of his horses.

"So you've quit the roundup?" he resumed to Shorty.

Shorty nodded and looked sideways at the Virginian.

For the Virginian knew that he had been fired for going to sleep while night-herding.

Then Balaam threw another glance on Pedro the horse.

"Hello, Shorty!" he called out, for the boy was departing. "Don't you like dinner anymore? It's ready about now."

Shorty forded the creek and threw off his saddle. He turned out Pedro, his buckskin pony, into Balaam's pasture. The Virginian also turned his horse into the pasture. He must stay at the ranch till the judge's horses should be found.

Balaam wanted Shorty to dine with him. And he could not exclude the Virginian, much as he would have enjoyed this.

"See any Indians?" he asked.

"Na-a!" said Shorty, scornful of recent rumors.

"They're headin' the other way," observed the Virginian. "Bow Leg Range is where they was reported."

"What business have they got off the reservation, I'd like to know," said the ranchman, "Bow Leg, or anywhere?"

"Oh, it's just a hunt, and a kind of visitin' their friends on the South Reservation," Shorty explained. "Squaws along and all."

"Well, if the folks at Washington don't keep squaws and all where they belong," said Balaam, in a rage, "the folks in Wyoming Territory will do a little job that way themselves."

"There's a petition out," said Shorty. "Paper's

goin' east with a lot of names to it. But they ain't no harm, them Indians ain't."

"No harm?" rasped out Balaam.

Dinner was ready, and they sat down.

"And I suppose," Balaam continued, still hot on the subject, "you'd claim Indians object to killing a white man when they run into him far from human help? These peaceable Indians are just the worst in the business."

"That's so," assented the easy-opinioned Shorty, exactly as if he had always maintained this view. "Chap started for Sunk Creek three weeks ago. Trapper he was; old like, with a red shirt. One of his horses showed up at the roundup Tuesday. Man ain't been heard from." He ate in silence for a while, evidently brooding in his childlike mind. Then he said, "I'd sooner trust one of them Indians than I would Trampas."

Balaam slanted his fat bullet head far to one side, and laying his spoon down (he had opened some canned grapes) laughed steadily at his guest with a harsh dose of irony.

The guest, perceiving he was seen through, smiled back rather miserably.

"Say, Shorty," said Balaam, his head still slanted over, "what's the figures of your bank balance just now?"

"I ain't usin' banks," murmured the youth.

Balaam put some more grapes on Shorty's plate, and drawing a cigar from his waistcoat, sent it rolling to his guest.

"Matches are behind you," he added. He gave a cigar to the Virginian as an afterthought, but to his disgust, the Southerner put it in his pocket and lighted a pipe.

Balaam accompanied Shorty when he went to the pasture to saddle up and depart. "Got a rope?" he asked the guest, as they lifted down the bars.

"Don't need to rope him. I can walk right up to Pedro. You stay back."

Hiding his bridle behind him, Shorty walked to the riverbank, where the pony was switching his long tail in the shade. Speaking persuasively to him, he came nearer, till he laid his hand on Pedro's dusky mane, which was many shades darker than his hide. He turned expectantly, and his master met his expectations with a piece of bread.

"Eats that, does he?" said Balaam, over the bars.

"Likes the salt," said Shorty. "Now, n-n-ow, here! You don't care to be bridled? Open your teeth! You'd like to play you was nobody's horse and live private? Or maybe you'd prefer ownin' a saloon?"

Pedro evidently enjoyed this talk, and the dodging he made about the bit. Once fairly in his mouth, he accepted the inevitable. Then Shorty turned and extended his hand.

"Shake!" he said to his pony, who lifted his forefoot quietly and put it in his master's hand. When the master tickled Pedro's nose, he wrinkled it and flattened his ears, pretending to bite. His face wore an expression of knowing relish over this performance. "Now the other hoof," said Shorty; and the horse and master shook hands with their left. "I learned him that," said the cowboy, with pride and affection. "Say, Pede," he continued, in Pedro's ear, "ain't you the best little horse in the country? What? Here, now! Keep out of that, you deadbeat! There ain't no more bread." He pinched the pony's nose, one quarter of which was wedged into his pocket.

"Quite a lady's little pet!" said Balaam, with the rasp in his voice. "Pity this isn't New York, now, where there's a big market for harmless horses. Gee-gees, the children call them."

"He ain't no gee-gee," said Shorty, offended. "He'll beat any cowpony workin' you've got. You can turn him on a half-dollar. Don't need to touch the reins."

Balaam knew this, and he knew that the pony was only a four year old. "Well," he said, "Drybone's had no circus this season. Maybe they'd buy tickets to see Pedro. He's good for that, anyway."

Shorty became gloomy. The Virginian was grimly smoking. Here was something else going on not to his taste, but none of his business.

"Try a circus," persisted Balaam. "Alter your plans for spending cash in town, and make a little money instead."

Shorty, having no plans to alter and no cash to spend, grew still gloomier.

"What'll you take for that pony?" said Balaam.

Shorty spoke up instantly. "A hundred dollars couldn't buy that piece of stale mud off his back," he declared, looking off into the sky with an exaggerated gesture.

But Balaam looked at Shorty, "You keep the mud," he said, "and I'll give you thirty dollars for the horse."

Shorty did a little professional laughing, and began to walk toward his saddle.

"Give you thirty dollars," repeated Balaam, picking a stone up and slinging it into the river.

"How far do you call it to Drybone?" Shorty remarked, stooping to investigate the bucking-strap on his saddle—though Pedro never bucked.

"You won't have to walk," said Balaam. "Stay all night, and I'll send you over comfortably in the morning, when the wagon goes for the mail."

"Walk?" Shorty retorted. "Drybone's twenty-five miles. Pedro'll put me there in three hours and not know he done it." He lifted the saddle on the horse's back. "Come, Pedro," said he.

"Come, Pedro!" mocked Balaam.

There followed a little silence.

"No, sir," mumbled Shorty, with his head under Pedro's belly, busily cinching. "A hundred dollars is bottom figures."

Balaam, in his turn, now duly performed some professional laughing, which was noted by Shorty under the horse's belly. He stood up and looked squarely at Balaam. "Well, then," he said, "what will you give for him?"

"Thirty dollars," said Balaam, looking far off into the sky, as Shorty had looked.

"Oh, come, now," Shorty complained.

He was fishing for an offer and this was exactly what Balaam wanted. "I'm not crying for your Pedro," he observed without emotion. "Only it struck me you were dead broke, and wanted to raise cash and keep yourself going till you hunted up a job and could buy him back." He hooked his right thumb inside his waistcoat pocket. "But I'm not cryin' for him," he repeated. "He'd stay right here, of course. I wouldn't part with him. Why does he stand that way? Hello!" Balaam suddenly straightened himself, like a man who has made a discovery. "What's the matter with that foreleg there?" said Balaam.

"Which? Nothin's the matter with it!" snapped Shorty.

Balaam climbed down from his fence. He passed his hand up and down the foreleg. Then he spit. "Mm!" he said thoughtfully and added, with a shade of sadness, "That's always to be expected when they're worked too young."

Shorty slid his hand slowly over the disputed leg. "What's to be expected?" he inquired, "That they'll eat hearty? Well, he does."

At this response the Virginian permitted himself to laugh aloud.

"Sprung," continued Balaam, with a sigh.

"Sprung!" Shorty said, with a bark of indignation. "Come on, Pedro, you and me'll spring for town."

He caught the horn of the saddle, and as he swung into place the horse rushed away with him. "O-ee! yoi-yup, yup, yup!" sang Shorty. He made Pedro play an exhibition game of speed, bringing him round close to Balaam in a wide circle, and then he vanished in dust down the trail.

Balaam looked after him and laughed harshly. He had seen trout dash about like that when the hook in their jaw first surprised them. He knew Shorty would show the pony off, and he knew Shorty's love for Pedro was not equal to his need of money. He called to one of his men, made a remark about the prolonged drought, and then walked to his dining-room door, where, as he expected, Shorty met him.

"Say," said the youth, "do you consider that's any way to talk about a good horse? You know that his leg ain't sprung any more than your leg's cork. Just as sound and strong as iron. Never stumbles. And he don't never go to jumpin' with you. He's kind and he's smart." And the master petted his pony, who lifted a hoof for another handshake.

Of course Balaam had never thought the leg was sprung. "Maybe there's two years' work left in that leg," he now observed.

"Better give your horse away, Shorty," said the Virginian.

"Is this your deal, my friend?" inquired Balaam. And he slanted his bullet head at the Virginian.

"Give him away, Shorty," drawled the Southerner. "His leg is busted. Mr. Balaam says so."

Balaam's face grew evil with fury. The Virginian, too, was not pleased. But he could not interfere. Already he had overstepped the code in these matters. He would have dearly liked—for reasons good and bad, spite and mercy mingled—to have offered a reasonable or even an unreasonable price for Pedro, and taken possession of the horse himself. But this might not be. In bets, in card games, in all horse transactions, onlookers must suppress their wisdom and hold their peace.

That evening Shorty again had a cigar. He had parted with Pedro for forty dollars, a striped Mexican blanket, and a pair of spurs. Undressing over in the bunkhouse, he said to the Virginian, "I'll sure buy Pedro back off him just as soon as I rustle up some cash." The Virginian grunted. He was thinking he should have to travel hard to get the horses to the judge by the thirtieth. Below that thought lay his aching disappointment and his longing for Bear Creek.

In the early dawn, Shorty stepped to the door carefully. Pedro stood in the pasture nearby. The cowboy slowly closed the door behind him. He sat down on the step, drew his money out, taking no comfort just then from its possession. Then he put it back, and after dragging on his boots, crossed to the pasture. There, he held a last talk with his pony, brushing the cakes of mud from his hide where he had rolled, and passing a lingering hand over his mane. Shorty glanced back to see that no one was yet out of the cabin, then put his arms round the

horse's neck. For a moment the cowboy's insignificant face was elevated by the emotion he would never have let others see. He hugged tight this animal, who was dearer to his heart than anybody in the world.

"Goodbye, Pedro. Goodbye." Pedro looked for bread.

"No," said his master, sorrowfully, "not any more. You know I'd give it to you if I had it. You and me didn't figure on this, did we, Pedro? Goodbye!"

He hugged his pony again, got as far as the fence, then returned once more. "Goodbye, my little horse, my dear horse, my little, little Pedro," he said, as his tears wet the pony's neck. Then he wiped them with his hand, and got himself back to the bunkhouse. After breakfast he and his belongings departed to Drybone. Pedro calmly watched this departure from his field. Horses must recognize even less than men the black corners that their destinies turn. The pony stopped feeding to look at the mail wagon pass by. His master sitting in the wagon could not turn his head.

BALAAM AND PEDRO

Resigned to wait for the judge's horses, Balaam went into his office and read nine accumulated newspapers. Then he rode out, and met his man returning with the troublesome animals at last. He hurried home and sent for the Virginian. He had made a decision.

"See here," he said, "those horses are coming. What trail would you take over to the judge's?"

"Shortest trail's right through the Bow Leg Mountains," said the foreman, in his gentle voice.

"Guess you're right. It's dinnertime. We'll start right afterward. We'll make Little Muddy Crossing by sundown, and Sunk Creek tomorrow, and the next day'll see us through. Can a wagon get through Sunk Creek Canyon?"

The Virginian smiled. "I reckon it can't, seh, and stay resembling a wagon."

Balaam told them to saddle Pedro and one packhorse, and drive the bunch of horses into a corral, roping the judge's two, who proved extremely wild. He had decided to take this journey himself. Judge Henry was indeed a more powerful man than

Balaam. By personally conducting the return of the horses, Balaam hoped to make up for his tardiness. Moreover, the sight of some New York visitors would be a good thing.

They forded Butte Creek, and crossed the well-traveled trail which follows down to Drybone. The long gray line of fence, almost a mile away, that ended Balaam's land on this side of the creek stretched along into the distance, adding desolation to the plain. Soon, the Virginian shut the last gate. He looked back at the pleasant trees of the ranch, and then followed in single file into the barrenness of No Man's Land.

No cloud was in the sky. The desert looked grim now, at noon. The sagebrush was dull, like zinc. Thick heat rose from the parched ground, and pale heat shrouded the distant peaks.

There were five horses. Balaam led on Pedro. As was his habit, he tilted his squat figure a little forward in the saddle, stiff, but solid as a rock. One of the judge's horses came next, dragging back continually on the rope by which he was led. After him ambled Balaam's wise pack animal, carrying the light burden of two days' food and lodging. She was an old mare who could still go when she chose. She gave no trouble to the Virginian who came behind her. He also sat solid as a rock, yet subtly bending to the struggles of the wild horse he led, as a steel spring bends and balances and resumes its poise.

They made slow time, finally stopping as the sky deepened to violet. The horses drank a long time from the sluggish yellow water. Its taste and warmth were equally welcome to the men. They built a little fire. When supper was ended, they smoked a short while in silence. Then they spread their blankets in a smooth place beside the water.

They had tied the judge's two horses in the best grass they could find, letting the rest go free to pasture where they wanted. When the first light came, the Virginian attended to breakfast, while Balaam rode away on one of the judge's horses to bring in the loose horses. They had gone far out of sight. When he returned with them, after some two hours, he was on Pedro. Pedro was soaking with sweat. Red froth creamed from his mouth. The Virginian saw the horses must have been hard to drive in.

"If you'd kept ridin' him, instead of changin' off on your horse, they'd have behaved quieter," said the foreman.

"That's good seasonable advice," said Balaam, sarcastically. "I could have told you that now."

"I could have told you when you started," said the Virginian, heating the coffee for Balaam.

Balaam had much to say about the outrageous conduct of the horses. He found them heading back for Butte Creek, with the old mare in the lead.

"But I soon showed her the road she was to go," he said, as he drove them now to the water.

The Virginian noticed the slight limp of the mare.

"I guess she'll not be in a hurry to travel except when she's wanted to," continued Balaam. He sat down, and sullenly poured himself some coffee.

"We'll be in luck if we make any Sunk Creek this night."

He went on with his breakfast, thinking aloud for the benefit of his companion. As for the Virginian, he made no comments, preferring silence to the discomfort of talking with a man like Balaam.

"Six o'clock, already," said Balaam, saddling the horses. "And we'll not get started for ten minutes more." Then he came to Pedro. "So you haven't quit fooling yet, haven't you?" he exclaimed, for the pony shrank as he lifted the bridle. "Take that for your sore mouth!" and he rammed the bit in, at which Pedro flung back and reared.

"Well, I never saw Pedro act that way yet," said the Virginian.

"Ah, rubbish!" said Balaam. "They're all the same. Each one's just laying for his chance to do wrong. Some'll buck you off, and some'll roll with you, and some'll fight you with their forefeet. They may play good for a year, but the Western pony is man's enemy, and when he judges he's got his chance, he's going to do his best. And if you come out alive it won't be his fault. You've got to keep them afraid of you. That Pedro horse there has been hand-fed, and fooled with like a damn pet, and what's that policy done? Why, he goes ugly when he thinks it's time, and decides he'll not drive any horses into camp this morning. He knows better now."

"Mr. Balaam," said the Virginian, "I'll buy that horse off you right now."

Balaam shook his head. "You'll not do that

right now or any other time," said he. "I happen to want him."

The Virginian could do no more.

Meanwhile Balaam began to lead Pedro to the creek for a last drink before starting across the dry earth. The horse held back on the rein a little, and Balaam turned and cut the whip across his forehead. A delay of forcing and backing followed, while the Virginian, already in the saddle, waited. The minutes passed, with no immediate prospect, apparently, of getting nearer Sunk Creek.

"He ain't goin' to follow you while you're beatin' his head," the Southerner remarked.

"Do you think you can teach me anything about horses?" retorted Balaam.

"Well, it don't look like I could," said the Virginian, lazily.

"Then don't try it, so long as it's not your horse, my friend."

Again the Southerner leveled his eye on Balaam. "All right," he said, in the same gentle voice. "But don't you call me your friend. You've made that mistake twice."

The road was shadeless, as it had been from the start, and they could not travel fast. No talk was exchanged between the two travelers. The cowpuncher had nothing to say and Balaam was sulky. So they moved along, silently enduring each other's company and the boredom of the journey.

After a time they ascended through the foothills. A little higher up, they came on a narrow gully with a bit of water that formed a stale pool among some willow thickets. They turned aside to water their horses, and found near the pool a circular spot of ashes and some poles. Beside these, a cagelike construction of willow wands had been built in the ground.

"Indian camp," observed the Virginian.

There were the tracks of five or six horses on the farther side of the pool, and they did not come into the trail, but led off among the rocks.

"They're about a week old," said Balaam. "It's part of that outfit that's been hunting."

"They've gone on to visit their friends," added the cowpuncher.

"Yes, on the Southern Reservation. How far do you call Sunk Creek now?"

"Well," said the Virginian, calculating, "it's mighty near forty miles from Muddy Crossin', and I reckon we've come eighteen."

"Just about. It's noon." Balaam snapped his watch shut. "We'll rest here till twelve-thirty."

When it was time to go, the Virginian looked musingly at the mountains. "We'll need to travel right quick to get through the canyon tonight," he said.

"Tell you what," said Balaam, "we'll rope the judge's horses together and drive 'em in front of us. That'll make speed."

"Mightn't they get away on us?" objected the Virginian. "They're powerful wild."

"They can't get away from me, I guess," said Balaam, and the arrangement was adopted. "We're the first this season over this piece of the trail," he observed presently.

His companion had noticed already, and agreed. There were no tracks anywhere. Soon the trail wound into a sweltering gully that seemed to attract the sun's rays and then hold the heat. One of the judge's horses chose this place to make a try for liberty. He suddenly whirled from the trail, dragging with him his less adventuresome fellow. Leaving the Virginian with the old mare, Balaam headed them off, for Pedro was quick. They came jumping down the bank together, but swiftly crossed up on the other side, getting much higher before they could be reached.

It was no place for this sort of game. The sides of the ravine abounded with jutting knobs of rock. The roots of short twisted pines made riding difficult. The Virginian helped, but used his horse with more judgment, keeping as much on the level as possible. He attempted to anticipate the next turn of the runaways before they made it. Balaam attempted to follow them close. He wheeled short when they doubled back. He made his way up the face of the slope, then veered back down to the point he had left. Whenever he felt Pedro begin to weary, he drove his spurs into the horse, forcing him to keep up the pace. It was no easy task to overtake and capture—on the side of a mountain—two animals who had been running wild for weeks, and who carried no weight. The difficulty of such work only served to heighten Balaam's stubbornness and rising temper. He had made up his mind not to give in.

The Virginian soon decided to move slowly

along, preventing the wild horses from passing back down the gully again. He was saving his own animal from useless fatigue. But Pedro was reeking wet, with his mouth open. Though he stumbled constantly, he galloped on. The cowpuncher kept the group in sight, driving the packhorse in front of him. The horses he followed reached the top of the gully but could not find a passage through its rocky rim to the levels above. As they descended once again, they gained ground, for Pedro had fallen twice.

Then the leader showed the cleverness of a genuinely vicious horse. He started kicking his companion with all the energy a short rope would permit. The rope slipped off. Without it, they quickly reached the top and disappeared. Leaving the packhorse for Balaam, the Virginian started after them and came into some high, flat ground. Beyond, the mountains began in earnest. The runaways were moving toward these at an easy pace. The Virginian followed for a moment. Then, looking back and seeing no sign of Balaam, he waited. The horses were sure not to go fast when they reached good pasture or water.

He got out of the saddle and sat on the ground, watching, till the mare came up slowly into sight, with Balaam behind her. When they were near, Balaam dismounted and struck Pedro fearfully, until the stick broke. Then he raised the splintered half to continue.

Seeing the pony's condition, the Virginian spoke, and said, "I'd let that horse alone if I were you."

Balaam turned to him, but he was completely enraged and did not seem to hear. "He played like he was tired," said Balaam, looking at the Virginian with glazed eyes. He turned again to the coughing, swaying horse, whose eyes were closed. Not having the stick, he seized the animal's unresisting head and shook it. The Virginian watched him a moment, and rose to stop such a spectacle. Balaam ceased, and, turning again in slow fashion, looked across the level, where the runaways were still visible.

"I'll have to take your horse," he said. "Mine's played out."

"You ain't goin' to touch my horse."

Again the words seemed not entirely to reach Balaam's understanding, so dulled by fury were his senses. He made no answer, but mounted Pedro. The failing pony walked forward mechanically, while the Virginian, puzzled, stood looking after him. Balaam seemed purposeless, and stopped in a moment. Suddenly he was at work at something. This sight was odd. For a few seconds it had no meaning to the Virginian as he watched. Then his mind grasped the horror, too late. Even though he sprang like a tiger to stop Balaam, the outrage was committed. Pedro sank motionless, his head rolling flat on the earth. Balaam was jammed beneath him. The man had struggled to his feet before the Virginian reached the spot. The horse lifted his head and turned it piteously round.

Then vengeance struck Balaam in one sudden blast. The Virginian hurled him to the ground, lifted

and hurled him again. Then he lifted him again, beat
his face, and struck his jaw. Balaam's strong ox-like
fighting was to no avail. He protected his eyes as best
he could against sledgehammer blows of justice. He
felt blindly for his pistol. That arm was caught and
wrenched backward, crushed, and doubled over. He
seemed to hear his own bones, and set up a hideous
screaming of hate and pain. Then the pistol at last
came out. At once, both the gun and the hand that
grasped it were instantly stamped into the dust. One
last time, Balaam was lifted and thrown so that he lay
across Pedro's saddle, a blurred, dingy, wet pulp.

Vengeance had come and gone. The man and
the horse were motionless. Around them, silence
seemed to gather like a witness.

"If you are dead," said the Virginian, "I am
glad of it." He stood looking down at Balaam and
Pedro, lying in the middle of the open tableland.
Then he saw Balaam looking at him. It was the
quiet stare of sight without thought or feeling,
almost frightful in its separation from any self. But
as he watched those eyes, the self came back into
them. "I have not killed you," said the Virginian.
"And I ain't goin' to do any more to you—if that's
a satisfaction to know."

Then he began to attend to Balaam with imper-
sonal skill, like someone hired for the purpose. "He
ain't hurt bad," he declared aloud, as if the man were
some nameless patient. "I reckon it might have put a
less tough man than you out of business for quite a
while. I'm goin' to get some water now." When he

returned with the water, Balaam was sitting up, looking about him. He had not yet spoken, nor did he
now speak. The sunlight flashed on the six-shooter
where it lay, and the Virginian secured it. "She ain't
so pretty as she was," he remarked, as he examined
the weapon. "But she'll go right handy yet."

Strength was in a measure returning to Pedro.
He was a young horse, and exhaustion from anguish
or overriding were not enough to affect him long.
He got himself on his feet and walked waveringly
over to the old mare, and stood by her for comfort.
The cowpuncher came up to him. Pedro, after starting back slightly, seemed to comprehend that he was
in friendly hands. It was plain that he would soon be
able to travel slowly if no weight was on him, and
that he would be a very good horse again. Whether
they abandoned the runaways or not, there was no
staying here for night to overtake them without
food or water. He left them to take care of themselves, determining meanwhile that he would take
command. The day was still high, and what its next
few hours had in store the Virginian could not say.
He took Pedro's saddle off, threw the mare's pack to
the ground, put Balaam's saddle on her, and on that
stowed her original pack. Then he went to Balaam,
who was sitting up.

"I reckon you can travel," said the Virginian.
"And your horses can. If you're comin' with me,
you'll ride your mare. I'm goin' to trail them horses.
If you're not comin' with me, your horse comes with
me, and you'll take fifty dollars for him."

Balaam was indifferent to this good bargain. He did not look at the other or speak, but rose and searched about him on the ground. The Virginian was also indifferent as to whether Balaam chose to answer or not. Seeing Balaam searching the ground, he finished what he had to say.

"I have your six-shooter, and you'll have it when I'm ready for you to. Now, I'm goin'," he concluded.

Balaam's mind was clear enough now. Though the rest of this journey would be nearly intolerable, it must go on. He looked at the pokerfaced cowpuncher getting ready to go, tying a rope on Pedro's neck to lead him. He looked at the mountains where the runaways had vanished. He could hardly believe he had gotten into such straits. He was helped stiffly on the mare, and the three horses in single file took up their journey once more. Soon they were in the mountains. The perpetual desert had ended. They crossed a small brook, where they lost the trail. The Virginian dismounted to find where the horses had turned off, and discovered that they had gone straight up the ridge along the water.

"There's been a man camped in here inside a month," he said, kicking up a rag of red flannel. "White man and two horses. Ours have went up his old tracks."

It was not easy for Balaam to speak yet, and he kept his silence. But he remembered that Shorty had spoken of a trapper who had started for Sunk Creek.

For three hours they followed the runaways over ever softer ground, climbing steadily. They reached some springs where the mud had not yet settled in the hoof prints they followed. Soon, they came through a corner of pine forest and down a sudden bank among quaking-aspen trees. Here the runaways were grazing at ease beside a stream. They saw them coming, and started on again, down the stream. The best the pursuers could do was to keep them in sight. Other streams flowed into the creek. It widened, making a valley for itself.

"This here's the middle fork of Sunk Creek," said the Virginian. "We'll be able to get back to our right road again where they join."

Soon a rude trail created by passing game ran along the stream. If the runaways stayed on this path, they would follow it down into the canyon. The only way out led to familiar ground. From there the horses would—without doubt—make for the judge's ranch on their own. But first, they had to reach the canyon before dark. The travelers came round a corner and from somewhere in the middle of it rose a buzzard. As it swept over the trail, something fell from its claw, a rag of red flannel. Each man looked at it as his horse went by.

"I wonder if there's plenty elk and deer here?" said the Virginian.

"I guess there is," Balaam replied, speaking at last. The travelers had become strangely reconciled.

"There's game almost all over these mountains," the Virginian continued. "This country's not been settled long enough to scare them out." So they fell into casual conversation, and for the first time were glad to have each other's company.

A new sound came from the pines above—the hoot of an owl. The call was answered from some other part of the wood. Soon they heard the same note, unexpectedly distant, like an echo. The game trail, now a clearer path beside the river, showed no sign of changing its course or fading out. The two men were relieved to see it continue.

The owls hooted again. Their music had something in it that caused both the Virginian and Balaam to look up at the pines and wish this valley would end. The sound never seemed to fall behind. It moved beside them among the trees. The faces of the travelers grew serious.

The sun sank beneath the tallest peaks at the same time the stream opened into a long wide meadow. The two men came out of the willows, and saw the runaways ahead, going up the hill to enter the woods.

"We must prevent that," said the Virginian and he dropped Pedro's rope. "There's your six-shooter. You stay on the trail, and camp down there"—he pointed to where the trees came to the water—"till I head them horses off. I may not get back right away." He galloped up the open hill and went into the pine.

Balaam dismounted and picked up his six-shooter. He took the rope off Pedro's neck and drove him slowly toward the woods. This would have to be their stopping place tonight. There was no way of knowing how far this forest of pines would extend before they would come out of it and reach another suitable camping ground. Pedro had recovered his strength, but he suddenly became restless. He shied and turned sharply round. As they approached the woods, Balaam got off. Pedro snorted, dashed into the water, and stood there. When Balaam followed, Pedro seemed to lose control of himself, and plunged into the middle of the river. Fearing he would escape, Balaam drew his six-shooter with the idea of turning him around. He would fire in front of the horse. The flash cut the gathering darkness and revealed the secret of all this—Indians. But the realization was too late. His bruised hand had stiffened, and his aim was off. Pedro fell over in the water, rose, and struggled up the bank on the farther shore. Balaam hurried there also to find that he had broken the pony's leg.

Now Balaam understood the owl calls that had haunted their journey. He knew that Pedro had sensed the trap lurking for them in the nearby woods. The fate of the trapper whose horse had returned without him might have been—might still be—his own. The Indians had waited in the woods they expected him to enter, wary of using their rifles in fear these travelers were part of a larger company. Safe under the cover of the pines, they had planned to drag the white man from his horse.

Balaam looked over the river at the ominous woods and then looked at Pedro. He probably owed his life to the horse he had first injured and now ruined. Pedro was lying on the ground, quietly looking over the green meadow. No sound of pain came from Pedro, whose friendly and gentle face remained turned toward the meadow. Once more Balaam fired his pistol. This time his aim was true and the horse rolled over, a bullet in his brain.

Balaam rejoined the old mare. He found his way along in the night till he came to the old trail—the road they would never have left but for him and his stubbornness. By Sunk Creek, where the canyon begins, he unsaddled the weary mare, letting her find pasture and water. Lighting no fire to betray him, Balaam crouched against a tree till light came. He thought about the Virginian in the woods. How would it help matters for Balaam to search for the Virginian? The cowpuncher would follow Balaam's tracks or not. They would meet where the creeks joined.

But they did not meet. Balaam could not bear the prospect of going on to the Sunk Creek Ranch. To come without the horses, to meet Judge Henry, to meet the guests of the judge's, looking as he did now after his punishment by the Virginian? How could he tell a story like this? Balaam made his way to a cabin he knew where he wrote a letter to the judge. This the owner of the cabin delivered. Balaam returned home, pleased with himself for alerting the judge to commence a search for the Virginian. As for himself, he had explained, a sudden illness would have made him a burden at Sunk

Creek. By the time Balaam returned to Butte Creek, the signs of the beating he'd taken were less noticeable. And there was Shorty, waiting!

Somehow the lost dog had been able to gather some ready money. "And so I come back, you see," he said. "I was figuring on getting Pedro back as soon as I could when I sold him to you."

"You're behind the times, Shorty," said Balaam.

Shorty looked blank. "You haven't sold Pedro, have you?"

"Them Indians," said Balaam, "got after me on the Bow Leg Trail. Got after me and that Virginia man. But they didn't get me."

Balaam wagged his bullet head to suggest that his escape was due to his own superior intelligence. The Virginian had been stupid, and so the Indians had got him. "And they shot your horse," Balaam finished. "Stop and get some dinner with the boys."

Having eaten, Shorty rode away in mournful spirits. For he had been so sure of riding and talking once more with Pedro, his friend whom he had taught to shake hands.

CHAPTER 27

GRANDMOTHER STARK

Except for its chair and bed, the cabin was stripped almost bare. Amid its emptiness, the tiny miniature of Grandmother Stark still hung, the last token of the home that had been. The picture was her final treasure waiting to be packed for the journey. In whatever room she had called her own since childhood, it had also lived. Till yesterday a Crow Indian war-bonnet had hung next to it. Opposite had been the skin of a silver fox. Over the door had spread the antlers of a black-tail deer. A bearskin stretched beneath it. The whole cozy log cabin had been furnished in this way, with trophies of the frontier. Yet her visitors had always stopped in front of the miniature.

Molly Wood was not going to teach school any more in Bear Creek, Wyoming. She was going home to Bennington, Vermont. When time came for school to open again, there would be a new schoolmarm.

This was the momentous result of that visit the Virginian had paid her. He had told her he was coming for his hour soon. From that hour she had decided to escape. She was running away from her own heart. She did not dare to trust herself face to face again with her powerful, determined suitor. She longed for him, and therefore she would never see him again. Her family, from her great-aunt on down, would forever say she had married below her station! So, she had written to the Virginian, bidding him goodbye, and wishing him everything in the world. At the same time, she was aware of taking everything in the world away from him. So, this was not the easiest of letters to write. But she had made the language very kind. And all because of that brief visit, when he had brought back to her two novels, *Emma* and *Pride and Prejudice*.

"How do you like them?" she had then inquired. He smiled slowly at her. "You haven't read them!" she exclaimed.

"No."

"Are you going to tell me there has been no time?"

"No."

Then Molly scolded her cowpuncher. He listened with undisguised pleasure.

"Why, it has come too late," he had told her when the scolding was over. "You can't learn a growed-up man to like such frilly books I reckon."

"So much the worse for you!" said Molly.

"No. I am pretty glad I am a man. Else I could not have learned the thing you have taught me. Here's some of them cactus blossoms you wanted," said the Virginian. "And I've brought a good horse

I've gentled for you. Taylor'll keep him till I need him."

"Thank you so much! But I wish—"

"I reckon you can't stop me from lendin' Taylor a horse. And you certainly will get sick schoolteachin' if you don't get outdoors some. Goodbye—till that next time."

"Yes, there's always a next time," she answered, as lighthearted as she could.

"There always will be. Don't you know that?"

She did not reply. Thinking about that moment, she now fell to work on her boxes. She played a sort of desperate dominos to try to fit in the last few objects. But here were a paperweight, a portfolio, and two books with no place to go. There, on her wall still, was the miniature, her little, silent ancestor. She appealed to Grandmother Stark for support and comfort across the century that lay between them. She stood in silent thought for a moment, and then turned again to her work. But after a half-hearted touch here and there she drew a long breath and walked to the open door. What use was there in finishing today, when she had nearly a week? Across the lane his horse—the one he had "gentled"—grazed lazily. She caught him, and led him to her gate. Mrs. Taylor watched the girl throw the saddle on with quick ease—the ease he had taught her. Mrs. Taylor also saw the sharp cut she gave the horse. She laughed grimly to herself in her window as horse and rider galloped into the beautiful sunny loneliness.

The poor horse was unaccustomed to Molly using a switch. The third time he was hit, he turned his head in surprise. She paid him no mind. He carried her over ground she knew by heart—Corncliff Mesa, Crowheart Butte, Westfall's Crossing, Upper Canyon. Bear Creek narrowed, its mountainsides drew near, its little falls began to rush white in midday shadow. Suddenly, the horse pricked up his ears. Unguided, he was heading for the trail over to Sunk Creek, when he heard a friend whinnying good day to him. He whinnied back and quickened his pace.

Molly came to life. What was Monte doing here? She saw the black horse she knew, saddled, with reins dragging on the trail as if the rider had dropped them to dismount. A cold spring bubbled out beyond the next rock. She knew her lover's horse was waiting for him while he drank. She pulled at the reins to turn and escape, but loosened her grip. Instead of fleeing, she rode boldly around the rock.

She came upon him by the spring. One of his arms hung up to its elbow in the pool. The other was crooked beside his head. His face was sunk downward against a rock. She could only see his black, tangled hair. As her horse snorted and tossed his head, she looked swiftly at Monte, as if to question him. Seeing now the sweat matted on his coat, and noting the white rim of his eye, she sprang and ran to the motionless figure. A patch of blood behind his shoulder stained the soft flannel shirt, spreading down beneath his belt. The man's whole strong body lay slack and pitifully helpless.

The hand she touched seemed neither warm nor cold. She felt for a pulse, as nearly as she could remember the doctors did. She could not tell if she imagined there was a beat. She leaned down and lifted his other arm and hand from the water. Only then did she see the patch near the shoulder she had moved grow wet with new blood. "I must not faint. I will not faint," she murmured aloud.

Suddenly her energy was restored. "The blood ran!" she exclaimed, as if to the horses. She moved to him, and put her hand in through his shirt against his heart.

Next moment she sprang up, got her small flask, and was back beside him. Here was the cold water he had sought. She put it against his forehead and drenched the wounded shoulder with it. Three times she tried to move him, so he might lie more easy. But his dead weight was too much. She sat close and raised his head to let it rest against her. Then she saw the blood that was running from in front of his shoulder also. She said no more about fainting. She tore strips from her dress and soaked them, keeping them cold and wet upon both openings of his wound. She drew her pocketknife out and cut his shirt away. As she continually cleaned the wound underneath, she watched his eyelashes, long and soft and thick. They did not stir. Near the pool were the charred remains of a fire he and she had once made here together. She built another fire now. When the flames were going well, she filled her flask-cup from the spring and set it to heat. Meanwhile, she returned to nurse his head and wound. Her cold water had stopped the bleeding. Then she poured her brandy in the steaming cup, and forced some between his lips and teeth.

Instantly, almost, she felt a tremble of life creeping back. His deep eyes opened upon her. She sat still and mute, wondering if perhaps he could not recognize her. Then he began to speak in slowly uttered words.

"I expected they were going to kill me." He stopped, and she gave him more of the hot drink. He took it, still lying and looking at her as if his senses were not quite regained. "I knew hands were touching me. I reckoned I was not dead. I knew about them soon as they began, only I could not interfere." He waited again. "It is mighty strange where I have been. No. Mighty natural." Then he lay back with his eyes upon her.

She quietly spoke his name in scarcely more than a whisper.

At this, something awakened in him. "It was you all along," he resumed. "It is you now. You must not stay—" Weakness overcame him, and his eyes closed. She tended to him. When he roused again, he began anxiously at once, "You must not stay. They would get you, too."

She glanced at him with a sort of fierceness, then reached for his pistol. In its chambers were nothing but blackened empty cartridges. She threw these out, drew six from his belt, loaded the weapon, and snapped shut its hinge.

"Please take it," he said, more anxious and more himself. "I ain't worth tryin' to keep. Look at me!"

"Are you giving up?" she inquired.

"Where is the sense in both of us—"

"You had better save your strength," she interrupted.

He tried to sit up.

"Lie down!" she ordered.

He sank obediently, and began to smile.

When she saw that, she smiled too, and unexpectedly took his hand. "Listen, friend," said she. "Nobody shall get you, and nobody shall get me. Now take some more brandy."

"It must be noon," said the cowpuncher, when she had drawn her hand away from him. "I remember it was dark when—when—when I can remember. I reckon they were scared to follow me in so close to settlers. Else they would have been here."

"You must rest," she observed.

She broke the soft ends of some evergreen, and putting them beneath his head, went to the horses. She led them to drink, and staked them so they could feed. To leave nothing undone that she could manage herself, she took the horses' saddles off. She brought the horse's blankets for him. But he pushed them away. He was sitting up against a rock now, stronger and asking for cold water. His head was fire-hot, and the paleness beneath his weather-beaten skin had changed to a deepening red.

"Only five miles!" she said to him, bathing his head.

"Yes. I must hold it steady," he answered, waving his hand at the cliff.

She told him to try and keep it steady until they got home.

"Yes," he repeated. "Only five miles. But it's fightin' to turn around." Half-aware that he was becoming lightheaded, he looked from the rock to her and from her to the rock.

"We can hold it together," she said. "You must get on your horse." She took his handkerchief from round his neck, knotting it with her own. To make more bandages she ran to the roll of clothes behind his saddle and tore a clean shirt in half. A handkerchief fell from it, which she seized also. Opening it, she saw her initials by the hem. Then she remembered again their first meeting, the swollen river, and the unknown horseman who carried her to the bank on his saddle and went away unthanked. At last, she knew where her long-forgotten handkerchief had gone that day. She refolded it gently and put it back in his bundle, for there was enough bandage without it. She said not a word to him, and he took a wrong meaning from the look she gave him.

"It don't hurt so much," he assured her (though extreme pain was clearing his head for the moment, and he had been able to hold the cliff from turning). "You must not squander your pity."

"Do not squander your strength," said she.

"Oh, I could put up a pretty good fight now!" But he stumbled trying to show her how strong he was, and she told him that, after all, he was still a child.

"Yes," he slowly said, looking after her as she went to bring his horse, "the same child that wanted to touch the moon, I guess." And during the slow climb down into the saddle from a rock to which she helped him he said, "You have got to be the man through this mess."

She saw his clenched teeth and his drooping muscles. He stayed on the horse, compelled by will alone. She walked beside him for support, leading her horse with a backward-stretched left hand. She counted off the distance to him continually—the landmarks nearing and dropping behind. Here was the tree with the wasp nest gone. Now the burned cabin was passed. Now the cottonwoods at the ford were in sight. He was silent, and held to the saddle horn, leaning more and more against his hands. Just after they had made the crossing he fell, slipping to the grass without a sound, his descent broken by her. He started to bleed a little. She dared not leave him to seek help. She gave him the last of the flask and all the water he craved.

Revived, he managed to smile. "You see, I ain't worth keeping."

"It's only a mile," she said. She found a log, and he crawled to that. From there he crawled to his saddle, and she marched on with him. For the next half-mile they went this way, the silent man on the horse, the girl walking by his side, cheering him forward. Suddenly he began to speak, "I will say goodbye to you now, ma'am."

She did not understand this at first.

"He is getting away," the Virginian continued. "I must ask you to excuse me, ma'am."

It was a long while since he had addressed her as "ma'am." Her concern grew when she saw him start to turn Monte and ride away. She caught hold of the bridle.

Now she understood. The Virginian was delirious. "You must take me home," she said, "I am afraid of the Indians."

"Why, you—why, they've all gone. There he goes. Ma'am—that horse—"

"No," said she, holding firmly his rein and quickening her step. "A gentleman does not invite a lady to go out riding and leave her."

His eyes lost their purpose. "I'll certainly take you home." With his eyes watching imaginary objects, he rode and rambled. The girl was silent, except to keep his mind from its half-fixed idea of the lost horse. At last she got him inside her cabin and set him down. He did not move, though his mind was wandering. She hurried to the Taylor's cabin only to find it locked and silent. She returned to her room, and already illness had spread over him. His face and indeed his whole body showed sickness in every line and limb. Clear and steady, she came to a decision. Supporting him over to her bed, she laid him on it. His head sank flat, and his loose, nerveless arms stayed as she left them. Then among her packing-boxes and beneath the little miniature, she undressed him.

He was cold. She got from her box her scarlet and black Navajo blanket and spread it over him. There was no more that she could do, and she sat down by him to wait. Among the many things that came into her mind was a word he said to her lightly a long while ago. "Cowpunchers do not live long enough to get old."

At the distant jingle of a wagon, she ran out of the cabin. She met the Taylors as they were returning. They heard her with amazement, and came quickly to the bedside. Then Taylor departed to spread news of the Indians and bring the doctor, twenty-five miles away. "I will look after him," said Mrs. Taylor, "and you'll need some looking after yourself."

But on returning from her cabin with what store of bandages and medicines she possessed, she encountered a rebel. Molly would hear no talk about saving her strength, would not be in any room but this one until the doctor should arrive. So, together the woman and the girl rinsed the man's wound and wrapped him in clean things, and did all the little that they knew—which was, in truth, the very thing needed. Then they sat watching him toss and mutter. The listeners now and then could piece out a reference from their own knowledge. "Monte," for example, was often addressed. Molly heard her own name, but invariably as "Miss Wood." And frequently he answered someone as "ma'am." As the night wore on, short lulls of silence intervened. The watchers began to hope that the fever was abating. But then the Virginian sat up in bed and looked steadily at Mrs. Taylor.

"Rise on your legs, you polecat," said he, "and tell them you're a liar."

The good woman gasped, then ordered him to lie down. He obeyed her with that strange double understanding of the delirious. Even while submitting, he muttered "liar," "polecat," and then "Trampas."

At that name, light flashed on Mrs. Taylor, and she turned to Molly. "You might as well know it," she said. "He would blame me for speaking of it, but where's the harm now? And you would never hear it from his mouth. Molly, child, they say Trampas would kill him if he dared, and that's on account of you."

"I never saw Trampas," said Molly.

"No, deary. But before a lot of men—Taylor has told me about it—Trampas spoke disrespectfully of you, and before them all he made Trampas say he was a liar. That is what he did when you were almost a stranger among us, and he had not started seeing so much of you. I expect Trampas is the only enemy he ever had in this country. But he would never let you know about that."

"No," whispered Molly. "I did not know."

In time, Mrs. Taylor offered some advice. "You had better go to bed, child. You look about ready for the doctor yourself."

"Then I will wait for him," said Molly.

So the two nurses continued to sit until darkness at the windows weakened into gray, and the lamp was no more needed. Their patient was rambling again. They waited for the doctor, not daring much more than to turn pillows and give what other ease they could. Then, at noon came a messenger, to say the doctor had gone on a visit some thirty miles beyond. Taylor had followed to bring him here as soon as might be. At this, Molly consented to rest and to take turns on watch. With the approach of the second night the Virginian's fever seemed to rise. It so raged that the women called in stronger arms to hold him down. There were times when he broke out in the language of the roundup, and Mrs. Taylor protested that Molly should not be hearing such language. "Why," said Molly, "don't you suppose I knew they could swear?"

Toward morning, as Mrs. Taylor sat taking her turn, he asked suddenly how long he had been sick. The wandering seemed to drop from him at that moment, leaving him altogether himself again. He lay very feeble, asking once or twice about his condition and how he came to be here. He remembered nothing about coming to the spring where he had been found.

When the doctor arrived, he pronounced that it would be long—or very short. He praised their clean water treatment. The wound was fortunately well up on the shoulder, and gave so far no bad signs. The strength of the patient had been as few men's were. Each hour was now an hour nearer certainty, and meanwhile the doctor would remain as long as he could. He had many inquiries to answer. Dusty fellows would ride up, listen to him, and reply, as they rode away, "Don't you let him die, Doc." Judge Henry offered to pay for any attention or medicine that might help his foreman. It seemed that the whole Territory was moved with concern and interest. The Indians who had done this were now in military custody. Newspaper editors immediately foresaw war arising out of this incident. But an editor can't make any more than two days' headlines from five Indians in a guardhouse awaiting punishment. What was true was that only through Molly alone (the doctor told her) had the wounded man gotten this chance—this good chance, he added.

"I'm afraid I'll be gone by the time he is well," said Molly, coldly. The discreet doctor simply noted that she would find Bennington quite a change from Bear Creek.

Mrs. Taylor said something and a change came over Molly. She exclaimed, "I shall stay as long as I am needed. I will nurse him. I want to nurse him. I will do everything for him that I can!"

"And that won't be anything, deary," said Mrs. Taylor, harshly. "A year of nursing don't equal a day of sweetheart."

The girl took a walk. She was of no more service in the room at present. She leaned over the pasture fence and watched the two horses—the one the Virginian had "gentled" for her, and his own

Monte. A call came from a neighbor for the doctor. In his going away to them, even under promise of quick return, Mrs. Taylor saw a favorable sign. When the doctor returned, he gave his opinion that all was even better than he could have hoped it would be. Here was now the beginning of the fifth day. The wound was healing. No further delirium had come, and the fever had abated. He believed the serious danger lay behind. The patient's recovery would take weeks—three, four, five. There was no saying how long yet. These next few days he must have utter quiet. He must not talk nor hear anything likely to disturb him. Then the time for cheerfulness and company would come, but gradually. So he departed, and sent next day some medicine and more direction regarding the wound and dirt. He would be calling again the day after tomorrow.

On that day, he returned to find two patients. Molly Wood lay in bed at Mrs. Taylor's. With little to do, and deprived of the strong stimulant of anxiety and action, her strength had quite suddenly left her. The chief treatment the doctor gave was a scolding. The doctor criticized her for taking on the work of several people when several people were at hand to do it for themselves, and this pleased Mrs. Taylor remarkably. As for the wounded man, he was behaving himself properly. Perhaps in another week he could be moved to a more cheerful room. Just now, with cleanliness and pure air, any barn would do.

"We are real lucky to have such a sensible doctor in the country," Mrs. Taylor observed, after the physician had gone.

"No doubt," said Molly. "He said my room was a barn."

"That's what you've made it, deary. But sick men don't notice much."

But, on a later day—and the interval was brief—Mrs. Taylor informed her that the sick man had noticed. "I could not tell him things liable to disturb him," said she, "and so I told him you were packing up for a little visit to your folks. He just looked at those boxes kind of silent like."

When the doctor came next, he told her that if she could play cards or read aloud, or otherwise offer distractions for him, she could be most useful. So she brought over a cribbage board, surprised by her unexpected hesitation at coming face to face again with the sturdy man she had saved and tended. He was not so sturdy now, but neat, with chin clean, and hair and mustache trimmed and smooth. He sat propped among pillows watching for her.

"You are better," she said, speaking first, and with uncertain voice.

"They have given me orders not to talk," said the Southerner, smiling.

"Oh, yes. Please do not talk—not today."

"No. Only this"—he looked at her, and saw her seem to shrink—"thank you for what you have done," he said simply.

She took tenderly the hand he stretched to her. Upon these terms they set to work at cribbage. She won, and won again, and the third time laid down her cards, scolding him for playing to lose.

"No," he said, and his eye wandered to the boxes. "But my thoughts get away from me. I'll be strong enough to hold the cards next time, I reckon."

Many tones in his voice she had heard, but never the tone of sadness until today.

Then they played a little more, and she put away the board for this first time.

"You are going now?" he asked.

"When I have made this room look a little less pitiful." And Molly busied herself once again with the personal effects destined for Vermont. Out they came. The bearskin was spread on the floor. The shelves grew comfortable with books. Some flowers were placed on the table.

"More like old times," said the Virginian, but sadly.

"It's too bad," said Molly, "you had to be brought into such a dreary looking place."

"And your folks waiting for you," said he.

"Oh, I'll pay my visit later," said Molly, putting the rug a trifle straighter.

"May I ask one thing?" pleaded the Virginian, and at the gentleness of his voice her face grew rosy. She fixed her eyes on him with a sort of dread.

"Anything that I can answer," said she.

"Oh, yes. Did I tell you to quit me, and did you load up my gun and stay? Was that a real business? I have been mixed up in my head."

"That was real," said Molly. "What else was

there to do?"

"Nothing—for such as you!" he exclaimed. "My head has been mighty crazy and that little grandmother of yours yonder, she"—he passed a hand over his forehead—"so many—or else one right along—well, it's all foolishness!" he concluded, with something almost savage in his tone. And after she had gone from the cabin he lay very still, looking at the miniature on the wall.

He was in another sort of mood the next time, cribbage not interesting him in the least. "Your folks will be wondering about you," said he.

"I don't think they will mind which month I go to them," said Molly. "Especially when they know the reason."

"Don't let me keep you, ma'am," said he. Molly stared at him. He spoke again, this time with that edge lurking in his slow words, "I'll never forget. How could I forget all you have done—and been? If there had been none of this, why, I already had enough to remember! But please don't stay, ma'am. We'll say I had a claim on your attention when you found me pretty well dead, but I'm gettin' well, you see—right quick, too!"

"I can't understand, indeed I can't," said Molly, "why you're talking so!"

He seemed to have certain moods when he would address her as "ma'am," and this she did not like, but could not prevent.

"Oh, a sick man is funny. And you know I'm grateful to you."

"Please say no more about that, or I shall go this afternoon. I don't want to go. I am not ready. I think I had better read something now."

"Why, yes. That's certainly a good notion. Why, this is the best chance you'll ever get to give me education. Won't you please try that *Emma* book now, ma'am? Listening to you will be different." This was said with softness and humility.

Uncertain precisely what he meant, Molly proceeded with *Emma*, indifferently at first, but soon with enthusiasm. She held the volume and read away at it, commenting briefly, and then, finishing a chapter, found her pupil slumbering peacefully. There was no uncertainty about that.

"You couldn't be doing a healthier thing for him, deary," said Mrs. Taylor. "If it gets to make him wakeful, try something harder."

When Molly next appeared, he said sadly, "I reckon I am a dunce." And he begged for pardon. "When I waked up," he said, "I was ashamed of myself for a plumb half hour." Nor could she doubt that he meant what he said.

"I am right glad you have come," he said. And as he saw her going to the bookshelf, he continued, "As regards that *Emma* book, you see—the doin's and sayin's of such folks are above me. But I think if you could read me something that was *about* something, I—I'd be liable to keep awake." And he smiled with a certain shyness.

"Something *about* something?" asked Molly, at a loss.

"Why, yes. Shakespeare. *King Henry IV.* The British king is fighting, and there is his son the prince. He certainly must have been a fine boy if that is all true. Only he would go around town with a mighty foolish gang. His father hated his traveling with trash like them. But the boy showed himself a man too. He killed a big fighter on the other side who was another fine one—and he was sorry for having it to do." The Virginian was just warming up. "I understand most all of that. There was a fat man kept everybody laughing. But the prince—that play is bedrock, ma'am! Have you got something like that?"

"Yes, I think so," she replied. "I believe I see what you would appreciate."

She read from Browning, her idol. This was better than *Emma*, he pronounced. "But the soldier should not have told the general he was killed," stated the cowpuncher.

"But that part at the finish—will you please say it again?"

So Molly read:

"You're wounded!" "Nay," the soldier's pride
Touched to the quick, he said:
"I'm killed, Sire!" And his chief beside,
Smiling the boy fell dead.

"What should he have told him, I'd like to know?" said Molly.

"Why, just nothing. If the soldier could ride out of the battle all shot up, and tell his general about their takin' the town—that was being gritty, you see. But that stuff at the finish—will you please say it again?"

His bandages, becoming a little bothersome, had to be shifted, and this turned their discussion from literature to Wyoming. Molly asked, had he ever been shot before? Only once, he told her. "I have been lucky in having few fusses," said he. "I hate them. If a man has to be killed—"

"You never—" broke in Molly. "Well," she added quickly, "don't tell me if—"

"I shouldn't wonder if I got one of those Indians," he said quietly. "But I wasn't waitin' to see! But I came mighty near finishing off a white man that day. He had been hurtin' a horse."

"Hurting?" said Molly.

"Hurtin'! But I will not tell you about that. It would hurt you to hear such things. But horses—don't they depend on us? Ain't they somethin' like children? I did not lay up the man very bad. He was able to travel almost right away. Why, you'd have wanted to kill him yourself!"

So the Virginian talked, not knowing what he was doing to the girl. Nor was she aware of what she was receiving from him in these Browning meetings every day.

Strength was flowing back into him each day, and Judge Henry's latest messenger had brought him clothes and mail from Sunk Creek. As a result, Molly found him waiting in a flannel shirt of a highly becoming shade, with a silk handkerchief knotted round his throat. He told her it was good to feel respectable again.

She had come to read to him. She threw around his shoulders the scarlet and black Navajo blanket. In his lap lay one of the letters brought over by the messenger. Though Molly was midway through a book that occupied his full attention— *David Copperfield*—his silence and absent look this morning stopped her. She accused him of not paying attention.

"Yes," he admitted, "I am thinking of something else."

She looked at him with an uneasiness he knew.

"It had to come," said he. "Today I see my thoughts most plainly since my head got clear. And now I must say these thoughts—if I can, if I can!" He stopped. His eyes were intent on her. One hand was gripping the arm of his chair.

"You promised—" trembled Molly.

"I promised you should love me," he sternly interrupted. "Promised that to myself. I have broken that word."

She shut *David Copperfield*, and grew white.

"Your letter has come to me here," he continued, gentle again.

"My—" She had forgotten it.

"The letter you wrote to tell me goodbye. You wrote it a little while ago—not a month yet, but it's away and away long gone for me."

"I have never let you know—" began Molly.

"The doctor," he interrupted once more, but

very gently now, "he gave orders I must be kept quiet. I reckon you thought tellin' me might—"

"Forgive me!" cried the girl. "Indeed I ought to have told you sooner! Indeed I had no excuse!"

"Why should you tell me if you preferred not to? You had written. You speak," he lifted the letter, "of never being able to repay my kindness. But you have turned the tables. I can never repay you! So I had figured I would just head back to Sunk Creek and let you get away. I saw the boxes. Mrs. Taylor is too nice a woman to know the trick of lyin', and she could not deceive me. I have knowed you were going away for good ever since I saw those boxes. But now here comes your letter, and it seems I must speak. I have thought a great deal, lyin' in this room. And—today—I can say what I have thought. I could not make you happy." He stopped, but she did not answer. His voice had grown softer than whispering, but yet was not a whisper. From its quiet syllables she turned away, blinded with sudden tears.

"Once, I thought love must surely be enough," he continued. "And I thought if I could make you love me, you could learn me to be less—to be more your kind. And I think I could give you a pretty good sort of love. But that don't help the little mean pesky things of day-by-day that make roughness or smoothness for folks tied together so awful close." He closed his eyes and drew a long breath. At last he looked at her again. "This is no country for a lady. Will you forget and forgive the bothering

I have done?"

"Oh!" cried Molly. "Oh!" And she put her hands to her eyes. She had risen and stood with her face covered.

"I surely had to tell you this all out, didn't I?" said the cowpuncher, faintly, in his chair.

"Oh!" said Molly again.

"I have put it clear how it is," he pursued. "I ought to have seen from the start I was not the sort to keep you happy."

"But," said Molly, "but I—you ought—please try to keep me happy!" And sinking by his chair, she hid her face on his knees.

Speechless, he bent down and enfolded her, putting his hands on the hair that had been always his delight. Presently he whispered, "You have beat me. How can I fight this?"

She answered nothing. The Navajo blanket fell over both of them. Without words, without even meeting eyes, the two pledged their devotion in this first new hour. So they remained long, the fair head nesting in the great arms, and the black head laid against it. The little Grandmother Stark in her frame kept her eye on the silent room, not quite familiar, not quite smiling.

CHAPTER 28

NO DREAM TO WAKE FROM

For a long while after she had left him, he lay still, stretched in his chair. His eyes were fixed upon the open window and the sunshine outside. There he watched the movement of the leaves upon the green cottonwoods. What had she said to him when she went? She had said, "Now I know how unhappy I have been." These sweet words he repeated to himself over and over, fearing in some way that he might lose them. "I have been asleep," he said. "But she was certainly here herself. Oh, yes. Surely. She always has to go away every day because the doctor says—why, she was readin'!" he broke off, aloud. "*David Copperfield*!" There it was on the floor. "How scared I am of myself! You're a fool. Of course it's so. No fever could make you feel like this."

He now noticed the miniature of Grandmother Stark. "You are awful like her," he whispered. "You're certainly awful like her. May I kiss you, ma'am?"

Then, staggering, he rose from his sick-chair. The Navajo blanket fell from his shoulders, and gradually he stood upright.

Helping himself with his hands, he moved slowly along the side of the room to the opposite wall. He reached the picture, and very gently touched Grandmother Stark's forehead with his lips. "I promise to make your little girl happy," he whispered.

He almost fell in bending to the portrait, but caught himself and stood carefully quiet. "Where is your strength?" he demanded. "I reckon it is joy that has wobbled your legs."

The door opened. It was she, come back with his dinner.

"My Heavens!" she said. Setting the tray down, she rushed to him. She helped him back to his chair, and covered him again. He had suffered no hurt, but she clung to him. At this moment he moved and let himself kiss her with more passion than he had kissed the miniature.

"I will be good," he whispered.

"You must," she said. "You looked so pale!"

"You are speakin' low like me," he answered. "But we have no dream we can wake from."

Had she surrendered on this day to her cowpuncher, her wild man? Was she forever wholly his? Had the Virginian's fire so melted her heart that no fracture in it remained? So she would have thought if any thought had come to her. But in his arms today, thought was lost in something more divine.

WORD TO BENNINGTON

They kept their secret for a while. At least they had that special joy of believing that no one in all the world but themselves knew what had happened between them. But I think that there was one person who knew how to keep a secret even better than these two lovers. Mrs. Taylor made no remarks to anyone whatever. Nobody in Bear Creek, however, was so extraordinarily cheerful and calm.

And when letters to Bennington would go out, Mrs. Taylor would inspect every one. Her eyes examined each envelope as if it were growing transparent beneath her eyes, revealing its great secret. But in truth these letters had no great secret to tell, until one day—yes, Mrs. Taylor would have burst, were bursting a thing that people did. Three letters were the cause of this emotion on Mrs. Taylor's part. One was addressed to Bennington, one to Dunbarton, and the third—here was the great excitement—to Bennington, but not in the little schoolmarm's delicate writing. A man's hand had traced those plain, steady vowels and consonants.

"It's come!" exclaimed Mrs. Taylor, at this

sight. "He has written to her mother himself."

That is what the Virginian had done, and here is how it had come about.

The sick man's recovery was achieved. The weeks had brought back not his whole strength yet—that could come only by many miles of open air on the back of Monte—but he was strong enough now to *get* strength. When a patient reaches this stage, he is out of the woods.

He had gone for a little walk with his nurse. They had taken (under the doctor's recommendation) several such little walks, beginning with a five-minute one, and at last today accomplishing three miles.

"No, it has not been too far," said he. "I am afraid I could walk twice as far."

"Afraid?"

"Yes. Because it means I can go to work again. This thing we have had together is over."

For reply, she leaned against him.

"Look at you!" he said. "Only a little while ago you had to help me stand on my legs. And now—" For a while there was silence between them. "I have never had a right down sickness before," he went on. "If any person had told me I could *enjoy* such a thing—" He said no more. She reached up, and no more speech was possible.

"How long has it been?" he next asked her.

She told him.

"Well, if it could be forever—if it could be forever with just you and me, and no one else to bother with—but any longer would not be doing right by your mother. She would have a right to think poorly of me."

"Oh!" said the girl. "Let us keep our secret a little longer."

"Not after I am back to work. Your mother must be told."

"It seems so—can't we—oh, why need anybody know?"

"Your mother ain't 'anybody.' She is your mother. I feel mighty responsible to her for what I have done."

"But I did it!"

"Do you think so? Your mother will not think so. I am going to write to her today."

"You! Write to my mother! Oh, then everything will be so different! They will all—"

Upon the fairy tale that she had been living with her cowboy lover broke the voices of the world. She could hear them from a distance. She could see the eyes of Bennington watching this man at her side. She could imagine the ears of Bennington listening for slips in his English. He would be wearing gloves, a smooth black coat and a vest instead of buckskin. How could they see the man he was? He would speak shortly and simply. They would say, "Oh, yes!" and "How different you must find this from Wyoming!" Then, after the door was shut behind his departing back, he would be totally underrated, and not in the least understood. Why should he be subjected to this? He should never be!

As these half-formed, distressing thoughts streamed through the girl's mind, she altogether forgot one truth. True it was that the voice of the world would speak as she imagined. True it was that in the eyes of her family and acquaintances this lover of her choice would be examined even more like a *specimen* than are other lovers upon these occasions. But, all accepted lovers have to face this ordeal of being treated like specimens by the other family. And if a chosen lover cannot stand being treated as a specimen by the other family, he's a very weak vessel, and not worth any good girl's love. That's all I can say for him.

Now the Virginian was scarcely what even his enemy would term a weak vessel. Molly should have known that he would indeed care to make a good impression in Bennington. His character was open for investigation. Judge Henry would vouch for him. This is what he would have said to his sweetheart had she revealed troubling thoughts. But she did not reveal them.

"Well, then," she sighed at last, "if you think so, I will tell her."

That sigh of hers, be it well understood, was not only because of those Bennington voices. It came also from bidding farewell to the fairy tale that she must leave now. The Virginian would be returning to Sunk Creek. No longer would she and he be living close together alone, unhindered, unmindful of all things.

"Yes, you will tell her," said her lover. "And I must tell her too."

"Both of us?" questioned the girl.

What would he say to her mother? How would her mother like such a letter as he would write to her? Suppose he should misspell a word? Would not sentences from him—written sentences—be a further barrier to his welcome acceptance at Bennington?

"Why don't you send messages by me?" she asked him.

He shook his head. "She is not going to like it, anyway," he answered. "I must speak to her direct. Otherwise, I would be shirking my duty."

Molly saw how true his instinct was here. A little flame shot upward from the glow of her love and pride in him. Oh, if they could all only know that he was like this when you understood him!

"Tell me what you're going to write," she said.

He smiled at her. "No."

"Aren't you going to let me see it when it's done?"

"No." Then a freakish look came into his eyes. "I'll let you see anything I write to other women." And he gave her one of his long kisses. "Let's get through with it together," he suggested, when they were once more in his sickroom, that room which she had given to him. "You'll sit at one side of the table, and I'll sit at the other. We'll go ahead, and pretty soon it will be done."

"Oh, dear!" she said. "Yes, I suppose that is the best way."

And so, accordingly, they took their places. The

inkstand stood between them. Beside each of them she placed enough paper for a presidential message. Pens and pencils were in great supply. Was this not the headquarters of the Bear Creek schoolmarm?

"Aren't you going to do it in pencil first?" she exclaimed, looking up from her blank sheet. His pen was moving slowly, but steadily.

"No, I don't reckon I need to," he answered, with his nose close to the paper. "Oh, damnation, there's an ink stain!" He tore his spoiled beginning in small bits, and threw them into the fireplace. "You've got it too full," he commented; and taking the inkstand, he tipped a little from it out of the window. She sat lost among her false starts. Had she heard him swear, she would not have minded. She rather liked it when he swore. He possessed that quality in his profanity of not offending by it. It is quite wonderful how much worse the same word will sound in one man's lips than in another's. But she did not hear him. She sat, her eyes fixed on that blank sheet before her, waiting. Then her gaze turned, with empty hopelessness, on the various objects in the room. While she sat accomplishing nothing, across from her the cowboy bent down, and the steady pen moved from phrase to phrase.

She became aware of his gaze. That strange color of seawater, which she could never name, shone in his eyes. He was folding his letter.

"You have finished?" she said.

"Yes." His voice was very quiet. "I feel like an honester man."

"Perhaps I can do something tonight at Mrs. Taylor's," she said, looking at her paper.

On it were a few words crossed out. This was all she had to show. At letter writing, the cowpuncher had greatly excelled the schoolmarm!

But that night, while he lay quite fast asleep in his bed, she was working in her room at Mrs. Taylor's. The next day, those three letters departed for the mail. And so, Mrs. Taylor could exclaim, "It's come!"

On the day before the Virginian returned to work at Judge Henry's ranch, he and Molly announced their news. What Molly said to Mrs. Taylor and what Mrs. Taylor said to her is of no interest to us, though it was of much to them.

But Mr. McLean happened to make a call quite early in the morning to ask about his friend's health.

"Lin," began the Virginian, "there is no harm in your knowing an hour or so before the rest, I am—"

"Lord!" said Mr. McLean, indulgently. "Everybody has knowed that since the day she found you at the spring."

"It was not so, then," said the Virginian, crossly.

"Lord! Everybody has knowed it right along."

"Hmp!" said the Virginian. "I didn't know this country was that rank with gossips."

Mr. McLean laughed. "Well," he said, "Mrs. McLean will be glad. She told me to give you her congratulations quite a while ago. I was to have 'em ready just as soon as ever you asked for 'em yourself."

Lin had been made a happy man some twelve months previous to this. And now, by way of an exchange of news, he added: "We're expectin' a little McLean down on Box Elder. That's what you'll be expectin' some of these days, I hope."

"Yes," murmured the Virginian, "I hope so too."

"And I don't guess," said Lin, "that you and I will do much shufflin' of other folks' children anymore."

He and the Virginian shook hands silently, and understood each other very well.

On the day the Virginian parted from Molly, his thoughts also dwelled on some serious news. The cattle thieves had grown more daring. Horses and cattle both were being missed, and each man began almost to suspect his neighbor.

"Steps will have to be taken soon by somebody, I reckon," said the lover.

"By you?" she asked quickly.

"Most likely I'll get mixed up with it."

"What will you have to do?"

"Can't say. I'll tell you when I come back."

So did he part from her, leaving her more kisses than words to remember.

And what was doing at Bennington, meanwhile, and at Dunbarton? Those three letters produced a great and painful uproar.

Molly had written to her mother, and to her great-aunt. That announcement to her mother took three hours and a half to write and filled eleven

pages. The letter to the great-aunt took only ten minutes. Its beginning, to be sure, did give the old lady a start; she had dismissed the cowboy from her probabilities.

"Tut, tut, tut!" she exclaimed out loud in her bedroom. "She has thrown herself away on that fellow!"

But some sentences at the end made her pause and sit still for a long while. "Ah, me," she sighed. "If marriage were as simple as love!" Then she went slowly downstairs, and out into her garden, where she walked long. "But if she has found a great love," said the old lady at length. And she returned to her bedroom, and opened an old desk, and read some old letters.

The next morning a letter arrived from Bennington. This had been written frantically by poor Mrs. Wood. As soon as she had been able to gather her senses after the shock of her daughter's eleven pages, she poured out eight pages to the eldest member of the family. There were good reasons for her distress. To begin with, Molly had written the opening page very carefully to gently prepare her mother. As a result, it made no sense whatever. Instead, it made Mrs. Wood's head swim, and filled her with a sickening dread. "Oh, mercy, Sarah," she had cried, "come here. What does this mean?" And then, with her elder daughter beside her, she turned to the second page and learned what it meant. "A savage with knives and pistols!" she wailed.

"Well, mother, I always told you so," said her daughter Sarah.

"What is a foreman?" exclaimed the mother. "And who is Judge Henry?"

"She is engaged to a sort of upper servant," said Sarah. "If it is allowed to go as far as a wedding, I doubt if I can bring myself to be present." (This threat she later made to Molly, with results that shall be described in their proper place.)

"The man appears to have written to me himself," said Mrs. Wood.

"He knows no better," said Sarah.

"Bosh!" said Sarah's husband later. "It was a very manly thing to do." The letter upset everything in the house at Bennington. All of Molly's declarations that her cowpuncher was held in universal esteem were wasted effort. In despair, Mrs. Wood wrote those eight childish pages to the great-aunt.

"Tut, tut, tut!" said the great-aunt as she read them. "You'd suppose," she said, "that the girl had been kidnapped! Why, she has kept him waiting three years!" And then she read more, but soon put the letter down with laughter. For Mrs. Wood had repeated in writing that early outburst of hers about a savage with knives and pistols. "Law!" said the great-aunt. "Law, what a fool Lizzie is!"

So she sat down and wrote to Mrs. Wood a wholesome reply about putting a little more trust in her own flesh and blood. She reminded her that General Stark himself had, as a military man, carried knives and pistols. He had occasionally taken them off, however, as did probably this young man in Wyoming. "You had better send me the letter he has written you," she concluded. "I shall know much better what to think after I have seen that."

Mrs. Wood got little comfort from this communication. It enraged her daughter Sarah. "She grows more difficult as she nears her old age," said Sarah. But the Virginian's letter was sent to Dunbarton, where the old lady sat herself down to read it with much attention.

Here is what the Virginian had said to the
unknown mother of his sweetheart:

Mrs. John Stark Wood
Bennington, Vermont.

Madam:

If your daughter Miss Wood has ever told
you about her saving a man's life here when some
Indians had shot him that is the man who writes
to you now. I don't think she can have told you
right about that affair for she is the only one in
this country who thinks it was a little thing. So I
must tell you it, the main points. Such an action
would have been thought highly of in a Western
girl, but with Miss Wood's raising nobody had a
right to expect it.

"Indeed!" snorted the great-aunt. "Well, he
would be right, if I had not had a good deal more
to do with her 'raising' than her mother ever had."
And she went on with the letter.

I was starting in to die when she found me.
I did not know anything then, and she pulled me
back from where I was half in the next world.
She did not know but what Indians would get
her, too, but I could not make her leave me. I am
a heavy man one hundred and seventy-three
pounds stripped and in full health. She lifted me
herself from the ground with me scarcely helping
for there was not much help in me that day. She

washed my wound and brought me to with her own whiskey. Before she could get me home I was out of my head but she kept me on my horse somehow and talked wisely to me so I minded her and did not go clean crazy till she had got me safe to bed. The doctor says I would have died all the same if she had not nursed me the way she did. It made me love her more which I did not know I could. But there is no end, for this writing it down makes me love her more as I write it.

And now Mrs. Wood I am sorry this will be bad news for you to hear. I know you would never choose such a man as I am for her for I have got no education and must write humbly about my upbringing. I wish I could make the news easier but truth is the best.

I am of old stock in Virginia. English and one Scotch Irish grandmother my father's father brought from Kentucky. We have always stayed at the same place as farmers and hunters never bettering our lot. We have fought when we got the chance, under Old Hickory and in Mexico. My father and two brothers were killed in the War Between the States. Always in our family it seemed one son would run away and I was the one this time. I had too much older brothering to suit me. But now I am doing well being in full sight of prosperity and not too old and very strong. My health has withstood the trials it has been put through. She shall teach school no more when she is mine. I wish I could make this news easier for you Mrs. Wood. I do not like promises. I have heard so many. I will tell any man of your family anything he likes to ask me, and Judge Henry would tell you about my reputation. I have seen plenty rough things but can say I have never killed for pleasure or profit and am not one of that kind, always preferring peace. I have had to live in places where they had courts and lawyers so called but an honest man was all the law you could find in five hundred miles. I have not told her about those things not because I am ashamed of them but there are so many things too dark for a girl like her to hear about.

I had better tell you the way I know I love Miss Wood. I am not a boy now, and women are no new thing to me. A man like me who has traveled meets many of them as he goes and passes on but I stopped when I came to Miss Wood. That is three years but I have not gone on. What right has such as he you will say. So did I say it after she had saved my life. It was hard to get to that point and keep there with her around me all day. But I said to myself you have bothered her for three years with your love and if you let your love bother her you don't love her like you should and you must quit for her sake who has saved your life. I did not know what I was going to do with my life after that but I supposed I could go somewhere and work hard and so Mrs. Wood I told her I would give her up. But she said no. It is going to be hard for her to get used to a man like me.

But at this point in the Virginian's letter, the old great-aunt could read no more. She rose, and went over to that desk where lay those faded letters of her own. She laid her head down and let her tears flow quietly upon them, "Oh, dear," she whispered, "Oh, dear! And this is what I lost!"

She wrote Molly the next day. And this word from Dunbarton was the one comfort among the harsh stings Molly was receiving. The voices of the world reached her in gathering numbers, and not one of them except that great-aunt's was sweet. Her days were full of hurts. And there was no one to kiss the hurts away. Nor had she heard from her lover yet. She only knew he had gone into remote country for his undertaking.

That errand took him far, over the Continental Divide into East Idaho. There, at his request, we met.

No guide led me to him. Starting from a little station on the railroad, he had charted my route by means of landmarks. I set out from the train in a dark storm that I might have seen—at one time—as an ill omen. But I had been living in cities and smoke. Idaho, even with rain, was delightful to me.

CHAPTER 30

A STABLE ON THE FLAT

At last the first landmark—a lone clump of cottonwoods—came into sight, about a mile from some distant buildings. That abandoned ranch, my resting place for the night, was a ruin—cabin, stable, and corral. Yet, having to eat and go to sleep in it fit perfectly the mood of my flesh and spirit. All of the city I had left with me was a newspaper half-crowded into my pocket. But for its possible help to build fires, it would have come no farther with me. I wanted not to be near human beings at all. To lie down with wild animals, with elk and deer, would have made my waking dream complete. But since such a dream could not be, the cattle—which were now only dots moving around the deserted buildings—were my proper companions for this evening.

Tomorrow night I should probably be camping with the Virginian in the foothills. I had come eastward across Idaho to make this journey with him back through the Teton Mountains. It was a trail known to him, and not to many other honest men. Horse Thief Pass was the name his letter gave it. Business (he was always brief) would call him over there at this time. He had designated for our meeting the forks of a certain little stream in the foothills which today's ride had brought in sight. If by a certain day—which was four days off—I had not reached the forks, he would understand I had other plans. Remembering my Eastern helplessness in the year when we had met first, I enjoyed thinking how I had come to be trusted. In those days I had not been allowed to go from the ranch for so much as an afternoon's ride unless tied to him by a string, so to speak. Now I was crossing unmapped spaces with no guide. The man who could do this could no longer be called a tenderfoot.

I approached ever nearer the moving dots of cattle and my lodging for tonight. Then my horse neighed. I felt his pace quicken. Twice he neighed, impatiently and long. Only then did I realize that those dots were not cattle. They were horses.

The buildings changed in appearance as they grew near. I could see their desolation more clearly. Around them the horses—all standing with ears erect—watched me in silence. The silence I had liked until now seemed suddenly to be too great. Then the door of the stable opened, and men came out and stood, watching me arrive. By the time I was dismounting, more were there. It was senseless to feel as unpleasant as I did, and I attempted to give them a natural sounding greeting. I told them I hoped there was room for one more here tonight. Some of them had answered my greeting, but none answered this. Just as I became sure I recognized several of their faces, the Virginian came from the stable. At that welcome sight, I expressed my relief instantly.

"I am here, you see!"

"Yes, I do see." I looked hard at him, for his voice held the same strangeness I felt in everything around me. He was looking at his companions. "This gentleman is all right," he told them.

"That may be," said one whom I now knew I had seen before at Sunk Creek, "but he was not due tonight."

"Nor tomorrow," said another.

"Nor yet the day after," a third added.

The Virginian fell into his drawl. "None of you was ever early for anything, I presume."

One answered, laughing, "Oh, we're not suspecting you in this."

And another, "Not even when we remember how thick you and Steve used to be."

Whatever jokes they meant by this he did not receive as jokes. I saw something like a frown pass over his face. But he now spoke to me. "We expected to be through before this," he began. "I'm right sorry you have come tonight. I know you'd have preferred to keep away."

"We want him to explain himself," put in one of the others. "If he satisfies us, he's free to go away."

"Free to go away!" I now exclaimed. "Gentlemen," I said, "I don't know why my movements interest you so much. It's quite a compliment!

May I get under shelter while I explain?"

No request could have been more natural, for the rain had now begun to fall in straight floods. Yet there was a pause before one of them said, "He might as well."

The Virginian chose to say nothing more. He walked beside me into the stable. Two men sat there together; a third man guarded them. At that sight I knew suddenly what I had stumbled upon. Rashly, I murmured to the Virginian, "You're hanging them tomorrow."

He kept his silence.

"You may have three guesses," said a man behind me.

But I did not need them. The clump of cottonwoods came into my mind, black and grim. No other trees high enough grew within ten miles. This, then, was the business that the Virginian's letter had so offhandedly mentioned. My eyes went into all corners of the stable. No other prisoners were here. I half-expected to see Trampas, and I half feared to see Shorty. Of late I had heard talk at Sunk Creek of breaking up a certain gang of horse and cattle thieves that stole in one Territory and sold in the next, and knew where to hide in the mountains between. And now forces had been gathered, a long expedition made, and here they were, successful under the Virginian's lead, but a little later than they figured on. And here was I, a little too early, and a witness as a result. My presence seemed a simple thing to account for. But when I had thus accounted for it, one of them said with good nature, "So you find us here, and we find you here. Which is the most surprised, I wonder?"

"There's no telling," said I, keeping as friendly as I could, "nor any telling who objects the most."

"Oh, there's no objection here. You're welcome to stay. But not welcome to go, I expect. He ain't welcome to go, is he?"

By the answers that their faces gave him it was plain that I was not. "Not till we are through," said one.

"Better sleep late tomorrow morning," a third suggested to me.

I did not wish to stay but I was helpless. I made no attempt to discover what kind of spy they imagined I could be. What sort of rescue could I bring in this lonely country? Again my eyes sought the prisoners. Certainly there were only two. One was chewing tobacco, and talking now and then to his guard as if nothing were the matter. The other sat in silence, not moving his eyes. He was dressed in a gray flannel shirt much like mine. I noticed how he continually moistened his dry lips. As I looked at these doomed prisoners, the one who was chewing quietly nodded to me.

"You don't remember me?" he said.

It was Steve! Steve of Medicine Bow! He now had a beard, but I recognized that it was indeed the pleasant Steve of my first evening in the West. Here he sat sentenced to die. A shock, chill and painful, deprived me of speech.

He had no such weak feelings. "Have you been to Medicine Bow lately?" he inquired. "That's getting to be quite a while ago."

I nodded. I would have liked to say something natural and kind, but the words got stuck. Steve looked me over and saw in my pocket the newspaper which I had brought from the railroad. He asked me would I mind letting him have it for a while? I gave it to him eagerly, begging him to keep it as long as he wanted.

He gave me a short glance and a smile. "Thank you," he said. "I'll not need it beyond tomorrow morning." And he began to search through it. "Jake's election is considered sure," he said to his companion, who made no response. "Well, Fremont County owes it to Jake." And I left him interested in the local news.

Dead men I have seen more than a few times. But I hope I shall never again have to be in the company of men waiting to be killed. By this time tomorrow the gray flannel shirt would be worn by a corpse. Until what moment would Steve chew? I managed to close my mind to such thoughts. But I asked to be allowed to pass the night elsewhere, suggesting the nearby cabin. The cabin leaked too much, I was told. I would sleep drier here.

The Virginian understood. "I am right sorry for your annoyance," he said. And now I noticed his mood was quite different from the ease of the others.

After the twelve hours' ride my bones were hungry for rest. I spread my blankets on some straw in a

stall by myself. But the longer I lay the more awake
I became. For a while the others sat, whispering cautiously. I became curious to hear them. Did I catch
the names of Trampas and Shorty spoken once or
twice? I could not be sure. I heard the whisperers
cease. To one after another sleep came, but not to
me. Twice through the hours the thieves shifted
their positions with clumsy sounds, exchanging
muted words with their guard. At last I heard someone get up and begin to dress. In a little while I saw
light suddenly through my closed eyelids. They had
swung in a lantern and found me by mistake. I was
the only one they did not wish to rouse.

They began to go out of the stable. My
thoughts went to the clump of cottonwoods. I lay
still with hands and feet growing steadily colder. I
wondered how they would do it. Would one have
to wait and see the other go through with it first?

The smell of smoke and the rattle of tin dishes
reached me. Breakfast was something I had forgotten. One of them was cooking it now in the dry
shelter of the stable. He was alone, because the talking and the steps were outside the stable. I could
hear the sounds of horses being driven into the corral and saddled. The coffee was ready, and almost
immediately the cook called them. As each man
came in, he shut the door behind him. At length
one spoke out bluntly, asking that the door be left
open on account of the smoke. What were they hiding from? he asked. The runaways that had escaped?
A laugh followed this little joke, and the door was

left open. Thus I learned that there had been more thieves than the two that were captured. Their suspicion of me made a bit more sense now. They were taking no chances, however remote.

I suddenly understood that they must all be sitting round the breakfast together, those who had to die and those who had to kill them. The Virginian never spoke. But I heard the voice of Steve. He discussed with his captors the various points of his capture.

"Do you remember a haystack?" he asked.

"That was Thursday afternoon," said one of the captors. "There was a shower."

"Yes. It rained. We had you fooled that time. I was laying on the ledge above to report your movements."

Several of them laughed. "We thought you were over on Spread Creek then."

"I figured you thought so by the trail you left after the stack. Saturday we watched you turn your back on us up Spread Creek. We were snug among the trees the other side of Snake River. That was another time we had you fooled."

They laughed again at their own expense.

Steve continued, "Would we head for Idaho? Would we swing back over the Divide? You didn't know which! And when we led you to that band of horses you thought was the band you were hunting—ah, we were a strong combination!" He broke off with the first touch of bitterness I had felt in his words.

"Nothing is any stronger than its weakest point." It was the Virginian who said this, and it was the first word he had spoken.

"Naturally," said Steve. His tone in addressing the Virginian was so different, that I supposed he took "weakest point" to mean himself. But the others now showed me that I was wrong in this explanation.

"That's so," one said. "Its weakest point is where a rope or a gang of men is going to break when the strain comes. And you was linked with a poor partner, Steve."

"You're right I was," said the prisoner, back in his easy, casual voice.

"You ought to have got yourself separated from him, Steve."

There was a pause. "Yes," said the prisoner, moodily. "I'm sitting here because one of us blundered." He cursed the blunderer. "Lighting his fool fire ruined the whole deal," he added. As he again heavily cursed the blunderer, the others murmured to each other various I told you so's.

"You'd never have built that fire, Steve," said one.

"I said that when we spied the smoke," said another. "I said, 'That's none of Steve's work, lighting fires and revealing to us their whereabouts.'"

It struck me that they were plying Steve with compliments.

"Pretty hard to have the fool get away and you get caught," a third suggested. At this they seemed to wait. I felt something curious in all this last talk.

"Oh, did he get away?" said the prisoner, then.

Again they waited. This time a new voice spoke, "I built that fire, boys." It was the prisoner in the gray flannel shirt.

"Too late, Ed," they told him kindly. "You ain't a good liar."

"What makes you laugh, Steve?" said someone.

"Oh, the things I notice."

"Meaning Ed was pretty slow in backing up your story? The joke is really on you, Steve. You'd ought never to have cursed the fire-builder if you wanted us to believe he was present. But we'd not have done much to Shorty, even if we had caught him. All he wants is to be scared good and hard, and he'll go back into virtuousness. That was his nature before he started traveling with Trampas."

Steve's voice sounded hard now. "You have caught Ed and me. That should satisfy you for now."

"Well, we think different, Steve. Trampas escaping leaves this thing unfinished."

"So Trampas escaped too, did he?" said the prisoner.

"Yes, Steve, Trampas escaped—this time; and Shorty with him—this time. We know it almost as if we'd seen them go. And we're glad Shorty is loose, for he'll build another fire or do some other foolishness next time. Then we'll get Trampas."

Their talk drifted to other points. I lay thinking of the struggle under the surface of their small talk.

Yes, the joke, as they put it, was on Steve. They were playing for names. He, being an honorable thief, was playing to hide names. They could only, among several likely confederates, guess Trampas and Shorty. It now struck me that after his single remark the Virginian had been silent throughout their shrewd discussion.

It was the other prisoner that I heard them next address. "You don't eat any breakfast, Ed."

"Brace up, Ed. Look at Steve, how hardy he eats!"

But Ed, it seemed, wanted no breakfast. And the tin dishes rattled as they were gathered and taken to be packed.

"Drink this coffee, anyway," another urged.

"You'll feel warmer."

My whole body turned cold at their words. It almost seemed like my own execution.

"I reckon if every one's ready we'll start." It was the Virginian's voice once more, and different from the rest. I heard them rise at his bidding, and I put the blanket over my head. I felt their tread as they walked out, passing my stall. The straw that was half under me and half out in the stable was stirred as by something heavy dragged or half lifted along over it. "Look out, you're hurting Ed's arm," one said to another, as the steps with tangled sounds passed slowly out. I heard another among those who followed say, "Poor Ed couldn't swallow his coffee." Outside they began getting on their horses. Their hoofs grew distant, until all was silence round the stable except the dull, even falling of the rain.

CHAPTER 31

THE COTTONWOODS

I do not know how long I stayed there alone. It was the Virginian who came back. As he stood at the foot of my blankets, his eyes—after meeting mine for a moment—turned aside. I had never seen him look as he did. Until this moment we had found no chance to speak alone.

"Seems to be raining still," I began after a little.

"Yes. It's a wet spell."

He stared out of the door, smoothing his mustache.

Again, I broke the silence. "What time is it?"

He brooded over his watch. "Twelve minutes to seven."

I stood and dressed.

"The fire's out," he said, putting some new sticks on the ashes. He offered me some coffee.

"Never mind," I said.

"We've got a long ride," he suggested.

"I know. I have crackers in my pocket."

I pulled on my boots and walked to the door. "It seems the clouds might lift," I said. And I took out my watch.

"What time is it?" he asked.

"A quarter of—it's run down."

While I wound it he seemed to be consulting his own.

"Well?" I inquired.

"Ten minutes past seven."

As I was setting my watch he slowly said, "Steve used to wind his all the time. I had to guard him till two." His spoke like someone in a trance.

Again I looked at the weather and the rain-covered plain. The eastern foothills where we were going were a soft yellow. Over the gray-green sagebrush moved shapeless places of light—spots where the storm was wearing thin. Wandering streams of warmth passed by slowly in the surrounding air. As I watched the clouds and the earth, my eyes fell on the distant clump of cottonwoods. Mists from the fading storm floated round them. They were indeed far away. I came inside and began rolling up my blankets.

"You will not change your mind?" said the Virginian by the fire. "It is thirty-five miles."

I shook my head, feeling a certain shame that he should see how unnerved I was.

He swallowed a hot cupful, then sat thinking. Presently he passed his hand across his brow, shutting his eyes. Again he poured out a cup, and emptying this, rose abruptly to his feet as if shaking himself free from something.

"Let's pack and quit here," he said.

Our horses were in the corral and our belongings

in the shelter of the cabin at this forlorn place. He collected them in silence while I saddled my own animal. In silence we loaded the two packhorses. Soon we mounted. As we turned onto the trail I gave a look back at my last night's lodging.

The Virginian noticed me. "Goodbye forever!" he interpreted.

"By God, I hope so!"

"Same here," he confessed. And these were our first natural words this morning.

"This will go well," said I, holding my flask out to him. Both of us took some, and felt easier for it.

At first, we could speak only of the weather, or that sort of thing. The thing we could not talk about spoke plainly in the air around us and in every syllable we uttered. We rode to get away from it, to leave it behind in the stable, to set ourselves free from it. Already relief had begun to stir in my spirits.

"You never did this before," I said.

"No. I never had to." He was riding beside me, looking down at his saddle horn.

"I do not think I could," I pursued.

Defiance sounded in his answer. "I would do it again this morning."

"Oh, I don't mean that. It's all right here. There's no other way."

"I would do it all over again the same this morning. Just the same."

"Why, so should I—if I could do it at all." I replied, thinking he had been defending their notion of justice.

He made no answer as he rode along, looking all the while at his saddle. But again he passed his hand over his forehead, frowned, and shut his eyes.

"I wonder how I would behave if I were condemned," I said next. Would I read the newspaper and discuss coming death as if I had lost a game of cards? Or would they have to drag me out? That poor wretch in the gray flannel shirt—"It was bad in the stable," I said aloud. A shiver went through me.

A third time his hand brushed his forehead, and I ventured some sympathy.

"I'm afraid your head aches."

"I don't want to keep seeing Steve," he muttered.

"Steve!" I was astounded. "Wh, why all I saw of him was splendid. Since it had to be. It was—"

"So, you're thinking about Ed. I'd forgot him. So you didn't enjoy Ed?"

At this I looked at him blankly. "It isn't possible that—"

Again he cut me short with a laugh almost savage. "You needn't to worry about Steve. He faced it bravely."

What then had been the matter that he should keep seeing Steve? For he seemed to be growing more troubled as I grew less. I asked him no further questions, however.

We went on for several minutes, he brooding always in the same fashion. At length, he resumed with the hard indifference that had before surprised me, "So you'd have been more comfortable if Ed had acted same as Steve. It certainly was bad seeing Ed take it that way, I reckon. And you didn't see him when the time came for business. Sure, a man may be such a confirmed outlaw that killing's the only cure for him. Still, he's your own species, and you don't want to have him fall around and grab your legs and show you his naked fear. It makes you feel ashamed. So Ed gave you feelings, and Steve made everything right easy for you!" There was irony in his voice, but it fell away at once into sadness. "Both was outlaws. But if Steve had played the coward, too, it would have been a whole heap easier for me." He paused before adding, "Steve was not an outlaw once."

His voice had trembled, and I felt his deep emotion now that action was over and he had nothing to do but think. His view was simple enough: you must die brave. There's no pity for a coward. Steve's perfect bearing caught his heart so that he even forgot his contempt of the other man.

But this was by no means all that was to come. He harked back to that notion of a prisoner helping to make it easy for his executioner. "Easy plumb to the end," he pursued, his mind reviewing the acts of the morning. "Why, he tried to give me your newspaper. I didn't—"

"Oh, no," I broke in. "I had finished with it."

"Well, he took dying as naturally as he took living. Like a man should. Like I hope to." Again he looked at the pictures in his mind. "No playacting.

No last words. Steve just told the boys goodbye as we led his horse under the limb—"

He stretched out his hand to point, but it fell, and he jerked his horse to a stand. My nerves sprang like a wire at his suddenness, and I looked where he was looking. There were the cottonwoods, close in front of us. As we had traveled and talked we had forgotten them. Now they were looming within a hundred yards. Our trail lay straight through them.

"Let's go around them," said the Virginian.

When we had come back to the trail he continued, "You did not have that thing to do. But a man goes through with his responsibilities—and I reckon you could."

"I hope so," I answered. Then he went on.

"Steve and I started punching cattle together maybe six years ago. We did everything together in those days—work and play. Steve had many good points once."

We must have gone two miles before he spoke again. "You probably didn't notice the way Steve acted to me?" It was a question, but he did not wait for my answer. "Steve never said a word to me all through. He shunned it. And you saw how neighborly he talked to the other boys. Steve shunned me. Did he think I was going back on him?"

"What if he did? You were not."

"No. Did you notice Steve would not give us any information about Shorty? That was right. I would have acted that way, too."

The sun was now shining warm two or three

minutes at a time, and gulfs of blue opened in the great white clouds. These moved and met among each other, and parted, like hands spread out, slowly weaving a spell of sleep over the day after the wakeful night storm. The earth lay basking and drying, and not one living creature, bird or beast, was in sight. Quiet was returning to me, but there was none for the Virginian. And as he reasoned matters out aloud, his mood grew more overcast.

"You have a friend, and his ways are your ways. You travel together, you spree together, and you suit each other down to the ground. Then one day you find him putting his iron on another man's calf. You tell him fair and square those ways have never been your ways and ain't going to be your ways. Well, that does not change him any, for it seems he's disturbed over getting rich quick and being a big man in the Territory. And the years go on, until you are foreman of Judge Henry's ranch and he—is dangling back in the cottonwoods. What can he claim? Who made the choice? He cannot say, 'Here is my old friend that I would have stood by.' Can he say that?"

"But he didn't say it," I protested.

"No. He shunned me."

"Listen," I said. "Suppose while you were on guard he had whispered, 'Get me off'—would you have done it?"

"No, seh!" said the Virginian, hotly.

"Then what do you want?" I asked. "What did you want?"

He could not answer me—but I had not answered him. So I pushed it further. "Did you want approval from the man you were hanging? That's asking a little too much."

But he had now another confusion. "Steve stood by Shorty. It was Shorty's mistake cost him his life, but all the same he didn't want us to catch—"

"You are mixing things," I interrupted. "I never heard you mix things before. And it was not Shorty's mistake."

He showed momentary interest. "Whose then?"

"The mistake of whoever took a fool into their enterprise."

"That's correct. Well, Trampas took Shorty in, and Steve would not tell on him, either."

But no common sense could turn him from the thread of his own argument. "Was it him I was deserting? Was not the deserting done by him the day I spoke my mind about stealing calves? I have kept my ways the same. He is the one that took to new ones. The man I used to travel with is not the man back there. Same name, to be sure. And same body. But different in—and yet he had the memory! You can't never change your memory!"

He gave a sob. I reined my horse up to his and put my arm around his shoulders. He was utterly overcome. "I knew Steve awful well," he said.

We had actually changed places. Early in the morning he had been firm while I was unnerved.

Now it was I who attempted to steady and comfort him.

I had the sense to keep silent. Presently he shook my hand, not looking at me as he did so. And he took to patting the neck of his pony. "You Monte horse," said he, "you think you are wise, but there's a lot of things you don't know." Then he made a new beginning of talk between us.

"It is kind of pitiful about Shorty."

"Very pitiful," I said.

"Do you know about him?" the Virginian asked.

"I know there's no real harm in him, and some real good. I know he has not got the brains necessary to be a horse thief."

"That's so. That's very true. Shorty should have stayed in Brooklyn, for he will be a novice his livelong days. You don't know about him? He has told me his circumstances. He don't remember his father. His mother was not much interested in him before or after he was born. He ran around, and when he was eighteen he got to be help to a grocery man. But a girl he ran with kept taking all his pay and teasing him for more. One day the grocery man caught Shorty robbing the till, and fired him. There wasn't no one to tell goodbye to, for the girl had to go to the country to see her aunt, she said. He still sends money back to that girl now. This ain't no country for Shorty."

"Perhaps he'll prefer honesty after his narrow shave," I said.

But the Virginian shook his head. "Trampas has

got hold of him."

The day was now all blue above, and all warm and dry beneath. We had begun to wind in and rise among the first slopes of the foothills, and we had talked ourselves into silence. At the first running water we stopped for a piece. I fell fast asleep right on the bare ground. My body was so deep in slumber that when the Virginian shook me awake I could not come back to life at once. It was the clump of cottonwoods, small and far out in the plain below us, that recalled me.

"It'll not be watching us much longer," said the Virginian. He made it a sort of joke. But I knew that both of us were glad when we rode into a steeper country, and lost all sight of the plain. He had not slept. His explanation was that the packs needed better balancing and that then he had gone up and down the stream in the hope of finding trout. But his haunted eyes gave the real reason. No matter what he claimed, Steve would stay with him for a long time.

CHAPTER 32

SUPERSTITION TRAIL

We did not make thirty-five miles that day, or twenty-five, for he had let me sleep. We made an early camp and tried some unsuccessful fishing. He promised trout tomorrow when we should be higher among the mountains. He never again touched on the subject that was on his mind. But while I sat writing my diary, he went off to his horse Monte. I occasionally heard the Virginian talking to that friend.

Next day we swung southward and headed for a short cut through the Teton Mountains known to but a few. We followed a stream with such good fishing that we took our time. The horses and I at least enjoyed ourselves. They found fresh pastures and shade in the woods. The mountains were all I needed when the fish refused to rise. This road of ours soon merged with the road they had taken to capture Steve and Ed. I noticed the footprints of many hoofs, rain-blurred but recent, the tracks of the people I had met in the stable.

"You can notice Monte's tracks," said the Virginian. "He is the only one that has his hind feet shod. There's several trails from this point down to where we have come from."

We reached the next higher level of the mountain, a space more open. There, rain-washed tracks appeared again in the soft ground.

"Someone has been here since the rain," I called to the Virginian, who was walking up behind the packhorses.

"Since the rain!" he exclaimed. "That's not two days yet." He came and examined the footprints. "A man and a horse," he said, frowning. "Going the same way we are. How did he come to pass us, and us not see him?"

"One of the other trails," I reminded him.

"Yes, but there's not many that knows them. They are pretty rough trails."

"Worse than this one we're taking?"

"Not much. How does he come to know any of them? And why don't he take the trail that's open and easy and not much longer? One man and a horse. I don't see who he is or what he wants here."

We got back into our saddles with the mystery unsolved. To the Virginian it was a greater one, apparently, than to me. Why should one have to account for every stray traveler in the mountains?

"That's strange, too," said the Virginian. He stopped, looking down at the trail. "Don't you notice?"

It did not strike me.

"Why, he keeps walking beside his horse. He don't get on him."

I had a natural explanation. "He's leading a packhorse. He's a poor trapper, and walks."

"Packhorses ain't usually shod before and behind," said the Virginian. Sliding to the ground, he touched the footprints. "They are not four hours old," said he. "This bank's in shadow by one o'clock, and the sun has not cooked them dusty."

It didn't seem peculiar to me that a man should choose to walk and lead his horse for a while. Nevertheless, I began to catch the Virginian's uncertain feeling about this traveler. So, when the Virginian suddenly stopped his horse again I called out sharply, "What's the matter now?"

He looked down at the trail, and then slowly turned round in his saddle, staring back steadily at me. "There's two of them," he said.

"Two what?"

"I don't know."

"You must know whether it's two horses or two men," I said, almost angrily.

But to this he made no answer, sitting quite still on his horse and contemplating the ground. The silence was like a spell on me, and I spurred my horse impatiently forward to see for myself. The footprints of two men were there in the trail.

"What do you say to that?" said the Virginian. "Kind of ridiculous, ain't it?"

"Very quaint," I answered, groping for the explanation. There was no rock here to walk over and step from into the softer trail. These second steps came more out of the air than the first. And my brain played me the evil trick of showing me a dead man in a gray flannel shirt.

"It's two, you see, traveling with one horse, and they take turns riding him."

"Why, of course!" I exclaimed and we went ahead a few paces.

"There you are," said the Virginian, as the trail proved him right. "Number one has got on."

As we rode the fresh hoof prints of the horse and the fresh footprints of the man preceded us. In the trees and in the opens, across the levels and up the steeps, they were there. And so they were not four hours old! Were they even that much? Might we not, round some turn, come upon the makers of them? I began to watch for this. I told myself to be steady.

We came to a place where the trail climbed so

abruptly that we once more got off to lead our horses. So likewise had those we followed done. As I watched the two different sets of footprints, I observed something. "One man is much heavier than the other."

"I was hoping I'd not have to tell you that," said the Virginian.

"You're always ahead of me! Still, my education is progressing."

"Pounds has got on," said he, "and Ounces is walking."

I glanced over my shoulder at him, and he nodded as he fixed the weather-beaten crimson handkerchief round his neck. Then he threw a stone at a pack animal that was delaying on the trail. "Damn your buckskin hide," he drawled. "You can view the scenery from the top."

"Do you think we'll catch up with those people?" I asked.

"Not likely. They're traveling about the same pace we are."

"Ounces ought to be the best walker."

"Uphill, yes. But Pounds will go down quicker."

The trail at last reached its highest point. Below us lay a bowl-shaped basin of land, a great cup of country—rocks, woods, opens, and streams. Tall peaks rose like spires around it, magnificent and bare in the last of the sun. We looked over this high world, letting our animals catch their breath. We stood between towering mountaintops, a half-circle of five miles or six, very wide in some parts. Our trail crossed over between two fantastic shapes of stone, like mushrooms. Banks of snow spread up here against the black rocks, but half an hour down the other side would find us back to the green and the woods. I looked down, both of us looked down, but we could see no one else.

"They'll be camping somewhere in this basin, though," said the Virginian, staring at the dark pines. "They have not come on this trail by accident."

A cold little wind blew down between our stone shapes, and upward again. Upward with it came fluttering a leaf of newspaper that caught against an edge close to me.

"What's the latest?" inquired the Virginian from his horse. For I had dismounted, and had picked up the leaf.

"Seems to be interesting," I next heard him say. "Can't you tell a man what's making your eyes bug out so?"

"Yes," my voice replied to him, and it sounded like some stranger speaking lightly nearby. "It's quite the latest, I imagine. You had better read it yourself." And I handed it to him with a smile, watching his expression, while my brain felt as if clouds were rushing through it.

I saw his eyes quietly run the headings over. "Well?" he inquired, after scanning it on both sides. "I don't seem to catch the excitement. Fremont County is going to hold elections. I see they claim Jake—"

"It's mine," I cut him off. "My own paper. Those are my pencil marks."

I do not think that a microscope could have discerned a change in his face. "Oh," he commented, holding the paper, and staring at it with a critical eye. "You mean this is the one you lent Steve, the one he wanted to give me to give back to you? And so them are your own marks." For a moment more he held it. "Well, you have got it back now, anyway." And he handed it to me.

"Only a piece of it!" I exclaimed, lightly. And as I took it from him his hand happened to touch mine. It was cold as ice.

"They ain't through readin' the rest," he explained easily. "Don't you throw it away! After they've taken such trouble."

"That's true," I answered. "I wonder if it's Pounds or Ounces I'm indebted to."

In this manner we joked as we rode down into the great basin. Before us, the horse and boot tracks showed plainly in the soft mud where melted snow ran half the day.

"Maybe we'll see their fire when they camp," said the Virginian.

We did not see their fire. We descended in the chill silence, while the mushroom rocks grew far and the dark woods approached. By a stream we got off where two banks sheltered us. A bleak wind cut down over the peaks. We pitched the tent this night, and I was glad to have it shut out the mountaintops. They showed above the banks where we camped. In the starlight their black shapes rose stark against the sky. They, with the pines and the wind, were a bedroom too unearthly this night. And as soon as our supper dishes were washed, we went inside with our lantern.

The Virginian sat reading the paper, while I arranged my blankets to make a warm bed. Then, since the paper continued to absorb him, I got myself ready, and slid between my blankets for the night.

He put the paper down. "I would do it all over again," he began. "The whole thing just the same. He knowed the customs of the country, and he played the game. No call to blame me for the customs of the country. You leave other folks' cattle alone, or you take the consequences, and it was all known to Steve from the start. Would he have me take the judge's wages and give him the wink? He must have changed a heap from the Steve I knew if he expected that. I don't believe he expected that. He knew well enough the only thing that would have let him off would have been a regular jury. For the thieves have got hold of the juries in Johnson County. I would do it all over, just the same."

Then, abruptly ending these memories, he went out of the tent. I heard him dragging a log to the fire. When it had blazed up, there on the tent wall was his shadow and that of the log where he sat with his half-broken heart. And all the while I supposed he was master of himself. I guess I supposed wrong.

I must have fallen asleep before he returned, for I remember nothing except waking and finding him in his blankets beside me. The fire shadow was gone, and gray, cold light was dimly on the tent. He slept restlessly, and his forehead was furrowed with lines of pain. While I looked at him he began to mutter, and suddenly started up with violence. "No!" he cried out and awakened, staring. "What's the matter?" he demanded. He was slow in getting back to where we were. Full awareness found him sitting up with his eyes fixed on mine. They were more haunted than they had been. His next words came straight from his dream. "Maybe you'd better quit me. This ain't your trouble."

I laughed. "Why, what is the trouble?"

His eyes still intently fixed on mine. "Do you think if we changed our trail we could lose them from us?"

I was thinking of a joking reply about Ounces being a good walker, when the sound of hoofs rushing in the distance stopped me. He ran out of the tent with his rifle. By the time I followed with mine he was up the bank, completely alert. But nothing came out of the dimness but our three stampeded horses. They crashed over fallen timber and across open ground to where their comrade grazed at the end of his rope. By him they came to a standstill, and told him, I suppose, what they had seen. All four now faced in the same direction, looking away into the mysterious dawn. We likewise stood. My rifle barrel felt cold in my hand.

"A bear, I suppose," said I, at length.

His strange look fixed me again, and then his eyes went to the horses. "They smell things we can't smell," said he, very slowly. "Can you prove they don't see things we can't see?"

A chill shot through me, and I could not help a frightened glance where we had been watching. But one of the horses began to graze. Finally, I had a reassuring thought. "He's already tired of whatever he saw," said I, pointing.

A smile came for a moment to the Virginian's face. "Must be a poor show," he observed. All the horses were grazing now. "It ain't hurt their appetites any."

We made our own breakfast then. The shock of Steve was working upon the Virginian. He like a brave swimmer against whom both wind and tide have plotted. In the solitude of these mountains, I was the only one who could throw him a lifeline.

"I reckon I made a fuss in the tent?" said he, feeling his way with me.

I threw him a rope. "Yes. Nightmare—indigestion—too much newspaper before retiring."

He caught the rope. "That's correct! I had a hell of a foolish dream for a growed-up man. You'd not think it of me."

"Oh, yes, I should. I've had them after too much lobster and champagne."

"Ah," he murmured, "too much! Too much of a thing is what does it." He glanced behind him. "Steve came back—"

"In your lobster dream," I put in.

But he missed this rope. "Yes," he answered, with his eyes searching me. "And he handed me the paper—"

"By the way, where is that?" I asked.

"I built the fire with it. But when I took it from him it was a six-shooter I had hold of, pointing at my chest. And then Steve spoke. 'Do you think you're fit to live?' Steve said. I was so angry at him, I reckon I must have told what I thought of him. You heard me, I expect?"

"Glad I didn't. Your language sometimes is—"

He laughed out. "Oh, I account for everything that's happened this morning same as you do. If we gave our explanations, they'd be pretty near twins."

"The horses saw a bear, then?"

"Maybe a bear. Maybe"—but here the tide caught him again—"What's your idea about dreams?"

My ropes were all out. "Liver—nerves," was the best I could do.

But now he swam strongly by himself.

"If my head is going to get shook up by a little old piece of newspaper . . ." he started without finishing. "I'm ashamed I burned that. I'm ashamed to have been that weak."

"Every man comes unstrung one time or another," I told him. My ropes had become pieces of straws. I spent the next hours trying to figure the right thing to say.

Once out of these mountains, I knew he could

right himself. But even I, who had no Steve to dream about, felt the silence of the peaks weighing on me.

Somewhere far in the basin there was a faint sound, and we stood still.

"Hush!" he said.

Nothing more followed.

"They have shot that bear," I remarked.

He did not answer, and we put the saddles on without talk. In no more than half an hour, we were moving again. It was not a new thing to hear a shot where wild game was in plenty. Yet in my mind, that shot sounded different from others. Perhaps I would not believe this today but for what I know now looking back. To make camp last night we had turned off the trail. Now we followed the stream down for a while, taking next a cut through the woods. In this way we came upon the tracks of our horses where they had been galloping back to the camp after their fright. They had kicked up the damp and matted pine needles very plainly all along.

"Nothing has been here but themselves, though," said I.

"And they ain't showing signs of remembering any scare," said the Virginian.

In a little while we emerged upon an open.

"Here's where they was grazing," said the Virginian; and the signs were clear enough. "Here's where they must have got their scare," he continued. "You stay with them while I circle a little." So

I stayed. The animals certainly were very calm at revisiting this scene. When you bring a horse back to where he has recently encountered a wild animal his ears and his nostrils are apt to be wide awake.

The Virginian had stopped and was signaling me.

"Here's your bear," said he, as I arrived. "Two-legged, you see. And he had a horse of his own." There was a stake driven down where an animal had been secured for the night.

"Looks like Ounces," I said, considering the footprints.

"It's Ounces. And Ounces wanted another horse very bad, so him and Pounds could travel like gentlemen should."

"But Pounds doesn't seem to have been with him."

"Oh, Pounds, he was making coffee, some-wheres up yonder, when this happened. Neither of them guessed there'd be other horses wandering here in the night, or they both would have come." He turned back to our pack animals.

"You'll not hunt for their camp to make sure?"

"I prefer making sure first. They might be expecting us at that camp."

He took out his rifle from beneath his leg and set it across his saddle at the ready. I did the same. Cautiously, we resumed our journey in a slightly different direction. "This ain't all we're going to find out," said the Virginian. "Ounces had a good idea, but I reckon he made a bad mistake later."

We had found out a good deal. Ounces had gone to bring in their single horse. Coming upon three more in the pasture, he had attempted to catch one and failed, instead driving them where he feared to follow.

"Shorty never could rope a horse alone," I remarked.

The Virginian grinned. "Shorty? Well, Shorty sounds as well as Ounces. But that ain't the mistake I'm thinking he made."

I knew that he would not tell me, but that was just like him. For the last twenty minutes, having something to do, he had become himself again.

We came out on a ridge from which we could look down. "You always want to ride on high places when there's folks around whose intentions ain't been declared," said the Virginian. And we went along our ridge for some distance. Then, suddenly he turned down and guided us almost at once to the trail. "That's it," he said. "See."

The track of a horse was very fresh on the trail. But it was a galloping horse now, and no boot prints were keeping up with it anymore. No boots could have kept up with it. The rider was making time today. Yesterday that horse had been ridden up into the mountains at leisure. Who was on him? There was never to be any certain answer to that. But who was not on him? We turned back in our journey, back into the heart of that basin with the tall peaks all rising like teeth in the cloudless sun and the snowfields shining white.

"He was afraid of us," said the Virginian. "He did not know how many of us had come up here. Three horses might mean a dozen more around."

We followed the backward trail in among the pines, and came after a time upon their camp. And then I understood the mistake that Shorty had made. He had returned after his failure, and had told that other man of the presence of new horses. He should have kept this a secret. Two cannot get away quickly upon one horse. So it was poor Shorty's last blunder. He lay there by their long dead fire, his lost-dog face looking upward, his thick yellow hair unparted as it had always been. The murder had been done from behind. We closed his eyes.

"There was no natural harm in him," said the Virginian. "But you must do a thing well in this country."

There was not a trace, not a clue, of the other man. We found a place where we could quickly cover Shorty with earth. As we lifted him we saw the newspaper that he had been reading. He had brought it from the clump of cottonwoods where he and the other man had visited, after our departure, to be sure of the fate of their friends—or possibly in hopes of another horse. Evidently, they had been able to escape with only one. All of the newspaper was there save the leaf I had recovered. But this paper had pencil writing on it that was not mine, nor did I, at first, take it in. I thought it might be a clue, and I read it aloud. "Goodbye,

Jeff," it said. "I could not have spoke to you without playing the baby."

"Who's Jeff?" I asked. But it came over me when I looked at the Virginian. He was standing beside me quite motionless. Then he put out his hand and took the paper, and stood still, looking at the words. "Steve used to call me Jeff," he said, "because I was Southern. I reckon nobody else ever did."

He slowly folded the message from the dead, brought by the dead, and rolled it in the coat behind his saddle. For a half-minute he stood leaning his forehead down against the saddle. After this he came back and contemplated Shorty's face awhile. "I wish I could thank him," he said. "I wish I could."

We carried Shorty over and covered him with earth, and on that laid a few pine branches. Then we resumed our journey. Before noon, we had already gone some distance on our trail through the Teton Mountains. But in front of us the hoof prints drew farther and farther from us. By the next afternoon somewhere we noticed they were no longer to be seen. After that they never came upon our trail again.

CHAPTER 33

THE SPINSTER
LOSES SOME SLEEP

Somewhere at the eastern base of the Tetons those hoof prints disappeared into a mountain sanctuary where many crooked paths have led. Not many cabins were yet built there. But the unknown rider knew he would find shelter and welcome among the outlaws who had come before him. Law and order might guess his name correctly, but there was no next step, for lack of evidence. In the shadows of those mountains he could wait until the rage for justice subsided. Then, carefully, he would let himself be seen again.

And now, as mysteriously as he had melted away, rumor passed over the country. No tongue seemed to be heard telling the first news. The news was just there one day, a matter of whispered knowledge. On Sunk Creek and on Bear Creek, and elsewhere far and wide, before men talked, men seemed secretly to know that Steve, and Ed, and Shorty would never again be seen. Riders met each other in the road and stopped to discuss the event and its bearing on the business of cattle ranching. In town saloons men took each other aside, and muttered over it in corners.

Thus it reached the ears of Molly Wood.

A neighbor joined her when she was out riding by herself.

"Good morning," said he. "Don't you find it lonesome?" And when she answered lightly, he continued, meaning well, "You'll be having company again soon now. He has finished his job. Wish he'd finished it *more*! Well, good day."

Molly thought these words over. She could not tell why they gave her a strange feeling. Then, entering the Taylors' cabin, she came upon several people who stopped talking abruptly, and were not skillful at resuming it. She sat there awhile, uneasily aware that all of them knew something she did not know, and was not intended to know. A thought pierced her—had anything happened to her lover? No, that was not it. The man she had met on horseback spoke of her having company soon again. How soon? she wondered. He had been unable to say when he should return, and now she suddenly felt that a great silence had enveloped him. It was not the mere silence of absence, of receiving no messages or letters, but another sort of silence. At this moment, that silence was weighing strangely upon her.

The next day it came out at the schoolhouse. During recess, she became aware through the open window that they were playing a new game outside. Lusty screeches of delight reached her ears.

"Jump!" a voice ordered. "Jump!"

"I don't want to," returned another voice, uneasily.

"You said you would," said several. "Didn't he say he would? Ah, he said he would. Jump now, quick!"

"But I don't want to," the voice shivered in a tone so dismal that Molly went out to see.

They had got Bob Carmody on the top of the gate by a tree, with a rope round his neck. Four little boys joyously held the other end. The rest looked on eagerly, three little girls clasping their hands, springing up and down with excitement.

"Why, children!" exclaimed Molly.

"He's said his prayers and everything," they all screamed out. "He's a rustler, and we're lynchin' him. Jump, Bob!"

"I don't want—"

"Ah, coward, won't take his medicine!"

"Let him go, boys," said Molly. "You might really hurt him." And so she broke up this game, but not without general protest from Wyoming's young voice.

"He said he would," Henry Dow assured her.

And George Taylor further explained, "He said he'd be Steve. But Steve didn't scare." Then George proceeded to tell the schoolmarm, eagerly, all about Steve and Ed while the schoolmarm looked at him with a rigid face.

"You promised your mother you'd not tell," said Henry Dow, after all had been told. "You've gone and done it," and Henry wagged his head in a superior manner.

In this way, the New England girl learned what her cowboy had done. She spoke of it to no one. She kept her misery to herself. He was not there to defend himself. Perhaps, in a way, that was better. But these were dark hours indeed to Molly Wood.

She recalled her visit to Dunbarton. At the first sight of her lover's photograph in frontier dress her aunt had exclaimed, "I suppose there are days when he does not kill people." Molly had answered—in good faith and good humor—"He never killed anybody!" Later, when he was lying in her cabin weak from his bullet wound, at a certain word of his there had gone through her a shudder of doubt. Perhaps in his many wanderings he had done such a thing in self-defense, or in the cause of popular justice. But she had pushed the idea away from her, back into the days before she had ever seen him. If this had ever happened, let her not know of it. Then, as a cruel reward for his honesty to her mother, the letters from Bennington had used his letter as a weapon against him. Her sister Sarah had quoted from it. "He says with apparent pride," wrote Sarah, "that he has 'never killed for pleasure or profit.' Those are his exact words, and you may guess their dreadful effect upon mother. I congratulate you, my dear, on having chosen a protector so careful in his killing."

Thus her elder sister had seen fit to write. Letters from less near relatives made hints at the same subject. So she was compelled to accept that he had killed. Yet still, still, those events had been before she knew him. He had been little more than a boy. No doubt it was to save his own life. And, she could bear the hurt of her discovery all the more easily because her sister's tone roused her to defend her cowboy.

But now!

"You're looking pale, dear," said Mrs. Taylor to her, a few days later.

"Am I?"

"And you don't eat anything."

"Oh, yes, I do." And Molly retired to her cabin.

That evening when Mr. Taylor came home to his family, George received a spanking. "And I suppose," said Mrs. Taylor to her husband, "that she came out just in time to stop 'em breaking Bob Carmody's neck."

The next day, Mrs. Taylor attempted the impossible. She took herself over to Molly Wood's cabin. The girl gave her a listless greeting. The older woman sat slowly down, and examined the comfortable room.

"A very nice home, dear," said she, "if it was a home. But you'll fix something like this in your real home, I have no doubt."

Molly made no answer.

"What we're going to do without you I can't see," said Mrs. Taylor. "But I'd not have it different for worlds. He'll be coming back soon, I expect."

"Mrs. Taylor," said Molly, all at once, "please

don't say anything now. I can't stand it." And she broke into wretched tears.

"Why, dear, he—"

"No, not a word. Please, please—I'll go out if you do."

The older woman went to the younger one and put her arms around her. But when the tears were over, they had not done any good. All storms do not clear the sky. Mrs. Taylor looked at the pale girl and saw that she could do nothing to help her find peace of mind.

"Of course," she said to her husband, "you might know she'd feel dreadful."

"What about?" said Taylor.

"Why, you know just as well as I do. And I'll say for myself, I hope you'll never have to help hang folks."

"Well," said Taylor, mildly, "if I had to, I'd have to, I guess."

"Well, I don't want it to come. But that poor girl is eating her heart right out over it."

"What does she say?"

"It's what she don't say. She'll not talk, and she'll not let me talk, and she sits and sits."

"I'll go talk some to her," said the man.

"Well, Taylor, I thought you had more sense. You'd not get a word in. She'll be sick soon if her worry ain't stopped someway, though."

"What does she want this country to do?" inquired Taylor. "Does she expect it to be like Vermont when it—"

"We can't help what she expects," his wife interrupted. "But I wish we could help *her*."

They could not, however; help came from another source. Judge Henry rode by the next day. To him good Mrs. Taylor at once revealed her concern. The judge looked grim.

"Must I interfere?" he said.

"Yes, Judge, you must," said Mrs. Taylor.

"But why can't I send him over here when he gets back? Then they'll just settle it between themselves."

Mrs. Taylor shook her head. "That would unsettle it worse than it is," she assured him. "They mustn't meet just now."

The judge sighed. "Well," he said, "very well."

Judge Henry sat thinking, waiting until school would be out. He did not at all relish what lay before him. He would like to have got out of it. He had been an honest judge. He had faced all of the responsibilities of his difficult office with courage and common sense. He had been a faithful servant of the law. Now he was invited to defend that which must seem a defiance of the law worse than the crime itself.

"I sent him myself on that business," the judge considered, uncomfortably. "I am partly responsible for the lynching. It has brought him one great unhappiness already through the death of Steve. If it gets running in this girl's mind, she may—dear me!" the judge broke off. "What a nuisance!" he sighed. For as all men know, he also knew that many things should be done in this world in silence, and that talking about them is a mistake.

But when school was out, he knocked at her door, ready—as he had put it—to sacrifice his character in the cause of true love.

"Well," he said, coming straight to the point, "some dark things have happened." And when she made no answer to this, he continued, "But you must not misunderstand us. We're too fond of you for that."

"Judge Henry," said Molly Wood, also coming straight to the point, "have you come to tell me that you think well of lynching?"

He met her. "Of burning Southern Negroes in public, no. Of hanging Wyoming cattle thieves in private, yes. You perceive there's a difference, don't you?"

"Not in principle," said the girl, dry and short.

"Oh—dear—me!" slowly exclaimed the judge. "I am sorry that you cannot see that, because I think I can. And I think that you have just as much sense as I have." The judge made himself very grave and very good-humored at the same time.

"What is the difference in principle?" she demanded.

"Well," said the judge, easy and thoughtful, "what do you mean by principle?"

"I didn't think you'd quibble," flashed Molly. "I'm not a lawyer myself."

The judge knew that he must give every word the girl said his perfect consideration. "I don't mean to quibble," he assured her. "I know the trick of escaping from one question by asking another. But I don't want to escape from anything you hold me to answer. If you can show me that I am wrong, I want you to do so. But," and here the judge smiled, "I want you to play fair, too."

"And how am I not?"

"I want you to be just as willing to be put right by me as I am to be put right by you. And so when you use such a word as principle, you must help me to answer by saying what principle you mean. For in all sincerity I see no likeness in principle whatever between burning Southern Negroes in public and hanging Wyoming horse thieves in private. We do not torture our criminals when we lynch them. We do not invite spectators to enjoy their death agony. We put no such hideous disgrace upon the United States. We execute our criminals by the swiftest means, and in the quietest way. Do you think the principle is the same?"

Molly had listened to him with attention. "The way is different," she admitted.

"Only the way?"

"So it seems to me. Both defy law and order."

"Ah, but do they both? Now we're getting near the principle."

"Why, yes. Ordinary citizens take the law in their own hands."

"The principle at last!" exclaimed the judge.

"Now tell me some more things. Out of whose hands do they take the law?"

"The courts' hands."

"What made the courts?"

"I don't understand."

"How did there come to be any courts?"

"The Constitution."

"How did there come to be any Constitution? Who made it?"

"The delegates, I suppose."

"Who made the delegates?"

"I suppose they were elected, or appointed, or something."

"And who elected them?"

"Of course the people elected them."

"Call them the ordinary citizens," said the judge. "I like your term. They are where the law comes from, you see. For they chose the delegates who made the Constitution that provided for the courts. There's your machinery. These are the hands into which ordinary citizens have put the law. So you see, at best, when they lynch they only take back what they once gave. Now we'll take your two cases that you say are the same in principle. I think that they are not. For in the South they take a Negro from jail where he was waiting to be duly hung. The South has never claimed that the law would let him go. But in Wyoming the law has been letting our cattle thieves go for two years. We are in a very bad way, and we are trying to make that way a little better until civilization can reach us. The courts, or rather the juries, into whose hands we have put the law, are not dealing the law. They are imitation hands made for show, with no life in them, no grip. They cannot hold a cattle thief. And so when your ordinary citizen sees this, and sees that he has placed justice in a dead hand, he must take justice back into his own hands where it was once at the beginning of all things. Call this primitive, if you will. But so far from being a *defiance* of the law, it is an *assertion* of it—the most basic assertion of self-governing men. There is your principle, Miss Wood, as I see it. Now can you help me to see anything different?"

She could not.

"But perhaps you are of the same opinion still?" the judge inquired.

"It is all terrible to me," she said.

"Yes. And so is capital punishment terrible. And so is war. And perhaps some day we shall do without them. But they are none of them so terrible as unchecked theft and murder would be."

After the judge had departed on his way to Sunk Creek, no one spoke to Molly upon this subject. But her face did not grow cheerful at once. It was plain from her fits of silence that her thoughts were not at rest. And sometimes at night she would stand in front of her lover's likeness, gazing upon it with both love and misgivings.

CHAPTER 34

TO FIT HER FINGER

When next I heard from him, the Virginian wrote for two rings.

After my dark encounter with what the Cattle Land could be, I soon had journeyed home. Steve and Shorty did not leave my memory, nor will they ever, I suppose.

The Virginian understood. The day I left him, he had noticed me looking at the plains and mountains in a sort of farewell.

"You will come back," he said. "If there was a tombstone for every man that fell in love with the freedom here, you'd see one every time you turned your head. It's a heap sadder than a graveyard—but you love it all the same."

Deep in him was sadness of course, as well as joy. For he had known Steve, and he had covered Shorty with earth. He had looked upon life with a marksman's eyes, very close. No one, if he has a heart, can pass through this and not carry some sadness with him forever. But he seldom shows it openly. Instead, it becomes part of him, enriching his cheerfulness and encouraging him to serve his fellow man all the better.

It was a cheerful duty he gave me. Rings could be had in Cheyenne. Denver offered a still greater choice. His duties may have allowed him to travel to either of these towns. But he was set upon having rings from the East. They must come from the best place in the country. Nothing short of that was good enough "to fit her finger," as he said. The wedding ring was a simple matter. Have them made from the purest gold possible, with her initials and his together engraved on the inside, with the day of the month and the year.

The date had been set for July third. Then, for sixty days and nights he was to be a bridegroom, free from his duties at Sunk Creek, free to take his bride wherever she might choose to go. And she had chosen.

Those voices from Bennington had done more than anger her. They had given her a purpose. Her sister would be given neither the chance to come nor to stay away. Had her mother even answered the Virginian's letter, there could have been some relenting. But the poor lady had not done so. She had sent messages—kind ones, to be sure—but only messages. If this had hurt the Virginian, no one knew it in the world, especially not the girl in whose heart it had left a cold, frozen spot.

So, meanwhile, she made her decree against Bennington. Wyoming, not Vermont, would be her wedding place. No Eastern eyes would be looking on when she made her vow to him and received his vow in return. Their voices would be spoken and that ring put on in this wild Cattle Land, where first she had seen him ride into the flooded river, and lift her onto his horse. It was this open sky that should shine down on them. On this frontier soil their feet would tread. The world would get its turn second.

She would spend a month with him by stream and canyon, far deeper into the mountain wilds than he had ever been free to take her before. Only after a month with a tent and sometimes only the stars above them would she take him to her mother and to Bennington. Then her old aunt over at Dunbarton would look at him, and be once more able to declare that the Starks had always preferred a man who was a man.

When the ring was fashioned, it was an opal—the birthstone for October, for Molly was born on the fifteenth of that month—but set with four small diamonds surrounding it, as diamonds are the birthstone for January, the Virginian's birth month. Her month stone joined with his, so that their luck and their love might be united.

He found the size of her finger one day when winter had departed, and the early grass was green. He made a ring of twisted grass for her, while she held her hand for him to tie it. He made another for himself. Then, after each had worn their grass ring for a while, he begged her to exchange. Later, he measured it most carefully. So the ring fit her well, and the lustrous opal thrilled his heart each time he saw it. June was near its end. That other plain gold ring, which, for safe keeping, he suspended round his neck day and night, seemed to burn with an inward glow that was deeper than the opal's.

So in due course the second of July arrived. Molly's anger at Bennington came to punish her in the end. She longed for her mother to be near her. But it was too late.

CHAPTER 35

WITH MALICE AFORETHOUGHT

Town lay twelve straight miles away from the lover and his sweetheart when they came to the top of the last long hill. Since morning they had ridden with neither horse ever ahead of the other.

At the sight of their journey's end, the Virginian looked down at the girl beside him. His eyes filled with a bridegroom's light. Hanging safe upon his breast, he could feel the gold ring that he would slowly press upon her finger tomorrow. He removed the glove from her left hand, and stooping, kissed the jewel in that other ring he had given her. The crimson fire in the opal seemed to mingle with the fire in his heart. He lifted her from the saddle for a moment as he held her to him. But his heart was troubled by the cold pang of loneliness which had crept upon her like a tide as the day drew near. None of her own people were waiting in that distant town to see her become his bride. She might pass friendly faces on the way, but all of them would be new friends, made in this wild country. Not a single face from her childhood would smile upon her. Deep within her, a voice cried for her mother far away in Vermont. Knowing she would see Mrs. Taylor's kind face at her wedding was no comfort now.

The town lay ahead amid the splendor of Wyoming: the watered fields, squares of green and yellow crops; the amber plains; the river stretching beyond sight; the Bow Leg Mountains with their still unmelted snows; three canyons from which flowed three clear forks which began the river. Over all this, silence hung like a harmony.

"How beautiful! How I love it!" whispered the girl. "But, oh, how big it is!" And she leaned against her lover for an instant. It was her spirit seeking shelter. Today, this vast beauty had in it for her something almost of dread. The small, comfortable, green hills of home rose before her. She closed her eyes and saw Vermont: a village street, and the post office, ivy covering an old front door, and her mother picking some yellow roses from a bush.

At a sound, her eyes quickly opened. Her lover had turned in his saddle, watching another horseman approach. She saw the Virginian's hand in a certain position, and knew that his pistol was ready. But the other merely overtook and passed them.

The man had given one nod to the Virginian and the Virginian one to him. Now he was already below them on the descending road. To Molly Wood he was a stranger. But she had seen his eyes when he nodded to her lover. She knew, even without the pistol, that this was not hatred at first sight. So she asked her lover who this was.

"Oh," said he, easily, "just a man I see now and then."

"Is his name Trampas?" said Molly Wood.

The Virginian looked at her in surprise. "Why, where have you seen him?" he asked.

"Never till now. But I knew."

"My gracious! You never told me you had mind-reading powers." And he gently smiled at her.

"I knew it was Trampas as soon as I saw his eyes."

"My gracious!" her lover repeated with charitable irony. "I better be mighty careful of my eyes when you're lookin' at 'em."

"I believe he did that murder," said the girl.

"Whose mind are you readin' now?" he drawled affectionately.

But he could not tease her off the subject. She took his strong hand in hers. "I know something about that—that—last autumn," she said, shrinking from words more plain. "And I know that you only did—"

"What I had to," he finished, very sadly, but sternly, too.

"Yes," she declared, keeping hold of his hand. "I suppose that—lynching," she almost whispered the word, "is the only way. But when they had to die just for stealing horses, it seems so wicked that this murderer—"

"Who can prove it?" asked the Virginian.

"But don't you know it?"

"I know a heap of things inside my heart. But

that's not proving. There was only the body, and the hoof prints—and what folks guessed."

"He was never even arrested!" the girl said.

"No. He helped elect the sheriff in that county."

Then Molly ventured a step inside the border of her lover's reticence. "I saw—" she hesitated, "just now, I saw what you did."

He returned to his tender irony. "You'll have me plumb scared if you keep on seein' things."

"You had your pistol ready for him."

"Why, I believe I did. It was mighty unnecessary." And the Virginian took out the pistol again, and shook his head over it, like one who has been caught in a blunder.

She looked at him, and knew that she must step outside his reticence again. She knew her cowboy lover, with all that he lacked, was more than she could ever be, even with all that she had. He was her servant, but her master, too. Therefore now, against the baffling smile he gave her, she felt powerless. And once again she ached for her mother to be near her today. She looked from her untamed man to the untamed desert of Wyoming, and the town where she was to take him as her wedded husband. But for his sake she would not let him guess her loneliness.

He sat on his horse Monte, eyeing his pistol. Then he showed her a rattlesnake coiled by some sagebrush. "Can I hit it?" he asked.

"You don't often miss them," said she, trying to be cheerful.

"Well, I'm told getting married unstrings some men." He aimed, and the snake was shattered. "Maybe it's too early yet for the unstringing to begin!" He thought for a moment and then sent three more bullets into the snake. "I reckon that's enough."

"Was not the first one?"

"Oh, yes, for the snake." And then, with one leg bent cowboy fashion across in front of his saddle horn, he cleaned his pistol, and replaced the empty cartridges.

Once more she ventured near the line of his reticence. "Has—has Trampas seen you much lately?"

"Why, no. Not for a right long while. But I reckon he has not missed me."

The Virginian spoke this in his gentlest voice. But his sweetheart turned her face away, and from her eyes she brushed a tear.

He reined his horse Monte beside her. Upon her cheek she felt his kiss. "You are not the only mind reader," said he, very tenderly. And at this she clung to him, and laid her head upon his breast. "I had been thinking," he went on, "that the way our marriage is to be was the most beautiful way."

"It is the most beautiful," she murmured.

He slowly spoke out his thought, as if she had not said this. "No folks to stare, no fuss, no jokes and ribbons and best bonnets, no public eye nor talkin' of tongues when most you want to hear nothing and say nothing."

She answered by holding him closer.

"Just the bishop of Wyoming to join us, and not even him after we're once joined. I did think that would be ahead of all ways to get married."

He paused again, and she made no reply.

"But we have left out your mother."

She looked in his face with quick astonishment. It was as if his spirit had heard the cry of her spirit.

"That is nowhere near right," he said. "That is wrong."

"She could never have come here," said the girl.

"We should have gone there. I don't know how I can ask her to forgive me."

"But it was not you!" cried Molly.

"Yes. Because I did not object. I did not tell you we must go to her. I missed the point, thinking so much about my own feelings. For you see—and I've never said this to you until now—your mother did hurt me. When I wrote her that letter telling all about myself, and how my family was not like yours, and—and—all the rest I told her, it hurt me never to get a word back from her except messages through you. I shared with her my hopes and my failings. I had said more than ever I've said to you, because she was your mother. I wanted her to forgive me, if she could, and feel that maybe I could take good care of you after all. It was bad enough to have her daughter quit her home to teach school out here on Bear Creek. Then I come along and make it worse. I have missed the point in thinking of my own feelings."

"But it's not your doing!" repeated Molly.

He had framed the whole matter as a hardship to her mother alone. He had saved her any pain of confession or denial. "Yes, it is my doing," he now said. "Shall we give it up?"

"Give what—" She did not understand.

"Our plans! Well, they're no more than plans. I hate the notion of changing, but I hate hurting your mother more. Or, anyway, I *ought* to hate it more. So we can shift, if you say so. It's not too late."

"Shift?"

"I mean, we can go to your home now. We can start by the stage tonight. Your mother can see us married. We can come back and finish in the mountains instead of beginning in them. It'll be just merely shifting, you see."

He could scarcely bring himself to say this at all. Yet he said it as if he were urging it. To put off his wedding day after his three years of faithful battle for it! To postpone the wedding journey he had arranged! There were the mountains in sight, the woods and canyons where he had planned to go with her. His horses, his tent, his rifle, all were waiting ready in the town for their start tomorrow. He had provided many dainty things to make her comfortable. Well, he could wait a little more, having waited three years. It would not be what his heart most desired. There would be the "public eye and the talking of tongues"—but he could wait. The hour would come when he could be alone with his bride at last. And so he spoke as if he urged it.

"Never!" she cried. "Never, never!"

She would not submit to such sacrifice on his part. Were they not going to her mother in four weeks? If her family had warmly accepted him—but they had not. It had gone too far, it was too late. She told her lover that if he said any more she would gallop into town separately from him. And for his sake she would hide deep from him this lone-liness of hers, and the hurt he had given her in refusing to share with her his trouble with Trampas, when others knew of it.

They descended the hill slowly together, pro-longing these last miles. Many rides had taught their horses to go side by side, and so they went now: the girl sweet and thoughtful in her modest attire; the man in his leather chaps, cartridge belt, and flannel shirt.

Having read his sweetheart's mind very plainly, the lover now broke his dearest custom. It was his code never to speak ill of any man to any woman. Now he did not say to her, "I'll tell you about this. You saw me get ready for Trampas because I have been ready for him for five years." He began far off from the point with his typical diplomacy.

"There's certainly a right smart difference between men and women," he noted.

"You're quite sure?" she replied.

"Ain't it fortunate? That there's both, I mean."

"I don't know about fortunate. Machinery

could probably do all the heavy work for us without your help."

"And who'd invent the machinery?"

She laughed. "We shouldn't need the huge, noisy things you do. Our world would be a gentle one."

"Oh, my gracious!"

"What do you mean by that?"

"Oh, my gracious! Get along, Monte! A gentle world all full of ladies!"

"Do you call men gentle?" inquired Molly.

"Now it's a funny thing about that. Have you ever noticed a joke about fathers-in-law? There's just as many fathers- as mothers-in-law, but which side are your jokes?"

"That's because the men write the comic papers."

"Hear that, Monte? The men write 'em. Well, if the ladies wrote a comic paper, I expect that might be gentle."

Here the Virginian gave a joyous chuckle in company with his sweetheart. "Yes, there's a big heap of difference between men and women," he said. "Take that fellow and myself, now."

"Trampas?" said Molly, quickly serious. She looked along the road ahead, and glimpsed the figure of Trampas still visible on its way to town.

The Virginian did not wish her to be serious— more than could be helped. "Why, yes," he replied, with a waving gesture at Trampas. "Take him and me. He don't think much of me! How could he?

And I expect he'll never. Once a man in the John Day Valley didn't think much of me, and by Canada de Oro I met another. It will always be so here and there, but Trampas beats 'em all. For the others have always expressed themselves. They aired their poor opinion of me.

"You see, I had to explain myself to Trampas a right smart while ago, long before ever I laid my eyes on you. It was just nothing at all. A little matter of cards in the days when I was apt to spend my money pretty reckless. And Trampas, he met me one night, and I expect he must have thought I looked kind of young. So he hated losin' his money to such a young-lookin' man, and he took his way of sayin' as much. I had to explain myself to him plainly, so that he learned straight away I was right older than I appeared.

"Well, I expect he hated that worse, having to receive my explanation with folks lookin' on, and him without any further ideas at the moment. That's what started his poor opinion of me, not havin' ideas at the moment.

"I'd almost forgot about it. But Trampas's memory is one of his strong points. Next thing— oh, it's a good while later—he gets to losin' flesh because Judge Henry gave me charge of him and some other punchers taking cattle—"

"That's not next," interrupted the girl.

"Not? Why—"

"Don't you remember?" she said, timid, yet eager. "Don't you?"

"Blamed if I do!"

"The first time we met?"

"Yes. My memory keeps that—like I keep this." And he brought from his pocket her own handkerchief, the token he had picked up at a river's edge when he had carried her from an overturned stage.

"We did not exactly meet, then," she said. "It was at that dance. I hadn't seen you yet; but Trampas was saying something horrid about me, and you said—you said, 'Rise on your legs, you polecat, and tell them you're a liar.' When I heard that, I think—I think it finished me." And Molly blushed.

"I'd forgot," the Virginian murmured. Then sharply, "How did you hear it?"

"Mrs. Taylor—"

"Oh! Well, a man would never have told a woman that."

Molly laughed triumphantly. "Then who told Mrs. Taylor?"

Being caught, he grinned at her. "I reckon husbands are a special kind of man," was all that he found to say. "Well, since you do know about that, it was the next move in the game. Trampas thought I had no call to stop him sayin' what he pleased about a woman who was nothin' to me—then. But all women ought to be somethin' to a man. So I had to give Trampas another explanation in the presence of folks lookin' on, and it was just like the cards. No ideas occurred to him again. And down goes his opinion of me some more!

"Well, today is the first time I've happened to see the man since the doings last autumn. He knows I can't prove he was with that gang of horse thieves. And I can't prove he killed poor Shorty. But he knows I missed him awful close, and spoiled his thieving for a while. So do you wonder he don't think much of me? But if I had lived to be twenty-nine years old like I am, and made no enemy, I'd feel myself a failure."

His story was finished. He had made her his confidante in matters he had never spoken of before, and she was happy to feel this much closer to him.

During the next several miles he was silent, and his silence was enough for her. Vermont sank away from her thoughts, and Wyoming held less of loneliness. More miles of the road lay behind them. In what was wilderness, scars of newly dug water ditches began to appear, and the first wire fences. Next, they were passing cabins and occasional fields. The free road became wholly imprisoned, running between unbroken stretches of barbed wire. Far off to the eastward a flowing column of dust marked the approaching stage, bringing the bishop, probably, for whose visit here they had timed their wedding. They began to meet citizens. Some recognized them and nodded, while some did not, and stared. Turning a corner into the town's chief street, where stood the hotel, the bank, the drug store, the general store, and the seven saloons, they were greeted heartily. Here were three friends—Honey Wiggin, Scipio le Moyne, and Lin McLean—all hoping to drink to the Virginian's health, if his lady wouldn't mind. The three stood grinning, with their hats off. Behind their good cheer the Virginian read some other purpose.

"We'll all be very good," said Honey Wiggin.

"Pretty good," said Lin.

"Good," said Scipio.

"Which is the honest man?" inquired Molly, glad to see them.

"Not one!" said the Virginian. "My old friends scare me when I think of their ways."

"It's bein' engaged scares you," retorted Mr. McLean. "Marriage restores your courage, I find."

"Well, I'll trust all of you," said Molly. "He's going to take me to the hotel, and then you can drink to his health as much as you please."

With a smile to them she turned to go on. He let his horse move with hers, but he kept an eye on his friends. Scipio's bleached blue eyes narrowed to a slit, and he said what they had all come out on the street to say, "Don't change your clothes."

"Oh!" protested Molly, "isn't he rather dusty and countrified?"

But the Virginian had taken Scipio's meaning. "Don't change your clothes." Innocent Molly appreciated these words no more than the average reader who reads a masterpiece, unaware that its style differs from that of the morning paper. Such was Scipio's intention, wishing to spare her from alarm.

At the hotel, she let her lover go with a kiss, and without a thought of Trampas.

At the hotel, the Virginian had civilized apparel proper for a genuine frontiersman when he comes to town. Only a green and unseasoned cowpuncher struts around in public wearing spurs and deadly weapons. But Scipio had told the Virginian not to change his clothes, therefore he went out with his pistol at his hip. Soon he had joined his three friends.

"I'm obliged to you," he said. "He passed me this mornin'."

"We don't know his intentions," said Wiggin.

"Except that he's hangin' around," said McLean.

"And fillin' up," said Scipio, "which reminds me . . ."

They strolled into the saloon of a friend, where, unfortunately, sat some foolish people. But one cannot always tell how much of a fool a man is, at sight. The Virginian and his friends stood at the bar, full of sentiment, empty of words, while memory and affection were busy in their hearts. All of them had seen rough days together, and they felt guilty with emotion.

"It's hot weather," said Wiggin.

"Hotter up at Box Elder," said McLean. "My kid has started teething."

Words ran dry again. They shifted their positions, looked in their glasses, read the labels on the bottles. They dropped a word now and then to the bartender. "I think there's a friend of yours in town this afternoon," he said to the Virginian.

"Did he mention he was my friend?"

The bartender laughed.

Honey Wiggin made the bridegroom a straight offer. "We'll take this thing off your hands."

"Any or all of us," said Lin.

But Scipio held his peace. His loyalty went every inch as far as theirs, but his understanding of his friend went deeper. "Don't change your clothes," was the first and the last help he would be likely to give in this matter. The rest must be as such matters must always be, man to man. To Honey and Lin, however, this seemed a very special case. Therefore they volunteered to help, an offer which might otherwise be seen as interfering in the affairs of another.

"A man don't get married every day," apologized McLean. "We'll just run him out of town for you."

"Save you the trouble," urged Wiggin. "Say the word."

The bartender now added his voice. "It'll sober him up to spend his night out in the brush. He'll quit his talk then."

But the Virginian did not say the word, or any word. He stood playing with the nickels.

"Think of her," muttered McLean.

"Who else would I be thinking of?" returned the Southerner. His face turned very serious. "She has been raised so different!" he murmured. He pondered a little, while the others waited.

A new idea came to the bartender. "I am acting mayor of this town," said he. "I'll put him in the calaboose and keep him locked up there till you get married and away."

"Say the word," repeated Honey Wiggin.

Scipio's eye met the proprietor's, and he shook his head about a quarter of an inch. The proprietor shook his to the same amount. They understood each other. It had come to that point where there was no way out, save only the ancient, eternal way between man and man.

"So he has talked about me some?" said the Virginian.

"It's the whiskey," Scipio explained.

"I expect," said McLean, "he'd run a mile if he was sober enough to appreciate his insults."

"Which we are careful not to mention to you," said Wiggin, "unless you inquire for 'em."

Some of the fools present had drawn closer to hear this interesting conversation. In gatherings of more than six there will generally be at least one fool. This company must have numbered twenty men.

"This country knows well enough," said one fool, who hungered for importance, "that you don't brand no calves that ain't your own."

The Virginian, unfazed, looked at him. "Thank you," said he, gravely, "for your endorsement of my character." The fool felt flattered. The Virginian turned to his friends. His hand slowly pushed his hat back, and he rubbed his black head in thought.

"Glad to see you've got your gun with you,"

continued the happy fool. "You know what Trampas claims about that affair of yours in the Tetons? He claims that if everything was known about the killing of Shorty—"

The bartender interrupted, agreeably. "Take one on the house. Your news will be fresher." And he pushed him the bottle. The fool felt less important.

"This talk had went the rounds before it got to us," said Scipio, "or we'd have headed it off. He has got friends in town."

Confusion knotted the Virginian's brows. The whole town knew that a man had implied he was a thief and a murderer. Now it knew that he knew it. But the case was surely peculiar. Could he avoid meeting the man? Soon the stage would be starting south for the railroad. He had already today proposed to his sweetheart that they should take it. Could he for her sake leave such accusations from such a man go unanswered? He had heard nothing with his own ears.

Into these thoughts the fool stepped once more. "Of course this country don't believe Trampas," said he. "This country . . ."

But he contributed no further thoughts. From somewhere in the rear of the building came a movement, and Trampas was among them, courageous with whiskey.

All of the fools now crawled out of the woodwork. One lay on the floor, knocked there by the Virginian, whose arm he had attempted to hold.

Others struggled with Trampas. His bullet smashed the ceiling before they could drag the pistol from him. "There now! There now!" they cut in. "You don't want to talk like that." Trampas was pouring out a tide of hate and insult.

All the while, the Virginian stood quiet by the bar. Many an eye of astonishment was turned upon him. "I'd not stand half that language," some muttered to each other. Still the Virginian waited quietly, while the fools reasoned with Trampas. But no earthly foot can step between a man and his destiny. Trampas broke suddenly free.

"Your friends have saved your life," he rang out, with obscenities. "I'll give you till sundown to leave town."

There was total silence instantly.

"Trampas," spoke the Virginian, "I don't want trouble with you."

"He never has wanted it," Trampas sneered to the bystanders. "He has been dodging it five years. But I've got him corralled."

Some Trampas supporters smiled.

"Trampas," said the Virginian again, "are you sure you really mean that?"

The whiskey bottle flew through the air, hurled by Trampas, and crashed through the saloon window behind the Virginian.

"I understood your answer without that, Trampas," said he.

"Get out by sundown, that's all," said Trampas. And turning, he went out of the saloon by the rear, as he had entered.

"Gentlemen," said the Virginian, "I know you will all oblige me."

"Sure!" exclaimed the bartender, heartily, "We'll see that everybody lets this thing alone."

The Virginian gave a general nod to the company, and walked out into the street.

"It's a terrible shame," sighed Scipio, "that he couldn't have postponed it."

The Virginian walked in the open air with thoughts disturbed. "I am of two minds about one thing," he said to himself uneasily.

Gossip ran in advance of him. Wherever he walked, the talk fell away until he had passed. Then they looked after him, and their words again rose.

"It don't trouble him much," one said, having read nothing in the Virginian's face.

"It may trouble his girl some," said another.

"She'll not know," said a third, "until it's over."

"He'll not tell her?"

"I wouldn't. It's no woman's business."

"Maybe that's so. Well, it would have suited me to have Trampas die sooner."

"How would it suit you to have him live longer?" inquired a member of the opposite party, suspected of being himself a cattle thief.

"I could answer your question, if I had other folks' calves I wanted to brand." This raised both a laugh and a silence.

Thus the town talked, filling in the time before sunset.

The Virginian paused at the edge of the town. "I'd sooner have a sickness than be undecided this way," he said. Then a grim smile came at his own expense. "I reckon it would make me sick—but there's not time."

Over in the hotel sat his sweetheart alone, away from her mother, her friends, her home, waiting his return, knowing nothing. He looked to the west. Between the sun and the bright ridges of the mountains was still a space of sky. The shadow of the mountains now stretched halfway toward the town. "About forty minutes more," he said aloud. "She has been raised so different." And he sighed as he turned back. As he went slowly, he did not know how great was his own unhappiness. "She has been raised so different," he said again.

Opposite the post office the bishop of Wyoming greeted the Virginian. His lonely heart throbbed at the warm, firm grasp of this friend's hand. The bishop saw his eyes glow suddenly, as if tears were close. But none came, and no word more open than, "I'm glad to see you."

But gossip had reached the bishop, and he was sorely troubled also. "What is all this?" said he, coming straight to it.

The Virginian looked at the clergyman frankly. "You know just as much about it as I do," he said. "And I'll tell you anything you ask."

"Have you told Miss Wood?" inquired the bishop.

The eyes of the bridegroom fell, and the bishop's

face grew at once more eager and more troubled. Then the bridegroom raised his eyes again. The bishop touched his arm, like a brother. "This is hard luck," he said.

The bridegroom could scarce keep his voice steady. "I want to do right today more than any day I have ever lived," said he.

"Then go and tell her at once."

"It will just do nothing but scare her."

"Go and tell her at once."

"I expected you was going to tell me to run away from Trampas. I can't do that, you know."

The bishop did know. Never before in all his wilderness work had he faced such a thing. He knew that Trampas was an evil in the country, and that the Virginian was a good. He knew that the cattle thieves—the rustlers—were gaining, in numbers and fearlessness. They had already led many weak young fellows to ruin. They had elected their own men to office, and controlled juries. They were a menace to Wyoming. His heart was with the Virginian. But he was not one to shirk his responsibility to serve the church.

"Am I right," he now slowly asked, "in believing that you think I am a sincere man?"

"I don't believe anything about it. I know it."

"I would run away from Trampas," said the bishop.

"That ain't quite fair, Bishop. We all understand you have got to do the things you tell other folks to do. You never talk like anything but a man, and you never set yourself above others. I saw you walk unarmed into that White River excitement when those two other parsons was afeared for their own safety. Damn scoundrels!"

The bishop instantly scolded the Virginian for using such language about brothers of the cloth, even though he disapproved of both of them and their doctrines. "Every one may be an instrument of God," he concluded.

"Well," said the Virginian, "if that is so, then Providence makes use of instruments I'd not touch with a ten-foot pole. Now if you was me, seh, and not a bishop, would you run away from Trampas?"

"That's not quite fair, either!" exclaimed the bishop, with a smile. "Because you are asking me to take another man's convictions, and yet remain myself."

"Yes, seh. I am. That's so. That don't get at it. I reckon you and I can't get at it."

"If the Bible," said the bishop, "which I believe to be God's word, was anything to you—"

"It is something to me, seh. I have found fine truths in it."

"'Thou shalt not kill,'" quoted the bishop. "That is plain."

The Virginian took his turn at smiling. "Mighty plain to me, seh. Make it plain to Trampas, and there'll be no killin'. We can't get at it that way."

"My friend," the bishop urged, and all his good, warm heart was in it, "my dear fellow—go away for one night. He'll change his mind."

The Virginian shook his head. "He cannot change his word, seh. Or at least I must stay around till he does. Why, I have given him the choice. Most men would not have took what I took from him in the saloon. Why don't you ask him to leave town?"

The good bishop was at a standstill.

"But you have helped me some," said the Virginian. "I will go and tell her. At least, if I think it will be good for her, I will tell her."

The bishop thought that he saw one last chance to move him.

"You're twenty-nine," he began.

"And a little over," said the Virginian.

"And you were fourteen when you ran away from your family."

"Well, I was weary, you know, of havin' elder brothers lay down my law night and mornin'."

"Yes, I know. Your life has been your own for fifteen years. But it is not your own now. You have given it to a woman."

"Yes, I have given it to her. But my life's not the whole of me. I'd give her twice my life—fifty—a thousand of 'em. But I can't give her—her nor anybody in heaven or earth—I can't give my—my—! There's no good in words. Goodbye." The Virginian shook the bishop's hand and left him.

"God bless him!" said the bishop. "God bless him!"

The Virginian unlocked the room in the hotel where he stored his tent, his blankets, his packsaddles, and everything he'd prepared for the bridal

journey in the mountains. From among his possessions he took a pistol, wiping and loading it. Then
from its holster he removed the pistol which he had
tried and made sure of in the morning. This,
according to his usual practice when going into a
risk, he shoved between his trousers and his shirt in
front. The untried weapon he placed in the holster,
letting it hang visibly at his hip. He glanced out of
the window again. The cottonwoods were no
longer in the sunlight. Fifteen of the forty minutes
were gone. "The bishop is wrong," he said. "There
is no sense in telling her." And he turned to the
door, just as she came to it herself.

"Oh!" she cried out at once, and rushed to
him.

He swore as he held her close. "The fools!" he
said. "The fools!"

"It has been so frightful waiting for you," said
she, leaning her head against him.

"Who had to tell you this?" he demanded.

"I don't know. Somebody just came and said it."

"This is mean luck," he murmured, patting her.
"This is mean luck."

"I wanted to run out and find you, but I didn't!
I didn't! I stayed quiet in my room till they said you
had come back."

"It is mean luck. Mighty mean," he repeated.

"How could you be so long?" she asked.
"Never mind, I've got you now. It is over."

Anger and sorrow filled him. "I might have
known some fool would tell you," he said.

"It's all over. Never mind." Her arms tightened their hold on him. Then she let him go. "What shall we do?" she said. "What now?"

"Now?" he answered. "Nothing now."

She looked at him without understanding.

"I know it is a heap worse for you," he went on, speaking slowly. "I knew it would be."

"But it is over!" she exclaimed again.

He did not understand her now. He kissed her. "Did you think it was over?" he said simply. "There is some waiting still before us. I wish you did not have to wait alone. But it will not be long." He was looking down, and did not see the happiness grow chilled upon her face, and then fade into fear. "I did my best," he went on. "I think I did. I know I tried. I let him say to me before them all what no man has ever said, or ever will again. I kept thinking hard of you—with all my might, or I reckon I'd have killed him right there. And I gave him a chance to change his mind. I gave it to him twice. I spoke as quiet as I am speaking to you now. But he would not hear me. And I expect he knows he went too far in the hearing of others to go back on his threat. He will have to go on to the finish now."

"The finish?" she echoed, almost voiceless.

"Yes," he answered very gently.

Her wide eyes were fixed upon him. "But—" she could scarcely speak, "but you?"

"I have got myself ready," he said. "Did you think—why, what did you think?"

She shrank back a step. "What are you going—"

She put her two hands to her head. "Oh, God!" she almost shrieked, "You are going—" He made a step, and would have put his arm round her, but she backed against the wall, staring speechless at him.

"I am not going to let him shoot me," he said quietly.

"You mean—you mean—but you can come away!" she cried. "It's not too late yet. You can take yourself out of his reach. Everybody knows that you are brave. What is he to you? You can leave him in this place. I'll go with you anywhere. To any house, to the mountains, to anywhere away. We'll leave this horrible place together and—and—oh, won't you listen to me?" She stretched her hands to him. "Won't you listen?"

He took her hands. "I must stay here."

Her hands clung to his. "No, no, no. There's something else. There's something better than shedding blood in cold blood. Only think what it means! Only think of having to remember such a thing! Why, it's what they hang people for! It's murder!"

He dropped her hands. "Don't call it that name," he said sternly.

"What other name when you have the choice not to!"

"He did the choosing," answered the Virginian. "Listen to me. Are you listening?" he asked, for her gaze was dull.

She nodded.

"I work here. I belong here. It's my life. If folks

came to think I was a coward—"

"Who would think you were a coward?"

"Everybody. My friends would be sorry and ashamed, and my enemies would walk around saying they had always said so. I could not hold up my head again among enemies or friends."

"When it was explained—"

"There'd be nothing to explain. There'd just be the fact." He was nearly angry.

"There is a higher courage than fear of outside opinion," said the New England girl.

Her Southern lover looked at her. "Certainly there is. That's what I'm showing in going against yours."

"But if you know that you are brave, and if I know that you are brave—oh, my dear, my dear— what difference does the world make? How much higher courage to go your own course—"

"I am goin' my own course," he broke in. "Can't you see how it must be for a man? It's not for their benefit, friends or enemies, that I have got this thing to do. If any man happened to say I was a thief and I heard about it, would I let him go on spreadin' such a thing? Don't I owe my own honesty something better than that? Would I sit down in a corner rubbin' my honesty and whisperin' to it, 'There! there! I know you ain't a thief'? What men say about my nature is not just merely an outside thing. If I let 'em keep on sayin' it, that's proof I don't value my nature enough to shield it from their slander."

She grew very white.

"Can't you see how it must be for a man?" he repeated.

"I cannot," she answered, in a voice that scarcely seemed her own. "If I ought to, I cannot. To shed blood in cold blood. When I heard about that last fall—about the killing of those cattle thieves—I kept saying to myself, 'He had to do it. It was a public duty.' But this . . ." she gave a shudder. "When I think of tomorrow, of you and me, and of—If you do this, there can be no tomorrow for you and me."

At these words he also turned white.

"Do you mean—" he asked, and could go no further.

Nor could she answer him, but turned her head away.

"This would be the end?" he asked.

Her head faintly moved to signify yes.

He stood still, his hand shaking a little. "Will you look at me and say that?" he murmured at length. She did not move. "Can you do it?" he said.

His sweetness made her turn, but could not pierce her frozen resolve. She gazed at him across the great distance of her despair.

"Then it is really so?" he said.

Her lips tried to form words, but failed.

He looked out of the window, and saw nothing but shadow. The blue of the mountains was now a deep purple. Suddenly his hand closed hard.

"Goodbye, then," he said.

At that word she was at his feet, clutching him. "For my sake," she begged him. "For my sake."

A tremble passed through his frame. She felt his legs shake as she held them, and, looking up, she saw that his eyes were closed with misery. Then he opened them, and in their steady look she read her answer. He unclasped her hands from holding him, and raised her to her feet.

"I have no right to kiss you anymore," he said. And then, before his desire could break him down from this, he was gone, and she was alone.

She did not fall. She stood motionless. And next—it seemed a moment and it seemed an eternity—she heard in the distance a shot, and then two shots. Out of the window she saw people beginning to run. At that she turned and fled to her room, and threw herself face downward upon the floor.

Trampas had departed from the saloon, leaving behind him his *ultimatum*. His loud and public threat was town knowledge already, would very likely be county knowledge tonight. After five years, here was the end coming—coming before dark. Trampas had got up this morning with no such thought. Now, he looked at the mountains, and saw their approaching shadow. And there somewhere behind him was the morning he could never go back to. The night that was coming he could not see, and his eyes and his thoughts shrank from it. He had given his enemy until sundown.

He could not trace the path which had led him to this. He remembered their first meeting—five years back, in Medicine Bow, and the words which at once began his hate. How had five years of hate come to play him such a trick, suddenly, today? Since last autumn he had meant sometime to get even with this man who seemed to stand at every turn of his crookedness, and rob him of his spoils. But how had he come to choose such a way of getting even as this, face to face? He knew many better ways; now his own rash words had trapped him.

Trampas had till sundown. He dared not leave town in all the world's sight after all the world had heard him. Even his friends would fall from him after such an act. Could he—the thought actually came to him—could he strike before the time set? But the thought was useless. Even if his friends could shelter him after such a deed, his enemies would find him. His own trap was closing upon him.

He came upon the main street, and saw the Virginian some distance off standing in talk with the bishop. He snuck between two houses, and cursed both of them. The sight had been good for him, bringing some rage back to his desperate heart. And he went into a place and ordered some whiskey.

"In your shoes," said the barkeeper, "I'd be afraid to drink so much."

Trampas's nerves were almost beyond the reach of intoxication. He swallowed some more, and went out again. He fell in with some of his brothers in cattle stealing, and walked along with them for a little.

"Well, it will not be long now," they said to him. And he had never heard words so grim.

"No," he heard himself say, "soon now." Their cheerfulness seemed unearthly to him, and his heart almost broke beneath it.

"We'll have one to your success," they suggested.

So with them he headed to another place. There, the sight of a man leaning against the bar made him flinch so much that people noticed. Then he saw that the man was a stranger whom he had never laid eyes on till now.

"It looked like Shorty," he said, and could have bitten his tongue off.

"Shorty is quiet up in the Tetons," said a friend. "You don't want to be thinking about him!"

They clapped him on the back and he left them. He thought of his enemy and his hate, trying to dredge some courage out of his rage and the drinks he'd had. He spotted Wiggin, walking with McLean and Scipio. They were watching the town, guarding against any foul play by Trampas's friends. They did not seem like real people to him.

Trampas looked at the walls and windows of the houses. Were they real? Was he here, walking in this street? Something had changed. He looked everywhere, and wondered what this could be. Then he knew. The sun had gone entirely behind the mountains. He drew out his pistol.

The Virginian, as a precaution, did not walk out the front door of the hotel. He went through back ways, and paused once. Against his breast he felt the wedding ring suspended by a chain from his neck. He drew it out and looked at it. He took it off the chain, and his arm went back to hurl it from him as far as he could. But he stopped, kissed it with one sob, and thrust it in his pocket. Then he walked out into the open, watching. He saw men here and there, and they let him pass as before, without speaking. He saw his three friends, and they said no word to him. But they turned and followed in his rear at a little distance, because it was known that Shorty had been found shot from behind. The Virginian gained a position where no one could come at him except from in front.

"It is quite a while after sunset," he heard himself say.

A wind seemed to blow his sleeve off his arm. He replied to it, and saw Trampas fall forward. He saw Trampas raise his arm from the ground and fall again. Then he lay there, still. A little smoke was rising from the pistol on the ground. He looked at his own, and saw the smoke flowing upward out of it.

"I expect that's all," he said aloud.

As he came nearer Trampas, he kept him covered with his weapon. The Virginian stopped a moment, seeing the hand on the ground move. Two fingers twitched, and then ceased. It was over. The Virginian stood looking down at Trampas.

"Both of mine hit," he said, once more aloud. "His must have come mighty close to my arm. I told her it would not be me."

He had scarcely noticed that he was being surrounded and congratulated. His hand was being shaken, and he saw it was Scipio in tears. Scipio's

joy made his heart like lead within him. He was near telling his friend everything, but he did not.

"If anybody wants me about this," he said, "I will be at the hotel."

"Who'll want you?" said Scipio. "Three of us saw his gun out." And he vented his admiration. "You were that cool! That quick!"

"I'll see you boys again," said the Virginian, heavily; and he walked away.

Scipio looked after him, astonished. "You might suppose he'd had poor luck," he said to McLean.

The Virginian walked to the hotel, and stood at the doorway of his sweetheart's room. She had heard his step, and was on her feet. Her lips were parted, and her eyes fixed on him. She did not move or speak.

"You have to know it," said he. "I have killed Trampas."

"Oh, thank God!" she said, and he found her in his arms. Long they embraced without speaking, and what they whispered then with their kisses does not matter.

Her New England conscience battled to the end, and, in the end, surrendered to love. The next day, with the bishop's blessing and Mrs. Taylor's broadest smile and the ring on her finger, the Virginian departed with his bride into the mountains.

AT DUNBARTON

For their first bridal camp he chose an island. Long beforehand he had set his heart upon it as the place. He had stopped at the island many times alone, and in all seasons. This time of year was when he liked it best.

For many weeks he had planned to bring her here after their wedding, on the day itself, to share his pines, his fishing rock, and the sheltered circle of his campground. Together they would smell the first true breath of the mountains, watch the sinking campfire, and listen to the water as it flowed round the island.

Until this wedding plan, it had by no means come home to him how deep a hold on him the island had taken. He knew that he liked to go there, but it was not his way to scan himself, his mind, or his feelings. Now he understood. He only fully appreciated his love of the place through his love of her. But he told her nothing of it. He kept his island as something she must first experience with her own eyes. He could not chance that by looking forward to it she would look for more than the reality.

385

As a result, when the houses of the town were shrunk to dots behind them, and they were nearing the foothills, she asked him questions. She hoped they would find a camp a long way from the town. She could ride as many miles as necessary. She was not tired. Should they not go on until they found a good place far enough within the solitude? Had he fixed upon any? And at the nod and the silence that he gave her for reply, she knew that he had thoughts and intentions which she must wait to learn.

Soon they entered the foothills, following a stream. The outstretching fences were no more. Now and then their path rose, giving them once again a view of the fields and houses down in the plain below. But as the hours passed, they were glad to see the traces of men passing from sight. The plowed and planted country—the quilt of many-colored harvests they had watched yesterday—lay in another world. No hand but nature's had sown these crops of yellow flowers, these willow thickets and tall cottonwoods. Somewhere in a passage of red rocks the last sign of wagon wheels was lost. They now rode a wild mountain trail. But it was still the warm air of the plains—bearing the sagebrush odor and not the pine—that they breathed. Full solitude was around them now, so that their words grew scarce, and when they spoke it was with low voices. They began to pass nooks and points she thought favorable for camping, with wood and water at hand, and pasture for the horses. But still he rode on in advance of her (for the trail was narrow) until he drew rein and pointed.

"What?" she asked timidly.

"The pines," he answered.

She looked, and saw the island, and the water enfolding it with ripples and with smooth spaces. The sun was throwing a light of deepening red gold on the pines. He pointed upward to the high mountains which they had approached, and showed her where the stream led.

"Tomorrow we shall be among them," said he.

"Then," she murmured to him, "tonight is here?"

He nodded. She gazed at the island and understood why he had not stopped before. Nothing they had passed had been so lovely as this place.

Side by side they rode to the ford and crossed, driving the packhorses in front of them. When they came to the sheltered circle, he helped her down where the soft pine needles lay. They felt each other tremble, and for a moment she stood hiding her head upon his breast. Then she looked round at the trees, and the shores, and the flowing stream, and he heard her whispering how beautiful it was.

"I am glad," he said, still holding her. "This is how I have dreamed it would happen. Only it is better than my dreams." And when she pressed him in silence, he finished, "Here I wanted us to see our first sundown and our first sunrise."

He invited her to explore the island, and he got to working. The packs and saddles came off the horses, which he turned loose on the pasture. The tent was unfolded first. He had long ago pictured where it should go, and how its white shape would look beneath the green of the encircling pines. After pitching the tent, he built the fire where its smoke would float outward from the trees and the tent. Near it he gathered the cooking things and his supplies, then prepared supper in the twilight. He had brought much, but for ten minutes he fished, catching trout. When she came riding over the stream at his call, there was nothing for her to do but sit and eat.

They sat together, watching the last of the twilight and the gentle arrival of dusk. The final afterglow of day left the sky. Through the purple which followed came the first stars, bright and wide apart. They watched the spaces between them fill, while near them the flames of their fire grew brighter. Then he sent her to the tent while he cleaned the dishes and made sure the horses had not strayed from the pasture. After darkness had fully settled in, he rejoined her. All had been as he had seen it in his thoughts beforehand: the pines with the setting sun upon them, the sinking campfire, and the sound of the water.

The tent opened to the east. From it they watched their first sunrise. He had seen this morning beforehand also: the waking, the gentle sound of the water murmuring ceaselessly, the growing day, the sense that the world was shut away far from them. So did it all happen, except that he whispered to her again, "Better than my dreams."

They saw the sunlight begin. When the sun itself came, lakes of warmth flowed into the air. "I am going into the stream," he said. Rising, he left her in the tent. This was his side of the island, he had told her last night. The other was hers, where he had made a place for her to bathe. When he was gone, she found it, walking through the trees and rocks to the water's edge. And so, with the island between them, the two bathed in the cold stream. He delayed long at his dressing, not willing to return to her unshaven. When he came back, he found her already busy at their camp. Blue smoke was floating out from the trees, and she was getting their breakfast. She looked at his eyes that were clear as the water he had leaped into, and at his soft silk neckerchief, knotted with care.

"Do not let us ever go away from here!" she cried, and ran to him.

They did not move camp that day, as they had planned. For six days and nights they stayed, finding no day or night long enough.

When at last they decided to leave the island to see more of the mountains, it was not a final parting. They would come back for the last night before their journey ended. Furthermore, they promised each other, like two children, to come here every year upon their wedding day. Like two children they believed that this would be possible. But in later years they did come, more than once. With each new visit they were able to say to each other, "Better than our dreams."

For thirty days they saw no faces except their own. When they were silent it was all stillness, unless the wind passed among the pines, or some flowing water was near them. Once, while they were well hidden, he showed her a bear, sitting with an old log lifted in its paws. She forbade him to kill the bear, or any creature that they did not require. He took her upward by trail and canyon. They explored woods untouched by men. They followed dwindling streams to their headwaters, lakes lying near the summit of the range, full of trout. Around them lay meadows of long grass and a thousand flowers, and above these nothing but peaks of rock and snow.

The mountains brought them together. At the end they loved each other doubly more than at the beginning. They did not want to go to Vermont and leave these mountains, but the day came when they had to turn their backs upon their dream. So they came out into the plains once more.

"If only you could," she said, laughing. "If only you could ride home like this."

"With Monte and my six-shooter?" he asked. "To your mother?"

"I don't think mother could resist the way you look on a horse."

But he said, "It's this way she's fearing I will come."

"I have made one discovery," she said. "You are fonder of good clothes than I am."

He grinned. "I certainly like 'em. But don't tell

my friends. They would say it was marriage. When you see what I have got for Bennington's special benefit, you—why, you'll just trust your husband more than ever."

She undoubtedly did. After he had put on one particular suit, she arose and kissed him where he stood in it.

"Bennington will be sorry," he said. "No wild-west show, after all." And he looked at himself in the glass with pleasure.

And Bennington probably was disappointed. To see him get out of the train merely a tall man with a usual straw hat, and a suit of a rather better cut than most in Bennington—this was dull. And his conversation—when he engaged in any—was suitable for inside the house.

Mrs. Flynt claimed, for any who would listen, that Sam Bannett had done so much better for himself. Sam had married a rich Miss Van Scootzer, of Troy. With their combined riches this happy couple still inhabits the most expensive residence in Hoosic Falls.

But most of Bennington soon began to say that Molly's cowboy could be invited anywhere and hold his own. The time came when they ceased to speak of him as a cowboy, and declared that she had shown remarkable sense. But this was not quite yet.

Did this bride and groom enjoy their visit to her family? Well—well, they did their best. Everybody did their best, even Sarah Bell. She found nothing to object to in the Virginian. She told Molly so. Her husband Sam did better than that. He told Molly he considered that she was in luck. Poor Mrs. Wood, sitting on the sofa, nervously spoke at length with her unusual son-in-law. She had to admit to Molly her astonishment at finding him so gentle. And he was undoubtedly very handsome. She believed that she would grow to like the Southern accent. Oh, yes! Everybody did their best. Dear reader, if you have ever had the occasion to be with a number of people all doing their best, you do not need me to tell you what a heavenly atmosphere this creates.

And then the bride and groom went to see the old great-aunt over at Dunbarton.

At Bennington they had managed to make the occasion of their arrival as completely mournful as any family party can be, with the window blinds up. "And with you present, my dear," said Sam Bell to Sarah, "the absence of a coffin was not felt."

But at Dunbarton the matter went off differently. They drove up to the gate in the afternoon. The great-aunt was in her garden, picking some August flowers. She called as the carriage stopped, "Bring my nephew here, my dear, before you go into the house."

As Molly stepped out of the carriage, she squeezed her husband's hand. "I knew that she would be lovely," she whispered to him. And then she ran to her aunt's arms, and let him follow. He came slowly, hat in hand.

The old lady advanced to meet him, trembling

a little, and holding out her hand to him. "Welcome, nephew," she said. "What a tall fellow you are, to be sure. Stand off, sir, and let me look at you."

The Virginian obeyed, blushing from his black hair to his collar.

Then his new relative turned to her niece, and gave her a flower. "Put this in his coat, my dear," she said. "And I think I understand why you wanted to marry him."

After this the maid came and showed them to their rooms. Left alone in her garden, the great-aunt sank on a bench and sat there for some time, weak with emotion.

Upstairs, Molly, sitting on the Virginian's knee, put the flower in his coat, and then laid her head upon his shoulder.

"I didn't know old ladies could be that way," he said. "Do you reckon there are many?"

"Oh, I don't know," said the girl. "I'm so happy!"

During the evening, the great-aunt did the chief part of the talking herself. She did not ask questions about Wyoming too soon. She reached that in her own way, and found out the one thing that she desired to know.

Pointing to the portrait of General Stark, she said, "He had a rough time of it now and then. New Hampshire was full of fine young men in those days. But nowadays most of them have gone away to seek their fortunes in the West. Do they find them, I wonder?"

"Yes, ma'am. All the good ones do."

"But you cannot all be—what is the name?—Cattle Kings."

"That's having its day, ma'am, right now. Now some of us are getting ready for the change."

"And what may be the change, and when is it to come?"

"The natural pasture is getting eaten off," he explained. "We'll soon have big pastures fenced, and hay and shelter ready for winter. What we'll spend in improvements, we'll more than save in wages. I am well fixed for the new conditions. When I took up my land, I chose a place where there is coal. It will not be long before the new railroad needs that."

Thus the old lady learned more of her niece's husband in one evening than the Bennington family in days. Through their conversation about Wyoming, the Virginian revealed his wide ranging ideas and his shrewd intelligence. He forgot to be shy. She sent Molly to bed, and kept him talking for an hour. Then she showed him old things that she was proud of, "because," she said, "we, too, had something to do with making our country. And now go to Molly, or you'll both think me a tiresome old lady."

"I think . . ." he began, but was not quite equal to expressing what he thought. His shyness had flooded him again.

"In that case, nephew," said she, "I'm afraid

you'll have to kiss me good night."

And so she dismissed him to his wife. "He'll do," she said to herself, nodding.

Their visit to Dunbarton was compensation for the miserable days at Bennington. The old lady gave much comfort and advice to her niece in private. When they came to leave, she stood at the front door holding both their hands a moment.

"God bless you, my dears," she told them. "And when you come next time, I'll have the nursery ready."

And so it happened that before she left this world, the great-aunt was able to hold in her arms the first of their many children.

Judge Henry at Sunk Creek had his wedding present ready. His growing affairs in Wyoming needed his presence in many places distant from his ranch, and he made the Virginian his partner. When the thieves prevailed at length, as they did, forcing cattle owners to leave the country or be ruined, the Virginian had prepared for this crash. The herds were driven away to Montana. Then, in 1889, came the cattle war, when, after putting their men in office, and coming to own some of the newspapers, the thieves brought ruin on themselves as well. In a broken country there is nothing left to steal.

But the railroad came, and built a branch to that land of the Virginian's where the coal was. By that time he was an important man, involved in many enterprises. He was able to give his wife all and more than she asked or desired.

Sometimes she missed the Bear Creek days. Sometimes she declared that his work would kill him. But it does not seem to have done so. Their eldest boy rides the horse Monte. And, strictly between ourselves, I think his father is going to live a long while.

AFTERWORD

About the Author

In Medicine Bow, Wyoming, there's a monument to Owen Wister, a society gentleman from the East famous for his writings about the West. With *The Virginian*, Wister helped create an international sensation, a legendary image of the cowboy in the American West. Wister offered a new kind of hero: quiet and skillful, decent and deadly, both a simple, modest cowpuncher and a dashing, romantic superman.

Wister's early life made him an unlikely candidate for helping create the American cowboy legend. He was born in 1860 into a fairly affluent family in Philadelphia, the son of a doctor and grandson of the famous actress Fanny Kemble. He studied in Europe before graduating from Harvard. Owen then enrolled in a Paris music school but after two years abandoned hopes for a musical career. Instead, he became a bank clerk in New York City. A breakdown brought this career choice to a standstill.

Wister first traveled to Medicine Bow in 1885, hoping to restore his health. He had been inspired, perhaps, by his college classmate and good friend Theodore Roosevelt, who had just started a working ranch in the Dakota Territory. The restless bank clerk was to return to Medicine Bow many times—he had fallen in love with the West.

After his life-changing visit to Wyoming, Wister entered Harvard Law School and graduated in 1888. Although he held a junior position in a Philadelphia law firm, Owen had little enthusiasm for law. Having already in 1882 published his first full-length work, he returned to this passion.

One evening in 1890, while dining with a friend at one of Philadelphia's most exclusive clubs, he had a brainstorm. No one had yet told stories of the West in serious fiction. Wister ran upstairs to the club's library and began what would become "Hank's Woman," published by *Harper's Magazine* in 1892. After writing a collection of western stories called *Red Men and White* and a biography of Ulysses S. Grant, Wister gained recognition as a writer. He continued to write stories of the West.

Over the years, Wister had filled journals describing his Wyoming adventures and those he had heard about. Many of the places and events Wister recorded became the basis for passages in his fiction. These journals served Wister well in his 1902 blockbuster *The Virginian*. A memorable night on the counter of the general store in Medicine Bow became an incident in the novel, for example. The liars, rustlers, bartenders, and cowboys that appear in this work are based on actual people.

The Virginian sold 50,000 copies in its first two months and made him world famous. It was well timed. Buffalo Bill's Wild West Show was at the height of its popularity, and the first movie to tell a complete story, 1903's *The Great Train Robbery,* was a western.

Owen Wister became a celebrity and started trends. It's said that Wister's 1906 book, *Lady Baltimore,* made white layer cakes popular. Wister socialized with famous people. He went hunting with his old friend Theodore Roosevelt. Wister's personal appearances for the ex-president in the 1912 election have been called the first celebrity political endorsement.

Wister never again wrote a book as popular as *The Virginian,* nor did he write much more about the West. But he remained a successful author until his death in 1938. His collected writing, published in 1928, filled eleven volumes. In 1958, Wister's Wyoming journals were published.

Interest in Wister and *The Virginian* has been long-lived. Four movie versions of *The Virginian* were made, the first based on Wister's successful stage adaptation. Long after Wister's death, his novel inspired a hit television show. Today, the Western Writers of America still honors lifetime achievement with the Owen Wister Award. Three never-before published Wister works were released in 2001. The citizens of Medicine Bow have even reconstructed Wister's vacation home and preserved the general store named after him. Visitors to the area can stay at the Virginian Hotel or the Trampas Motel.

With *The Virginian*, Owen Wister popularized a new variety of fiction that has since been further developed by authors from Zane Grey to Larry McMurtry. Movie westerns like Academy-Award winners *Dances with Wolves* and *The Unforgiven* continue to thrill audiences. You could say that Owen Wister was the father of all westerns. And when you call him that, smile.

About the Book

Cowboy. What comes to mind when Americans hear the word?

A tall, slim fellow with fringed leather chaps, coiled rope in hand, spurs on his boots, and a pistol at his hip? That's how Owen Wister describes the Virginian.

A strong, shy man more comfortable with his horse than with people? That's the Virginian and his faithful Monte.

A showdown between the good guy and the bad guy on the dusty streets of a small town? Wister was first to put that plot element in a serious work of literature.

A masculine code of behavior? That was the code by which the Virginian lived.

Today, the cowboy image still echoes in advertising, politics, fashion, fiction, and film. Yet, the era of the true cowboy lasted only about twenty years. Why did he make such an enduring impression? Credit *The Virginian*, one of the most widely read books of the twentieth century.

Many Americans of Wister's time wanted to believe that they were cowboys at heart. By 1902, more and more Americans lived in crowded cities and worked in repetitive factory jobs. Like them, the cowpuncher was a workingman. He survived, thrived, and tamed the wilderness with his own hands: roping, branding, building, repairing fences, digging ditches, and herding cattle. Unlike them, he roamed the open spaces, facing constant challenges. The cowboy represented the triumph of instinct over intelligence, common sense over book learning, the rugged individual over the citified and prettified. On the frontier, true democracy flourished. There, the people, mistrustful of government and overregulation, made and enforced the law.

Though Wister was important in spreading the cowboy legend, he did not invent it. The narrator of *The Virginian*—a stand-in for Wister and most of the book's readers—must have read the shamelessly exaggerated western dime novels of the day. He thinks he knows how cowboys treat a tenderfoot from back East:

> I recalled some terrible tales about people who had traveled to the West. Was I about to be invited to dance on the platform to the music of pistol shots aimed at my feet?

The invitation never arrives.

The misinformed Easterner has much to learn. When he discovers he must still travel two-hundred and sixty-three miles to get to the judge's ranch, he wonders how "they count distance in this country." His city ways leave him blind to the "great sunset light of Wyoming."

The first thing to make a strong impression on him is a cowboy "like a tiger, smooth and easy, as if his muscles flowed beneath his skin." In action he is extremely capable, a man who "knows his business."

Moments after seeing this fellow's skill with a rope, we witness him engaging in very clever banter with Uncle Hughey:

> "Now, how could I forget you was fifty," he murmured, "when you have been telling it to the boys for the last ten years!"

The Virginian might seem like a simple cowpoke, but he has brawn and brains, and he's not afraid to use them. The Virginian displays remarkable sophistication:

> This handsome, uneducated son of the soil kept his distance with cold and perfect courtesy. No polished person could have done it better.

The narrator believes cowboys "live nearer nature, and they know better." They have all the right qualities without the phony "outward trappings." The Virginian has surprising depth. "Beneath the quiet of this man was a volcano." He even cleans up nice:

> The Virginian's entrance produced a slight silence. He had done wonders at the wash trough. He had even brushed his clothes. With all the roughness of his dress, he was now the neatest of us.

But most importantly, the Virginian shows

readers how to live by the unwritten western code of conduct. A cowboy doesn't interfere in the business of others:

> In bets, in card games, in all horse transactions, onlookers must suppress their wisdom and hold their peace.

A real man "goes through with his responsibilities." Whatever he does, he "must do a thing well." He must never "speak ill of any man to any woman" or strut "around in public wearing spurs and deadly weapons." A real man "must die brave. There's no pity for a coward." And he deals with his problems in "the ancient, eternal way between man and man."

The Virginian was the first western hero to have his inner life revealed. Preparing to face Trampas, the Virginian is not as definite as he must have seemed on the outside. The code is clear for a western man, but now there is a woman to consider. Only minutes before the climactic showdown, our hero remains unsure. He says, "I'd sooner have a sickness than be undecided this way."

But Wister's book needed more than a compelling hero to become a phenomenon. The Virginian provided the muscle. But romance, humor, and nostalgia create the novel's beating heart.

Wister understood the appeal of romance. The charm of the roller-coaster affair between the unemotional cowboy and the Vermont schoolmarm rests on a simple twist. After their first meeting, when he rescues her, she has "thoughts of maidenly resentment toward her rescuer and of maidenly hope to see him again." For the tough cowpoke, love begins at first read. After looking over Molly's letter to the people of Bear Creek, "the seed of love had floated across wide spaces and was biding its time in his heart." From that moment on, he pursues her. On the other hand, Molly—a hopeless romantic searching for the perfect love—tries her best to deny her intense attraction to the cowpuncher.

Sometimes Wister's language can remind you of popular romance novels:

> Had she surrendered on this day to her cowpuncher, her wild man? Was she forever wholly his? Had the Virginian's fire so melted her heart that no fracture in it remained?

But he also writes with sensitivity and restraint. His depiction of the first day of the couple's honeymoon is intimate, romantic, and sensual, without any sex:

> They felt each other tremble, and for a moment she stood hiding her head upon his breast. Then she looked round at the trees, and the shores, and the flowing stream, and he heard her whispering how beautiful it was.

"I am glad," he said, still holding her. "This is how I have dreamed it would happen. Only it is better than my dreams."

Much of the novel's humor comes from the romance and the colorful cast of supporting characters: the wise Scipio, the pompous Reverend MacBride, and the practical joker Lin McLean. Here's Lin describing his unsuccessful courting of Molly:

. . . she chattin' cheerful and askin' me a heap of questions all about myself every day, and I not lyin' much neither.

The Virginian also tapped into the nostalgia Americans were already feeling for the vanishing frontier. Much of this is done with subtlety. For example, as the happy couple approaches Medicine Bow for their wedding, Wister notes:

In what was wilderness, scars of newly dug water ditches began to appear, and the first wire fences.

More and more such fences appear until "the free road became wholly imprisoned."

The cowpokes on the job express their awareness of the changes underway:

They came upon the schoolhouse, roofed and ready. It symbolized the dawn of a neighborhood. The feel of it struck cold on the free spirits of the cowpunchers. They told each other that, what with women and children and wire fences, this country would not long be a country for men.

They declare that "if this here Territory is goin' to get full of family men and empty of game," they'll have to find another place to go. Readers knew there was already no wild place left to which they could escape from the arrival of modern civilization.

The western itself had become almost invisible by 1938 when Wister died. But it was not a final outcome. The very next year, the movie *Stagecoach* was released and became a critical and box office success. Its star, John Wayne—playing a character modeled after the Virginian—helped make the cowboy more popular than ever.

Today once again, the popularity of the western has faded, though its influence has not. When the western comes back—and it will—it will once again be reinventing what Owen Wister first created in *The Virginian*.